BOOK **TWO** OF MISMATCHED MATES

MISGUIDED Motives

MELODY TYDEN

For Cadence

Chapter One

~Abby~

My suitcase was nearly packed when Oliver's voice called out from the living room. "Hurry up, Heels! We're going to be late."

Shoving a few last things in, I zipped the case up before rushing out to where he was waiting, his own bag already in his hand. "I would have been more organized if you had told me more than ten minutes ago we were going somewhere," I pointed out.

"Then it wouldn't have been a surprise," he teased as he took my suitcase from me, hoisting it up as if it weighed nothing. To him, it probably did. He was tall, muscled and strong, the epitome of an Alpha werewolf. "Come on, everyone's waiting."

"Wait, everyone?" I called out after him as he stepped out into the dorm hallway and I hurried to keep up. "Who's everyone?"

All I knew was that ten minutes ago my mate had told me he was taking me on a spur-of-the-moment trip to celebrate writing our last final exams for the college year, and now he was saying there were more people coming? I still had no idea where we were going or for how long.

"Oliver James West." I used his full name to get his attention and, as I expected, he stopped immediately. "Tell me what's going on right now."

He turned back to me with his eyebrows raised, a smirk on his face and a smile in his warm grey eyes. "Abby Eleanor Flintoff," he said, mocking my serious tone. "No. What part of the word 'surprise' is tripping you up here? You'll see when we get there."

"Eleanor?" I repeated in disbelief as he turned back and started walking again. "My middle name is not Eleanor."

"Elaine?" he guessed as he pushed the door open, heading out into the quad outside our dorm. I'd been staying with him in his dorm room for the last few months, ever since I accepted him as my mate, and though it was technically against school rules, no one had called us out on it. I supposed that was what happened when your dad donated a ton of money to the college like Oliver's dad did.

"It's not Elaine either," I huffed in disapproval. We'd been together for four months now and he usually paid attention to these kinds of things. "Do you really not know?"

He turned back to me with an amused glint in his eyes. "Of course I know. I just figured you'd move faster if you were angry with me, Abby Elyse Flintoff."

He leaned down to kiss me and any annoyance I might have had with him immediately melted away. His kiss was electric, just like always, and I would have happily lost myself in it if it weren't for the catcalls and whistles that rang out around us.

I broke away to find a large group of our friends standing outside a stretch Hummer limo. There were Whitney and Jack, of course, my former roommate and her boyfriend, along with my friends Liz and Melanie, and a couple of other guys from Oliver's football team, Caleb and Lincoln.

"Save it for the hotel, you guys," Whitney teased, her arm tucked around Jack's.

"Hotel?" I repeated, looking at Whitney in surprise. "What hotel? Where are we going?"

Oliver shook his head. "That won't work. They've all been instructed to ignore all your questions. Now let's get going, we don't want to miss our flight."

"Flight?" That word came out as almost a squeak. I'd never been on a plane before. What on earth did Oliver have up his sleeve?

Nearly an hour later we pulled up at the airport with me having made absolutely no headway at getting any information out of anyone. They all seemed to think it was great fun that Oliver hadn't told me what was happening, so I had to accept that I wasn't going to make them crack.

Surely at the airport someone would have to tell me where the plane was going? There must be a sign or something, I was certain of it.

But to my surprise, we bypassed the main terminal entirely, going instead to a smaller building where Oliver checked us all in before we headed out to a plane waiting on the tarmac.

"Is this a private plane?" I asked, my surprise growing by the minute.

"My dad uses it sometimes for Jade Moon pack business," Oliver told me, speaking quietly so none of the others would overhear the reference to his pack. "He's letting us take it for the weekend."

The weekend. Okay, that was the first concrete piece of information I had about his plans.

"How long have you had this all planned?"

If he had a private plane and all of our friends were ready to go, it couldn't have been very spur-of-the-moment at all.

"About a month," he admitted a little bit sheepishly. "I just wanted to do something a bit special with our human friends before we go back to the pack for the summer."

That made sense. Since none of the rest of our group knew that Oliver and I were werewolves, it wasn't like we could really invite them to hang out with us at Oliver's pack house. Oliver had promised his dad that he would be home for the whole summer to be more active in the pack and make sure everything was on track for when he took over as Alpha in another year's time. He only had one year of college left and then he'd be returning home for good.

I still had three more years to go, but we were already looking at options for remote learning for me to finish up my degree once Oliver had graduated. We both knew there was no way we could be apart for any real length of time. We could hardly stand to be apart for a day.

I couldn't imagine my life without him, which was crazy to think about when I remembered how I had once thought we must have been mismatched.

Now I know better. He is my perfect match in every way.

Except when he keeps secrets from me. I poked him in the ribs as we got to the stairs to the plane, making him jump. "Just tell me where we're going."

He simply laughed. "Not a chance, Heels. You'll see when we get there."

~Oliver~

I suspected Abby was getting a bit annoyed that I wouldn't tell her my plans for the weekend, but I knew if I told her where we were going, she'd immediately figure out why I'd picked that location and then the whole surprise would be ruined. I was going to have to hold out a little bit longer, though she didn't make it easy when she turned those beautiful pale blue eyes of hers on me.

We passed the time on the flight by chatting with our friends, all of whom were excited to be finished with classes for the year and to have a short getaway before the summer started. Most of them would be going home for the summer like I was, though some were staying in town to work. Whitney and Jack had both got jobs at the local mall and Liz was doing a summer placement with the town's newspaper. The three of them had got a short-term lease on a house off campus until the fall, when we'd all go back to the dorms together.

Whitney and Liz weren't really likely friends, but then Abby and I hadn't been an entirely obvious match either. Whitney was a cheerleader and Abby's old roommate, and she and I had very briefly dated. Her boyfriend Jack was on the football team with me while Liz was a classmate of Abby's who had once had a fling with the same professor that Abby did.

Said out loud like that, it all sounded a bit crazy and probably shouldn't have been the basis for a friendship, but somehow it was. The whole group of us were pretty close. They were some of my favourite people in the world, even if they were human.

Because that was another thing we didn't have in common. None of our friends knew that Abby and I were werewolves.

At college, we could almost forget about our packs and our responsibilities, but this summer was going to be different. Back at my pack, I would have to catch up on everything that was going on and everything I'd missed while I'd been away. We hadn't really spent much time back there since the pack had decided to accept me as their future Alpha despite the fact that I wasn't the biological son of the current Alpha. I knew that Marissa, the daughter of our former Beta, had moved to Abby's old pack to be with her mate, the son and heir to their Alpha, but I didn't know anything about how that was going and if there was still any tension between our two packs after the fight we'd had a few months ago.

We had a lot to catch up on.

Part of me was looking forward to it but I knew that Abby was a bit nervous. Despite how well our relationship was going, she was still not totally comfortable with the idea of being my Luna once I took over as Alpha from my dad.

But hopefully this summer would be a good chance for her to get to know everyone and see just how perfect she would be for the role. I didn't have any doubts about it. She had a hundred different qualities that made her a perfect Luna, she just needed to see it for herself.

Finally the plane began its descent and Abby peered curiously out the window. I watched her face, waiting for the moment that the clouds cleared and she could see what was below.

The first look was almost disbelief. "Is this... San Francisco?"

"What gives you that idea?" I teased her as the sun poked through the clouds to hit the Golden Gate Bridge below us.

She looked out the window for a moment more, her brow furrowed in confusion, until suddenly her eyes lit up and she turned that smile of hers on me, that amazing smile that always made me feel like the luckiest fucking man on the planet.

"Really?" she squealed.

She didn't even need to say it. I knew exactly what she was thinking, and she was right, so I nodded my confirmation and she threw her arms around me.

"Oliver, this is amazing! I can't believe you did this." Her eyes shone with happiness as she pulled back and returned to the window. Then she turned back to me with a bit more caution. "You got tickets, right?"

She was talking about tickets to the Bay Book Festival, the biggest literary fair of the year and the one she'd been excitedly telling me about for the last month at least. Several of her favourite authors were going to be there and never in a million years did she think she would actually get to go.

For a moment I thought about teasing her or keeping her in suspense, but it felt too cruel so I just gave in and told her the truth. "VIP passes, all three days."

Her arms wrapped around me again, and this time she kissed me too. As soon as our lips connected, the sparks of our mate bond fired into action, sending a shiver of electricity all the way through me. My arms circled her waist as I pulled her closer to me, slipping my tongue into her mouth and she gave a little sigh, my favourite sound in the whole world.

"I told you she'd kiss him!" Whitney exclaimed from behind us. "That's five bucks! Pay up."

The laughter of our friends made Abby and I pull apart reluctantly.

"To be continued at the hotel," I promised in her ear.

"It better be," she whispered back before turning to the rest of the group. "So does that mean we're all going to the festival?"

They laughed again. "Sorry, Abby," Jack said. "Me and Whitney and the guys have other plans, but Liz and Melanie are going with you."

Abby turned to her book-loving friends and they started to gush over which authors they wanted to see and which lectures to go to. I watched her with a mix of affection and amusement until Jack leaned over and tapped me on the shoulder and I turned to look at him instead.

"You sure you don't want to get out of this?" he stage-whispered to me. "We can always break you out so you can come see the game with us tomorrow." They were planning on catching a baseball game the next afternoon.

I just shook my head at him. "Too late for that. She's got me wrapped around her finger."

He snorted in agreement as I looked back at my beautiful mate. What I'd said was completely true, but I left out the second, and best, part of it.

Which was that I wouldn't have it any other way.

~Abby~

I was still buzzing with excitement as we got to our hotel and checked in. It was just down the street from the convention centre where the book festival was being held and I knew Oliver must have chosen it on purpose for that reason. Whitney and Jack were sharing a room, Liz and Melanie had another one and Caleb and Lincoln a third. Oliver made sure they were all taken care of before he got our own room sorted, just like the Alpha-to-be he was.

As I watched him charming the receptionist, I couldn't wipe the grin off my face. In moments such as this, I sometimes still felt I should pinch myself to make sure this really was my life and this amazing man really belonged to me. And not only was he mine, but he cared enough about me to organize a trip like this which was all about something that I wanted to do.

I couldn't wait to get to our room and show him my appreciation.

Finally everyone was all checked in and we said good night to our friends, agreeing to meet up with them all for breakfast the next morning. Then Oliver and I headed to our room, him carrying both our bags because he insisted on it.

No sooner had I stepped into the open door of the room than I found myself swept off my feet. Oliver had somehow managed to get inside after me, lock the door and drop the suitcases before I'd had a chance to do anything.

"This is our first holiday together," he pointed out as he carried me towards the bed, his face nuzzled in my neck. "The first of many."

"I hope so," I agreed, already feeling a little breathless with need as his lips brushed against his mark on my neck.

"And the first time I get to make love to you in a new state," he pointed out as he laid me on the bed, covering my body with his in an instant. "The first one to check off our list."

The idea of him keeping a list made me laugh. "You really think we're going to check off all fifty?"

"Oh, I know it, Heels. And a whole bunch of different countries too. We've got a lifetime of adventures ahead of us."

"You're all the adventure I need, Alpha," I said, and his eyes darkened as they did whenever I called him that.

In a flash, his mouth was on mine and this time there was no one to interrupt us. Clothes went flying and soon we were naked, all except for my glasses which Oliver pulled off last. "There you are," he growled in approval. He liked to tell me that seeing me without my glasses on always made him hard because it was the way he saw me whenever we're in bed together.

He started to move his kisses down my body, but I quickly grabbed his shoulders and rolled him over, catching him off guard. Now I was on top and it was my turn to kiss my way down his chest.

"Fuck, Abby," he moaned. "If you do that, I'm not going to last for very long."

I couldn't help giggling. "Like that's ever been a problem for you." One of the best things about having a werewolf mate was the quick recovery time between erections. He didn't need to last when he could just go again. "Besides, you're the one who deserves a reward for putting this whole trip together."

His chuckle was warm and low. "Well, when you put it that way..."

He trailed off as my lips reached the tip of his cock, already hard and ready for me. I ran my tongue across the head of it, smiling as it jumped towards me eagerly. I'd already accumulated months of experience at finding out exactly what made him react the most and I put it to good use now.

First, I licked all the way down to the base of his shaft, my tongue running along the hard ridge, and then I worked my way back up, flicking my tongue from side to side as Oliver sighed in pleasure. When I got back to his head, I sucked just the tip into my mouth, hard enough to hollow out my cheeks, and he inhaled sharply.

"Someday you really are going to kill me," he groaned.

I released him just long enough to answer him. "Death by blow job? At least you'd die a happy man."

He started to laugh, but it turned into a strangled choke as I took him in deep with no warning at all, his cock hitting the back of my throat. Using my hand in tandem, I began to pump him in earnest, and he was absolutely right. It wasn't very long at all before he came and once I swallowed every drop, I kissed my way back up his body. Oliver's hands dug into my hair as he pulled me up to his mouth, kissing me deeply and possessively.

"My turn now," he said, trying to push me onto my back, but I held firm, keeping him down.

"This is still my thank you," I reminded him. "And I want to give you the ride of your life."

He growled again, this time in anticipation and I could feel his cock already stirring beneath me. It only took a couple more minutes of kissing before he was stiff again, and as I sank down onto him, we both sighed together. That feeling of him entering me, the amazing sparks between our bodies and feeling them from the inside, it was something that would never get old.

Oliver's hands intertwined with mine as I lifted my body up until just the very tip of him was in me, and then sank back down on him again. "Fuck, yes," he moaned. I couldn't have said it better myself.

We continued that way for a little longer until my own need grew too great, the pressure building so high it demanded a release. I dropped my hands to his shoulders and used his solid strength to steady myself as my hips moved faster, stroking his hard cock with my inner walls.

"Oliver!" His name flew from my lips as my orgasm took me, and I could feel him shuddering beneath me too, as perfectly in sync with me as always.

Collapsing onto him as pleasure washed over me, his warm arms embraced me, stroking my back gently as we both caught our breath.

"If this is the reward, I'll take you to any damn book festival you want," he muttered, and we both laughed.

I loved how he could always make me laugh, almost as much as I loved how he could always make me come. Finding a man who could do one of those things was rare enough, but having one who could do both was simply perfection.

Eventually we ordered some room service and then made love again before finally falling asleep.

When morning came, I could hardly contain my excitement. Oliver and I got dressed and had breakfast with the rest of our group and then Jack, Whitney, Caleb and Lincoln went off to do whatever they had planned while Liz, Melanie, Oliver and I headed to the Bay Book Festival.

As soon as we walked in, I felt like a kid in a candy store, hardly knowing which way to look first.

"I think there's a check-in table over here," Oliver said, pointing to the far wall. "I'll go see what's there, you guys can get started."

He wandered away from us while Liz, Melanie and I hurried to the first booth. It was for one of the top literary agents in the country and Liz and I were a little starstruck. We were in a lot of the same writing classes together and we both had ambitions of being published authors someday. We chatted with the woman from the agency for a few minutes until something caught my eye from across the room and I turned away to take a closer look.

Oliver was in a heated discussion with someone, his face set in a scowl that I had hardly ever seen on him before. I didn't recognize the person he was speaking to, and I couldn't imagine what had him so upset.

"Excuse me," I murmured to the woman at the booth and my friends. "I'll be right back."

Just as I started to walk over to where the two men were standing, someone bumped into me and the stack of books he was carrying fell to the ground.

"Oh, I'm so sorry," the man apologized. "I didn't see you there."

"I'm fine," I assured him. "It was my fault. Please, let me help you."

I stooped down to pick up the books and suddenly Oliver was in front of me. "Need some help, Heels?" he teased as he crouched down to assist me. "I can't leave you alone for two minutes, huh?"

Surprised at his sudden appearance and his casual tone after the argument I had just witnessed, I looked him over and frowned. He was wearing a blue t-shirt, which I remembered him putting on this morning now that I thought about it, but a second ago, when I saw him arguing with the other man, he'd been wearing a black one. Confused, I glanced back over to where the other man had been, but there was no one there.

"Heels?" Oliver's voice pulled me back to him. "You okay?"

"Yeah," I answered, still a little unsure as I picked up the last book and handed it back to the man it belonged to, then turned back to my mate. "Were you just talking to someone?"

He gave me a confused look of his own. "At the check-in desk, you mean?"

"No, I mean a big man with dark hair and a scar on his face."

Oliver still looked uncertain as he shook his head. "Wasn't me. Do we need to get your glasses checked?"

My glasses were fine, I knew that. But I was also certain I had seen him, or at least someone who looked almost exactly like him. I realized now that, besides the different coloured shirt, if it really had been Oliver, I would have been able to feel his agitation through our mate bond. Strong emotions were usually shared between us, and though the man I had seen was visibly upset, I hadn't felt anything, which must have meant it wasn't Oliver after all.

This was all very strange.

"You might have a doppelgänger here," I warned him. "I swear there was someone over there who looked just like you. Let's keep our eyes open."

He laughed at that, his handsome face relaxing into his easy grin. "If you say so. I think you just want two of me."

His teasing made me smile so I teased him right back. "Not a bad idea, actually. I can think of a few ways that might come in handy."

With another laugh, we went back to my friends who were still at the booth where I'd left them, but I couldn't help glancing back over my shoulder one more time, looking for the men I had seen arguing before, but there was no sign of either of them.

Chapter Two

~Oliver~

As we wandered through the festival, Abby kept looking around at all the other men, looking for this supposed double of mine.

"If you don't stop checking out all the other guys, Abby, I'm going to get a complex over here."

She blushed at my teasing, though she tried to hide it with a dirty look. "I'm just curious! You don't understand, he looked exactly like you."

I gave her an indulgent smile but I was sure she was exaggerating. There were a lot of men in the world with short, dirty blonde hair and a football player's build. Okay, maybe most of them didn't hang out at book festivals, but that didn't mean they weren't out there. And besides, from a distance she and Liz looked a lot alike too with their dark, wavy hair and glasses. It didn't strike me as nearly as unusual as she was making it out to be that there was someone here who looked like me.

The day went by quicker than I expected it to since it was so much fun to see Abby so excited. We went to a few readings, the girls all got copies of new books signed by some of their favourite authors and they even took part in a one-hour writing challenge. The winners were going to be announced at the end of the festival.

"What did you write about?" I asked Abby once they'd finished.

She gave me a far too innocent smile. "Oh, a completely fictional story about a werewolf getting shot with a poisoned arrow and her brilliant chemist mate who saved her life."

"Seriously?" I laughed, shaking my head. I was glad we could joke about it now, but it had been fucking terrifying when it happened.

She shrugged, trying to hold back her own laugh. "They say to write about what you know."

Finally the festival began to close down for the day and we headed for the door. "If you ladies don't mind," I said to Liz and Melanie. "I've got something planned for my girlfriend tonight. We'll see you back at the hotel later."

They both gave Abby a quick hug, and I heard Liz whisper to her how lucky she was. Most guys wouldn't have heard it, but most guys don't have wolf hearing. As soon as they were gone, I turned to Abby and took her hand. "So just how lucky are you?"

She tried to give me a look of disapproval for my eavesdropping, but there was far too much affection in it for it to have any sting. "Pretty damn lucky," she told me.

I took her down to a restaurant right on the water with a view of the bay and the bridge, where we shared a wonderful meal of fresh seafood and wine. As I looked across the table at my beautiful, intelligent, funny mate, I couldn't help feeling that no matter what her friends said, I was the lucky one here.

The sun was setting as we left the restaurant, casting golden beams across the water, and we sat for a while to watch the colours dancing in the waves.

"This is so nice, Oliver," Abby whispered to me, her eyes fixed on the water. "It almost feels like our lives at home aren't even real."

I recognized the hint of worry in her voice. "Hey." I waited until she looked up at me, her pale blue eyes meeting mine almost sheepishly. "Our real lives aren't so bad. This summer's going to be great. You'll get to know the whole pack and they'll get to know you. They're going to love you, Abby, I promise."

She shook her head at me. "You can't promise that."

"I can," I contradicted her. "I know them and I know you. It's all going to work out."

She nodded but I could tell she still didn't fully believe me, and there wasn't anything I could say that was going to convince her. She was just going to have to wait and see for herself.

"Come on, let's head back to the hotel," I suggested, standing up and offering her my hand. "There's a perfectly good bed going to waste."

That made her smile, at least. She took my hand and we started heading up the hill away from the water, chatting more about the festival as we went.

It was only a couple of blocks later that I first felt a bit uneasy, getting a distinct feeling that we were being watched. I took a quick look around us but there was nothing out of the ordinary. There were quite a few people out on the street as it was a beautiful evening, but none of them seemed to be paying any extra attention to us. I sniffed the air, looking for signs of other wolves, but there were no unusual scents.

Trying to shake off the strange feeling, I focused back on Abby as we kept walking, but less than half a block later I was almost certain we were being followed though I couldn't say exactly why I felt that way. I spun around but, once again, there was no one there.

"Oliver?" Abby's voice was warm and concerned. "Are you okay?"

I didn't want to alarm her. If she wasn't feeling anything strange, it was probably all in my head. I really couldn't see anything to be worried about anyway, it was just an odd feeling I had.

"It's nothing," I told her. "Just thought I heard something."

We resumed our climb up the hill, nearly back at the hotel by now, but as we passed the next alley, we were suddenly surrounded by a group of men who pulled us into the alley with them.

"Abby!" I called out. Two men were holding onto her and the sight of their hands on her nearly drove my wolf mad. A loud growl rumbled from my chest and the men holding onto me quickly tightened their grip.

"Calm down," the one on my right side instructed. "We don't want the girl. Come with us quietly and she'll be free to go."

Go with them? Where? Why? This made no sense, but they had chosen the wrong couple to mess with. I might not be armed in the traditional sense but I had my own weapons.

With another growl, I began to shift, and the man who had spoken to me swore loudly. "He's changing! Quick, the needle!"

Something sharp pierced the skin at the back of my neck just as I began to take my wolf form, and I heard Abby cry out.

"No! Oliver!"

I tried to answer her but before I could get any words out, the world went black.

~Abby~

Shock ran through me as Oliver collapsed in front of me. He'd been on the verge of shifting, the fur starting to sprout across his body and his claws coming out, but whatever they'd given him in the syringe had not only knocked him out, it had reversed the shift too. By the time the men holding onto him had propped him back up again, he was completely back to his human form.

These men obviously knew what we were but they weren't werewolves themselves, I would be able to smell it if they were. So who were they and what did they want with Oliver? Why did they want him to go with them?

The man holding the syringe looked over at me now, a hard look on his face. "If he'd just come quietly, I wouldn't have had to do that. It's your call now. You walk away from here and we'll let you go. If you try anything stupid, you'll get a needle of your own, and since we don't need you, we'll just leave here in this alley all alone."

I had no doubt that he was serious. What was I supposed to do? I couldn't just let them take Oliver but there were five of them and only one of me. Even if I managed to shift before he jabbed me, I couldn't take them all on and get Oliver away as well.

I was going to have to be smart about this.

Looking over Oliver's unconscious form, I could see the outline of his phone in his pocket, and I started to get an idea. Shortly after we'd moved in together, Oliver's friend Kevin had set us both up with tracking systems on each other's phones as a precaution. He meant it to be used in case one of our phones was stolen, not if the person holding it was taken, but the principle was the same.

So long as his phone was on him, I could find out where he was.

With that in mind, I tried to relax my stance and look submissive. "Okay, I'll go."

The man nodded in satisfaction. "That's the right decision. Now get out of here."

The men holding me released me and shoved me back towards the street. My chest ached at the thought of letting Oliver out of my sight and I couldn't help glancing back as I took a few steps. Four of the men were lifting him now and carrying him in the other direction, but one of them turned back to make sure I was really leaving.

My heart pounding, I went around the corner so they would think I'd gone, then peered back into the alley just in time to see them take a left turn at the other end. Moving as quickly and quietly as I could, I ran down the alley after them and peeked around the corner again. A large white van was parked next to the curb and they were loading him into the back of it.

Frantically, I scanned the streets for a taxi, but there weren't any. There was, however, a man getting into his car a short way down the street in the opposite direction, so I ran for him instead.

"This is going to sound crazy," I said with no introduction. "But I need to follow that van. Can you help me, please?"

The man gave me a rather nervous look. "Why do you need to follow it?"

"They have my boyfriend," I told him, fully aware of how insane I sounded but not able to do anything about it. "Please, he's in trouble."

The man's expression turned harder. "Look, miss, I don't want to get involved in anything."

"His life could be in danger," I tried, but I could tell it wasn't helping. He obviously thought I was crazy. "Please, I can pay you."

He got into the car without bothering to answer me this time, locking the doors behind him.

Damn it. I could hear the doors of the van being slammed shut down the street and my stomach lurched painfully. What could I do now?

"I can take you," a new voice from behind me said.

I spun around to find a woman, at least ten years older than me, with bright red hair, a leather jacket and several piercings in the parts of her body that I could see. Her appearance was unusual, but it didn't startle me nearly as much as her scent did.

She was a werewolf too.

~Oliver~

My head was throbbing as I regained consciousness and there was a strange buzzing noise in my ears. I started to open my eyes, then immediately squeezed them shut again as the light was far too bright.

"He's waking up," a deep voice said. It sounded vaguely familiar but it took me a moment to place it. Finally the scene in the alley came rushing back to me and I forced my eyes open no matter how painful it was.

I was in a small room with brick walls and a concrete floor. There was a single rectangular window high on one wall, providing a bit of outside light. Bright fluorescent lights flickered overhead, which explained the buzzing sound I could hear, and I was sitting on a metal chair that appeared to be bolted to the floor, with ropes wrapped tightly around my chest, keeping me upright while I was unconscious.

There was no sign of the man who had just spoken, the same one who had talked to me in the alley, but the door to the room was wide open so he must have just stepped outside.

'Abby?' I reached out to her through our mind-link as panic flooded my body. The last thing I had seen was her being restrained by two of the men. Was she here? What had they done with her?

There was no reply and adrenaline rushed through me as I went to shift to my wolf form. The shift would break me out of these ropes easily enough.

But despite all the blood pumping through my veins, nothing happened. I tried again, and again there was nothing, not even the tingle on my skin that was usually the first sign of my fur starting to grow.

"Stop struggling."

My head snapped up to see the man from before standing in the open doorway with two of his goons behind him.

It was the first time I was able to get a good look at him since there had been too much going on in the alley to pay any attention to what he looked like. He was human, obviously, probably in his mid-30s. He had short, dark hair and a matching beard, and what looked like a long scar across one cheek. He had the build of a fighter, and if I'd had to make an on-the-spot guess, I would have put my money on him having a military background.

"You can squirm all you want but you're not shifting for a while," he said as he walked into the room, leaving the other men at the door. "Your mind-link's been silenced too. You've got nothing to do and nowhere to go, Elijah, so you and I can have a good, long talk."

I was so busy trying to figure out how on earth they had stopped me from shifting that it took me a moment to realize what he'd called me.

"Elijah?" I repeated. "That's not my name."

The man smirked at me. "Eli, then? I didn't realize we were on such friendly terms."

I tried to growl at him but the sound came out much weaker than usual. "I don't know what any of this is about, but my name isn't Elijah, it's Oliver. And where the fuck is my mate?"

The last words came out shouted and normally with my Alpha authority, even humans would be a little affected, but this man showed no signs of it. It was almost like I didn't have a wolf at all.

"The girl's fine," he told me, still with that annoying smirk on his face. "I didn't realize you had a mate though, I thought she was just another of your hookups. If I'd have known she was special, I would have hung on to her. Maybe that would have given you a little more incentive to cooperate."

He moved closer, lowering himself down so he was eye-level with me.

"Now let's get to the point. Where's the book, Elijah?"

Book? What fucking book?

"I don't know what you're talking about," I answered him in the same cool tone he was using with me. "And again, my name is not Elijah. Are you deaf as well as stupid?"

He sighed, standing back up again. "I really wanted to do this the easy way. I thought putting your wolf to sleep for a while would be enough, but you want to play hardball? We can do that."

He gestured to one of the men still standing by the door, who stepped forward and handed the guy in front of me a switchblade.

"What do you think, Elijah?" he asked, flipping the knife open. "Will your mate be happy with you if you come back with that pretty face of yours all messed up? Without your wolf to help you heal, I could give you a nice, permanent scar, just like mine."

He gestured to his face as if he was proud of the jagged line there, and I swallowed hard. Clearly, I wasn't about to intimidate this guy. I was going to need to try something else.

"Look, let's back up a second here," I said, inclining my head as a peace offering. "There's obviously been some kind of misunderstanding. As I already told you, my name's Oliver. Oliver West. I'm here for the weekend with my mate, I don't know you, and I don't know anything about any book."

As soon as the word 'book' came out of my mouth, I had a flash of realization. *My double.* Abby said she saw someone at the book festival who looked just like me. Fuck, maybe she wasn't kidding. Maybe this double, whoever he was, really did exist.

I decided to share that bit of information too. "We were at the Bay Book Festival today and my mate thought she saw someone who looked like me. Maybe that was this Elijah that you're looking for. All I know is, it's not me."

The man was giving me a calculating look, clearly not buying a word I was saying. "Well, there's an easy enough way to tell for sure, isn't there? Let's see your tattoo."

My tattoo? How the hell did this guy know about my tattoo? I had a wolf and a jade moon tattooed on my side to represent my pack, but it wasn't something that a stranger should know about. None of this was making any sense to me but if seeing it would somehow convince him that I wasn't this Elijah person, I was fine with that. "You'll have to untie me," I pointed out. "I can't lift my arm like this."

The man gave me a funny look. "That won't be necessary."

He moved around to the back of my chair and pulled the neck of my shirt down. There was a moment of silence, followed closely by a loud curse. "You fucking idiots!"

That wasn't directed at me, obviously, since there was only one of me. The two men in the doorway shifted their weight nervously as he took a few steps towards him.

"He doesn't have the mark! This isn't him."

Mark? What mark? The only mark I had was my mark from Abby, and it wasn't on the back of my neck. No wolf had their mark there.

What the hell was he talking about?

"He looks just like him," one of the men offered nervously. "And he was at the festival. How were we supposed to know?"

His reward for that answer was a punch to the face that knocked him straight to the ground. The other man winced but made no move to help his colleague who staggered back to his feet unsteadily.

"I can't fucking believe this," the man who'd been speaking to me muttered before facing me again. "What did you say your name was?"

"Oliver West," I repeated, grateful that at least they seemed to be believing me now. "Look, mistakes happen. Let me go and I'll forget the whole thing."

He gave an almost rueful smile. "I wish I could do that, Oliver, but I'm afraid you've seen too much. No one's supposed to know I can shut down a wolf."

I was still very curious how he had done that in the first place but this didn't seem the best time to ask. "I won't say anything," I promised.

"I'd like to believe you," he replied, still looking almost regretful. "But I can't take that chance. This just wasn't your lucky day."

He handed the knife back to the man who had given it to him and reached into the back waistband of his pants, pulling out a gun instead, and my stomach dropped. This couldn't be happening. Even with my wolf, surviving a gunshot wound would be difficult. Without him, I had no chance.

The man raised the gun, aiming it directly at me. "I really am sorry. For you, and your mate too."

Abby. My heart was pounding in terror but the only thing I could think of was her. Was I really never going to see her again? It felt like I had just found her and there were so many things we were still meant to do together. I couldn't believe this was how it was going to end.

With her image lodged firmly in my mind, I closed my eyes, waiting for the inevitable click of the trigger.

~Abby~

"Who are you?" I asked the werewolf in front of me, the rather punk-rock-looking woman who had just offered me a ride.

She raised an eyebrow at me curiously. "Do you really care? I thought you just wanted to follow your mate."

Oliver. My eyes flew back to the van which was just pulling away with him inside. She was right. It didn't matter who she was or why she was here: if she was going to help me keep him in sight, I was going to have to trust her.

"Let's go."

With a half-smile of approval, the woman pointed to a motorcycle parked just behind the car I'd been trying to talk my way into. "You know how to ride?"

I didn't answer her, walking quickly over to the bike instead and grabbing the helmet that was hanging off the handlebar. "They're leaving, come on!"

She grabbed another helmet from the bike box and climbed on the front of the bike while I quickly hopped on behind her. By the time we were moving, the van was at the end of the street already and taking the corner.

"Go right!" I shouted at her and she turned her head to the side with a sarcastic tilt.

"I don't need a backseat driver," she yelled back. "I can see them. Just hold on."

Revving the bike, she accelerated into the corner, taking it at such an angle that I could almost feel my leg brush the pavement. Maybe this wasn't the best idea, getting on this bike with someone I knew absolutely nothing about, but it was the only idea I had, so I was going to have to just hang on and hope for the best.

She stayed a car or two behind the white van as we moved through the city streets, up and down hills, through what felt like a complete maze to me, until finally they turned off into a commercial area made up of warehouses and small office buildings.

She slowed down then as no other cars turned off with us and it would have been too obvious we were following them if she kept the same speed. It made sense as she did it, but I wasn't sure I would have thought of it. I couldn't help thinking she must have done this kind of thing before.

We were able to keep them just in sight as they pulled into an empty parking lot in front of a small, square building. At the same time, we pulled over and the woman I was with grabbed her phone to make it look like that was the reason we'd stopped. It didn't prove necessary though, as no one seemed to be paying any attention to us. The men quickly exited the van and one of them opened the door to the building while the others carried Oliver inside. Only when they were completely out of sight did she put her phone away and we moved forward again. She pulled over and parked her bike on the side of the street just past the building we wanted.

"So what's your plan?" the woman asked me as she got off the bike and took her helmet off, shaking out her unnaturally red hair.

I had no idea what my plan was. I'd only gotten as far as making sure I knew where Oliver was, and now I wasn't sure what to do next. I could really use some help, so I asked the woman for it, flat out. "I don't suppose you'd be willing to help me out a little more?"

She gave me a smirk that suggested she had expected that question. "I'm here anyway, aren't I? What's your name?"

"Abby," I introduced myself. "What's yours?"

"Storm," she replied, and then laughed when I raised my eyebrows in surprise. "Not my birth name, obviously, but I choose my own path in life. And right now, my path seems to have led me to you. So what's your plan, Abby?"

I tried to think about this logically, just like I knew Oliver would if he were in my shoes.

"There are at least five of them," I said, thinking out loud. "And maybe more inside. We don't have any weapons except our wolves, so at some point we're going to have to shift."

She nodded in agreement then gestured towards the building. "There are several ways in, but it would help if we knew exactly where he was in the building."

That was something I could do. I pulled out my phone, opened the tracking app and zoomed in as far as it could go. The little dot representing Oliver's phone was towards the back of the building, in the right corner, and I showed it to Storm now.

"Good," she said, sounding impressed. "That's helpful. Let's go check it out."

Trying to look as innocent as possible in case anyone was watching, we made our way around the side of the building. The room in the back right corner, the one that Oliver must be in, only had one window and it was quite high off the ground. Storm examined it carefully, judging the height and distance.

"I can make that jump in my wolf form," she concluded. "Can you?"

I wouldn't know for sure until I tried, but I was highly motivated. "I'll make it," I promised.

She nodded. "Okay. Then we just need to find something to break the window first. The glass doesn't look very thick, it should be easy to break if we have something hard enough."

Together we scoured the surrounding area, but there was nothing obvious, no bricks or stones that might be useful. I kept reaching out to Oliver through my mind-link as we searched but there was no reply. He must still be unconscious, I figured. If anything worse than that had happened to him, I would have felt it.

When a few minutes had passed and we were still coming up empty, I looked back towards the street. "What about the bike helmet?"

Again, that little half-smile crossed her face. "Smart. Go grab it, I'll wait here."

I did as she said, running back to her bike and grabbing the helmet I'd been wearing. As I got back to the rear of the building, Storm was on her phone, talking to someone, but she hung up as soon as she saw me. "Got it?" she asked.

Something about the quick way she ended the call made me a little uneasy, but I couldn't waste time by stopping to question it now. We needed to get in to see Oliver as soon as possible.

"How's your throwing arm?" she asked next, looking between the helmet in my hands and the window.

If Oliver were here in my place, he would have no problem, I thought, remembering all his precision throws as the college football team's star quarterback. But athletics were really not my strong suit.

"Not great," I admitted. "What about you?"

Storm took the helmet from my hands and bounced it a little as if judging its weight, then she looked back up at the window. "Yeah, I think I can manage that. Step back so the glass doesn't hit you."

I quickly took a couple of steps back as Storm wound up to throw it, but then she suddenly stopped and looked back at me.

"I guess we better strip first, if we want to have any clothes when we get back out?"

That was a good point. I didn't usually shift out in the open like this so it wasn't something I was used to worrying about. I scanned the area quickly, looking for any security cameras that might pick us up, but there didn't seem to be any, so we both stripped down to our underwear and I shifted to my wolf as she wound up again.

This time she released the helmet with force and precision, and it hit the window directly in the middle, shattering it instantly. Sounds of surprise from inside quickly reached our ears, and she nodded at me. "Go get him, Abby."

Taking a running leap, I jumped through the open window.

Chapter Three

~**Oliver**~

The gunshot I was expecting never came. Instead there was a loud crash along with the sound of glass shattering, and I opened my eyes just in time to see a motorcycle helmet hit the ground as the men at the door shouted out in surprise.

"What the...?" the man with the gun muttered, looking away from me, but before he could finish the thought, a wolf leapt gracefully through the window, its eyes falling immediately on him and the gun in his hand. The wolf's jaws snapped down on his arm before he had a chance to react, and a second later another wolf appeared, this one slightly bigger and more red in colour.

I had no idea who the second wolf was, but the first one was completely familiar to me. *Abby.*

My brilliant mate, saving my ass once again.

The two men who'd been standing at the door both turned tail and ran as the red wolf growled at them, leaving only the man who'd been threatening me, with his arm stuck in Abby's mouth. The gun he'd been holding had fallen to the ground. As he struggled against Abby's grip, the red wolf shifted into a tattooed, red-haired woman I had never seen before. Her tattoos covered so much of her body it wasn't even immediately apparent that she was naked. She grabbed the gun off the floor and aimed it at the man who'd been about to shoot me with it.

"Call your men," she ordered, sounding calm and completely in control of the situation. "Tell them we're walking out of here with you and if they try to stop us, you die."

His jaw clenched and I could see the simmering rage in his eyes. Still, he reached down to pull out some kind of communication device that had been attached to his belt. His words were clipped as he relayed the order and requested acknowledgement, which was quickly received.

"Let him go now, Abby," the woman said next. "Go get your mate."

I was more grateful to see them than I'd ever been to see anyone but still incredibly confused about what was happening. How did Abby and this woman know each other? How did they find me?

Abby released the man's arm and padded over to me, still in her wolf form, and used her sharp canine teeth to gnaw through the ropes that were restraining me. I jumped to my feet as they fell to the floor.

"Let's get out of here," I suggested sharply. Their appearance was nothing short of a miracle and I didn't want to test my luck by staying another second.

The woman with the gun led the way, checking around each corner to make sure no one was lying in wait, but the coast seemed to be clear as we exited the building into an empty parking lot.

"Here, take over a second," she said to me, thrusting the gun into my hands as Abby shifted and re-dressed in the clothes she must have left here. The other woman didn't bother getting dressed, but she did pick up her clothes and tuck them under her arm. I held the gun steady, pointed at the man who was glowering at me now, his frustration almost palpable.

When she had her clothes sorted out, the woman retrieved the gun from me, and with my arms free, I finally got to embrace my courageous mate.

"Thank you, Abby," I whispered to her. I had no idea how she had got here, but I owed her my life. She was incredible.

"What's wrong with your wolf?" she asked, looking up at me in concern. "I can't feel you."

"It's just temporary," I told her. At least I hoped it was. "Whatever they injected me with, it put him to sleep."

"Let's save the catching up for later," the woman said to me, still aiming the gun at the man. She addressed him now with a smirk of familiarity. "We'll meet again, I'm sure."

"I'm sure we will," the man agreed, his face and his voice filled with hostility before the woman punched him hard in the face, knocking him out in one fell swoop.

That was impressive. I wasn't sure I could have done it any better. Whoever this woman was, she clearly knew what she was doing. With the woman still holding onto the gun to provide cover for us, we left the man behind and went back to the street where there was a motorcycle waiting.

"What's the plan?" I asked them, looking between Abby and the woman and the single bike. "We won't all fit on there."

"You can take it," the woman said. "Go to this address. I'll shift and run there, I know how to avoid being seen."

Pulling a Sharpie from a compartment on the bike, she wrote an address on my arm. Then she placed the gun on the ground, handed her clothes to Abby and her keys to me, and shifted back into her wolf before picking the gun back up in her mouth. In a flash she was gone, ducking between buildings as she ran down the street.

I looked at Abby in total confusion and she shrugged back at me. "I honestly have no idea who she is," she told me. "But if she wanted to hurt us, she could have done it with that gun just now. So we might as well go where she told us to and maybe then we can get some answers."

I supposed that was the best plan and, in any case, we should definitely get out of here before any of those men came back. Abby and I both climbed onto the bike and she pulled out her phone to look up the address as we drove and shouted directions at me since my mind-link still wasn't working.

It wasn't too long before we arrived in front of a house with the address that was written on my arm. I couldn't say for sure what I had been expecting to find, but it certainly wasn't a mansion behind large iron gates. As we pulled up to the driveway, something on the bike beeped and the gates began to swing open on their own.

Who the hell is this woman?

I drove the bike up the drive and parked it outside the huge front door. Abby and I both climbed off and I turned to her, finally able to take a proper look at her for the first time since she'd arrived to save me. "Are you okay?"

She gave me a rather wry smile. "You're the one who was injected with something and tied up and held at gunpoint. I think I should be asking you if you're okay."

"I'm alright. I still can't feel my wolf at all but hopefully it won't be for much longer."

Abby nodded, her brow lined with concern. "I hope not either. What on earth did they want with you?"

I let out a huffed laugh as I thought back to it. "They thought I was someone else. I think they thought I was the guy you saw at the festival this morning, the one who looked like me."

Abby's eyes widened. "Seriously?"

Before I could answer, the door in front of us opened and the woman from before appeared, back in her human form and fully dressed already in a t-shirt and ripped jeans. She must have sprinted the whole way to get here before us and have time to dress. "Were you guys planning on coming in or were you just going to stand out here all day?"

I looked back at Abby and she simply shrugged as if to say she didn't know anything more than I did. We both headed inside, following the woman into a huge entrance hall with at least six doors leading into other rooms and a large staircase that wound its way up to the next level.

She led us into an elegant, formal sitting room through one of the doors and I looked around curiously at the antique furniture and expensive-looking paintings on the walls. Everything about the room seemed completely at odds with the woman's casual appearance. I had a million

questions as we all sat down but she asked one of her own before I had a chance to begin.

"How long have you been hiding the fact that you found your mate, Eli?"

Not this again. I was going to clear this up right now.

"Look, I don't know who this Eli person is. Apparently I look like him and that's why those men wanted me. But my name is Oliver, this is my mate Abby, and this is our first day in San Francisco. We're just visiting for the weekend and we have no idea what the hell is going on, so I'm really hoping you can fill us in."

The woman's eyes widened as I spoke. "Fuck. You really aren't him, are you? You don't sound the same but you look just like him."

Abby turned to me with a satisfied smirk. "I told you."

She really had, but that wasn't what I was most worried about right now. "Thank you for helping to get me out of there. I don't mean to sound rude, but I am really fucking confused right now and I would love some answers. Who are you, and who, exactly, is Elijah?"

~Elijah~

The club was dark as I made my way inside and it took a moment for my eyes to adjust. My hand ran subconsciously across the tattoo on the back of my neck as I waited. It showed a trail of words leading to a golden light in the distance, a golden future I'd been seeking for a very long time, and at last, it felt like I was on the right path.

It was still early enough in the evening that the club was fairly empty so once I could see clearly, it didn't take me long to find the person I was looking for. I slid into the booth across the table from him as we gave each other a nod of greeting.

"You're sure you weren't followed?" my Beta asked, his eyes darting to the door and back again.

"Positive."

I was more than a little surprised not to have been. I'd taken all kinds of precautions just in case I was, circling blocks, backtracking and going through the protocol I'd laid out for myself in advance, even though there was no sign of anyone on my tail.

After running into Darryn Reeves this morning at the book festival and the confrontation we'd had, I had to change my initial plans. Originally I'd hoped to get the book and get out again, as simple as that. But once I saw him there, I knew if he or any of his team did follow me and managed to catch me, they'd take the book, so I made sure that the one I was carrying was a decoy. If they had taken it, it would have fooled them temporarily, but it wouldn't have done them any good in the long run.

Meanwhile I handed off the real book, the one everyone was after, to my Beta Julian with instructions to meet me here with it now.

And then I somehow managed to lose my shadows anyway, making all my precautions unnecessary. I couldn't quite understand where they'd gone but I wasn't about to look a gift horse in the mouth. I was here and clear, that was what was important, and I laid the decoy copy on the table now. "You've still got the original, I hope?"

Julian's face filled with panic for a moment and my heart nearly stopped. I couldn't guess what my face looked like but the expression on it made him laugh before he reached down to pick up the book from the bench next to him. He placed it on the table too, sliding it across to me. "Sometimes you're too easy to tease, Eli."

I growled at him and he immediately bowed his head in apology, feeling the power of my disapproval. Normally I didn't mind the odd joke but this was no laughing matter. This was the piece of the puzzle we'd been seeking out for the last five years, and if one of the other people who was also looking for it had got to it first, all the time we'd spent would have been wasted. There was nothing funny about that.

But now I really had it. After all this time, the book was here in my hands.

Almost reverently, I picked it up and flipped the cover open. Written inside was a list of names of people the book had belonged to. My eyes went immediately to the bottom of the list and the name scrawled there in a rather childish script. The book's last owner.

Nicole Williams. My mother's name.

Those two words were pretty much the only thing I really knew about her.

"You're sure this is it, right?" Julian asked, leaning over across the table to try to see what I was looking at.

"It has to be," I replied. "There can't be two of them."

Other than the decoy sitting next to it on the table, of course. But the one in my hands, this was no fake. This was the real thing, I had no doubt, and I was desperate to dig into it now but I had to remember we were still in public. Even if I hadn't been followed here directly, it wasn't worth taking any chances. I hadn't come this far to mess up now.

"We should head out tonight," I told Julian. "Get back to the pack territory before anyone has a chance to catch up with us."

He nodded in agreement and we both stood up. As we walked out the door, I pushed down that other feeling that had been following me all day.

My mate had been at the festival too, I was almost sure of it. The overpowering scent, the feel of being pulled towards her, it was all just as I expected it to be when I finally met her, but the timing couldn't be worse. I was nearing the end of the quest that I'd dedicated myself to for so long and the last thing I needed was to get distracted now. So when I started to feel the mate pull, I didn't even look for her. I left before she could find me, and now I was leaving town too.

Whoever she was, she was just going to have to wait.

~Abby~

Storm leaned back in her chair, looking between the two of us as Oliver demanded answers.

"As I've already told your mate, my name's Storm. As for the rest of it, it might be safer for you not to know," she told us frankly. "You've already seen first-hand the dangers of getting involved."

That was true but I knew Oliver wouldn't be satisfied with that. He had a scientific curiosity about everything and this was a mystery that would drive him crazy if he never got to the bottom of it.

He told Storm as much now. "We're already involved, whether we want to be or not. So now I want to know who those men were, who you are, who Elijah is, and what book they're looking for."

Storm's eyes widened as Oliver mentioned a book, and I repeated the word in my head curiously. 'Book?'

'Heels?' Oliver's voice echoed in my head. 'I heard that.'

Thank the goddess, his wolf must be waking up. No sooner had I thought so than I picked up on his agitation too. He was more shaken up by all of this than he was letting on externally. Not that I blamed him at all, of course. What he'd just been through was more than a little traumatic. I placed my hand on his thigh to help calm him, and he covered it with his own hand gratefully, giving mine a little squeeze.

"What do you know about the book?" Storm asked warily.

"Nothing," Oliver answered truthfully. "That's the point. All I know is that they were looking for a book and they thought Elijah had it. They thought I had it, since they thought I was Elijah."

Storm sighed. "Alright, look. I can understand that you feel you deserve some answers so I'll tell you the basics. But after that, I really suggest that you just forget all of this ever happened and go back to your own lives."

I could tell from the way that Oliver's jaw clenched that he didn't agree, but he nodded curtly anyway, obviously trying to get her to reveal anything at all.

"So there's a book," she began. "A very valuable book to certain people. For many years, nobody knew where it was, but recently there were rumours that it was going to be offered for sale today at the Bay Book Festival. There are at least three different people who want it. Darryn Reeves is the man you had such a nice introduction to today, he's one of them. Elijah's the second, and my employer is the third."

I tried my best to sort through all that in my head. "So Darryn didn't get the book," I surmised, since he had asked Oliver for it. "And I'm guessing you don't have it either, so does that mean Elijah's got it?"

Storm sighed again. "It certainly looks that way, which means I'm going to have to find him."

Oliver nodded, having obviously reached the same conclusion. "Sounds good. And we're coming with you."

~Oliver~

As soon as I said Abby and I were going along to find Elijah, Storm immediately shook her head.

"No way. It's going to be tough enough for me to track him down, I can't be babysitting the two of you as well."

Abby looked just about as offended by that as I felt, and Storm gave a nod of acknowledgement in Abby's direction.

"I'll admit, the way you chased down your mate today was pretty badass, but I work alone, always have and always will. Sorry. If you want to find Elijah, you'll have to do it on your own."

As frustrating as that answer was, I could understand where she was coming from. She didn't know us, after all, and certainly didn't owe us anything. On top of that, she'd already helped save my life, even if she only did it because she thought I was someone else.

"That's fair," I agreed. "But can you at least give us some clues? His full name? What pack he's from? Anything that would help us get started."

"Why do you care?" Storm asked in reply. "It's honestly better for you to stay out of it."

"I care because apparently there's somebody out there with my face," I pointed out. "I'd like to know who he is."

"And if this guy is caught up in dangerous things, Oliver could still be in danger," Abby added. "We need to understand what's going on so we can protect ourselves."

Storm sighed again. She did that quite a lot, I'd noticed, though I wasn't sure if it was simply a habit of hers or if we were particularly exasperating. "If Elijah's got the book, he won't be sticking around and neither will Reeves, so I'm sure you're in the clear for as long as you're here. However, I do also see your point. I'll tell you a little bit about him but if things go wrong, don't say I didn't warn you."

She pulled a phone out of her pocket and tapped on the screen for a minute before handing it to me, and my jaw dropped as I got a look at the photo on the screen.

This guy didn't just look like me. If I didn't know any better, I would think it *was* me.

Was it really possible for a complete stranger to have such a strong resemblance? Or was it possible there was something else going on here?

"You see why I thought it was you?" Abby's voice was soft in my ear as she leaned over my shoulder to take a look at the photo too.

"I do," I had to admit. "Is there some kind of successful cloning project I don't know about?"

I was only half-joking, but Storm smiled as she took the phone back from me. "If one of you is a clone, who's to say which one is the real one? Maybe you're the clone and you never knew it."

'He could be related to you,' Abby's voice suggested in my head via our mind-link. 'Through your biological father?'

The same thought had crossed my mind as soon as I laid eyes on the picture. I had found out a few months ago, back when Abby and I were still getting to know each other, that the man who raised me and I'd always thought was my father was not actually my biological dad. He'd offered to tell me the name and pack of the man whose genes I had inherited, but with everything going on with school and football and getting to know Abby and preparing to take over the pack, it honestly hadn't been top of my list of priorities.

I wished now that I knew a little more.

And in any case, I didn't want to bring any of this up in front of Storm. We still had no idea exactly how much we could trust her. 'He could be,' I agreed with Abby, still communicating through our link. 'Let's see what else we can find out.'

"You know I can tell that you're talking to each other, right?" Storm was looking back and forth between me and Abby with an expression of amusement on her face. "I can see your eyes cloud as you mind-link. This is exactly why I'm not taking you along with me. Amateur mistake."

Once again, that was a valid point, but I ignored it to move on to what I really wanted to know. "So he's basically my double, I can see that, but you still haven't told us who he is."

"His name's Elijah Reynolds," she said, glancing back at the photo on her phone one last time before switching the phone off and putting it back in her pocket. "He's Alpha of the Seven Hills pack."

He was an Alpha? That certainly increased the likelihood of him being related to me since my biological father was also from Alpha blood, as was my adoptive dad.

"Where are they located?" Abby asked.

"Oregon," Storm answered. "I don't know exactly where though, so that's as much as I can tell you."

A memory stirred in my mind, snippets of my mother telling me a story about the forests in Oregon and the huge redwood tree forests she would run through. She must have grown up there but I realized now that I didn't even know the name of the pack she had come from, nor had I ever thought about how she met my dad when they lived so far away from each other.

As a child, it was hard to think of my parents as people with past lives of their own. I had never asked those kinds of questions, but now it seemed like it was well past time I started learning more about them, and about my biological dad's family too.

"I wouldn't waste your time going there right now anyway," Storm continued. "If he's got the book, he won't be going home."

That brought me back to the other big question we hadn't discussed yet. "What's the deal with this book? Why is it so special?"

She just shook her head. "That's definitely above your pay grade, Oliver. Find Elijah if you want, but trust me, you don't want to get mixed up in anything else about this book. The people who are after it aren't messing around."

I already knew that. As I remembered the man pointing the gun at me earlier, my heart rate spiked again, and Abby immediately leaned into me, feeling my agitation through our link.

"Maybe we should head back to the hotel now," she suggested to me softly. "We can sleep on this and decide what to do tomorrow."

"That's an excellent idea," Storm agreed. She pulled out her phone once again and tapped it a couple of more times. "There's a taxi coming for you now, it'll drop you off wherever you need to go. It's already paid for."

"And you're really not going to tell us anything about yourself?" I asked her one last time, glancing again around the room at all the expensive décor.

"That is also above your pay grade, but I will give you this."

Standing up, she went over to a small writing desk at one side of the room, which was obviously an antique. From one of the drawers, she pulled out a small business card and walked back over to us, handing it to Abby.

"If you find yourself in trouble again, you can reach out to me. At least thanks to you, I know that Elijah has the book. My employer wouldn't have been pleased if I lost track of it, so I owe you one. You can collect that favour when you need to."

I glanced at the card as Abby held it in her palm. It was black with a storm cloud etched in gold and a phone number. That was all, no name or any other information.

Storm walked us back to the door and opened it for Abby and I to step outside. "Take care of yourselves," she said. "And remember, before you start digging too deep, make sure you can handle whatever you uncover."

With those rather cryptic words, she closed the door behind us, leaving Abby and I on our own once again.

Chapter Four

~**Abby**~

Oliver was quiet on the taxi ride back to the hotel and by the time we got up to our room he'd still only said a few words since we left Storm's house. I could feel his turmoil and, other than helping him get the answers he wanted, I could only think of one way to help him right now.

"Take off your clothes," I instructed him once we were inside. "And lay down on the bed."

That got his attention, at least, and he raised his eyebrows at me in amusement. "Really, Heels? Not even a kiss first?"

I shook my head at him with a disapproving smile. "Don't get your hopes up. You're tense and worried so I'm going to give you a massage."

I could almost see his muscles start to relax just at the mention of it. "That sounds amazing," he said, flashing me a grateful smile.

As quickly as possible, he stripped before lying face down on the bed while I grabbed some lotion from the bathroom then climbed on top of him, straddling his waist.

"You don't want to take your clothes off too?" he suggested, his voice slightly muffled in the pillows.

"I don't want you getting too excited," I teased him as I squirted some lotion onto his back and began to press my fingers into his tight muscles. "You need to relax. Now tell me exactly what happened."

Between little moans of pleasure as I hit particularly good spots, Oliver relayed everything I had missed and I told him about how I had come across Storm in the first place.

"She must have been following us too, thinking I was Elijah," Oliver suggested. "It felt like someone was following us after we left the restaurant but it couldn't have been the men that took me because they were waiting ahead in the alley."

That made sense. It obviously wasn't a coincidence that she had shown up right when I needed her, she must have been there for a reason.

And now that he'd mentioned Elijah, I focused back on him. "So what theories have you come up with so far about who he might be?"

"I think he must be related to my biological dad," Oliver said, which matched up with what I'd already suggested. "Storm said Elijah's from Oregon and I think that's where my biological dad's pack is located. We know that he was someone my mom knew from when she was growing up, and I think she was from there too"

"That's a lot of 'I thinks'," I couldn't help pointing out.

"It is," he agreed with a bit of a sigh. "I'm going to have to ask my dad about it. My real dad, I mean. Patrick."

This certainly was all a little bit confusing to keep track of.

"Do you want to go home early then?" I asked. I knew my mate. Once his curiosity was aroused about something, he wouldn't rest until he got answers. "We could leave in the morning."

"That's not necessary," he assured me. "If everyone's off chasing Elijah now, we should be safe, like Storm said, and I don't want you to miss the rest of the festival or for our friends to miss out on their trip either."

He was always so considerate. Once again, I paused for a moment to appreciate how lucky I was in my mate, and suddenly tears filled my eyes. Oliver immediately sensed my change of mood through our link and he twisted around to look at me.

"What's wrong, Heels?"

"I'm just so glad you're okay," I whispered to him, finally letting myself think about just how close he had been to being seriously injured, or worse. With all the adrenaline and excitement of the chase and rescue, I hadn't really let it sink in yet.

Somehow he managed to get out from beneath me and have his arms around me before I even realized what was happening. "It's going to take more than that to take me away from you," he promised, his warm grey eyes looking deep into mine. "Especially when you keep saving me right in the nick of time."

I wasn't sure if he moved towards me or I moved towards him, but in an instant our lips were together and I was kissing him with all the worry and fear and love and hope I had inside me. A growl of answering emotion sounded from deep in his chest, letting me know his wolf was well and truly back. Before long my clothes had joined his on the floor, my glasses were off, and he was entering me with even more urgency than usual.

"I was scared, Abby," he admitted to me as his hips rolled against me. "Scared I'd never get to see your face again as I do this."

He pulled out of me for a moment just to fill me back up again deeply, making me cry out in pure pleasure and need for him.

"I want to still be doing this when we're eighty," he moaned, and I had to laugh for just a minute, until he thrust into me again, and again, until there were no thoughts left in my head but how perfect he felt and how perfect he made me feel, until the world exploded around me.

We fell asleep still tangled up in each other and we were woken the next morning by a knock on the door.

"Shit," Oliver groaned as he grabbed his phone to check the time. "We're late."

Moving as quickly as we could, we got ready and joined our friends for breakfast.

"Late night?" Whitney asked us in a teasing tone as we sat down at the table. "Or is the book festival really that exciting?"

Oliver and I exchanged glances. Obviously we couldn't tell them what really happened without revealing much more about ourselves than we wanted to. "It took more out of us than we expected," I replied vaguely. "What did you guys get up to yesterday?"

They filled us in on their day as we ate and then we were all off again. The second day of the festival was just as good as the first and the evening was far less eventful, thankfully. The whole group of us went out to a nice club for drinks and dancing and it was all completely normal. Almost before I knew it, we were back at the convention centre for the third and final day of the festival, waiting for the results of the writing contest from the first afternoon. They were giving prizes to the top five entries and Liz's piece was chosen as number five. Oliver, Melanie and I cheered for her enthusiastically as she went up to collect her prize, and then the next two winners were announced.

That only left two spots, and I was beginning to feel a little discouraged. Maybe my story had been a little too fantastical, even though it was actually a real-life account?

"Second place and honourable mention goes to... Abby Flintoff."

My feet left the ground before I even fully registered what the man had said as Oliver swept me up into a giant bear hug. "I'm so proud of you, Heels." He grinned at me, giving me a quick kiss before he let me go so I could head up to the stage.

Looking out over the crowd after I'd collected my award, it was just a blur. I tried to find Oliver but I couldn't see him in the sea of faces. As I attempted to scan the room once more, a movement at the back of the crowd caught my eye and I immediately froze.

It was Elijah. It had to be. Once again, he looked just like Oliver, except he was dressed in a dark leather jacket while I knew Oliver was wearing a grey button-down shirt that matched his eyes. I had complimented him on it this morning as he put it on.

And not only was he here, but Elijah was staring right at me, his gaze intense. Did he know who I was? Did he know about Oliver?

'Oliver, he's here!' I called out through our mind-link. 'Elijah's by the back door.'

'Really?' His reply was about as breathless as it was possible for a thought to get. 'I'm going there now.'

The last winner was announced and, after some applause, the crowd began to disperse. I lost sight of Elijah in the crowd and I still couldn't find Oliver either. After exchanging pleasantries with the other winners and thanking the judges, I made my way back off the stage.

'Oliver?' I called out to him in my head.

"Right behind you," his voice said out loud, nearly making me jump out of my skin.

"Did you find him?" I asked as I turned around, looking for any sign of Oliver's mysterious double.

Oliver shook his head in frustration. "No, there are too many people. I wonder why he came back though. Storm seemed fairly certain he wouldn't."

She really did. There must be something she didn't know, and it was just one more thing to add to our long list of questions that still remained unanswered.

~Elijah~

As I stepped back into the conference centre where the book festival was being held, I still wasn't entirely sure what I was doing back here. Julian and I left San Francisco the other night just as we planned but with every mile put between us and the city, the tightness in my chest got worse. My wolf was restless and I was finding it hard to concentrate on anything. The words on the pages of my mother's book swam before my eyes as I tried to focus, and finally I had to close the book and try to get some sleep as Julian drove north along the highway.

By the time I woke up, the sun was coming up and we were pulling onto our pack's land. The sentry on duty saluted us both as we drove by and soon I found myself at my desk in my office with the book in front of me, ready to devour it at last, but I still couldn't make sense of the words. My brain was refusing to cooperate.

After about an hour there was a knock on the door and I slammed my palms down on the desk in frustration. "What?" I snapped.

The door opened to reveal the rather nervous face of my Gamma Lucas. "Sorry to disturb you, Alpha, but we've had a message from that woman who calls herself Storm. She sent it through the usual secure channels."

That didn't make me any happier. Storm might be less of a nuisance than Darryn Reeves but I still didn't have the patience for her today. Although at least listening to her message would give me something to do other than stare at the same paragraph in the book over and over again.

"Send it through to me," I instructed with a sigh. Lucas nodded in acknowledgement and closed the door behind him. A few moments later the video appeared on my desktop and I opened it up, the audio from my speakers filling the room.

"Sorry I missed you in San Francisco, Eli," she began with her usual smug look that always made me feel like she knew something that I didn't. "I was hoping we could catch up. I understand you have the book now but I'm sure you don't have the first idea how to interpret it. My previous offer still stands: we can work together to find the artifact. You know Reeves will stop at nothing to get to it before you do, so if you want to live long enough to see it for yourself, I suggest you consider my offer carefully."

There was nothing particularly new in that message, nothing she hadn't said to me before, so I reached over to close the video window. Just before I hit the X in the corner, she added one more thing.

"Although we didn't meet up, I did happen to come across another werewolf who looks exactly like you. Have you got a twin you haven't told me about?"

With one final smirk from Storm, the video cut off.

What the hell was that about? Was she lying so I'd be curious and make contact with her, or had she actually met someone who looked like me? I was confused, but in the end I decided it was just one of her mind games to try to entice me into getting in touch with her, so I put it out of my mind.

Soon it was time for lunch and then I had a bit of pack business that needed my attention before I finally had time to sit down with the book again. But just as before, as soon as I tried to start reading, my mind started racing and my wolf wouldn't let me rest.

As frustrated as I was, I knew exactly what the problem was.

It was all because of my mate.

It was driving my wolf crazy that we'd just walked away and left her there. I had done it so that I wouldn't be distracted, but clearly that hadn't worked. I'd never been so distracted in my whole fucking life.

Finally, I had to give in and I called Julian back to my office. "I'm going back to San Francisco," I told him abruptly, and his eyes widened in surprise.

"What? Why? Did you forget something?"

That was one way of putting it. "I just need to go back. I'll go alone though, you can stay here and look after things until I get back."

"What if you run into Reeves?" Julian asked with real concern.

"He won't be there anymore," I asserted confidently. "He won't expect me to hang around, so he'll be looking for me elsewhere. And even if he is there, I'll avoid him. I always have before."

Julian conceded that point, clearly resisting the urge to bring up the number of close calls I'd had, and after going over a few more things with him, I got back in the car and headed back down to California. It was late by the time I arrived so I checked into a motel on the outskirts of the city and first thing in the morning, I headed back to the book festival. It was the only place I knew my mate might possibly be, though what the odds were that she'd be there again, I couldn't begin to guess.

I was just starting to scan the room, sniffing the air carefully, when a man on a stage started calling out names and people from the crowd went up to join him. It seemed like he was announcing the winners of some kind of contest. I didn't know exactly what was going on, but it didn't really matter. I was only here to see if my mate was still here. The ideal scenario, as far as I could see it, was that I looked for her and didn't find her. Then I would be free to go back to what I was supposed to be doing and my wolf could calm the fuck down since I had at least made an effort.

But just as I was about to look away from the stage, my eyes fell on a woman who was climbing the stairs to join the man standing there, and an utter certainty filled me.

She was my mate.

Shit.

Not only was she here, but I'd missed her name too. I hadn't been paying attention when the man called it out and I cursed myself now for not listening more closely.

She looked out over the crowd with a rather shy smile and as her eyes got closer to me, my heart began to beat faster. *Seriously?* I shook my head at my own body's reaction. She wasn't even that attractive, not if I thought about it objectively. I'd been with women who were far more sexy, so why should my heart be pounding like a lovesick schoolboy's when I looked at her?

Then her eyes landed directly on me and I felt a pull towards her stronger than anything I'd ever felt before. *Mine,* my wolf growled in my head even as I tried my best to resist.

Before I even had a chance to register what her reaction was, another woman stepped onto the stage, stepping directly into my line of vision between me and my mate, and I frowned as I got a closer look at her. She looked incredibly similar to my mate: the same dark, wavy hair and glasses. They could have been sisters, definitely, if not quite twins. And after just a moment, her eyes locked on me too, widening as they did so.

What the hell was going on? I didn't feel anything towards this woman, so why was she looking at me like that? *And why won't she get out of the way so I can see my mate again?*

Then her eyes clouded over for just a second and I realized she must be a werewolf. *Fuck.* Who was she talking to and did it have to do with me? Maybe I wasn't as safe here as I thought. Darryn Reeves wouldn't be working with wolves, I was sure enough of that, so was there someone else after me now too? Or was she with Storm, perhaps? I'd never known Storm to have backup though. This didn't make any sense.

No matter who she was with or how much it upset my wolf, I wasn't going to stand around and wait to be caught. I took off out the door instead, ignoring the pounding of my heart and the blood rushing through my ears.

It wasn't until I was already a block away from the convention centre that I realized there was one big thing I'd missed: my mate's scent. Even with the distance between us, I had detected the faint smell of honeysuckles from her that I'd smelled the other day. But it hadn't hit me until now that it was the only scent I picked up from her.

There was no wolf scent at all, which could only mean one thing.

My mate is human.

~Liz~

My whole body felt like it was on fire and I was fighting hard to keep down the blush in my cheeks.

It wasn't just from being on stage in front of all these people, although that was a challenge for me too. I never particularly liked being the centre of attention, but the weird sensation had only started when I was looking out over the crowd as the other winners were called and I saw him watching me.

Oliver? He had moved to the back of the room for some reason and he was staring right at me with an intensity I'd never seen from him before. Even though there was a whole room and hundreds of people between us, it almost felt like electricity when our eyes connected.

I'd never felt anything like that before, and certainly not with him. What could it mean?

I'd always had a little bit of a crush on Oliver. That was no secret from anyone, especially not from Abby. Hell, I even asked her once if he had a twin brother she could set me up with, and who could really blame me? He is one fine-looking man and a total sweetheart to boot. If Abby wasn't one of my best friends, I would have hated her for having the good luck to land a guy like him.

But a harmless little crush was all it was. I would never, ever act on it, and I knew that Oliver didn't feel anything for me other than friendship. He was one hundred percent besotted with Abby, that lucky, lucky girl.

So why on earth was he staring at me like that right now?

Then Abby got up on stage as well and I realized she must have won an award too though I hadn't actually been paying attention. I applauded and cheered for her as she stepped in front of me to get the certificate, and then when I looked back to where he'd been standing, Oliver was gone.

As the ceremony ended, I took some deep breaths to slow my heart rate but it didn't help very much. I was still extremely confused as I followed Abby back down off the stage.

Then Oliver appeared beside her, speaking to her in a quiet voice, with eyes only for her, as always, and I frowned in confusion.

I was sure when I'd seen him watching me, he was wearing a leather jacket, but now he didn't have any jacket on at all. And come to think of it, I didn't remember him wearing a jacket earlier today either.

What is going on?

There was no way I could ask Oliver about it without melting into a puddle of self-consciousness, but I pulled Abby aside as we started to head towards the exit. "Does Oliver own a leather jacket?"

She gave me a bit of a funny look. "I don't think so. Why?"

I decided to level with her, at least part way. "I could have sworn I saw him in the crowd when we were onstage, but he was wearing a dark leather jacket."

Abby's eyes widened. "You saw him too?"

Too? What does that mean? I must have looked as confused as I felt because Abby quickly explained.

"That wasn't Oliver. There's someone else here who looks a lot like him. I noticed him on the first day but we haven't been able to track him down again."

Relief flooded through me at her reply. It wasn't Oliver, so he *wasn't* trying to hit on me in front of my friend that he was dating. That was definitely a good thing.

That relief was quickly followed by a little rush of excitement. Did that mean there was someone out there who looked almost exactly like Oliver who might actually be interested in me? What were the odds of that? It would be an incredible stroke of luck, and I hadn't had any luck with men ever since Liam, which wasn't exactly lucky either. I was more than ready to find someone new.

But this was San Francisco and we were supposed to be going home right away. I didn't even know this guy's name or where he was from, or if it was even me he'd been staring at. The whole idea seemed completely hopeless. Now that he'd disappeared, how was I ever going to find him again?

~Oliver~

Liz seemed reluctant to leave the festival for some reason, but Abby and Melanie and I were ready to go so we headed back to our hotel to grab our bags. The rest of the group was already waiting for us along with the taxis and soon we were back at the airport and on the plane heading home.

Although I'd done my best to mute all the questions in my brain over the last two days, I hadn't been completely idle. I'd already been in touch with my friend Eric back in the Jade Moon pack and he'd taken a few of the wolves from our pack to my dorm room on campus and packed up the rest of our things so that Abby and I didn't have to go back there when we landed. We could head straight to the pack house instead and hopefully first thing in the morning we could sit down with my dad and start to try to figure out some of the mystery surrounding Elijah.

After saying goodbye to our friends at the airport and promising to keep in touch over the summer, Abby and I got in the waiting car that had been sent from the Jade Moon pack for us. It was late by the time we got there and the pack house was quiet as most people had already turned in for the night.

I had a surprise for Abby that I'd been planning to show her the next day when we arrived, but with the change of plans, it was going to have to be now. Heading up the stairs to the top floor where my childhood bedroom was located, I walked in first and then turned around quickly to see her reaction.

I wasn't disappointed. Abby's mouth fell open as she took in the room which had been completely transformed since the last time we were here. Gone were the posters of half-naked women and pictures of me with old girlfriends. The first time she was in this room and saw them, it made me wince to imagine what kind of message it sent about me. Now it was a proper adult's bedroom in shades of blues and greens, Abby's favourite colours.

I wanted her to feel a part of this pack and part of the future that we would have here together, and I thought this would be a good place to start.

"When did you do all this?" she asked in amazement, looking around to take in all the details.

"Eric and the guys did all the work," I admitted. "I just gave them a bit of direction. But I figured if we're staying here the whole summer, we might as well be comfortable. Do you like it?"

She gave me her beautiful, soft smile. "I love it, Oliver. Thank you."

I kissed her gently then pulled away before my body could react like it always did around her. "You know I want to test out the new bed with you, Heels, but would you mind if we wait until tomorrow?"

I hadn't said anything to her, but I hadn't slept very well while we were in San Francisco. Every time I closed my eyes, I could see the men who had captured me, holding onto Abby and injecting me with whatever they'd given me before, only this time they were going to take her and there was nothing I could do about it.

I'd tried my best to hide the anxiety it was causing me from her but I knew she could tell something was a little off, just like I always could with her.

"Of course," she agreed now, giving me one more quick peck on the lips before heading over to the closet to get her pajamas. "It's late, let's get some rest."

My sleep was better now that I knew we were back on our pack land and no one could get to us without going through a hell of a lot of pack security. When morning came I was feeling energized and more than ready to start getting some of my questions answered.

We grabbed a quick breakfast in the kitchen, saying hello to a few of the pack members that were hanging around, and then we headed to my dad's office.

"Oliver, Abby, it's good to see you," he greeted us warmly. It had taken my dad a little while to accept Abby when we first met, not least because he was being blackmailed to try to get me to reject her, but now he was one of her biggest fans. I knew he was excited to have us both home for the summer.

"Hey, Dad," I replied and Abby gave him a little wave.

"Hi, Alpha Patrick." She smiled at him and he smiled back. It was still a little weird to me to see them so friendly with each other, but I was really happy they were getting along.

"What brings you here so early?" he asked curiously as we all took a seat around his desk. "I wasn't expecting you until later today."

"We had a change of plans," I admitted. "There's something I need to talk to you about."

"Oh?" His curiosity was even stronger now. "What is it?"

I took a deep breath. "I'm ready for you to tell me about my biological father."

Chapter Five

Alpha Patrick's shoulders tensed when Oliver asked to know more about his biological dad, but he did his best to keep calm.

"Of course," he replied to his son evenly. "I told you I'd be happy to tell you when you were ready and I meant it."

Oliver nodded in appreciation. "I know. I wasn't ready before but I think I am now."

I squeezed his hand in support, the hand that was holding mine as we sat beside each other in the Alpha's office. It was here in this room just a few months ago that Oliver had first learned the man in front of us wasn't his biological father. Alpha Patrick had told us a little bit about the situation surrounding Oliver's birth then, but there was still a lot we didn't know.

I could see the curiosity in the Alpha's eyes, wondering what had brought on this sudden desire for the information that Oliver had been avoiding until now, but he didn't question it. He leaned back instead and took a breath before he started speaking.

"His name is Adrian," he began, keeping his gaze focused on Oliver. "He's the Alpha of the Seven Hills pack, or at least he was at the time. I have no idea if he still is. We haven't exactly kept in touch."

The Seven Hills pack. That was the pack Storm had mentioned, where Elijah was Alpha. If Oliver's dad had been Alpha before him, it seemed more than likely that Elijah was also Adrian's son, which made sense given how much they looked alike. It certainly seemed like we were on the right track for finding him.

"Is that the pack Mom was from?" Oliver asked, and his dad nodded.

"That's right. They're out in Oregon, not too far from where you were this weekend, actually. Your mom was the daughter of the Beta there, kind of like your own mate."

He gave me a smile at that, but I could see a hint of sadness in his eyes as he spoke of Oliver's mother. He must still miss her, I thought. Oliver and I had spoken about how hard it must be for his dad to be on his own all these years, especially since he rejected his second chance mate so that no one would find out that he wasn't able to have children and that Oliver wasn't really his son. And then that information had come out anyway, so in the end, he had nothing to show for the sacrifice he'd made. It made me sad to think about it too.

"How did you meet her?" Oliver asked curiously. "That's practically on the other side of the country."

Alpha Patrick's lips turned up just a little at the memory. "My father signed up to a program that was being trialed at the time where Betas and Gammas from different packs spent some time in other friendly packs to exchange ideas and efficiencies about the best way to run things. It was a rather idealistic experiment and obviously it fizzled out eventually. But we were one of the packs that took part, and our Beta went to the Seven Hills pack for a few weeks while theirs came here, and he brought his daughter with him."

My heart melted a little as I pictured the scene in my head. "So you knew she was your mate as soon as she arrived?"

The Alpha gave me an indulgent look, clearly hearing the excitement in my voice. "Not right away. She was still seventeen when she got here, but a week later she turned eighteen and we had a big party for her since she was away from home. That was when we found out we were mates."

How exciting. I could see the whole scene so clearly in my head, a younger Patrick, not Alpha yet, and the visiting Beta's daughter, seeing each other across the crowded dance floor, being pulled together by the magical mate bond. They must have been so happy to find each other. I could picture the wonder in their eyes and the sparks that ignited the first time their hands touched.

My imaginings were quickly dashed though. "She wasn't thrilled about it at first," Alpha Patrick continued, a touch of amusement in his eyes. "She even considered rejecting me. She had been dating someone else in her own pack and they had hoped they would be mates. But the more time we spent together, the more it became impossible to resist the connection between us, and just a few days before she was meant to go home, she finally accepted me and stayed here instead."

Oliver and I exchanged smiles. We certainly knew all about how impossible it was to resist someone who was truly meant for you.

"And then, as I've already explained to you, when we were unable to conceive, she reached out to Adrian for help. He had recently become Alpha of the Seven Hills pack, so he had the Alpha blood we needed. They had grown up together as children of Alphas and Betas often do, so they were friends. He was surprised at the request, of course, but he agreed to help us and we travelled there together. Once she was pregnant, we came back home and I've never seen him again."

"Was he mated at the time?" Oliver asked, and I understood the reason for the question. He was trying to establish a timeline for when Elijah would have been born, but Alpha Patrick quickly shook his head.

"No. I don't imagine there are many mates who would be understanding enough to let their mate do something like that."

"You were," I pointed out softly. It couldn't have been easy for him, emotionally or physically, to let his mate sleep with another man. For a mated werewolf pair, infidelity of any kind caused real physical pain along with any emotional wounds that might form.

He gave a nod of acknowledgement to that before looking back at Oliver with affection. "Yes, I was willing, but I got a son out of it. It was more than worth it."

The muscles in Oliver's cheek twitched, which I knew was a sign that he was trying not to get emotional. I knew just about every little tell on his body by now.

He brought the conversation back to Alpha Adrian, still trying to figure out how Elijah fit in. "Did he find his mate shortly afterwards, then? Does he have children of his own?"

Alpha Patrick shrugged. "I honestly don't know. As I said, I never saw him again. Your mother kept in touch with him from time to time, I believe, but I never heard from him, not even after she died. I'm not sure he even knows that she is dead, although perhaps he assumed as much when he stopped hearing from her."

That didn't particularly help us. Elijah had to be very close to the same age that Oliver was, but if Alpha Adrian hadn't been mated, maybe he wasn't as closely related as we'd originally thought. Maybe if Adrian didn't have any children of his own, it was his nephew or another relative who had taken over as Alpha?

Oliver was silent for a moment, thinking things over, and the Alpha spoke again.

"Are you going to reach out to him?"

He was trying hard to sound casual, but I could hear the small note of concern in his voice.

"I think so," Oliver replied honestly, finally telling his dad the reason we were asking in the first place. "While we were in San Francisco we came across a wolf who looks incredibly like me. We thought he might be a blood relative of mine, so I guess the easiest way to find out would be to speak to Alpha Adrian himself, and I think I'd rather do it in person. Do you mind if we use the plane again for a few days?"

Alpha Patrick quickly agreed. "That's fine. If you like, I can also give you the name of your mother's best friend from the pack. If you're going anyway, I'm sure she would like to meet you and she might be able to answer some of your questions too. Now to mention she probably has a lot of stories about your mother that you've never heard before."

Oliver nodded, smiling a little wistfully. "That would be nice, actually. Thanks, Dad."

He knew, just as I did, that this had to be a little difficult for Alpha Patrick, both to talk about what had happened and to think about Oliver spending time in his biological father's pack.

In recognition of that, he gave his dad a stronger smile in an attempt to reassure him. "We'll only be gone a day or two. We've got a lot to do here at home this summer after all, so we'll be back before you know it."

That seemed to be just what Alpha Patrick needed to hear and he relaxed a little at Oliver's words. "Sounds good. In that case, have a good trip, and I'll see you when you get back."

~Elijah~

I was at war with myself for the whole drive home. My fingers drummed on the steering wheel incessantly and my eyes darted back and forth as my thoughts chased each other around my head.

Finding my mate hadn't cleared anything up for me. If anything, it made things worse.

What the hell am I supposed to do now?

Taking a human as my mate was not an option. It didn't fit in with any of my plans at all. I was just a few short steps away from being the most powerful Alpha this country had ever seen and there was no way having a human Luna was going to help me. On the contrary, she would be a liability, a weak point for me, something my enemies could use against me, and I was certain I was going to have a lot of enemies. You couldn't get to the kind of position I had in mind without pissing a few people off.

This was what I'd been planning and preparing for ever since I heard about the existence of the artifact five years ago and realized my own connection to it. My destiny was immediately clear to me that day and everything I'd done since then had been for the purpose of fulfilling it.

So what kind of cosmic joke was being played on me that my mate should suddenly appear now that I was almost within reach of possessing my goal, when I could least afford the distraction, and that she should be a human too?

This must be some kind of test for me, and I was determined not to fail it, no matter how much my wolf whined or pouted at me.

If you're so convinced you don't need her, then why didn't you reject her?

I growled at the unwanted thoughts that kept materializing in my head. I didn't need to reject her, I told myself. Since she was human, she probably had no idea that werewolves even existed. The rejection would mean nothing to her so it wasn't necessary. It was better to just leave her behind and pretend the whole thing had never happened. Then, when I had achieved my goal and was ready to have my own heirs, I could take a mate of my own choosing, one that would suit my new position.

That was the sensible thing to do. In a way, maybe this was actually a good thing. After all, having the mate bond with this human woman prevented me from getting stuck with anyone else, someone who would actually recognize our bond for what it was.

Or at least it would be a good thing if I could get rid of the lump in my throat and the tightness in my chest that the distance between us seemed to be causing.

It wasn't quite dark yet when I got back to my pack land, and Julian was still in my office. We went over what had happened since I left and I could see him shooting me furtive glances from time to time. It was obvious he wanted to ask me what I'd gone back to San Francisco for, but in the end he didn't bring it up and I wasn't about to volunteer the information. So far, I was the only person who knew about my mate and that was the way I intended to keep it.

When we were done catching up, I relieved him of his duty and he left me alone in my office. My mother's book was safely locked away in my wall safe where I'd left it this morning, so I retrieved it now and sat down again at my desk, determined to make some headway with it this time.

The book was handwritten and very old. All the things I'd heard about it suggested that it was written by some of the first European werewolves that came to North America, hundreds of years ago. One of them had brought with them a powerful artifact and the book told not only the legend of how they came to be in possession of it, which could also be found in several other places, but it had the one thing that all the other sources didn't: the location where the artifact had been hidden.

Those early settler wolves had been threatened by the supernatural creatures that were native to this continent, wendigos and skinwalkers and the like, and so they had hidden the artifact for safekeeping. Unfortunately they were then wiped out and the location was assumed to have died with them. The power of the artifact was thought to be lost forever.

Or at least that's what everyone thought until the existence of this book was revealed just five years ago.

Someone amongst the pack of wolves that had brought the artifact over with them had written the book in fear of their extinction and sent it back to Europe, to a relative in another pack there. It had been passed down through generations for hundreds of years until the meaning of it became obscured and the people who owned it assumed it was just another old book, something that a young girl would write her name in, never knowing the treasure that she possessed.

I had stumbled across the legend of the artifact entirely by accident while at a conference with my dad. There was an eccentric wolf there giving a lecture on it and most people thought he was crazy. My dad was convinced it was a waste of time to go and listen to him and tried to talk me out of it, but it piqued my curiosity for reasons I couldn't quite explain, so I attended the lecture anyway while my dad was busy with other meetings. The whole idea of it fascinated me in a theoretical sense, like something out of Indiana Jones or Pirates of the Caribbean, something mythical and mystical that was an adventure far removed from real life.

And then the wolf mentioned the name of the last known person to have possessed the book: Nicole Williams.

It wasn't an uncommon name, but as soon as he uttered it, I knew it in my heart. *It was my mother.* It was her book and her family that were part of the legend, which meant all of it was my legacy too.

This book belonged to me and so did the artifact it led to. I was completely convinced of it. I had never known her, but perhaps this was what she had left me instead. It would be the one thing of hers that I got to claim as my own.

Now if only I could get the other people who wanted the artifact to agree.

Taking a deep breath to clear my head, I tried to read the book once more, and at least this time, the words stayed in one place. My wolf might not be happy that we'd left our mate behind, but he seemed to recognize that now that I knew she was human, there was no way I was claiming her, so he let me be, sulking off in a quiet corner of my mind.

I lost track of time as I read through the pages of the book in its odd old-English script. Storm was right that it required some deciphering but I had studied the legends long enough that I could make out most of it. I wasn't quite as helpless as she liked to believe I was.

And then I got to a page talking about protecting the 'source of power' and my heart began to beat faster. Those were the words that were often used to describe the artifact. No one knew exactly what the artifact was but its purpose was clear enough: whoever possessed it would possess a power greater than any wolf could ever have on their own.

And since the book was talking about it now, this must be the part that explained where the artifact had been hidden. I leaned closer to the page as if that would make the words easier to read, struggling between wanting to devour the whole thing at once and needing to absorb each word.

At the junction of the river and the sea, whither men have built and winds destroyed, the source hath been secured.

The full moon wilt illuminate the path. Both the key and the receptacle will be needed but only one can be preserved.

Once found, only a worthy wolf can claim the power held within.

Frantically I flipped the page over, but there was no more. The next page was on a different subject, so those few lines appeared to be all I had to work with.

Taking a deep breath, I went back to the previous page and leaned back in my chair. It might not be much, but that was the clue I had spent the last five years looking for.

Now what the fuck did it mean?

~Oliver~

Early the next morning, Abby and I were in a rental car, heading south of Portland towards the border of the Seven Hills pack. We had flown back yesterday afternoon but by the time we arrived it was too late to make an unannounced visit to the pack land so we simply found a hotel where we could spend the night before setting off early this morning.

Abby teased me that I was showing off with the private plane now and that it would have saved us a lot of time if we'd just called my dad from San Francisco instead of flying all the way home and then back to the west coast again. That was true, though I hadn't really expected that we would just turn around and come back. However, once it was clear that my dad didn't know anything about Elijah, I didn't really see what other choice we had.

His ignorance on the subject made me more curious than ever. If Elijah wasn't my half-brother, and based on what my dad had said, I didn't really see how he could be, then how did we look so much alike? Why was he Alpha? There had to be something we were missing.

I probably could have tried to contact the Alpha's office ahead of time to let them know I was coming but I had a gut feeling that the element of surprise would work in our favour. Storm had implied that Elijah was caught up in some rather dangerous things so I figured we had a better chance of finding him if we turned up without any warning. I was hoping so, at least.

I had prepared a cover story to get us past the border guards but it didn't end up being necessary. As soon as we approached, slowing to a crawl outside the small booth, the guard on duty peered through the windshield, saluted, and raised the barrier across the road to grant us entry. I nodded back at him and drove through.

"Oliver!" Abby gasped in surprise, turning around to look back at the guard through the back window. "We can't just go in. He must have thought you were Elijah."

"Of course he did," I agreed, grinning at her. "It gives us an advantage, Heels, and I'm going to use it."

That hadn't been my plan, but if the opportunity presented itself, I was going to take it.

"But as soon as we get out of the car, they'll smell that we're not from here," she pointed out. "Won't we be in trouble when they find out we didn't check in?"

"How are they going to know that unless the guard says something?" I argued back. "And if you were him, would you admit that you just let us in without checking us first?"

She had no response to that other than letting out a small huff of air, which I recognized as her signal of surrender. She wouldn't always tell me when I was right, but that little puff told me anyway. I knew all of her little noises and what they meant, and I loved almost all of them. The only ones I could do without were the ones she made when she was really annoyed with me, which luckily didn't happen too often.

We drove down a winding dirt road through an old forest full of huge trees. These must be the trees my mother had told me about, I thought, glancing up from the road to see how they pierced the sky above us. After another ten minutes, a large log cabin-style building that could only be the pack house came into view.

We pulled up in front of the house and got out of the car. There were two men guarding the front door and as soon as they saw me, they bowed their heads.

"We didn't expect you back so soon, Alpha," one of them said to me before sniffing the air curiously.

That was one useful bit of information, even if it was disappointing. Elijah wasn't here. And this man, just like the guard at the border, assumed I was him, even with my different pack smell.

Maybe I can play along for just a little while longer. It was worth a shot, anyway.

"I ran into some trouble," I answered, trying to use enough of my own natural Alpha authority to sound convincing. "Got into a bit of a scrape with another pack and now I've got their scent all over me."

Was that lie going to be enough to fool him? He sniffed once more, but then nodded his head and I could feel Abby relax a little beside me.

"I'm going to my office," I continued, seeing just how far I could take the ruse. "Have Alpha Adrian sent to see me there."

Abby inhaled sharply beside me but I kept my gaze steady and commanding, hoping that the men would focus on me and not on her.

"Alpha Adrian?" the man repeated curiously.

Shit. Was that suspicious? Maybe he was dead, or didn't live here anymore? There were a lot of possibilities, but I was in too deep now to change my story though, so I stuck with it.

"Yes. Immediately."

To my relief, the man nodded again and bowed to us, and Abby and I quickly walked inside.

"How are we going to find his office?" she whispered to me. We had found ourselves inside a large entrance hall which was, thankfully, completely empty at the moment. I'd been in enough pack houses to know that the Alpha's office was usually on the ground floor. Beyond that, it was going to have to be a bit of trial and error.

Before I could choose a direction though, a man came towards us, walking with enough purpose that I had to guess he'd been told we were here. "Good morning, Alpha," he said, bowing his head. His nose twitched a little as he raised his head again and I knew he was curious about the scent, but I didn't bother to explain it this time. I figured if we were inside the house, he would assume we'd already passed through security, and I hoped his eyes would overrule his nose.

"Good morning," I responded firmly. "Can you show my guest to my office? I'll be there in a minute."

"Of course," he agreed, looking over at Abby curiously as well.

Once again, I figured it was safer to offer no explanation, so I let them go, watching which direction they went before walking firmly towards the back of the house where I assumed the kitchen would be. Luckily, I was right. Keeping my cool, I went in to wash my hands, figuring that was a good enough excuse for my presence there. There were more people in there who bowed and greeted me, and I simply nodded at them, not bothering to say anything this time.

The less I spoke, the better.

After drying my hands off, I went back to the hallway I'd seen Abby go down and followed her scent to the open door of Elijah's office. Abby was already seated inside as the man who had brought her here offered to get her a drink.

"We don't need anything," I told him. "Make sure no one disturbs us until Alpha Adrian arrives."

A flash of confusion crossed his face, but he quickly hid it and bowed once more, leaving the room and closing the door behind him.

As soon as we were alone, Abby gave me a disapproving look. "Oliver, this is dangerous! Why not just tell them who we are and what we want?"

"Catching them off guard is going to be the best way of getting the truth," I told her. I couldn't really explain why I felt that so strongly, but I did. "If Elijah was here, I would have spoken to him directly, but since he's not, I'm just borrowing his authority for a little while."

"And what would your pack do if Elijah showed up there pretending to be you?" she asked with real worry in her voice. "If they discovered him, they would assume he was trying to infiltrate the pack, or worse! It's not worth it, Oliver. We should come clean."

I could see her point but I also felt like we were in a bit too deep to turn back now. "It will be fine, Abby," I assured her. "We'll speak to Alpha Adrian and I'll explain to him who I am and why I've come. I'm sure he'll understand."

Once again, it was just a gut feeling that told me he would, but it was strong enough that I trusted it. My instincts rarely steered me wrong.

As we waited, I took a look around the room, trying to figure out a little more about the man who shared my face. There were no personal photos or mementos of any kind. The desk had a computer on it and nothing else. The furniture was all dark and solid, no splashes of colour anywhere.

He must not have a mate yet, I figured. There was absolutely no sign of a woman's touch in here.

Finally there was a knock on the door. "Come in," I called out, my heart beating a little faster at the prospect of coming face to face with the man whose DNA I carried. But when the door opened, it wasn't the former Alpha who stood there. Instead there were four large men who quickly advanced on me and Abby.

"What are you doing?" I tried to protest with all the Alpha authority I possessed, but it was clear the game was up. For the second time in the last few days, Abby and I found ourselves restrained, and my stomach sank. *Fuck.* What kind of danger had I just put her in? This was like my recent nightmare come to life.

The man who had greeted us earlier came in through the still open door and regarded Abby and I grimly. "I don't know who you are," he said to me. "But you're definitely not Alpha Elijah."

There didn't seem any point in lying about it any longer, though I wasn't sure exactly what had given me away. "I'm not," I agreed. "But I can explain."

"You will," he agreed, a rather sinister smile crossing his face. "To her."

He turned back towards the door and a woman entered dressed in leather from head to toe and carrying what appeared to be a silver-tipped flail. Despite her clothes and the youthful cut of her hair, a closer look at her face revealed that she was actually quite a bit older than me. Closer to my parents' age, probably.

There was a cold look on her face as she walked into the room. "You've chosen the wrong pack to mess with," she said, looking first at Abby.

Then her eyes moved over to me and they widened in genuine surprise as her lips parted.

"Oliver?"

Chapter Six

~Abby~

I was starting to feel like I had whiplash from all the abrupt changes of mood since we'd arrived here. Oliver hadn't warned me that he was going to impersonate Elijah when we arrived, so that was my first surprise. At first people were bowing to him, and then we were in trouble and now this woman appeared who, even though I had never seen her before, seemed to know exactly who Oliver was.

I could tell by Oliver's expression that he didn't recognize her either and his next question quickly confirmed my suspicions. "Who are you?" he asked, his eyes scanning the woman for clues to her identity. She was clearly someone of importance in the pack. The other wolves seemed to defer to her, giving her a wide berth that had little to do with her leather jacket and high-heeled boots.

She didn't answer him but turned to the Seven Hills wolves instead. "Leave us," she instructed. "I can take it from here."

The man who had accused Oliver looked like he wanted to protest, but a single raised eyebrow from the woman in front of us subdued him into submission. The wolves holding me and Oliver let go and they all moved back to the door.

"I'll be right outside," the man said, giving Oliver and I one last glare before he closed the door behind him.

As soon as we were alone, the woman threw the flail she was carrying onto the Alpha's desk and wrapped her arms around Oliver in a tight hug. I wasn't sure who was more surprised, me or him, but a low growl rumbled in my throat before I even realized I meant to do it.

The woman laughed as she released Oliver and turned to me with more than a little amusement. "You must be Oliver's mate then. I'm Jenny."

Understanding dawned on Oliver's face and I breathed a sigh of relief too. Jenny was the name Alpha Patrick had given us for Oliver's mom's best friend.

That explained a lot.

"I'm Abby," I introduced myself, holding out my hand to shake hers, but she ignored it, giving me a quick, firm hug as well.

"I'm delighted to meet you both," she said, her face breaking into an easy smile that was completely at odds with the hardened look she'd been wearing when she came in. There was even a softness in her eyes as she looked back at Oliver. "Your mom told me so much about you but I didn't think I'd ever get to meet you myself."

Oliver blinked a couple of times, clearly caught off guard by her words. "My mom talked to you about me?"

"All the time," she confirmed. "Until she died, of course. I'm sorry about that, by the way."

Oliver simply nodded, not quite sure what to say to that, so I stepped in. "I'm sorry for you too. You must have been very close."

Jenny gave me a wistful smile. "We were. I missed her very much when she left the pack, and then even more when she died."

She gave her head a little shake, as if shaking away the sadness.

"But enough about me. What are you doing here, and why the hell were you pretending to be Eli?"

"I didn't really plan to impersonate him," Oliver admitted sheepishly. "It just seemed like the easiest way to get what I wanted."

"Which was...?" Jenny prompted.

"To talk to Alpha Adrian," Oliver elaborated. "My father."

Jenny exhaled dramatically. "Well, that explains it."

Oliver and I exchanged glances. "Explains what?" I asked.

"Why they knew you weren't Elijah. You might have fooled them about the scent, but Eli wouldn't be asking to talk to the former Alpha."

There was obviously something we were missing here but before we could ask, Jenny gestured to the chairs in the room.

"Let's sit down. I'm sure you've got a few questions and I'd love to get to know more about you too."

We accepted the offer gratefully. Oliver and I took a seat next to each other while Jenny sat across from us as comfortably as if we were all old friends instead of complete strangers.

"I do have a lot of questions," Oliver admitted. "I hardly know where to start, but I'm curious about what you just said. Why wouldn't Elijah want to talk to Adrian?"

"They haven't really spoken in a couple of years," Jenny explained, her mouth twisting into a bit of a smirk. "When you take a wolf's Alpha position by force, it doesn't really leave you on the best of terms."

Once again, Oliver and I looked at each other curiously. Elijah had become Alpha through a challenge? Did that mean he wasn't Adrian's heir after all? Then why did he look so much like Oliver?

There still had to be more to the story.

"Does Adrian still live in the pack then?" Oliver asked. "I was hoping to speak to him."

"He doesn't, but I can tell you where to find him."

Well, that was a piece of good luck then. I was extremely grateful that we'd run into her. This all could have ended much worse than it had if she hadn't been the one brought in to question us.

"Does he... know about me?" Oliver asked, and the touch of vulnerability in his voice melted my heart. "I mean, I know that he knows I exist, but does he know about me like you do?"

"I don't know what Nicole told him about you," Jenny said. "They did stay in touch and I know they talked about Elijah, but I'm not sure how much they talked about you. She always wanted to keep her life at the

Jade Moon pack separate from the one here, as much as possible. I was really the only one who had access to both parts of her life."

Oliver had gone very still as he processed her words. "Why did they talk about Elijah?" he asked quietly.

Jenny looked surprised by the question and her eyes moved back and forth between me and Oliver curiously. "Well, you know who Elijah is, right? I assumed you must, since you came here pretending to be him."

Again, Oliver seemed a little overwhelmed, so I spoke up in his place.

"We know that he and Oliver look very similar," I said. "And we know that he's the Alpha of this pack. But we don't know who he is to Oliver or to Alpha Adrian. That's actually what we came here to find out. It's why we were looking for Alpha Adrian in the first place."

Jenny exhaled again, her cheeks puffing out as she blew the air through the lips. "I see. Well, you don't need to find him to tell you that. I can tell you instead."

"Tell me what?" Oliver asked, his voice still low and quiet.

I suspected he already knew the answer, just as I did, but it still didn't seem entirely possible until Jenny spoke the words.

"He's your twin brother."

~Oliver~

I heard the words that Jenny said but I still couldn't quite believe them. How could I have a twin brother? Or rather, how could I have one and not know about it?

Sensing my turmoil, Abby spoke on my behalf yet again. "Alpha Patrick never told us about a twin," she said, her own voice laced with confusion. "Why would he keep it a secret?"

Jenny sighed, leaning forward with her forearms on her knees as she looked between us. "Because he doesn't know. It was a secret from him too. The only people in the world that knew about it were Alpha Adrian, your mother, and me. And with your mother gone, that only leaves two of us who knew, until now."

I still didn't know which of the many questions in my head to ask next, but Jenny spoke again before I could get any of them out.

"Who did you think he was?" she asked, sounding a little bit amused now. "He looks exactly like you. Everyone here thought you were him."

Well, sure, if you say it like that, it sounds obvious. But I still didn't understand how it was possible.

"How could my dad not know?" I asked, not sure if she would even know the answer to that, but I needed to ask it anyway. "Wouldn't the pack doctor have said something? Couldn't he hear the babies' heartbeats?"

Wolves have incredibly sensitive hearing. I'd heard that when pups were close to term, it was possible to hear their heartbeat through the mother's stomach. I'd already imagined listening for it with Abby when the time came for us.

"Your mom didn't use the Jade Moon pack doctor," Jenny explained. "She used me."

"You?" Abby asked curiously. "You're a doctor?"

Jenny nodded, a slight smirk on her face. "In a past life, yes." She looked back over at me. "When your mom conceived, I went back to the Jade Moon pack with her. Alpha Adrian wanted to be sure she was safe and cared for."

I couldn't help bristling at that. "My father would have cared for her."

Jenny smiled at my reaction. "Of course, and he did. But Alpha Adrian felt responsible for her wellbeing too after the time they'd just shared together."

The reminder of my mother's infidelity made me wince. Even though my dad had agreed to it, it was still difficult to imagine. I couldn't imagine letting anyone else touch Abby, no matter what the situation was.

"Alpha Patrick had to go away on business about a month into the pregnancy," Jenny continued. "So I did the first ultrasound without him there and that's when we discovered there were two babies."

"And she didn't tell Alpha Patrick?" Abby prompted, leaning forward onto the edge of her seat. She always loved a good story, whether it was in a book or in real life, and this one certainly had all the elements of a page turner. Or at least it would if it wasn't about my own life.

"She didn't set out to keep it from him at first," Jenny explained. "But she decided to call Alpha Adrian first to let him know, since the children were genetically his, after all. And that's when he made the request."

"The request?" I repeated dully. I was beginning to see where this was going, though I still could hardly believe it was real.

"To keep one of the babies as his own," she said, confirming what I suspected. "He didn't have a mate at that time and no heir. It made a certain amount of sense."

"But what about when he found his own mate?" Abby asked. "Wasn't she upset that he already had a child from another woman?"

"She might have been," Jenny said with a shrug that seemed a little forced. "If he had ever found her. But since he didn't, the pack was grateful that he had his heir at least."

New questions were popping into my head at an alarming rate but I tried to focus back on the narrative around my mother's pregnancy. "So my mom agreed to give him one of the babies," I guessed, filling in the blanks. "And she never told my dad?"

"She didn't think he would approve," Jenny admitted bluntly. "She had her own reasons for agreeing too, but that's the reason she didn't tell him. She didn't want to fight with your dad and she also felt that she owed Adrian for helping them out. Obviously no one could have expected twins and it didn't seem fair to her that Patrick should get two heirs and Adrian none. So yes, she agreed, and she agreed to keep it secret. And Adrian also never told anyone here who Elijah's mother was. The only people who know that are me and Elijah himself."

"So Elijah knows about Oliver?" Abby jumped in. "He knows he has a twin brother?"

Jenny shook her head. "No. He simply knows that Nicole was his mother and that she was mated to someone else. He doesn't know who her mate was or that Oliver exists."

My head was spinning trying to keep track of all the secrets and who knew which facts.

"And my dad really never knew?" I asked. I was harping on this point, I knew, but I still couldn't understand it.

Jenny leaned back now and gave a rather soft smile. "When your mom shared her decision with me, I agreed to stay and be her doctor until the babies were born. During subsequent ultrasounds, I was able to hide the second baby. I even came up with a long medical excuse as to why it might sound like two heartbeats, but in the end it wasn't needed. Your heartbeat and Elijah's were always in perfect sync. It sounded like one."

"And what about when they were born?" Abby asked. "How did he not know then?"

"Oliver was born first," Jenny explained. "I handed him to Alpha Patrick and then told him I needed to treat your mother for a slight complication with the delivery. I assured him it was nothing serious and sent him out of the room to go show off his new son to his waiting pack. Then I delivered Elijah and secreted him away to the wet nurse who had already been employed. The next day, the nurse, Elijah and I flew back to the Seven Hills pack and Alpha Adrian took over Elijah's care. Alpha Patrick never had any idea."

So many secrets. So many things hidden, especially from me and Elijah. What would it have been like for him, growing up with only his father, knowing that his mother had given him up? Did he resent her for it? Did he even know that she was dead?

"I believe that the Alpha was going to tell Elijah about you eventually," Jenny said. "But as I said, they haven't spoken much since the takeover."

That was a whole other can of worms we had yet to open. And as helpful as Jenny had been, that was one story I would prefer to get right from the source.

"Thank you for telling me all of this," I told her sincerely. "And I would love to talk to you more about my mother another time, but for right now, I'd really like to finish what we came for. Where can we find Alpha Adrian?"

~Elijah~

Staring up at the massive house behind the iron gates, I was sure I must be in the wrong place. But when I double checked the address on my phone, this was definitely the address Storm had sent me. What the hell was she doing in a place like this?

Granted, I didn't know exactly who Storm was, but she'd always struck me as a bounty hunter type, bouncing from place to place and job to job. She was the only one of the three major players after the artifact who didn't want it for themselves. All the evidence from our previous encounters indicated that she was only in it for the money, which was why I had finally given in and agreed to meet with her when I found myself at a dead end with the clue in my mother's book.

But now, looking at the house, I was more than a little confused. If this was her house, she obviously didn't need the money after all. So what was her real motivation for being involved? Was there more going on here than I realized?

I was going to have to tread very carefully.

As soon as I pressed the buzzer at the gate, it began to swing open. I looked around until I saw the camera and gave it a small nod of acknowledgement before walking in. The front door opened before I even got to it and Storm appeared.

"Where's your backup?" she asked, scanning the street in front of the house.

"You told me to come alone," I reminded her as I approached.

"And I know you're not that stupid," she retorted just as drily. "So where are they?"

Suppressing a sigh, I pointed to the car down the street where my Beta Julian and Matthew, one of my head warriors, were waiting. I'd left my Gamma Lucas in charge of the pack with instructions not to contact us unless something truly apocalyptic was happening. Anything else, he could deal with on his own. Nothing was more important to me right now than the mission I was on.

Storm pulled out her phone and tapped something on the screen and I guessed that she was programming some kind of target on the car. That was quickly confirmed as she turned to me with a smirk. "You try anything stupid and they'll be taken out faster than you can blink. Understood?"

I nodded, holding up my hands in surrender. "I'm not looking for a fight. You said you'd help and I'm here to take you up on that. That's all this is."

"If that's true, Eli, then you've got nothing to worry about." She stepped back and held the door open for me. "Come on in."

I followed her into the impressive mansion, taking a curious look at all the furnishings and finishings. "Is this your house?"

Storm laughed in genuine amusement. "You know, your double was just as curious about this place as you are. I guess the two of you share more than just a face."

Her words took me completely by surprise. I had pretty much convinced myself that there was no truth to what she'd said about meeting someone who looked like me, that it was all part of the game to get me to come and see her. But now that I was here, why was she bringing it up again? Was it actually true? I couldn't see what she had to gain by lying about it.

"Why was he here at your house?" I asked, trying not to come straight out and ask who he was. If she knew how curious I was, she'd use it against me, the same as I would do to her. It was better to try and keep my questions less focused while still getting some information.

"I helped to save him from Darryn Reeves," she explained as she led me into a sitting room and gestured for me to take a seat on the formal sofa. "Reeves thought he was you and snatched him after the book festival. Probably would have killed the poor guy too if we hadn't got there in time."

This was all news to me, but as soon as she said it, it finally made sense to me why no one had followed me after the festival. They must have thought they were following me but they ended up with this other guy instead. The resemblance really must be significant if Reeves had been fooled. He was no amateur.

And there was one other thing she'd said that stuck out at me.

"We?" I repeated. She'd said he might have been killed if "we" didn't get there in time. But as far as I knew, Storm always worked alone. I'd never seen her with a partner or even a sidekick.

She leaned her head to one side in acknowledgement. "Me and the guy's mate."

His mate? At the mere mention of the word, my wolf howled in my head, reminding me yet again that I still hadn't taken any steps towards claiming my own. He was getting to be worse than a fucking alarm clock, going off on me nearly every hour. And every time he started up, my body felt the effects too, a wave of weakness washing over me. I was almost beginning to regret my decision to leave her behind. It was affecting me far more than I had expected it to. Maybe I would have to try to track her down eventually and reject her after all, although I had to admit I had no idea where I would even start to try to locate her.

For now, I tried to focus back on what Storm had just said. She'd helped this other guy's mate rescue him from Reeves. So he was a werewolf too? The more information she gave me about him, the stranger it all seemed.

But in the end, all of this was merely a distraction. I was here for one reason and one reason only.

"You said you could help me interpret the book," I reminded her bluntly, bringing us back to the topic at hand. "I've found the passage I think is the key but I don't know what it means."

A smile of satisfaction crossed her face. "Finally. I was beginning to think this job was never going to end. Show it to me."

"Not so fast," I warned her. "We need to set some ground rules first."

Storm crossed her arms and leaned back, her usual look of amusement on her face. "I'm listening."

"I'll share the text with you," I offered. "And we can work together to figure out the location. But after that, all bets are off. The artifact still belongs to me."

"Unless I get to it first," she countered, teasing me with that cocky smirk of hers.

I ignored the provocation and continued with my conditions. "If either of us are in danger from Reeves, we'll help each other out, but only until the immediate threat is past. After that, we're on our own again."

"Careful, Eli," she taunted. "I'm going to start to think you care about me if you get all worried about my safety."

Returning her smirk with one of my own, I added my last provision. "And when I retrieve the artifact first and this whole search comes to an end, you'll agree to come and work for me."

That took her genuinely by surprise. For a moment, the arrogant look fell from her face, but only for a moment. In the next second, it was back again stronger than ever.

"You think you can handle a woman like me, Eli? Little wannabe dictators aren't really my type."

I growled at her. "Not that kind of work," I muttered through clenched teeth. "I'll need people with your skill set when I start to expand my territory. You've impressed me, Storm, and to be perfectly frank, I prefer having women in my team. They're more trustworthy."

And easier to manipulate, I added in my mind. I'd used my head of security Jenny's attachment to my mother to ensure her support for years, even though I suspected deep down she would have preferred to side with my father. She'd always deferred to him in the past.

Emotional attachments make you weak. That's what growing up without a mother had taught me, and it was why I kept my own emotions firmly in check whenever possible.

Storm laughed once again. "So you're sexist as well as having delusions of grandeur. Good to know."

My face remained stony as I glared back at her. "You don't have to like me or even agree with me. I'm not suggesting that we be best friends. You just need to accept my proposal if you want me to show you the text."

Her eyes searched my face carefully for a moment, though what she was looking for, I wasn't sure. Finally, she gave a shrug. "I suppose I don't have much choice, do I? You're the one with the book. So let's move this along, Eli. Show me what you've got."

~Abby~

Armed with Alpha Adrian's address, Oliver and I drove back off the Seven Hills pack land. The man who had exposed our deception glared at us as we drove off but we had Jenny's assurances that he wouldn't directly contradict her order to let us go. Although he was the pack Gamma, Jenny was the head of security, so her word on matters of security was final, subject to overrule only by the Alpha himself, who, of course, wasn't at home at the moment.

Just before we left the office, Jenny told Oliver about some letters Nicole had sent to her just after Oliver and Elijah were born. She hadn't read them in years and couldn't remember all the details but she thought they might help to explain his mother's frame of mind at the time if he wanted to read them. He gratefully accepted, so now he had those to look forward to as well.

But first we were going to pay his biological father a visit, at long last.

Oliver was uncharacteristically quiet as we drove and I could only imagine what he was making of everything we'd just learned. I waited for him to speak on his own, but when he didn't, I made a gentle enquiry.

"How are you feeling?"

He grimaced while still keeping his eyes on the road. "I honestly don't know, Heels. I mean, I might literally have an evil twin. How am I supposed to be feeling?"

"Nobody said he's evil," I scoffed, though I wasn't sure exactly how serious Oliver was being. "It's actually kind of exciting, really. Maybe you'll get along really well. Didn't you always want a brother?"

It was something he had told me before, how it was a bit lonely for him growing up as an only child. He'd always had a big group of friends but he felt it wasn't quite the same thing. Whereas I came from a big family, but had never felt particularly close to them, so to me, the idea of being an only child wasn't all that bad.

"I did want a brother," Oliver confirmed. "But what do we know about this guy so far? He took some book that people were ready to kill me for, Storm told us to stay out of whatever he's involved in because it's dangerous, and now we know that he challenged his own father for control of the pack. Overall, that's not really sounding like someone I want to be buddies with."

Those were all fair points, but I had to remind him of the lesson we'd both learned together not that long ago. "People aren't always what they appear to be, Oliver. There might be good reasons behind everything he's done. You have to give him a chance."

He grunted in acknowledgement of that but I could tell he wasn't fully convinced. "Let's see what Alpha Adrian has to say first, though I'm not particularly thrilled with him either right now. It sounds like he was at least partly responsible for my mom keeping Elijah a secret from my dad in the first place."

That was another good point. There was still a lot we didn't know.

The address we'd been given wasn't too far from the pack land. An unmarked road took us through another part of the same forest to a small log cabin, similar in style to the pack house we'd just visited but on a much smaller scale.

We had only just managed to park and get out of the car when the front door to the house opened, and my mouth fell open as I got a look at the man standing there.

There was no doubt we had found the man we had come to see.

He was pretty much just an older version of Oliver. His physique and body shape were just the same. His dirty blond hair had started greying around the temples so that it almost matched his sharp, grey eyes, which were currently narrowed in Oliver's direction.

"To what do I owe this pleasure?" he called out sarcastically. "Did the pack finally kick you out?"

Obviously he thought Oliver was Elijah. Oliver knew that as well as I did, I was sure, but he still swallowed almost nervously as he took in the man in front of him. What was he feeling, seeing his biological father for the first time? I wished there wasn't a whole car between us so I could offer him my support.

I was also ready to explain who we were if Oliver needed a moment, but it wasn't necessary. He spoke up before I had the chance. "I think you've mistaken me for someone else, Alpha Adrian."

Now it was the Alpha's turn to have his jaw drop. "It can't be," he muttered, almost to himself. His eyes went to me curiously for just a moment before returning to his son. "Oliver?"

Oliver nodded, his lips drawn together tightly. "That's right. And this is my mate, Abby."

Alpha Adrian looked over at me again and gave me a slight nod before looking back at Oliver, his body language loosening considerably from when he thought Oliver was Elijah. "Well, this is certainly a surprise," he understated. "Please, come in."

He held the door open for us as Oliver and I walked inside and then directed us to a small sitting room. I couldn't help comparing it to the grandeur of the pack house we had just been in. What was it like for him to be separated not only from his son but from the pack he had led and the life he had there?

I couldn't help feeling a bit of sympathy for him even though we still didn't know the full story.

We all took a seat on the worn leather furniture and Alpha Adrian looked Oliver over curiously, as if he was unable to look away.

"Forgive me for staring," he said. "It's just uncanny how much you look like Elijah. I know you're identical twins, of course, but it's still something else entirely to see it right in front of me. It's almost... miraculous."

His awe was a little bit endearing but I was surprised that he would assume Oliver knew who Elijah was after everything we'd just been told. Seeming to read that surprise in my face, Adrian gave me a small nod of acknowledgement.

"I figured you wouldn't have known where to find me if you didn't go to the pack first," he pointed out. "So I assume you already ran into Eli."

"We haven't actually met him yet," Oliver answered, his voice tighter than usual. "But I'm aware of him, yes."

He didn't add that we'd only really learned about him less than an hour ago, so Adrian nodded again. "I see. Well, I am surprised to see you, Oliver. I figured after all this time that either you didn't know about me or you had decided you weren't interested in meeting me. I could understand either way."

"I found out about you a few months ago," Oliver told him, his words far more stilted than usual. "My father told me."

Adrian flinched slightly at the word 'father' but he didn't interrupt.

"But it was Elijah that brought us here today," Oliver continued. "We want to know more about him. Why is he Alpha? What happened between you?"

Adrian let out a long breath. "That's quite a long story. Are you sure you don't want me to explain something more simple, like the meaning of life?"

That almost made me laugh, it was so much like something Oliver would have said. Was it possible for a sense of humour to be passed down in someone's genes?

Oliver, however, didn't crack a smile. "Just give me the highlights for now."

Adrian gave Oliver an appraising look, obviously sensing his discomfort with the whole situation, but he didn't argue with him. "Alright. Well, the short version is, he wanted money and pack resources, and I said no. So he challenged me for my position and he won."

Well, that was a little too short. We still needed more information than that.

"What did he want the money for?" I asked before I could stop myself, then shot Oliver an apologetic look. "Sorry." I had been trying to let him do the talking, but my curiosity got the better of me.

"It's fine, Abby," he said. His voice was still restrained but he gave me the briefest of smiles before looking back at Adrian. "It's a good question. What was the money for?"

"Well, that's where it gets complicated," Adrian explained. "What exactly do you know about your mother's book?"

Chapter Seven

Adrian's words ricocheted around my head. My mother's book? Was this the same book Elijah was at the festival for, the one those humans had kidnapped me over? What did that have to do with Elijah taking over the pack?

And what the fuck was so special about this book in the first place?

As always, Abby could feel me getting upset and reached over to put her hand on mine. "We've heard of a book," she answered for the both of us. "But we didn't know it had anything to do with Oliver's mom or what's special about it."

It really was like she was in my head sometimes, even when we weren't linking directly. I turned my hand over so our fingers entwined and the sparks of our bond helped to both calm me and give me strength.

I could use all the strength she could spare right now. It was more than a little surreal to be sitting across from this man who looked so much like me. When I was younger, I noticed how people always said my friends looked like their dads. No one ever said that about me, but they must have said it about Elijah.

"So you don't know the legend?" Adrian asked, looking between the two of us. "Or anything about the source of power?"

I simply shook my head. I didn't have a clue what he was talking about. "I've never heard those words in that order before."

Adrian's lips twitched upward at my wry answer, but there was something else lurking in his eyes, something almost haunted. "I wish I could say the same. I think we'd all have been better off if it had never existed."

I was about to tell him to just spit it out already when Abby spoke up, her hand squeezing mine. "Could you tell us the legend, Alpha?"

That was more polite than I would have been and I was grateful to have her here to keep things going smoothly.

Adrian leaned back as if settling in for the long haul. "Well, the story starts about four hundred years ago…"

"Four hundred years?" I nearly choked on the words. When he said it was complicated, I didn't think he meant four hundred years' worth of complications. How long was this going to take?

He chuckled at my alarm. "Don't worry, I won't go day-by-day. Essentially, there was a group of werewolves that came over from England with some of the early settlers. Some people say they were a pack looking for a new home. Others maintain that they were exiled by the Alpha King at the time, and others argue that they were just individual wolves from different packs that wanted to start a new life. Whatever the case may be, just before they left, one of them managed to steal an artifact from the Alpha King and secreted it away with him on the ship."

"What was the artifact?" Abby asked, leaning forward eagerly, already wrapped up in the story.

"That's the big question," Adrian admitted. "Nobody knows exactly what it was. But apparently, without it, the Alpha King lost his authority and his kingdom was overrun within days of its theft. Rumours spread that the King's power had actually derived from the artifact itself, and whoever possessed it would be able to bend all wolves to their will just as the King's bloodline had previously done."

"That seems like quite a leap of logic," I couldn't help pointing out. Although I was aware of the supernatural elements of our world, my scientific brain couldn't help weighing in too, and I couldn't see how anyone's authority could have come from an old object, no matter what it was. Alpha authority was passed down in our blood or won in battle. It wasn't conferred on us by any dusty antique.

"Indeed," Adrian agreed, to my surprise. "But people were more superstitious then. And whatever the artifact was, the wolves who brought it with them valued it enough that when their lives were threatened, they took the time to hide it away and to write the location of it down so that, if anything happened to them, someone else would be able to retrieve it."

"And they wrote it in this book?" Abby guessed, almost breathless in her enthusiasm.

"That's right," Adrian said, giving her a nod of acknowledgement. "It was sent back to the family of one of the wolves involved. They were still living in England at the time, and their surname was Williams."

My mother's family. "So the book was eventually passed down to my mother?"

"Yes." Adrian grimaced a little at some memory only he could see. "She showed it to me when we were young, or at least I'm fairly certain she did. She had this very old book that she used to like to play with, but her parents would get upset if they saw her with it and tell her it wasn't a toy. I never read it then, of course, I had no idea what it was. But knowing what I know now, I assume that must have been it."

It was strange to hear this man I'd never met before speaking about my mom in such a familiar way, but obviously, he had known her well. Better than I had. They were friends growing up, my dad had said, and then, he would have known her more intimately later on.

I cleared my throat in an attempt to stop my mind from hopping aboard that particular train of thought. "So this book is meant to show the location of this magical artifact, and whoever finds it will be able to rule over all wolves."

"That's the basic idea," Adrian confirmed. "Though it's all nonsense, if you ask me."

Well, at least we agreed on that.

"But there are people who take it very seriously indeed. People like Eli, and a few others as well."

Finally, we were getting to the heart of the matter. "So Elijah wanted money to... what? Buy the book? Go on a treasure hunt for this artifact?"

My tone was slightly sarcastic which only made Adrian smile. "Pretty much, yes. He has spent a lot of time and money and the pack's resources on this quest, hoping that it will all pay off when he gets the artifact and claims what he sees as his rightful position as the new Alpha King."

It was worse than I thought. I had been half-joking about the evil twin thing in the car with Abby but from the sounds of it, my brother might actually be crazy.

"Alpha," Abby cut in softly. "We think Elijah has the book now. Do you know how he would have got it? Why didn't it go to Oliver from his mother?"

That question hadn't even crossed my mind yet but it was a good one. Why had I never even heard of this book before now?

Adrian looked back at me. "Actually, I was hoping you might be able to tell me that. Nic... that is, your mother... definitely took it with her when she left the pack. What happened to her things after she... died?"

He stumbled over the word 'died' as if it was painful, and I suddenly remembered what my dad had said, about how he wasn't even sure Adrian knew she was dead. But Jenny said they had talked often about Elijah, so he must have known something was wrong at some point when he didn't hear from her.

There were still a lot of unanswered questions but for now, I tried to focus back on the one he'd just asked me: what happened to my mother's things? "My dad got rid of everything," I said slowly, pulling memories from my brain I didn't even know I had. "A few months after she died, he got really worked up about it and wanted everything out of the pack house. I remember someone going into her closet and taking out all her clothes. It was all donated to charity. I don't think he even looked through anything, he just told them to take it all."

"I see." Adrian's words were short and succinct, and I could tell he didn't approve. But everyone grieved in their own way, so I wasn't going to blame my dad for that. "So someone must have eventually recognized the age of the book if not its precise value and put it up for sale. That's how it got to the festival."

My eyes narrowed. "How do you know about the festival?" I asked suspiciously. "I thought you and Elijah weren't on speaking terms."

"We're not," Adrian confirmed. "But I have other sources, people who are keeping an eye on him to try to make sure he doesn't do anything too stupid. Despite everything, he's still my son, and the only family I have."

He gave me an inscrutable look as he said those words, which made me slightly uncomfortable. I was not anywhere near ready to call either him or my brother my family yet.

"Can I ask another question?" Abby piped up again, and Adrian nodded. "How did he defeat you? You're obviously still strong enough to fight him and I'm sure you're more experienced too."

He smiled a little at that, giving Abby an appreciative look before turning back to me. "You've got yourself a very clever mate here."

"I do," I agreed, but I wasn't about to let him distract me. "And I'd like to know the answer to her question as well."

"It's simple enough," Adrian replied with a shrug. "I should have had the upper hand but he played on my weakness."

My eyes scanned his body before I was even aware I was doing it, looking for any obvious defect, but there was none. "What weakness?"

"Not a physical one," he clarified, clearly having noticed my inspection. "An emotional one. As I was about to bring him down, he mind-linked me to ask what his mother would think of us fighting that way over something of hers that should naturally belong to him anyway. He asked if she would be disappointed in me. It made me pause just long enough for him to get the upper hand."

So Elijah was crazy *and* manipulative. Perfect. This just kept getting better.

"Couldn't you have issued a new challenge?" Abby asked. "When the time had passed?"

There were a lot of rules surrounding Alpha challenges, but in a case where the contest was decided by defeat rather than death, the losing side was usually allowed to make one additional challenge after a set period of time.

Adrian ran a weary hand across his face. "I could have, I suppose. But that fight showed me the lengths he would go to, so I decided it was better to let him win and try to keep an eye on things in other ways."

That brought me back to another question I had. "You said you've got sources who keep you informed on his movements?" Adrian nodded again. "Then I want to know where he is. I want to go and speak with him."

I needed to see him face to face. It felt more important to me with every passing minute.

"That might be tricky right now," Adrian warned me. "He's in pretty deep with his search for the artifact. Now that he's got the book, things seem to be coming to a head."

"We can handle any danger," I asserted as confidently as I could. "I just need to know where to find him."

"I can't tell you that exactly," Adrian said, and then quickly held up his hands as I opened my mouth to protest. "But I know someone who can."

He stood up and went over to a drawer in one of the small tables in the room and rifled around in it for a few moments before returning and handing me a business card.

A very familiar looking card, the double of which was still in Abby's pocket.

Storm.

~Elijah~

Storm and I were both bent over different books when her phone rang, the heavy metal song that was her ringtone sounding completely out of place in the silence of her library. She pulled the phone out to look at the display and her eyebrows raised ever so slightly in surprise.

"I need to take this," she told me, standing up and heading towards the door. "Don't break anything while I'm gone."

I rolled my eyes behind her back as she left, my jaw clenched. This wasn't the first time she'd spoken to me like I was a child. I thought that when I won the Alpha position from my father, respect would automatically come with it, but outside of my own pack that wasn't always the case. Sometimes it felt like I had spent my whole life proving myself. Even my own mother hadn't cared for me enough to be part of my life. I'd had to fight for every scrap of attention and recognition I ever got from anyone.

But that will all change once I have the artifact.

I took a couple of deep breaths to let the annoyance leave my body so I could focus back on what I'd been reading. It had been hours already that we'd been reviewing these books and the sky was dark outside, but I wasn't going to rest until I found something to go on.

Storm agreed with me that the first part of the passage I'd found was probably literal.

At the junction of the river and the sea...

We agreed that the sea would have to be the Atlantic Ocean, since that was the major body of water the wolves would have crossed to reach North America. So now we just had to determine which river the passage referred to, out of hundreds of large ones and thousands of smaller ones all along the coast.

That was pretty much where I had gotten stuck when I'd been reviewing the passage on my own. But when I showed it to Storm, or at least showed her the photo of the book I'd taken with my phone, since there was no way I was letting anyone outside my pack near the actual book, she quickly jumped on the next part of the passage.

...whither men have built and winds destroyed...

She brought me here to the library in her house where there was an impressive collection of history books and maps. Armed with the maps and a list of all major wind-related events that took place during the early settlement of the continent, we were trying to narrow the options down.

I was currently looking at the path of the Great Colonial Hurricane of 1635. There was no exact date anywhere in my mother's book to indicate when it was written, but this fit the general timeline of early English settlement and the hurricane was certainly strong enough that it would have destroyed anything that men at the time had built.

I was a bit annoyed at myself that I hadn't put that much together on my own, but it really didn't matter. Here in her library, Storm had more resources than I did and I was certain I could lose her when it came down to it, so it didn't hurt me to take advantage of her offer of help now and get myself to the end of this search a little faster.

The hurricane had travelled up along the east coast before finally making landfall on Long Island and then moving up across Connecticut and Massachusetts. Looking at the major rivers in the area, I could see the Charles River in Massachusetts, which was a definite possibility, but that whole area was very built up now. If the artifact had been hidden there, there was a good chance its hiding place no longer existed or was buried beneath a much more modern settlement. I had to believe that wasn't the case. My gut told me it was still out there waiting to be found. I felt certain I would know if it wasn't.

I moved back down across the land mass, looking for other rivers, and my finger came to a rest on the Thames River in Connecticut. Something twigged in the back of my mind, and I quickly mind-linked Julian who was still on his stakeout in the car on the street outside.

'Alpha,' he greeted me, sounding hopeful. 'Are you finished?'

'Almost,' I told him, also hoping that was true. 'I need you to look something up for me in the book.'

The actual book was still safely locked away in the safe back in my office but Julian and Matthew had images of all the pages on their phones, in case I needed them. I didn't have them on my own phone, just in case Storm somehow managed to take it from me or copy the information from it.

I was aware of how the game was played, and nobody was going to pull one over on me.

I directed him to the pages where I thought I remembered reading about the journey the wolves had made from the Old World to the New. I hadn't paid too much attention to it as it didn't have to do with the source directly, but something made me think it might be helpful now.

'It mentions a waterway,' I told him, trying to remember exactly what I'd read. 'Can you find it?'

There was a moment's pause before he answered me. 'Yeah, you're right. It says 'it was difficult to fathom having travelled all this way to find ourselves beside a waterway bearing the same name as the one we had departed from. The name was all it had in common though, its aspect...' He trailed off. 'It just goes on to describe the river. Do you want me to keep going?'

'No, that's fine,' I told him, fighting the smile that was trying to take over my face. 'That's what I needed. I'll be out very soon.'

The Thames. If they left England from London, they would have travelled out on the Thames, and then found themselves beside a completely different Thames River upon arrival. The hurricane passed almost directly over the spot where the river met the ocean.

It made sense. It all fit. *Finally things were coming together.*

Just as I cut the link, Storm came back into the room. "Did I miss anything?" she asked with her trademark smirk.

"I'm still stuck," I lied, forcing myself to sound frustrated. "There are too many possibilities and I'm starting to see double. I think we should call it a night and pick up the search again in the morning."

She looked surprised at my proposal, but to my relief, she didn't argue. "That's fine with me. I don't know where you're spending the night, but just to be clear, my bed's not an option."

She thinks she's so funny. I narrowed my eyes at her to show I wasn't amused, but it only made her laugh.

"Go get some rest then, Eli," she said, slapping me on the shoulder. "I don't get up before ten, so don't bother coming back before then."

I shrugged her hand off and headed out. As soon as I was back outside, I linked with my men again. 'Meet me at the club.' I didn't need to specify which one I meant since Julian and I had just been there a few days earlier.

I made my own way there separately from the other two just in case anyone decided to follow me, doing my usual trick of backtracking and watching for tails, but I seemed to be in the clear. By the time I arrived at the club, Julian and Matthew were already on their second or third drink and had a trio of beautiful women at the table with them.

"You must be Eli," one of them greeted me as I walked over, giving me an inviting smile. She was blonde and tanned in that typically Californian way, her shirt hanging off one shoulder and her long legs crossed just to draw attention to them. "We've been waiting for you."

It was obvious what kind of night Julian and Matthew had in mind and normally I would have been happy to do the same. We couldn't fly out until the morning now anyway, so some company for the night wasn't a bad idea. But as I looked over the woman's body again, my mind suddenly flashed back to a very different woman. One with dark hair and glasses and a rather cute little nose.

My mate.

My wolf began to howl again as soon as she crossed my mind, and I shut my eyes against the sound. *Not this again.* He'd actually stayed silent most of the day to let me concentrate, but now he seemed determined to make up for it.

"Eli?" Julian was giving me a funny look when I opened my eyes again. "Everything okay?"

It should be. There was no reason I couldn't spend the night with this woman if I wanted to. My mate, if I could even call her that, was human, and I certainly hadn't marked her, so she wouldn't feel anything if I chose to be with someone else.

So why was there an annoying, niggling feeling of something like guilt in the back of my mind at the thought of it?

"It's been a long day," I told them all. "I'm just going to have a drink and call it a night. But you all enjoy yourselves and I'll see you in the morning."

Leaving them all behind, I went to the bar and ordered myself a drink. It had just been placed in front of me when someone else slid into the seat next to me, making me jump as her shockingly red hair came into view.

"Do you really think I'm that stupid, Eli?" Storm asked as I groaned into my glass. "Obviously you figured something out. What was it?"

"How did you find me?" I snarled at her, avoiding the question. I was sure I hadn't been followed.

"Tracking chip," she said cheerily, patting my shoulder where she had slapped it earlier. "You're not getting rid of me that easily. I agreed to your conditions so you have to stick to your end of the deal too. We track this thing down together."

"Why do you even care?" I asked her, genuinely curious about the answer. "The source doesn't mean anything to you."

"It doesn't," she agreed, still sounding far too pleased with herself. "But it means something to my employer. That's all you need to know. Now, where are we headed?"

~Letters from Nicole~

Dear Jenny,

It feels strange to be writing to you after having you here with me for so many months when I could just call down the hall and talk to you whenever I wanted.

I miss you more than I can say. Not only because of how much I loved having you here, which I did, but also because you were the only one that I could confide in. With you gone, I'm starting to feel like I'm going mad.

Maybe this letter feels a bit old-fashioned, but talking over the phone feels too dangerous. If someone from the pack overheard the things I want to talk to you about, if Patrick ever found out, I don't know what I would do. He would be so hurt, and the last thing I ever want to do is hurt him.

I never wanted to hurt anyone.

Adrian called me last night and I could hear Elijah crying in the background and Jenny, my heart hurt so much it felt like it would break apart right then and there. I know he was crying out for me, even if he doesn't know it. It feels like a part of myself has been cut off and taken away, but I have to pretend to all the rest of the world that it's fine. Not just fine, I have to pretend things are wonderful, because Patrick is so happy that we have our son at last, the pack is so happy for us, and Oliver deserves a happy mom too, but half the time I want to just lie on the floor and weep for my baby that was taken from me.

And I know, I know... you don't have to say it! I was the one who made the choice. I agreed that Adrian could take him but I didn't know it would feel like this. I couldn't imagine anything that would feel like this.

I tell myself over and over, hundreds of times a day, that it will get easier. I know that Elijah is loved and cared for. Adrian wants him and loves him and you will be there to keep an eye on him too. It has all worked out as we planned. Patrick has his heir and Adrian has his heir too.

And the boys... well, you know my feelings on that. Twins in my family have always brought bad luck. Keeping them apart is not only right for their fathers, it is right for them too.

It is just me that feels all wrong.

And the little boy I won't see again.

I pray every night to the Moon Goddess that Adrian will find his mate and that she will raise my son and love him as her own. It's hard to think of him with another mother but it's better than thinking of him with no mother at all.

Please be there for him when you can, Jenny. Comfort him when he's crying and encourage him when he needs it, at least for now.

Oliver is doing so well, he is a perfect baby. Patrick adores him already and shows him off proudly to everyone who shows the slightest interest. I sometimes wonder if he forgets he's not really his son. I hope that Oliver takes after me so that no one will ever question why he doesn't look like his dad at all.

I know the day will come when I can look at him and not see the missing half of him too, but that day hasn't arrived yet. I pray that it will come soon.

All my love,

Nicole

Dear Jenny,

Thank you for your letter, it made me smile which is something I haven't done much of lately.

But speaking of smiling... Oliver smiled at me for the first time today! His eyes are already turning from blue to grey, just like Adrian's. I think Patrick was secretly hoping they would stay blue like his, but it looks like it's not meant to be.

Is Elijah smiling too? I would ask Adrian, but the last time we spoke, things were very tense. He only wanted to talk about our past. No matter how many times I tell him that there is no chance of me ever leaving Patrick, he refuses to give up hope. In fact, I think he is becoming even more determined. He said that the fact that Patrick is unable to have children and that I came to him and that we made these two beautiful boys together only proves that we were meant to be together all along. He says we can't fight destiny. No matter what I say, I can't convince him otherwise.

I wish I could talk to my mate about all of this, but there are too many things I have kept from him for too long. I'm terrified that if he learned the whole truth and how I have lied to him, his love for me would dim, and I couldn't bear that, not when I love him so desperately.

I know it makes me weak and cowardly, and I truly hate myself for it some days. But I'm in so deep now, I can't see the way back up to the surface. I can only swim down.

You asked me in your letter what Patrick knows about my past with Adrian? The truth is that he doesn't know any of it.

If I had told him the truth about Adrian from the beginning, maybe this would have all been different. On the day Patrick and I met and I told him that I was already seeing someone, he asked me who it was. What if I had just said the words then? What if I had told him that it was Adrian that I had pledged my heart to?

It didn't seem important at the time. I had no intention of accepting Patrick so what did it matter to him who the other man was?

And then when things changed and I began falling for him, it didn't seem right to tell him about Adrian before I had a chance to end things with Adrian properly.

Each day seemed to move faster and almost before I knew it, we were talking about finding an Alpha who would help us to conceive. You also asked me in your letter why we didn't simply use in vitro fertilization. That was at Patrick's insistence. We fought over this, badly, our only true fight where we didn't speak to each other for days. I screamed and shouted at him that I did not want to sleep with anyone else! How could I when it would hurt the man I loved so much? And the idea of any other man touching me that way was simply repellent. But Patrick insisted that we couldn't go through doctors, that it wasn't secure enough. He insisted this had to be a secret, that if anyone from the pack ever found out they would not accept the child as his heir, and he was convinced this was the only way.

I'm not certain when the idea of asking Adrian first came to me. There were many ways in which he was the obvious choice. He was on the other side of the country so there was very little chance that, should the child bear a resemblance to him, anyone would ever make the connection. He had the Alpha blood we were looking for, of course. And though I still didn't want to be with any man other than Patrick, at least Adrian was familiar to me. We had loved each other once. I knew he would be gentle and patient with me.

But I still hadn't told Patrick that Adrian was the man I had intended to mate with before we met, and how could I tell him then? He would have thought I still had some kind of feelings for Adrian and as a result would refuse to consider him. But that wasn't why I chose him. It was almost entirely a matter of comfort and convenience.

I'm sure you can imagine how surprised Adrian was when I made the request. We had hardly spoken since the night I told him I was accepting Patrick. But he agreed to meet with me anyway, and... well, you know the rest.

And then we found out about the twins and I confided my fears to him, about the things that had happened to twins in my family in the past. That was when he first suggested that he simply take one of them.

He grew so excited by the idea of having an heir of his own when there was still no sign of his mate that it was difficult to refuse him.

And yet I did. I tried to. But then he used my omissions to Patrick against me. He threatened to tell my mate how I had kept our relationship a secret from him and he asked me to think about how that would look to Patrick.

I knew exactly how it would look. Even though it wasn't the truth, it would look like I had returned to a former lover because I wanted to, not because Patrick had been so desperate for his heir.

Adrian wouldn't let up. Every day he called me and told me how much he would treasure and care for our child and he reminded me of the sad fate of all the twins in my family's past, and in my weakness, I gave in. I told myself I was doing it for Adrian, so that he could have his heir too, and for the boys, so they would be safe.

But really I was doing it to protect myself. I see that more clearly with each passing day, but I don't know how to fix it, Jenny. It's too late.

I have made my bed and now I have to lie in it.

Well, look at that. I started this letter with happy news and the intention of writing you a happy letter, but it seems I'm not capable of it, at least for now.

Please keep writing with news of Elijah and send me pictures if you can. I know he looks just like Oliver, but he is not the same. I need to see my other boy too.

All my love,

Nicole

Chapter Eight

~Oliver~

I already had our bags packed by the time Abby came out of the shower.

"Oliver?" She looked confused but also completely beguiling wrapped only in the towel, her hair still damp. If it were any other time, I wouldn't be able to resist pulling the towel off her and taking advantage of the situation, but my mind was far too troubled to be thinking about that right now. "What's going on?"

She must feel my anger because I knew she couldn't see me from that distance with her glasses off.

"We're going home," I told her. "I need to talk to my dad. My other dad, I mean."

I walked over to hand her the clothes I'd left out for her but instead of taking them from me, Abby grabbed hold of my arm.

"Hang on," she said, her voice soothing as her pale blue eyes tried to focus on me. "Tell me what happened. Ten minutes ago we were going to spend the night here and wait to hear from Storm in the morning. What changed?"

She was right, that had been the plan. After leaving Alpha Adrian's house, we got back in the car and Abby gave Storm a call, putting her on speaker phone so I could hear as well. She explained that we had just spoken to Elijah's father, that we were looking for Elijah now, and that Adrian had given us her number.

Storm gave an amused-sounding huff. "To be honest, I thought I'd seen the last of you two. But I do owe you a favour, and if Adrian's sending you my way, that's all the more reason for me to help."

"So you know where he is?" I pressed, wanting to get to the point.

Her sigh echoed through the phone. "Actually, Elijah's at my house right now."

Abby and I looked at each with wide eyes. What was he doing at Storm's house? And when was anything going to start making sense to me? Even after the information Jenny and Adrian had given us, I still had so many unanswered questions.

"We're on our way," Abby told her, but Storm quickly shut down that idea.

"Don't bother coming here, we won't be staying long. We're close to figuring out our next move and then we'll be heading out. But I've got your number now, so as soon as I know where we're going, I'll let you know."

"We?" I repeated, trying to figure out why they were together at all. "You're going together?" I hadn't had the impression from anything she'd told us before that they were working together.

"It's a temporary truce," she explained drily. "Forged by circumstance, not by personal preference."

So she didn't like Elijah either, apparently. Was there anybody out there who had anything good to say about my brother?

"Just sit tight," she told us. "It's getting late so we won't be leaving until the morning anyway, and that's if we even figure out where we're supposed to be going. I'll be in touch."

She hung up and Abby and I looked at each other in silence for a moment. So many times, words weren't needed between us, I could read what she was feeling in her face and she could do the same with me. In this unspoken exchange, she knew I wasn't going to give up and I knew she had my back, no matter what.

"I guess we can go back to the same motel we stayed at last night," I suggested out loud. "At least we'll be close to the airport if we need to fly somewhere once we hear from Storm."

And that had been the plan when we'd checked in and when Abby went to have a shower before bed. But then a message had come in on my phone and now, after reading through the letters Jenny had sent me, I needed to go home.

What had changed, Abby asked me. Everything had changed. Ever since we got to that book festival, my life felt like it was unravelling. Everything I thought I knew about my parents and my family was being called into question.

But I didn't need to explain that to her. That much, she already knew. What she needed now were the specifics.

"Jenny sent me a couple of my mom's letters," I explained. "She took photos of them and sent them to me. You can read them on the plane, but for now, we have to go."

Jenny said she was sure she had more letters, but these were the ones she could find for now. As soon as I read them, I called the airport and the pilot. I had more questions for Adrian, of course, but right now, I didn't particularly trust him to tell me the truth. My dad, however, I could demand answers from, so that's where we were heading.

Once we were settled on the plane, I gave my phone to Abby so she could read the letters for herself.

I watched her face as she read them, watched her brow furrowing and her eyes widening as I was sure mine must have done when I read them too. When she finally handed the phone back to me, there were tears in the corners of her eyes.

"Wow," she said softly. "It's even more complicated than we thought."

In spite of everything, that nearly made me laugh. It seemed impossible for things to get more complicated and yet they had.

"I know you're angry," she continued. "But who are you angry with?"

"Honestly? All of them," I blurted out, feeling my anger rise again as I thought about it. "Alpha Adrian manipulated my mom into giving up

Elijah. And he had the nerve to sit in front of us this afternoon and complain about Elijah using emotional blackmail against him? I don't believe he's as innocent as he's claiming to be. And my dad's not a lot better, forcing his mate to sleep with someone else when she really didn't want to? That is not okay at all. And my mom lied to my dad almost from the day they met. How can she talk about how much she loves him if she didn't even trust him enough to tell him the truth?"

I had been getting more worked up as I went on, not even realizing that by the end I was practically shouting in frustration, until Abby winced at my last words and I immediately reached out to take her hand.

"I'm sorry, Heels, I shouldn't be taking this out on you. It's not your fault."

"I understand why you're upset," she assured me. "And I think talking to Alpha Patrick is a great idea, but let's try not to jump to any conclusions."

"How am I jumping to conclusions?" I asked, gesturing to the phone still in my hand. "These are her own words."

"But it's still just one person's perspective," she reminded me. "And sometimes people's actions might seem misguided from the other side, or based on how things turned out, but unless we know what was really in their heart, we'll never know for sure."

"It's too late to ask my mom," I pointed out bitterly. "These letters are as close as I'm going to get, and I don't know if I even like the woman in them."

This wasn't the mother I remembered. But then, I had only known her as a mother, not as a real person with hopes and fears of her own.

"Well, let's look at the letters again," Abby suggested gently, taking my phone back from me and beginning to read through them again out loud. Hearing my mom's words in Abby's voice was very strange, but it also made her sound a little more real. A little more human and a little more vulnerable.

When she got to the part about how my mom hadn't told my dad about Adrian when they first met, Abby looked up at me almost sheepishly. "You know, this isn't so different from us. I was already seeing someone when we met and I refused to tell you who it was."

I grimaced at the reminder. I hadn't thought about Abby's ex, Liam, for a long time and the thought of him now did nothing to calm my nerves. Even though he'd gotten exactly what he deserved for taking advantage of Abby and Liz and many others before them, losing his job and his fiancée and his reputation, I still didn't like to waste any time on him.

"By not telling you, I was protecting him as much as myself, or maybe even more. Your mom is pretty harsh on herself here, saying she did it only for herself, but I don't think that's true. I bet she was worried that your dad would do something if he found out. After all, Alpha Patrick's not exactly the least intimidating guy I've ever met."

She shuddered a little bit at the memory of how my dad used to be with her, and I had to admit that everything she said was true. If Abby had told me who she was seeing before she accepted me, I probably would have gone and confronted him, and my dad likely would have done the same.

"And when she talks about bad things happening to twins," Abby carried on. "I think it's more serious than she lets on here. I think she was truly scared about it and I bet that played more of a role in her decision than anything Alpha Adrian said or could have said to her."

She lapsed into silence as she reviewed the letters again, and I felt a surge of admiration for her. "How do you do that, Heels?"

"Do what?" she asked, looking up at me innocently.

"Always see the good in people." She had a natural compassion that never failed to amaze me.

"Well, I've had some practice. I had to find the good in you, didn't I?" she teased me, and I was surprised to find myself smiling.

She knew just how to make me feel better too.

"Let's try to get some rest," she suggested now. "We won't know anything else until we talk to your dad so there's nothing we can do until then. And I have a feeling that no matter what we find out, tomorrow's going to be a long day."

~Abby~

We landed in the early morning and got back to the Jade Moon pack house in time for breakfast. A few of Oliver's friends were hanging around in the kitchen when we went in to get some food and they all greeted us enthusiastically.

"I thought you were getting back a couple of days ago," Eric said, flashing me a smile before turning back to Oliver.

"We've been in and out," Oliver answered, his reply and his whole bearing far more stiff than usual. "And we'll be leaving again. I just need to talk to my dad about something."

He moved over to the fridge to grab us some food, leaving Eric with a concerned look. "Is everything okay?" he asked me quietly.

It really wasn't my place to share anything that was going on so I just gave him the most convincing smile I could. "It will be. We just have a few things we need to sort out."

After a quick breakfast, we headed to Alpha Patrick's office where the Alpha was already busy with the day's work. I realized as we walked in that I had hardly ever seen Oliver's dad in the pack house when he wasn't in his office. Did he ever take any time off? What did he do for fun?

Those clearly weren't the questions on Oliver's mind as he walked right up to his dad's desk, put his hands flat on it and leaned across to him, taking Patrick by surprise before he could even say hello.

"I think there were some things you left out when you told me the story of my conception."

Patrick was never one to be easily intimidated but his eye twitched a little beneath his son's accusing glare. "You spoke to Adrian."

It wasn't a question, just a statement of acknowledgement, but it seemed to be missing the point. Oliver was upset about what his mom had said about him forcing her into sleeping with another man, not anything Adrian told us.

"We did," Oliver confirmed, his voice still tinged with anger. "And we learned a few things we need to tell you about. But first I want you to explain to me why you forced her into this arrangement in the first place? You made it sound like it was something you agreed on together, but that's not what she said."

A brief look of confusion and maybe even hurt flashed across Patrick's face. "She told Adrian that I forced her into it?"

I could see where his confusion was coming from, since Oliver hadn't mentioned the letters yet, so I decided to jump in before they misunderstood each other any further. "Alpha, we didn't discuss that with Alpha Adrian. But Oliver saw some letters that his mom sent to her friend Jenny and in them she talked about the fight you had."

The confusion on his face melted into a bit of understanding and perhaps a little remorse. He sighed and gestured to the chairs opposite him. "Sit down."

Oliver pushed him off the desk and grabbed one of the chairs roughly, pulling it over to him rather than going to it. Everything in his body language suggested that he was still on the offensive, but he held his tongue and let his father speak.

"I don't know exactly what she said in the letter," Patrick started. "But yes, when I first suggested this rather unusual kind of surrogacy arrangement, we did have a fight about it. A pretty big one. She accused me of not loving her as much as she loved me if I could even think about letting her share a bed with another man."

Oliver grimaced a little, the talk of his parents' sex life clearly a little uncomfortable for him. But we were all adults here, and I knew how badly he wanted answers, so I encouraged the Alpha to keep going. "I can kind of see her point," I admitted gently. "If Oliver suggested something like that, I would be hurt too."

Patrick nodded at me appreciatively. "Yes, and I can see that now. But at the time I thought she was completely missing the point. I thought the fact that I was suggesting it at all showed how much I loved and trusted her. If I had any doubts about the strength of our bond, I never would have suggested it."

There was some logic in that too. Once again, I really could see both sides.

"She said you didn't do in vitro fertilization because you were concerned about someone finding out?" Oliver asked. His voice was still firmly controlled, but his posture was a little more open. He was listening to his dad, at least.

"That was part of the reason," Patrick agreed. "If anyone had found out, it would have cast doubt over your legitimacy immediately, and it would also make me look weak to the pack. People weren't as accepting of things like that twenty years ago. And the other part was that I didn't want to put her through months or even years of invasive procedures and possible disappointments, not when there was absolutely nothing wrong with her. The problem was entirely mine. If we planned it carefully enough, she could be pregnant within a week. It seemed far less stressful for her in the long run."

That also made sense, but Nicole's letter hadn't mentioned anything about that.

"Did you explain that to her?" Oliver asked, clearly thinking along the same lines that I was.

"Probably not as well as I could have," Patrick admitted. He ran his hand down his face, grabbing hold of his chin as he reached the bottom. "Your mom and I were a volatile pairing at times. She was very emotional and I was practical. It led to conflict more often than I would have liked. I explained my reasoning to her logically, but she needed an emotional explanation more, and I didn't see that at the time."

"How was your argument resolved?" I asked. It seemed to me they were at an impasse. Someone would have had to give in first.

"It took almost a week," Patrick told us. "Almost a week of her not speaking to me and my wolf going crazy. But finally, she came to me and told me she had thought of one person that she would be comfortable asking. Of course, I immediately knew who she meant."

"You did?" Oliver sounded as surprised as I was. Nicole's letter said Patrick didn't know anything about her past relationship with Adrian, and the things he had told us the last time we were all together in this room seemed to back that up.

Patrick gave a wry smile. "She never knew that I knew about Adrian. I ran into him randomly at a meeting we were both attending, about a year after your mother accepted me. He introduced himself to me and when he asked about Nicole, I simply knew it. There was envy in his voice and possessiveness in his eyes that could only be because of past intimacy."

"And you weren't upset?" I asked in amazement. That idea shocked me more than anything else he had said so far.

He shrugged. "What did I have to be upset about? She chose me. If she wanted to keep the identity of her past lover a secret from me, she must have had her reasons. I trusted her completely and never doubted her love for a second. That was one thing I'm not sure she ever knew, probably because I never told her properly."

The regret was thick in his voice and I could see Oliver softening further. "So she came to you and suggested that she have Adrian's baby," he said. "And you were okay with that, knowing their past relationship?"

"Yes," Patrick said simply. "It was what I expected her to decide when I first suggested it. I would never have forced her to be with anyone she didn't want to be with. But I knew that she already had a history with Adrian, that it wouldn't be entirely unpleasant for her. I loved her enough that I wanted the experience to be as positive for her as it possibly could be."

This was a level of selflessness or perhaps detachment I could hardly fathom and clearly Oliver was struggling with it as well.

"And when it actually happened?" he pressed. "When they slept together and you felt the pain, you didn't regret it then?"

Patrick's face twisted a little as though he were feeling the pain again now. "Of course I hated it. When the time came for her to go to his bed, in secret so that nobody from his pack knew about it either, I shifted and ran into the woods so that I wouldn't lash out at anyone. The pain was overwhelming, but I still felt it was worth it in the end."

"And you weren't afraid about any old feelings being rekindled with them being together?" I couldn't help asking. How could he not have been jealous at all?

"Afraid? No," he said, shaking his head. "As I said, I trusted her entirely. If she enjoyed it at the time, that was fine. It was better than the idea of her hating it. And I knew that she would come back with me afterwards, and she did. So no, to answer your earlier question, Oliver, I never regretted it. Not when it worked out just as I'd hoped it would."

"Not exactly as you hoped," he muttered, and Patrick's brow creased.

"What do you mean?"

Oliver glanced over at me as if asking me if he should go ahead and tell Patrick the rest. My philosophy ever since Oliver and I had got together was that it was always best to be as truthful as possible, so I nodded at him now, encouraging him to go ahead.

"There's something you don't know," Oliver said, giving his dad a much more sympathetic look than any he'd given him since we arrived this morning.

He exhaled deeply while I held my breath, waiting to hear the words he would choose.

"Mom didn't just get pregnant with me. There was another baby."

Patrick's face turned ashen as his eyes searched Oliver's face for any sign of a lie. "What?" he whispered as if the word was some kind of curse. "There couldn't have been."

"It's not likely," Oliver agreed. "But apparently it happened. Abby saw him in San Francisco. That's what started us on this path in the first place."

Patrick was still struggling to understand. "Saw who?" he asked, his eyes flitting between me and his son.

Oliver answered for both of us. "My twin brother."

~Oliver~

Maybe I should have softened the blow. I knew it would be as big a shock to my dad as it was to me to learn I had a twin brother we'd never known about. I knew he would be surprised and hurt and angry, and probably a few other things too.

But the one thing I didn't expect was the look of understanding that crossed his face. Even though there were still some traces of disbelief there, he was taking it far better than I had anticipated. Far better than I still was, to be honest.

"She had twins?" he asked softly, speaking more to himself than to me or Abby as his eyes moved back and forth, seeing things in his mind that I couldn't begin to guess at. "And she gave one of them to Adrian?"

I nodded, still thrown off by his reaction. Why wasn't he furious? His mate had lied to him and kept a whole other child hidden from him! He should be raging, but he wasn't. He simply looked... sad.

"She must have been so scared," he continued, still talking so quietly I could barely hear him. I wasn't sure that I was meant to.

"Scared because she kept it from you?" I asked, trying to make sense of what he was saying.

My dad looked at me in surprise when I spoke, almost as if he'd forgotten I was there. "What?"

We were clearly not on the same wavelength, and once again, Abby stepped in to try to bridge the gap. "Why would she have been afraid, Alpha?"

Her letters had already given us a clue about that and my dad confirmed it now. "Because of what always happens to twins in her family."

The way he said it sent a chill through me, and Abby's words on the plane came back to me. *I think it's more serious than she lets on,* she'd said. Perhaps she was right.

"What happens to them?" I asked. It couldn't be anything *that* serious. After all, Elijah and I were both alive and well. Or at least alive. I wasn't sure how well he was.

But my dad's answer quickly proved me wrong.

"One of them kills the other. Each and every time."

Abby gasped, her hand reaching out for me instinctively. I quickly grasped it with my own, letting her feel my warmth and strength. 'I'm just fine, Heels,' I told her through our link. 'You don't have to worry.'

Despite my soothing words, I couldn't deny the anxiety that those words caused me too. If that was true, it was a damn good reason to keep us apart. My mom's actions were finally starting to make a tiny bit of sense.

"Why do they kill each other?" Abby managed to ask, her voice still a little choked with fear and surprise.

"It's not always on purpose," my dad explained. "In fact, it usually isn't. She told me all about it when we first started trying to have children. I made a joke that I would love to have twins or even triplets and get a big family started all at once. She went completely pale and rigid before confessing to me that twins had always been accompanied with bad luck in her family. And that's really what it sounded like, just horrible luck. Accidents where one twin unintentionally does something that kills the other. The family has called it a curse, though we both found the word distasteful."

"What about if the twins were raised separately?" I asked. "If this kept happening, surely they must have tried that." My mom couldn't have been the only one who thought of it.

"They did," my dad confirmed. "But in each case, once they met, something happened to one of them. Again, it was usually an accident, but she knew of at least one case where the twins were kept apart into adulthood, and then when they finally met, having been told of the curse in advance, one of them murdered the other so that he wouldn't be the one to die."

That could hardly be more fucked up. I couldn't imagine doing something like that, but as I thought back to everything I knew about Elijah, I also couldn't be completely sure if he wouldn't. But then he would have to know about the curse to make that connection, and I didn't know how he would. If Adrian hadn't told him about me, why would he tell him about the curse? And that was if Adrian even knew about it at all.

Now, more than ever, I really needed to talk to my brother.

"Have you already met him?" my dad asked. There was a bit of worry in his own voice that surprised me. My dad wasn't kidding when he described himself as practical and logical. I wouldn't expect him to be the kind of person who believed in curses.

"Not yet," I replied honestly. "But I intend to."

"Oliver..." Abby began, her voice filled with worry, but I cut her off with a shake of my head.

"This has all been kept hidden for way too long, Abby. I need to see him for myself and he deserves to know about me too. Even if it's just one time, I need to meet him."

Maybe the things my dad had just said should have dimmed my conviction on this point, but if anything, they had made me more determined. Whatever this artifact was, whatever the curse was about, it was part of our legacy, part of both of us. It seemed vital to me that we figure it out together.

"I wish she had confided in me," my dad said softly, making Abby and I both turn back to him. "It must have been a very difficult decision for her. I wish I could have helped her."

"Why wouldn't she have told you?" I asked, trying to keep my own voice calm as well. I wasn't so angry with him anymore at least, and I was starting to understand my mother's choice a little better too, though I still didn't agree with it or the fact that she had kept it all a secret.

My dad grimaced. "There are some things I haven't told you about your mom, Oliver. I didn't ever really intend to. I don't want to tarnish the memories you have of her."

"I think it's a little late for that now," I told him drily. "After all of this, I don't know how it could get much worse. Just tell me everything, Dad. No more secrets."

He closed his eyes tightly for a moment before nodding in agreement. "You're right. I'm just so used to not talking about it. You have to understand Oliver, things were different twenty years ago. These days, people are a bit more accepting of it, but back when I first met your mother and through our whole mating, it was still seen as quite taboo."

"What was?" He wasn't making any sense to me again.

"Mental illness."

My mom was crazy? Maybe that's where Elijah gets it from.

Those dark thoughts stayed in my head where no one else heard them, thankfully. Outwardly, I tried to be a bit more composed. "What kind of illness?"

"The doctors never gave it a name. We could have seen a specialist of course, but your mom insisted she didn't want to, for the same reason we didn't attempt the in vitro treatment. There was too much stigma attached to it and she didn't want the pack to respect her less. But she suffered from depression and paranoia at times. I knew that's why she never told me about Adrian. She was completely convinced that I would leave her if I knew, and I was worried that if I just told her that I already knew, she'd have a breakdown."

"I don't remember her like that." I didn't have a lot of memories of my mom, but they were generally happy ones.

"She always did her best to hide it from you. If anything, she over-compensated, being cheerful and sunny around you all the time. But privately, she suffered a lot, and she had a particularly bad spell right after you were born. I thought at the time that it was baby blues combined with her usual struggles, but obviously it was more than that. She must have been mourning being away from her other son."

Abby's hand squeezed mine in empathy. I had almost forgotten I was still holding it, but I was grateful she was still there.

"And there's one more thing I need to tell you," my dad said, his deep blue eyes fixed on me with both determination and trepidation.

Now what? His demeanour suggested it was important, but after everything we'd already discussed, I didn't know what was left. "What is it?" I asked, eager to get all the secrets out once and for all.

"It's about how she... died," he said, wincing at the word almost in the same way that Adrian had the day before.

"She was sick," I reminded him. That's what I had always been told. "I remember visiting her in the hospital."

My dad nodded. "She was sick, but not physically. She was in the hospital because of her mental illness. And in the end, it wasn't enough."

Abby gasped once again beside me, but I hadn't made the connection yet. "What do you mean?"

My dad took a deep breath before giving me a sad and sympathetic look. "She didn't die from any illness, Oliver. She killed herself."

Chapter Nine

~Elijah~

"Why won't you just tell me where we're going?"

It had to be the tenth time Storm had asked me that, and I was quickly losing patience.

"Because you don't need to know. I'm taking you along, aren't I? I'm keeping up my end of the deal, so you'll see when we get there."

We were already aboard the private plane, the two of us along with Julian and Matthew, who had both arrived looking a little worse for wear from their night out. That didn't bother me. We had a five hour flight to get to Connecticut, so they could sleep it off now and be alert and ready to go when we landed. They were both doing exactly that right now, their snores echoing off the plane walls.

My plans were almost ruined this morning when we arrived at the airport and the woman at the desk pulled me aside to speak to me privately. "I'm very sorry, Mr Reynolds," she said apologetically. "But we've been asked not to extend you any further credit on this account. Your bill from the last quarter hasn't been paid yet."

Fuck. I knew things were getting tight in the pack finances but I really didn't need this right now. We were so close. Once I had the artifact and the other packs began to submit to us, we'd have more money than we would know what to do with. I just needed a little more time.

"I'm sure it must be a mistake," I assured her, dialling up my charm as I flashed her a confident smile. She was older than me but not by too much, and there weren't very many human women who could resist my Alpha magnetism when I really turned it on. "It's incredibly important to me that we make this flight today, but I will have my assistant look into the bill just as soon as we get back."

Her eyes moved down to my lips as I spoke and I knew I had her. She looked back up at me with a small smile. "I suppose we can make an exception this time. But it really will need to be paid after this."

I leaned in a little closer. "You can be sure of it, Ms...?"

"Abrams," she murmured, her pupils dilating. "Kelly Abrams."

"Kelly." I said her name softly as I gave her a wink. "Perhaps I'll deliver the payment personally when I get back."

"Where are you going?" she asked.

"Hartford," I answered honestly. There was no need to lie. "But if everything goes well, I'll be back very soon."

She couldn't even manage to respond to that other than to nod at me, and I went back to the others to board the plane. *Humans are so weak,* I thought as I mounted the stairs to the plane. *So easy to manipulate.* Just another reason to be glad I had lost track of my mate.

Or at least that's what I tried to tell myself every time she crossed my mind, which was far too often for my liking.

"I need to let my employer know where I am," Storm told me, bringing my thoughts back to the present. "I'm required to check in with them at regular intervals."

"You can tell your employer that you're on a plane," I suggested sarcastically. There was no way I was telling her where we were going before we got there. She could arrange for people to be waiting for us there or who knows what. I had no idea what kind of resources she had available to her, but after seeing her house, I was sure they were extensive. Hell, at this rate, I might need to hit her up for a loan if we didn't find the artifact soon.

But that wasn't going to be necessary, I told myself firmly, because we were going to get it today. This was the day I'd been waiting for and working towards for the past five years.

"What's your plan if we run into Reeves?" she asked, finally accepting that she wasn't going to get an answer out of me about our destination.

The truth was that I didn't have much of a plan about that. I was mostly hoping that we were too far ahead of him for him to catch up with us. If all went well, we'd have the artifact in hand while he was still trying to figure out where we went.

"What do you know about him?" I asked her, hoping she wouldn't notice that I hadn't answered her question.

"Reeves? Not much." Storm shrugged as she stretched her legs in the spacious cabin. "Ex-military, hates wolves, has a lot of money. Probably the same things you know."

I did know that much, but I was still curious. "Why does he hate werewolves so much? How does he even know about us? And where does his money come from?"

Again, Storm shrugged. "Your guess is as good as mine. I kinda figured he had a bad experience with a wolf once. He seems like the kind of guy to hold a grudge. And as for the money, I have no idea where he got it from, but he's got enough to fund his little team and their research too."

"Research?" That was something new. I wasn't sure what she was talking about.

"Ways to fight against wolves," she explained. "That guy they took, the one that looks just like you, they shot him up with something that put his wolf to sleep. It made him pretty much human."

That wasn't good. Being made human was about the worst thing I could think of. "Permanently?"

She shook her head. "No. Just for about an hour or so, but long enough for them to get the drop on him. So whatever you do, don't underestimate him."

I didn't intend to, but I was still pretty certain that he wouldn't be a threat if we could be efficient in our search. He didn't have the book, so he must still be looking for me. Without the book, he had nothing.

"We can't let him get the artifact," Storm continued. "If the legends are true and it really does confer some kind of power, he's the last guy who should have it. I can't imagine what he wants to do to all of us."

"*If* the legends are true?" I asked incredulously. "Are you telling me you've been looking for the source for years and you don't even believe in it?"

Storm gave me another shrug, a gesture that I was already beginning to tire of. "Who knows? I'll believe it when I see it. But where Reeves is concerned, it's not worth taking any chances."

Since she had no further useful information, I left her alone, finding another spot on the plane where I could have some privacy to review the pages of my mother's book on Julian's phone. I had been reading it all very carefully, looking for any clues as to what we might be looking for and where it would be.

I had found a few things of interest, but there was one particularly odd thing I'd come across. It was a page of mourning, dedicated to a young child. I could only assume it was the child of the wolf who wrote the book. In it, he lamented the child's early death and begged the Moon Goddess to spare the child's twin. Then he wrote beneath it:

It seems the King's curse held some power after all. My mate insists the source should be returned, that it is the only way to end it. I am undecided.

The King must be the Alpha King. Had he cursed my family when they took the source from him? What was the curse?

This hadn't come up in any of the legends I'd heard about the source. I trusted the book more than any of the other legends, but I had no idea what it might be referring to.

For the first time, a sense of unease crept in. What if the source really was cursed? Was that why they had all been wiped out?

Then just as quickly, I shook my head at myself. This was not the time to get cold feet. I could figure it out once I had the source. I would have armies at my disposal that those early wolves couldn't have dreamed of. I would be perfectly fine.

At last we landed in Hartford. I'd already arranged for a car to pick us up there and drive us to New London, the city at the mouth of the Thames river. But when we parked on the tarmac and I looked out to where the driver was waiting for us, a chill immediately went down my spine.

"Storm."

She looked up as I called her name and I gestured for her to come over. She peered out the window beside me and her mouth set in a straight line, confirming my fears.

"Reeves."

How was he here? It wasn't possible... unless someone at the airport in San Francisco tipped him off? I groaned as my mind went back to the desk agent I thought I'd charmed. Had that all been a distraction? And I'd fucking told her where I was going.

"So what's the plan, chief?" Storm asked me, far too cheerily.

"What the fuck are you smiling about?" I growled back at her. "He's just as big a threat to you."

"I would guess he doesn't even know I'm here," she contradicted me. "You're the one with the book, so he's looking for you. But if you're smart, you can use the fact that he doesn't know about me to your advantage."

"How?" I muttered. I didn't see her point, but I didn't want her to know that.

"Go out and let him take you and your men," she suggested. "While I get some backup."

My eyebrows shot up. "*That's* your plan?"

"Have you got a better one?"

I glared at her for a moment while she smiled back at me innocently. The unfortunate truth was that I didn't. Goddess help me, I was going to have to trust her.

"Fine," I growled in agreement. "But whoever you get to help you, make sure they're human."

That was the first thing I'd said that caught her off guard. "Human? Why?"

"He'll be expecting wolves," I pointed out. "He won't be expecting humans to come for me. They can create a distraction."

She nodded, looking impressed. "Not bad, kid."

I growled at her again. I hated when she called me a kid, but she just laughed before reaching into her bag and placing another microscopic tracking chip on me.

"They won't find that, but it'll help me find you. Now get on out there and greet your adoring fans."

"And you'll come for me soon?" I asked, just wanting to hear her say the words.

"Of course," she smirked. "Just as soon as I track down some humans who are willing to help. How hard could it be?"

~Abby~

For the second time in the course of this conversation, it felt like all the air had been sucked out of the room. The first was when Oliver told his dad about Elijah, and now, Alpha Patrick had just said that Oliver's mom had committed suicide.

The look of confusion and heartbreak on Oliver's face was almost enough to bring me to my knees, but he needed my strength right now. Falling apart wouldn't help him. Instead, I leaned into him, tightening my grip on his hand as he processed what he'd just been told, letting him take whatever comfort from me that he could.

"How could that have happened?" Oliver asked, his voice small and quiet and so unlike him. "Wasn't she being watched?"

That was a good question. If the Luna had been in the hospital, surely someone knew the reason why. Wouldn't they have taken precautions?

"She was," Alpha Patrick answered. "But not every second, apparently. I stayed with her as much as I could but I still had the pack to run. I left her in the hospital's care and I've regretted it every day since."

The guilt in his voice was palpable and my heart went out to him too. There was so much hurt in their past, both of these men who seemed to the outside world like they had it all completely together. I suppose you could never really know what a person had been through based on what you could see.

"How did she do it?" Oliver asked. The question made me wince, but I didn't blame him for wanting to know. So much had been hidden from him for so long, he wanted the whole truth now.

Alpha Patrick seemed to agree because he didn't avoid the question at all.

"She slit her wrists."

My eyes closed in horror and pain, the same emotions I could feel coming from Oliver through our link. The woman in the letters we read had loved her sons and her mate desperately. What must she have been going through to think killing herself was the best choice?

"So," the Alpha added after a minute went by with no one saying anything. When I glanced at Oliver, there were tears in the corners of his eyes. "I try not to judge any of the choices she made, even something as big as what you just told me. It's impossible for me to know what it was like in her head."

I couldn't have said it better myself.

Suddenly my phone rang out, the unexpected noise making us all jump. "Sorry," I quickly apologized to both of them, pulling it out to silence it. "I'll just..."

I stopped in mid-motion as Storm's name flashed across the screen, and I showed it to Oliver instead. He quickly nodded at me, blinking away the tears in his eyes. "Answer it."

"Hello?" I said after accepting the call and putting it on speaker phone again.

"Hey, Abby." Storm's greeting was almost too casual. "I don't suppose you guys are anywhere near Connecticut right now?"

Oliver and I looked at each other in surprise. The Jade Moon territory was in upstate New York, not far away at all. How did she know where we were? We had never said anything about where we lived.

"Why?" I asked cautiously, not sure how much I should reveal.

"Elijah's got himself in a bit of trouble," she continued, still sounding a little too cheery considering what she was saying. "I need some humans to come and help bail him out, and I don't know anyone in the area. I thought I'd check and see if you knew anyone."

So she didn't know where we were? This was just a random coincidence? Once again, I felt completely off balance.

"Why do you need humans?" Oliver cut in.

"Oh, hi, Oliver," Storm greeted him too. "This'll make more sense to you, I bet. Reeves has Eli."

Reeves? The guy who had kidnapped Oliver before? That couldn't be good.

Oliver seemed to agree. "How did that happen?" he asked before quickly shaking his head. "No, never mind, that's not important. So you need humans... to get past their anti-wolf security?"

Storm gave an impressed whistle. "You and Eli are on the same wavelength, apparently. That was his idea."

There was clearly a lot we were missing here, but Oliver was already standing up. "We'll find some people," he told her. "Text us the location and we'll be there as soon as we can."

I stood up too, though I wasn't sure what he was thinking. Storm agreed to Oliver's request and signed off, and I hung up the phone.

"Sorry, Dad," Oliver said to his father. "We need to go."

Alpha Patrick didn't try to stop us, but I didn't miss the look of concern on his face either. "Be careful, Oliver. I don't know how much of this twin curse business is true, but your mother certainly believed it was. The few times we talked about it, she got very upset."

Oliver promised we'd be careful and then we headed out to the parking lot where my car was waiting. Only when we were buckled up and headed off the pack land did I get a chance to ask him where we were going. "What's your plan?"

Obviously he had one, but unusually for us, I had no idea what was going on in his head.

"There are only a few humans that I really trust," he told me. "So we're going to have to ask them."

"You don't mean..." I trailed off in surprise, certain he couldn't be suggesting what it sounded like.

But he was. "Whitney and Jack," he confirmed. "Can you think of anyone else?"

I couldn't, not anyone that I trusted as much as I trusted them. But how were we going to explain this to them?

"Are we going to tell them what we are?"

His lips tightened in determination. "I think we're going to have to. I don't know how much time we have, Heels, and this is the best plan I've got."

"What about Liz? Are you going to tell her too?" I asked. They were all living together right now, so if she was home, it would be difficult not to include her.

"If I have to," was Oliver's firm reply.

We were in town in record time and pulling up in front of the house that Whitney, Jack and Liz were sharing for the summer. Oliver and I hopped out of the car and he bounded up the steps to the front door, knocking on it before I could even ask him exactly what he was planning on saying.

It was Liz who answered the door. "O-Oliver?" she stuttered in surprise before peering around him to see me. "Oh, hi, Abby. We weren't expecting you guys."

"Are Whitney and Jack home too?" Oliver asked, stepping past her into the house without waiting to be invited in.

"Uh, yeah, they're just getting ready for work," Liz answered, shooting me a curious look as I followed in behind him. "What's up?"

"They're going to have to call in sick," Oliver replied, avoiding her question. "We need you guys today. But first, there's something we need to tell you."

~Liz~

For just a second when I opened the door and saw Oliver standing there, I thought it was the guy from San Francisco, the one who looked just like him.

The one I hadn't been able to get out of my head ever since that day.

I could still feel the intensity of his eyes as he stared at me from across the room and the strange way my body had reacted. I hadn't fully appreciated it at the time because I thought it was Oliver, but now that I knew it wasn't, the connection between us intrigued me even more.

Unless it was all in my head. It wouldn't be the first time that had happened, after all. I thought Liam and I had a special connection too, and look how that turned out. For all I knew, that guy at the book festival might have been looking at someone else entirely and not at me at all.

But it still didn't stop me from hoping, or my heart from fluttering when I opened the door and I caught sight of the man standing there, at least until I realized that there was no way that guy was going to randomly appear at my door on the other side of the country.

It had to be Oliver. That made much more sense, and I managed to stutter out a greeting without giving away my disappointment.

When he said he had something to tell us all, I ran upstairs and knocked on Whitney and Jack's door. So far living with them had been good, except that the house we had found was quite small, so my room was just across the hall from theirs and sometimes at night it was a little too easy to hear what was going on in their room.

I didn't begrudge them having a little fun, of course. It was just that it made my empty bed seem even emptier. After my experience with Liam, I hadn't had any luck with men. Whitney suggested it was because I had erected defensive walls around myself in my mind and men could see them. However, this was the same girl who chose her outfit for the day based on the dreams she'd had the night before, so I wasn't so sure about mental walls and all of that. But one thing I was certain about was that I had made it through a whole year of college and was still a virgin, and it was more than a little frustrating.

There was a muffled laugh from inside the room now before the door opened and Whitney's face appeared, trying to hide her grin. "Hey Liz, what's up?"

"Oliver and Abby are here," I told her, pretending I didn't notice the mostly naked Jack in the background. As Whitney was fully clothed, it wasn't too hard to guess what they'd been up to. "They want to talk to us."

"Is everything okay?" she asked as Jack grabbed a shirt and pulled it over his head.

I shrugged. "No idea, but Oliver said you need to call in sick to work, so I think he's got something planned."

I couldn't guess what Oliver was up to now. That trip to San Francisco had been amazing, but I didn't think he'd be doing anything like that again so soon. Maybe he was finally going to invite us over to his house? He was always pretty secretive about where he lived, but based on the amount of money his family seemed to have, I was sure it must be impressive.

Whitney and Jack followed me down the stairs, back to where Abby and Oliver were still standing in the living room.

"Hey, man," Jack greeted him as they gave each other one of those weird half-handshake, half-hug things that guys do. "What brings you to town? I thought you were going to be too busy for us all summer."

He was joking, of course, but Oliver didn't crack a smile. "We've got something we need to talk to you about. You should probably sit down for this."

That sounded serious. Maybe everything wasn't okay after all?

Whitney, Jack and I all took a seat next to each other on the sofa while Oliver and Abby remained standing. Abby looked slightly nervous while Oliver was just focused. I wasn't sure I'd ever seen him looking so serious before.

"We don't have a lot of time," he started. "But we need your help."

"What's going on?" Jack asked. "Are you guys in some kind of trouble?"

"Kind of," Oliver answered, to my surprise. "Or at least someone we know is. We need to go and help him, but we need you to come too."

None of this was making any sense to me. "What do you need us to do?"

"We just need you to create a diversion," he explained. "We can figure it out on the way there." He was obviously in a hurry, but he wasn't giving us much to go on. I still had no clue what he was talking about.

"Why us?" Whitney piped up. "Don't you have friends at home who could help you?"

Oliver and Abby exchanged glances before she nodded at him and Oliver turned back to us with a sigh. "We do, but we need some friends who aren't like us. We need people who are... human."

This time it was Whitney, Jack and I who looked at each other, their faces reflecting my own confusion back to me. What was that supposed to mean? Was this some kind of joke?

"And what are the two of you if you're not human?" I asked, trying to figure out the game.

"We're... werewolves."

There was dead silence in the room for a moment before the three of us on the sofa burst out laughing all at the same time.

"You had me going for just a second," Jack laughed, smacking the back of the sofa in amusement. "If you had said something a little less crazy, I might have fallen for it. Like aliens!"

"Or angels!" Whitney giggled.

"Or vampires," I added. *How I wish vampires were real.* I had so many vampire books in my library, they were my guilty pleasure when I wasn't reading books for school.

"How are vampires less crazy than werewolves?" Oliver was looking a little offended, which only made us laugh harder.

"Well, vampires were people first who have been turned into vampires," I explained, reviewing all my knowledge on the subject in my head. "They're just people who had something happen to them. But werewolves are like a whole other species, and they've got a wolf inside them? Like two beings sharing one body? It's just weird."

"It's not weird," Oliver protested, still looking less than pleased with our reaction.

"Yes, it is," Whitney said, backing me up. "It sounds like some kind of multiple personality disorder."

"And if I could turn into an animal, I would definitely want to be something cooler," Jack added. "Who wants to be a big dog?"

"A wolf is not a dog!"

Oliver's outraged objection struck us all as funny again and we couldn't help laughing more. But even as I laughed, I began to notice that Abby wasn't laughing at all, or even smiling. She didn't seem to think it was funny, and that was strange. She usually loved a chance to tease her boyfriend.

"We're wasting time," I heard her murmur to Oliver, and he nodded back at her.

"Alright," he said with determination. "You guys don't believe me?"

"Uh, no, bro, we definitely don't believe you." Jack laughed again, but I was starting to get a funny feeling about this. Abby was still way too serious.

Then Oliver pulled off his shirt and everyone's laughter died off. *What is he doing?*

My eyes were drawn to the tattoo on his side. I had seen it once before when we all went swimming at the lake last month, but I had tried not to stare. Now that I was seeing it again, I remembered it was a wolf, which seemed kind of a strange thing to have tattooed on your body.

Unless...

No, that's just crazy. I wasn't going to let myself go there.

Then Oliver unzipped his jeans and pulled them down, and my cheeks immediately flushed red at the sight of him in nothing but his underwear. It really should be illegal for anyone to look that good. My mind immediately went back to the mystery guy from San Francisco. Did he look as much like Oliver beneath his clothes as he did with them on?

Whitney and Jack were both looking a little stunned right now too.

"What are you doing, Oliver?" Whitney asked uncertainly. She had slept with him once, I remembered, just before he and Abby got together. And Jack had probably seen him naked in the locker room after a football game before. I supposed that meant I was the only one in the room who hadn't seen Oliver naked. Was that about to change?

In the end he didn't take his boxers off, though I wasn't sure if I was relieved or disappointed about that. Instead, he stepped forward into the middle of the room, where we could all see him clearly and then, without taking his eyes off us, his body began to change.

First, his nose grew longer. Not quite like Pinocchio, but that was the first thing that crossed my mind as I squinted behind my glasses, trying to make sense of what I was seeing. Then the hairs on his arms and chest grew longer, and thicker, until it began to cover his whole body, almost like... fur.

His body bent then, his front half reaching to the ground as his arms and legs adjusted in length until they were even.

Things happened faster and faster and I lost track of all the individual changes until, almost before I knew it, where Oliver had once stood, there was a large, black wolf.

Chapter Ten

~Abby~

The looks on our friends' faces were actually pretty funny. In any other circumstances, I would have laughed. But after everything we had just learned about Oliver's mom and the twins curse and all the rest of it, not to mention the fact that we still had to go and try to help rescue Elijah, the best I could muster right now was a smile.

Jack's mouth had fallen open, Whitney's eyes were bugged out and Liz had turned completely pale, like she'd just seen a ghost rather than a man she'd known for months turn into a wolf in front of her.

Alright, if you say it like that, it does sound a bit weird.

Oliver took a step towards them in his wolf form and Whitney immediately shrieked, scrambling further back onto the sofa as Jack put a protective arm around her. Liz, on the other hand, leaned forward, examining my mate's wolf closely, as if she couldn't quite believe her eyes.

She probably couldn't. It must be a huge shock to all of them.

Not wanting to scare them any more, Oliver returned to me and I handed him his clothes, which he took with his mouth into the next room so he could shift back and get redressed. I picked up the shredded pieces of his underwear from the living room floor as all three of our friends watched me in stunned silence.

"That didn't really just happen," Jack said slowly, looking between me and the other two girls. "Did it?"

"It did," I assured him, wanting to keep this moving along. "Oliver is a werewolf, and so am I. We can shift into wolves and there are a few other things that make us different from humans, but deep down, we're still exactly the same people you've known all year. You don't need to treat us any differently."

"And there are more of you?" Whitney squeaked, her eyes still wide. "All over the place?"

I nodded. "There are quite a lot of us, yes. But most of them live with their packs and don't interact with humans unless they have to. Oliver and I being here at the college with you guys is a bit unusual."

Liz opened her mouth to ask something, but I had to cut her off. We'd already been here too long.

"We really need to get going. I'm happy to answer any other questions you have in the car, but we should leave now."

All three of them nodded silently, too stunned to refuse. I knew it hadn't fully sunk in yet, even though they had just seen a man shift with their own eyes. It wouldn't be easy for them to accept it when they'd gone their whole lives thinking creatures like us didn't exist.

With his clothes back on, Oliver led the way back to the car where our friends piled in the back and he set out towards the coordinates that Storm had sent us.

"So there are some men who have kidnapped a friend of ours," Oliver told them once we were underway. "These men are human but they know about werewolves. They know that's what he is, and they might be expecting more wolves to turn up, but they won't be expecting you guys."

"What do you need us to do?" Liz asked from the back corner. Whitney was sitting in the middle between Liz and Jack, still looking the most shell-shocked out of the three of them. I wished I could reach back and give her a hug and tell her it was okay.

"Just create a distraction," Oliver explained, answering Liz's question. "Pretend to be lost and ask for help. These guys are dangerous, I'm not going to lie to you, but I don't believe they would do anything to innocent humans who just happened to be in the area. They'll probably try to get rid of you quickly, so you'll need to keep them busy as long as you can."

"And then you'll go in and rescue your friend?" Jack asked.

"Right," Oliver confirmed. "There's at least one other werewolf who will help us, and I don't know if she has any others with her. But for the distraction to work, we need humans."

"And you guys have always been... not human?" Whitney asked, sounding a little embarrassed about the question. "You weren't turned into werewolves or something?"

I fielded that one. "We were born this way, though our wolves don't appear until we turn 18. So I haven't had mine for very long. And no, we can't turn humans into werewolves, so you don't have to worry."

I gave her a smile so she knew I was joking, and she smiled back, though it was a bit tentative. I suspected she was thinking about how we'd shared a room for the whole first half of the year and she'd never known there was anything different about me. I couldn't really imagine how she was feeling.

"Nobody else at the college knows what we are," Oliver added. "And most humans don't know we exist at all. We keep to ourselves because when it comes down to it, humans are a far greater threat to us than we are to them. Just like every other species on the planet."

Our friends all nodded at that, which almost made me laugh. Nobody tried to defend humanity.

"So is that why you and Oliver got together?" Liz asked me. "Because you're both werewolves? Could you tell when you met?"

Oliver and I exchanged glances. Going into how we knew we were mates and all the rest of it seemed like it might be a bit of an information overload for them right now. I decided to stick to the basics.

"We knew we were both werewolves," I told her. "We can smell the difference between wolves and humans. Our noses are more sensitive than humans' noses. But we didn't get together just because we're both werewolves. We can be in relationships with humans too. I was with Liam at the time, remember?"

That was a rhetorical question. I knew she remembered, and Liz quickly nodded in confirmation. "Of course. And Oliver was..."

She gasped loudly, making all of us jump as she grabbed Whitney's arm beside her.

"Whitney!" she squealed. "You had sex with a werewolf!"

Whitney's eyes went wide as she stared at the back of Oliver's head and this time I couldn't help laughing at the stunned and dismayed look on her face. My laughter made Oliver laugh, and soon our friends were all laughing with us, the sound of our combined laughter filling the small interior of the car.

I was so glad they could laugh about it. This whole situation *was* pretty ridiculous. And at least if they were laughing, they must be feeling a little less shocked.

"It's not as weird as it sounds," I managed to get out when I caught my breath. "Werewolves and humans cross-mate all the time. When we're in our human forms, we're pretty much human. There aren't any differences in our anatomy."

"It's really weird to just talk about this like it's all normal," Jack admitted, and Oliver nodded his head sympathetically.

"I know. And I'm sorry we had to spring it on you like this. We wouldn't have asked if we didn't really need your help."

That brought us back to the reason we were all in the car right now, and we spent the next half hour going over the cover story that Whitney, Jack and Liz would use to distract the people who were guarding Elijah, wherever he was being held.

It wasn't much later that we were pulling into the parking lot where Storm was waiting for us along with another wolf I'd never seen before, a very large, tattooed specimen of a man whose eyes were glued to Oliver from the second he got out of the car.

"This is Matthew," she introduced us as we all walked over. "He's part of the Seven Hills pack."

That explained why he was staring at Oliver like he'd just seen a ghost. My mate looked exactly like his Alpha.

"Eli and his Beta Julian were both taken," Storm explained. "Matthew and I were able to avoid detection and also keep any traces of the book away from Reeves and his men. So they'll be questioning Eli and Julian about it, torturing them maybe, but they shouldn't be able to get anything. These are the humans?"

She looked over at our friends who were all hanging back a bit shyly, though whether they were intimidated by Storm's or Matthew's appearances or the fact that there were another two werewolves with us, I wasn't sure. I was more caught off guard by the casual way she'd mentioned that Eli and Julian might be getting tortured right now, like it was no big deal.

Oliver quickly introduced Whitney, Jack and Liz. "They're friends of ours. Their safety is our top priority. If we have to abort the whole thing to keep them safe, we do it."

Storm nodded. "Fine with me. Matthew?"

He didn't look thrilled with that, probably because it would mean abandoning his Alpha and Beta, but he nodded as well anyway.

"They've taken them to an abandoned building just around the corner," Storm told us now. "I've got a tracker on Eli so I know exactly where he is. We'll go in as close to the room as we can, just like we did in San Francisco, Abby."

She gave me a smile of acknowledgement and I smiled back. That seemed like a lifetime ago already, not just a few days. I certainly never thought I'd be doing anything similar again quite so soon.

"They'll be armed, so don't stay in one place for too long. Protect yourselves first, help others second. And if it looks hopeless, we pull out. Any questions?"

Storm looked around the group at each one of us in turn. When everyone shook their heads, she put her sunglasses on and flashed us all a smile, as if this was all some kind of game.

"Alright, then. Let's go."

~Elijah~

The bones in my cheek cracked yet again as the fist of the man in front of me slammed into my face. *Isn't he getting tired of this yet?* I breathed deeply against the pain and the slight sting as my body healed itself, the bones stitching themselves back into place beneath my skin.

When I got off the plane with Julian, Reeves approached us and I did my best to play along. I needed him to take us and not worry about the plane where Storm and Matthew were hiding along with the phones that contained the shots of the book.

"Thought you could lose me, did you, Eli?" he smirked at me from a safe distance. He and Storm had the same habit of acting like they knew something I didn't, and I hated the look on both of them.

"Thought you were smarter than to come after me," I replied, using the same condescending tone of voice that he did. "You really think you and your friends here can take on a pissed off Alpha and Beta wolf?"

"Oh, I don't need to take you on," he replied, looking far too pleased with himself. "I just need you to get in."

The door of the van next to him slid open, and the next thing I knew Julian and I were both shot with some kind of fucking blow dart, and the last thing I remembered was hitting the ground.

When we woke up, we were in the same filthy room we were still sitting in now, our ankles and wrists tied to the chairs we were sitting in with silver chains.

The silver took me by surprise. I'd expected him to use the wolf-silencing injection that Storm had warned me about, but that wasn't what he had in mind. He wanted us to keep our wolf abilities, or at least the healing ones. That let him torture us longer and harder without actually causing us any damage other than the pain of constant injury and recuperation. It had been going on for at least an hour now, maybe longer. I'd lost track of time.

"I know you found something, Eli," Reeves said to me as the man who'd hit me took a step back. "You wouldn't be here if you didn't. Just tell me what it is."

"You haven't given me any incentive to," I pointed out, spitting some of the blood from my mouth onto the floor. "You won't kill either of us while we know where the book is, and we aren't talking, so this is all a big waste of time."

"Time's something I've got plenty of," Reeves taunted me. "And when he gets tired of hitting you, I've got a whole other roster of guys to sub in. We can do this as long as it takes. You're the one who seems to be in some kind of hurry."

I just gave him an unimpressed look. "Bring it on."

He smirked at me again, but I could see the frustration lurking in his eyes before he turned back to the other man. "Get the knives and move on to the Beta."

I sighed and let my head fall down as my face continued to heal itself. "He's not going to talk either. I know how to train my men."

"Maybe he won't talk," Reeves agreed. "But you'll get to listen to him scream."

I shrugged. "Is that supposed to bother me?"

Reeves let out a low whistle. "That's cold, Eli. I thought you Alphas were supposed to take care of your packs."

"The members of my pack can take care of themselves," I told him. "Just like I can."

I'd been doing it since I was a kid. My dad had always been busy and since I had no mother, I was left on my own most of the time. I learned quickly how to rely on no one but myself.

"Because you're doing such a good job of that now," he agreed, smirking at me one more time before turning to Julian. "You got anything you want to say before we get started?"

Before Julian could reply, Reeves' walkie-talkie crackled with static. "Boss, there's three people approaching the building. Humans."

My heart rate kicked up a little bit as I tried not to show it. Were these the humans that Storm had found? Did that mean she was here? It was about fucking time.

Reeves' brow furrowed. "Get rid of them," he ordered into the device, pausing a second before adding one more instruction. "Bring backup to the front door just in case."

Perfect. That was just what I had hoped for. They would go to the front, leaving other entrances unguarded. We should be out of here in a matter of minutes.

I decided to make the most of the time I had left with Reeves. "What do you want the source for anyway? What would you do with it?"

He gave me a self-satisfied smile as he placed his walkie-talkie back in its holder. "I would have thought that was obvious. I'm going to build myself a wolf army."

The chilling glee in his tone sent a shiver down my spine. "To do what?"

"To take all you bastards out from the inside."

Storm's guess back on the plane must have been right. This was some kind of personal grudge. "What did we do to you?"

Fire flashed in his eyes, but he gave me a pithy answer. "Your existence is insult enough."

That obviously wasn't true. This was something personal, and that made him more dangerous. When something is personal enough, it makes a person unpredictable.

Like me.

Gathering all the strength I had left, everything that wasn't being sapped by my silver restraints, I tipped the chair forward until I was on my feet, and then threw myself, chair and all, directly at Reeves.

"Fuck," he gasped as we fell to the ground, me and the chair on top of him. "Get him off me!"

The other guy in the room quickly called for backup, which was just what I wanted. Between the humans at the front and the guys coming in here now, that should leave all the other entrances unattended.

And sure enough, while the guy who'd been beating me and the two guys he called in were still trying to lift me off Reeves, a loud growl sounded down the hall, and just a few seconds later, three wolves appeared in the door.

The men quickly dropped me back to the floor as they scrambled for their weapons, but not before I got a decent look at the wolves. One I recognized as Matthew. The other was so red that I assumed it must be Storm. And the third one I'd never seen before, but it was big and black. *Just like my own wolf.* If I didn't know better, I would have thought it was me.

"There are knives on the table over there," I shouted out. Matthew was trained in all kinds of weapons and I knew he'd know how to use them. He quickly shifted and grabbed them while the other two wolves went after the men's weapons, managing to get them to drop their guns before they could get any shots off. Reeves had got back to his feet now, but his left arm was hanging limply. I suspected I must have dislocated it when I landed on him.

"Let us go," I ordered from my rather inelegant position on the floor. "And we'll let you live."

"You're still outnumbered," Reeves tried to argue. "The others will be checking in any second."

"And if they get here before we're gone, then you all die," I countered just as firmly. "Matthew?"

With not much more than a flick of his wrist, the knife from his hand flew through the air and buried itself in Reeves' dislocated shoulder.

"Son of a bitch!" he yelled, grabbing the handle and pulling the knife out. He held the bloody end of it over me so that the blood dripped onto my face as he scowled down at me. "You can't outrun me, Eli."

I just smiled at him innocently. "How will we know until you let me try?"

With an impressive growl of his own, for a human, he gave in. "Collins, untie them."

The man who'd been beating me before walked over to Julian first and then to me, loosening our chains enough that we could slip free. I flexed out my hands, noting the burn marks on my wrists which were going to take a while to heal and I held one of them up in front of Reeve's face so he knew exactly what pain I'd been in.

"Next time we meet, one of us isn't walking away."

"Fine with me," he snarled back.

"Let's move," Julian ordered. The black wolf, who I still couldn't identify, stepped into the hall just as a gunshot sounded from the far end and Julian quickly pulled him back. "Fuck, that must be the others."

I wasn't worried. I just turned to Matthew and gave him a nod. He picked up the guns that the men in the room had been carrying, and charged out into the hallway. A few rounds were fired from both sides, but sure enough, in a few seconds, Matthew's voice rang out. "All clear."

I turned back to Reeves one last time. "Think about what I said before you come after us."

He didn't reply, so I simply shook my head and walked out of the room with the others.

"This way," Matthew directed us once we were in the hall, taking us to a back door that was half off its hinges. That must have been how they got in. He shifted back into his wolf as Julian and I ran after the three wolves, down the street as I checked behind us, making sure we weren't being followed. Thankfully, I couldn't see anyone.

A large van was waiting for us there, and a petite brunette with glasses jumped out of the front seat as we approached. My heart sped up again and I had to do a double take at the sight of her. For just a second, I thought she was my mate, but the lack of the mate scent and the fact that she had her own wolf scent quickly told me I was wrong.

But as soon as I processed the fact that she wasn't my mate, I realized that I had seen this woman before. She was the one from the book festival, the one who had been on stage with my mate.

What the fuck was she doing here?

"Everyone get in," she said. "You can shift once we're safe."

Her eyes scanned me curiously, but she said no more, pulling the back door open for us all to climb in.

And that's when it hit me. An overwhelming scent of honeysuckles and sweetness that I'd only smelled a couple of times before. My wolf howled for joy inside me as I locked eyes with the woman inside the van.

My mate.

Chapter Eleven

~Liz~

This was definitely not the way I thought this day was going to go when I woke up this morning. I was supposed to have the day off, so while Whitney and Jack went to their jobs, I was going to go lie in the sun in our little backyard with a good book and a cold drink.

Now I was somewhere in Connecticut, walking up to an abandoned building where there were men inside, probably armed based on what Oliver said, and we were supposed to be creating a distraction so that our werewolf friends could rescue some other werewolves being held inside.

This was completely insane.

Oliver had gone with the man and woman we'd met before while Abby was keeping an eye on us from a safe distance. She said if we got in any trouble, she'd come out in her wolf form and distract the men from us since they'd be far more interested in her than they would be in us. I still couldn't quite believe that Abby could turn into a wolf too, even though we'd seen Oliver do exactly that.

It wasn't something you ever expect your friend to be able to do.

But I had to put all that out of my mind as we wandered up to the front door, arguing with each other about which way we should go, just as we'd practiced. Before we even reached the door, it swung open and two large men appeared. "What are you doing here?" one of them asked us suspiciously.

I couldn't really blame him for being suspicious. We were out in the middle of nowhere after all, but we stuck to our prepared story.

"Thank goodness we found someone," I exclaimed loudly, giving Whitney and Jack my best glare before turning to the guy who'd spoken with a sweet smile. "Could you help us? We're lost and these two keep arguing about which way we should go."

"Where are you trying to go?" the other one asked, and the first guy gave him an incredulous look.

"We don't have time for this," he muttered under his breath.

"It'll just take a minute," the second one argued before turning back to me. "Go ahead, sweetheart."

Sweetheart? Not likely, but I forced myself to smile. "Thank you so much. Guys, where are we trying to go?"

"East," Jack replied at the same time Whitney said, "North."

That set them off fake-arguing again, while I rolled my eyes at the men at the door. "You see the problem? They've been like this all day."

Just then, two additional men showed up, and my heart beat a bit faster. Did they know what we were up to?

But Jack pulled out his phone with the address we'd chosen as the place we were trying to find, and soon all four of them were bent over the map, arguing about the best way for us to get there.

I shot Whitney a disbelieving look when I was sure they couldn't see me. Was it really this easy? I could only hope that Oliver and the others were having as much luck as we were.

No sooner had I thought it than the first guy seemed to remember himself and he snatched Jack's phone, handing it back to him. "Just go back two blocks that way to the main road and get a taxi."

"But what about..." Whitney tried, but the guy was already herding the others back inside and soon the door was closed in our faces.

We all glanced at each other nervously. Was that enough time?

A sharp whistle sounded out, and we all turned to find Abby gesturing us over, so we ran over to her. "That was perfect," she told us all enthusiastically. "You guys did great. They're in."

"How do you know?" I asked in confusion. She couldn't see where the others had gone any more than I could.

"Oliver and I can communicate sort of telepathically," she admitted sheepishly, then laughed as our mouths all dropped open again. "It's a long story. Come on, let's get back to the vehicles."

There was the car that we'd arrived in, but it wasn't going to be able to fit all of us, so the scary-looking red-haired woman had given Abby the keys to a large van that she was using. Abby hopped in the front while Whitney, Jack and I got in the back.

"The wolves are going to get in the back with you," Abby warned us. "But don't worry, they're harmless. We'll just get somewhere safe before they shift back."

Great. A bunch of wolves were getting in the van with us. *Nothing odd about that.*

After a couple of minutes, Abby opened her door and jumped out again. I could hear her muffled voice from outside, and then she opened the back door to where we were. There was Oliver and a guy I didn't recognize, along with three wolves.

Just breathe, I reminded myself. *They're just people, people who don't want to hurt you.*

Oliver just stood there staring at me for a minute, almost like he'd never seen me before, so I gave him an odd look in return. "Are you coming in or what?"

Still looking thrown off, he climbed into the van followed by the others, including the wolves. There wasn't a lot of room for all of us, so he had to slide over right next to me. My skin seemed to almost tingle with electricity as he drew nearer. *Maybe there's static electricity on the seats?*

"You..." he said, looking down at me still with that very unsure look. "You helped to rescue me?"

His voice sounded a bit different than usual. Deeper somehow, more gravelly. Maybe it was from whatever happened inside? Did they run into trouble?

"Did you need rescuing?" I teased, trying to ignore the weird way my body was reacting. I was still feeling all tingly just from his closeness. It was starting to freak me out. "I thought you were the rescuer, Oliver."

"Oliver?" he repeated, the lines between his eyebrows deepening in confusion. "Why would you call me that?"

I quickly glanced around to see if anyone else was hearing how weird he was being, but no one was paying attention to us. Abby and the other guy who was in his human form right now were driving and navigating, Whitney and Jack were talking to each other quietly, and the wolves were... well, wolves.

"Because it's your name?" I replied, trying to smile at him and not show how confused I was too.

The way I was feeling was so strange, it was almost like...

It was almost like the way I felt in San Francisco when I locked eyes with the guy who looked like Oliver.

It couldn't be... could it?

A gasp left my lips before I could stop it, and he stared down at them like he was in some kind of trance.

"You're not Oliver, are you?" I asked breathlessly, backing away from him just a little, mostly so that I wouldn't give in to the overwhelming temptation I was having to throw myself directly into his arms.

His eyes returned to my eyes and a hint of a smile crossed his lips. "Not last time I checked. My name is Elijah."

Elijah. It wasn't a name I had ever considered particularly sexy before, but right now I thought it might be the sexiest thing I had ever heard. What on earth was he doing here? Did Oliver and Abby know him?

Is he a werewolf too?

"I'm Liz," I managed to introduce myself, amazed that I got the words out with the way my insides were going crazy. Butterflies wasn't a strong enough word for what was happening in my stomach. Somehow the guy

I'd been daydreaming about for days was sitting next to me, and from the way he was looking at me, I hadn't been imagining anything in San Francisco. His gaze really had been meant for me.

"What are you doing here with a bunch of wolves, Liz?" Each word out of his mouth was more enticing than the one before, and when he said my name, I nearly melted right then and there. But his question also told me that he clearly knew about werewolves too. I was more confused now than ever.

"They're my friends," I stuttered out. "Abby and Oliver."

Confusion clouded his features again. "Oliver is your friend," he repeated curiously. "But you thought I was him?"

I nodded. Didn't he know why? "You look just like him."

His eyes left me for the first time since he got in the van and found the large black wolf that sat in the back instead. Now that I turned to look at him too, I realized that it must be Oliver. That was how he'd looked when he showed us his wolf earlier, back at our house.

And the wolf version of Oliver was staring right back at us.

"Who are you?" Elijah asked the wolf before looking around the whole van suspiciously. "What is this?"

"Stay calm," Abby called out from the front seat. "We're going to pull over just up here so the wolves can shift back, and then we can all talk."

She made it sound like there was something serious to talk about. Once again, I was completely confused, feeling like I was missing quite a lot. But I didn't have a chance to find out anything else before the van pulled over and the door was opened and we were all piling out. Elijah quickly walked away from me, like he couldn't get away from me fast enough, and got straight into a heated whispered discussion with the guy who had been driving. Whitney and Jack got out too, closing the door behind them, apparently so the wolves could change back into people and put their clothes back on.

This was all so bizarre.

Meanwhile, Abby came up to me and gave me a curious look. "What were you talking to Elijah about?"

"You know him?" I asked her, avoiding the question. It wasn't that we had said anything particularly important. It was the way he had made me feel that mattered. "Why is he here?"

"That's a really long story," she told me. "But the way he's looking at you..."

I blushed as she trailed off. She could see it too? So it really wasn't just in my head.

I didn't get a chance to answer before the van door opened again, and the red-haired woman and the large man from earlier climbed out, followed by Oliver.

There really are two of them.

I glanced over at Elijah, who was staring at Oliver like he'd seen a ghost. Had they really not met each other before? Then why were we here at all?

What in the world was going on?

~Elijah~

Storm must have set me up. That was the thought drowning out all others as I jumped out of the van and pulled Julian to the side.

"I don't know what's going on," I told him under my breath. "But I think she planned all of this. We need to get out of here."

That was the only thing I was relatively certain of. Everything else was still an unanswered question. Was Storm working with Reeves? How the fuck did she know about my mate? And who was this guy who looked like me, in both human and wolf form? Where had she found him and what was he doing here? Storm was trying to achieve something by bringing everyone here, but I had no idea what she had to gain.

I couldn't remember ever feeling as completely off balance as I did right now, and it had all started when the van door opened and my mate suddenly appeared, her sweet scent nearly knocking me over. Looking right at me, she gave me a teasing smile, as if she'd been expecting me. "Are you coming in or what?"

Her tone and her words threw me for a loop. Did she know who I was to her? She was human, she shouldn't be feeling any mate pull, or even if she felt something, she shouldn't know what it was. So why was she here at all? And had she actually helped to distract Reeves' men? I had expected Storm to track down some ex-con thugs to do that, not some tiny human woman who Reeves' cronies could have snapped in half if they felt like it.

Just the thought of anything happening to her made my stomach twist and my wolf struggle to break loose. *Fuck.* Why was I feeling like this? I'd already decided I wasn't going to have anything to do with her, but I certainly hadn't expected her to show up and help rescue me.

Why would she do that for me?

And then she called me by another name, and when we cleared up who I was, she leaned away from me, and once again, my body went haywire but this time it was with jealousy. Did she have feelings for this other guy? Was that why she sat closer when she thought I was him?

And why did I care?

Okay, maybe she was more attractive than I had originally thought from across the room at the book festival. Her eyes behind her glasses were an unusual hazel colour, seeming to switch between light brown and green depending on whether she was looking directly at me or not. Her lips were full and a deep red colour, impossible not to notice. Her hair looked soft on her shoulders, and I suddenly had an image of running my fingers through it, pulling her head back as I sank my teeth into her neck...

Whoa, where the fuck did that come from?

Trying to focus, I looked back up at her and asked her why she was there. Then she said she was friends with the guy she'd mistaken me for, and suddenly I remembered the wolf who looked like me. Was that him? Was he actually here?

And that's when everything began to feel like entirely too much of a coincidence. How did Storm just happen to have my mate and this guy, whoever he was, on standby? It wasn't possible. She must have planned this from the beginning, but why? There was still way too much that wasn't making sense to me.

"We can neutralize them all," Julian muttered back to me as we stood apart from the others. "Just give me and Matthew the order."

I growled at him before I could stop myself. That was my mate he was talking about, after all. He instantly bowed his head in submission, but I could see the confusion in his eyes, and I had no idea what to tell him about my own behaviour. I'd just told him we needed to get away, and then I snapped at him for trying to come up with a plan.

I couldn't even explain it to myself.

I turned back to confront Storm as she came out of the van, but as soon as she got out, the other guy got out behind her, and everything else seemed to fade away for just a moment.

It isn't possible. How could there be someone who looked so much like me? It had to be some kind of trick, but I still wasn't sure what the point of it was.

He walked right over to me, his face set in a grim expression I recognized. I'd seen it often enough in the mirror.

"Elijah," he said, looking me over just as curiously as I was looking at him. "I'm Oliver."

I had figured that out already, based on what my mate had said. His voice was a little different to mine, and he had a different pack smell, of course. But those were the only differences I could spot. Physically, we were truly identical.

"What is this?" I asked, my eyes flicking around to the other people standing around us, but everyone else looked just as surprised as I was. Their eyes all moved back and forth between the two of us, like they were seeing double. Everyone was hanging on our every word. "Who are you and why are you here?"

"I've been trying to find you," he replied. "Ever since San Francisco, when those men we just rescued you from thought I was you."

I'd almost forgotten about that, but I could see why that would have spiked his interest.

"I went to your pack," he continued. "And spoke to your father."

My eyebrows raised in surprise. He talked to my dad? Why? What was so important that he had to track me down right away?

"What do you want?" I asked, trying to get to the point. "Are you after the source?"

I needed things to start making sense, and soon.

But Oliver merely blanched at my words. "No, I don't care about that."

If that was true, then he was an idiot, but it still didn't explain why he was here. "So what do you care about?"

His lips tightened for a moment as he debated what to say, but finally he spoke again. "Let me introduce myself properly. My name is Oliver West of the Jade Moon pack. The man who raised me is Alpha Patrick West."

I hadn't asked for his life story. When was he going to get to the fucking point?

And then he did. "And my mother was Nicole Williams."

For the second time in a matter of minutes, the edges of my vision went grey, so that all I could see was directly in front of me. My heart sped up and my whole body felt cold.

"Nicole Williams," I repeated flatly. We had the same mother? I knew she had been mated to someone other than my father but I never knew she had other children. The thought stung me, even after all these years, but I tried not to let my emotions rule me. There were still too many other questions. It didn't explain how much we looked alike. Unless...

Suddenly the way he phrased his earlier sentence took on new significance. *The man who raised me*, he said. Not his father.

"My father..." The words caught in my throat, threatening to cut off my air.

Luckily he filled in the blank I had already guessed at so I didn't have to. "Is my biological father. I'm your twin brother, Elijah."

The words were spoken quietly enough, but they still forced me to take a step back, and from the corner of my eye, I saw my mate move towards me, almost as if she wanted to support me. The other woman held her back, the one who looked so much like her.

"That's your mate?" I asked, looking over at the two women.

Oliver followed my gaze for a second before nodding. "Yes. That's Abby."

His voice and his face softened as he said her name. Was it just a coincidence that our mates looked so much alike, or did it have to do with the fact that we were twins? I realized it was far from the most important question right now, but there were so many thoughts in my head, I seized on it as one that might be the easiest to answer.

It was far easier than some of the other ones, anyway. *Like why our mother kept Oliver and not me.*

"So what do you want?" I asked, trying to get myself back under control. I did not need this distraction right now, not when I was so close to finding the artifact. Someone had to be doing this to me on purpose.

Oliver looked a little taken aback by the question. "I wanted to meet you. I thought you might be interested in knowing that I exist. I didn't know about you either, not until San Francisco."

"It's just like *The Parent Trap*," one of the other humans whispered, thinking she was being quiet. I glared over at her to let her know she wasn't, and the pretty blonde shrank back against the wide man next to her. I hadn't really paid any attention to those two in the van, I'd been so distracted by my mate, but now I had to wonder who they were and what they had to do with all of this. But yet again, those were questions that could wait. The source was all that mattered.

"I'm not really interested in a family reunion right now," I told Oliver as bluntly as I could, turning back to face him. "I'm kind of in the middle of something here."

"I know," he confirmed with determination in his voice too. "But there's more that we need to talk about. And if you're not going to talk to me until you find what you're looking for, then I'm going with you to find it."

~Oliver~

I wasn't sure what I was expecting Elijah's reaction to be, but indifference wasn't really one of the options I had considered. When he first saw me, he was surprised, of course. He stared at me just like I had stared at him in the van when I was still in my wolf form. It was incredibly odd to be looking at a mirror image of myself. In fact, I'd been so distracted by his appearance that I hadn't even heard anything he and Liz were talking about until she said my name and he looked over at me.

And just now, when I first mentioned our mother's name, he seemed a little overwhelmed, like I would have expected. For a second, I thought I saw a hint of vulnerability in his eyes. But then he started asking about my mate before announcing that he basically didn't have time for me.

He wasn't exactly rolling out the welcome mat into his life.

But I had to cut the guy a bit of slack as well. It was a lot for me to take in, and I had learned the information gradually over a few days, while he had it dumped on him all at once. Maybe he just needed a bit of time to process it.

Be that as it may, I had no intention of letting him out of my sight right now, especially if there was any truth to the twin curse. We needed to talk about that, and I wanted to know exactly what he intended to do with this 'source of power' if and when he found it.

As far as I was concerned, he was dangerous, not only to me but possibly to other wolves in general. I needed to know more.

I could almost see the wheels turning in his head, trying to work out whether it was worth it to argue this point with me or not, but finally he shrugged. "Fine, you can all come if you want, but if there's any trouble, you're on your own. You've already seen the kind of dangers involved, and if Reeves catches up to us again, my team and I aren't going to worry about any of you."

His eyes slid back over to Abby for just a second as he said that, and I frowned. Why was he so interested in her? The way he'd asked me if she was my mate struck me as odd, and this quick glance didn't make me feel any better. If he was going to try to use her to hurt me somehow, maybe it was best if she didn't come along.

'Don't even think about it,' Abby's voice rang out in my head. 'I know that look, Oliver West, and I'm coming with you.'

She really could read me like a book. I shot her an apologetic smile. 'Of course you are. But what about everyone else?'

Abby gave the others an appraising look. 'Liz needs to come too,' she said firmly, to my surprise. 'So we might as well bring Whitney and Jack.'

Why did Liz need to come? I wasn't sure, but this wasn't the time to argue with my mate, so I simply nodded my agreement and turned back to Elijah. "That's fine. I'll take care of my people."

"Let's get moving then," he announced to everyone. "It's about 45 minutes to where we're going."

Well, that was something at least. It would give us a bit of time to talk.

But to my surprise, when we went to get back to the van, Abby held out her hand to stop me. "Can you sit up front with Storm, at least for a little while? I need to talk to Elijah."

She needed to talk to him? I thought I needed to talk to him more than anyone else, but I also trusted her completely. If she was asking me to do this, there must be a damn good reason.

Reluctantly, I got in the front of the van instead. There were three rows of seats in the back, and Whitney, Jack and Liz squeezed into the one closest to the front. Elijah's two pack members took the middle row and Abby and Elijah got in the back, though he didn't look particularly pleased about it.

I wasn't really pleased about it either. I still didn't trust him even a little bit, and I hoped that she knew what she was doing.

~Abby~

It was really surreal to be sitting next to my mate's twin brother. Although I'd seen him from a distance at the book festival, it was even more obvious from up close just how similar they were. If it weren't for his scent, I could almost believe he was Oliver.

The only real difference was in their eyes. Oliver's grey eyes were warm and open while Elijah's were guarded and cold.

What had he been through to make him that way? And how was I going to break through the walls that he'd put up around himself?

That's what I needed to figure out, and that's why I'd insisted on being the one to sit with him, even though I knew Oliver was desperate to speak to him too. But hopefully if I could gain his trust even a little, I could open the door not only for my mate, but for my friend as well.

Because I was pretty sure I knew what was going on between them even if Liz herself didn't have a clue.

"Liz is your mate, isn't she?" I asked quietly as soon as we were back underway.

Elijah's eyes immediately shot to the back of her head, two rows ahead of us, before returning warily to me. "How do you know that? Did she tell you?"

Obviously I was right. And it looked like my second suspicion was right as well: he didn't intend to tell her about it. I had guessed that from the way he ran away from her as soon as the van door had opened.

"She doesn't know," I told him honestly. "But I saw the way you were together, and I know my friend. She's feeling something for you even if she doesn't fully understand it."

His lips tightened into a thin line. "It doesn't matter. I can't think about a mate right now."

That was what I expected too, but my eyebrows still raised in a bit of amusement. He was obviously in denial. "If there's one thing I know about, it's that the mate bond doesn't care if you think you're ready for it. It doesn't care if you have other stuff going on in your life. It's going to grow and grow and drive you crazy until you do something about it."

His grimace told me that he already had some idea what I was talking about. "So you and... Oliver... didn't want to be mates either?"

He stumbled over his brother's name like it was difficult for him to get out, but I ignored that for now to answer his question. "I didn't want to accept it. I even tried to reject him, but he won me over because, no matter what I thought at the time, we were truly meant to be together. I don't know exactly what you're going through right now, of course, but for your own sake, please don't make any rash decisions. Give it a bit of time and get to know her. And if you decide to reject her, the least you can do is be kind about it. She's been through enough already."

His brow furrowed at that and he glanced over at her again, as if the thought of Liz enduring any kind of hardship caused him pain, and that gave me a bit of hope. Maybe he was capable of deeper feelings than I initially thought possible.

Which brought me back to the other reason I wanted to talk to him. "You also need to give Oliver a chance."

Any traces of emotion vanished from Elijah's face as he put his walls firmly back up. "I didn't ask for a brother," he pointed out. "And I'm not a child who needs a companion. We've got nothing in common besides our faces."

I had to agree based on what I'd seen so far, but I didn't know how he could be so convinced of that when they had just met.

"Don't you want to know what happened?" I suggested tentatively. "Or how you ended up separated?"

There was a flash of curiosity in his eyes, but he quickly pushed it back down. "It doesn't matter. It happened. It's in the past."

I didn't believe that for a second. He wanted to know. He just wouldn't admit it.

But it wasn't my place to tell him that anyway. All I could do was lay the groundwork, which I'd tried to do. Now it was up to Oliver to do the rest.

'You ready?' I linked to my mate up in the front seat and he immediately turned back to face me. 'He's all yours.'

Chapter Twelve

Talking to Abby made me a little uncomfortable for a few different reasons. First, she looked an awful lot like my mate which kept my mind on the fact that Liz was sitting just a short distance away, as if her scent alone wasn't enough to keep her foremost in my mind.

Then there was the way Abby kept examining me like I was some kind of lab specimen. I understood it must be weird for her too, since I looked not just a lot like her mate but exactly like him, but it didn't mean she needed to scrutinize me quite so intently.

And finally, there were the things she said. When she talked about the mate bond growing, I couldn't even pretend I didn't know what she meant. It had been getting stronger since the day we met, even when Liz and I were apart and I didn't have a clue where or how to find her. And now that my mate was almost within touching distance, my wolf was going insane and it was taking a great deal of effort just to stay in my seat and not move closer to her.

I didn't like anything having this kind of power over me. I needed to be in control of my own actions, not reliant on anyone else.

Other people always let you down. The only person I could trust was myself. I'd learned that a long time ago and it wasn't a lesson I intended to forget.

Then Abby asked if I didn't want to know what happened with Oliver and I, and why we didn't know about each other until now, and once again, I had to push down the natural curiosity I was feeling. Of course I wanted to know. Who wouldn't? But what was the point? It wasn't going to change anything now. My mom chose him over me, that much was clear, and I couldn't see how anything else really mattered.

Abby stood up suddenly as she finished speaking and I saw Oliver get up at the same time. "Where are you going?" I asked, though I was pretty sure I already knew the answer.

"You need to talk to your brother," she said in that empathetic way of hers that almost made me feel like she cared about me, which was ridiculous. Of course she didn't. She didn't even know me, and she would be on her mate's side over mine anyway. As far as I was concerned, the whole world was divided into 'us' and 'them', and Abby was definitely a 'them'.

And Liz... well, I was less certain about her. But she was with them, wasn't she? That still confused me. How did she come to know about werewolves and all of this in the first place?

Abby and Oliver both climbed over seats and around each other like they were taking part in some kind of complicated dance, until finally he dropped into the seat next to me.

"That looked like more trouble than it was worth," I pointed out drily. I didn't just mean getting to the seat. He had gone to a lot of trouble to track me down at all and I didn't understand why.

He ignored my sarcasm and dove right in. "Look, we don't have a lot of time, and there's a lot we need to discuss."

I obviously wasn't getting rid of him for now, so I simply spread my arms open in invitation. "Go ahead."

"What were you told about your birth?" he asked me to begin with. "What do you know about our mother?"

Our mother. He said that as if she had ever been any kind of a mother to me at all.

"Not much," I replied vaguely. He could talk if he wanted to but I didn't intend to share anything with him if I didn't have to. If he thought we were going to have some kind of heart-to-heart, he was about to be sorely disappointed.

Oliver nodded. "I figured as much. I don't have all the answers either, but I'll tell you what I know. Our biological parents, my mother and your father, were involved with each other when they were young. Then she came to my dad's pack where she turned eighteen and they found out they were mates. So she broke up with your dad to be with her mate."

None of this was news to me. My dad had told me the same thing, and how she had eventually come to regret her decision and returned to him. That's when she got pregnant. Then her mate came and either begged her or blackmailed her – I was never sure which – to return with him, which she did. Then he hid her away until she gave birth to her bastard son, me, and I was sent back to live with my dad.

My mother had chosen her mate over my dad and over me. He had always made that perfectly clear to me.

But if all that was true, then where did Oliver fit in? That was what I couldn't quite figure out right now.

"My parents couldn't have children of their own," Oliver continued. "Or, to be more precise, my dad couldn't father a child, so they reached out to Alpha Adrian for his help."

My brow started to furrow but I quickly caught it, keeping my face neutral so I wouldn't betray my surprise. That was a deviation from the story my dad had always told me.

"They went together to your pack where our parents slept together until she was pregnant," Oliver said, wincing a little over the words, since it was our parents he was talking about. "Then they returned home. It was a little while later that she found out she was carrying twins."

"So it was your dad who didn't want me?" I couldn't help asking. Was that why I was sent back? Because he only needed one? That made a bit of sense, although it still meant my mother didn't want me. It didn't really change anything.

But Oliver shook his head. "No, not at all. He probably would have been thrilled to have two sons. But my mom... our mom... never told him that there were two babies."

This was getting a little unbelievable. "How could he not know?"

For the first time, Oliver almost smiled. "That's what I asked too. But apparently my mom and Jenny worked together to hide it from him. Because your dad asked to have one of us, to raise as his own, and she agreed."

Jenny knew about all of this? A memory stirred somewhere deep in my brain, of Jenny comforting me after I hurt myself as a little boy. "Your mom would be so proud of you," she'd said. "She loves you, you know."

I didn't know, and I didn't know how she could have known that either. But then my father's voice rang out in my memory, loud and angry, demanding to know what she'd said to me and what else she'd been hiding from him.

I didn't see Jenny for a long time after that. And when she came back, she was... different. She never talked to me about my mom again.

I didn't know if that was significant, but the one thing I did understand was that I had still been given away. She could choose to keep one of us, and she chose Oliver and not me. She knew I was out there the whole time and she never tried to see me.

"Your dad sounds pretty clueless," I pointed out, trying to distract myself from all the thoughts and feelings trying to claim my attention.

To my surprise, that made Oliver smile. "He was in love. That can make you clueless sometimes."

He glanced up at his mate with real affection, and I couldn't help looking over at Liz too.

That was just what I was afraid of. Clueless was the last thing I needed to be, not when everything I'd been working for was almost within my reach.

"But there was another reason she decided to separate us," Oliver carried on, oblivious to my train of thought. "Besides the simple fact that your father asked her to."

I couldn't think of any reason that would be good enough to explain it, but I humoured him anyway. "What was that?"

"She believed we were cursed," he replied bluntly. "And that we still are. She was completely convinced that if we ever met, one of us would die."

~Liz~

My head was spinning as we set off in the van towards... well, actually, I had no idea where we were going. All I knew was that I was in a van full of werewolves, two of whom were my friends, and one who was...

Actually, I didn't know how to explain what Elijah was to me either. But now I knew that he was Oliver's twin brother.

I was shocked when Oliver told Elijah that they were twins, and it was obvious that Elijah was too. How did neither of them know they had a twin brother before? I glanced at Abby to see if this was a shock to her too, but she didn't look surprised at all, just concerned. And I was concerned too as I watched Elijah react to the news. I could almost feel his pain and confusion inside me, which was crazy, but that's how it felt. I tried to go to him, even though I didn't know what I intended to do when I got there, but Abby stopped me before I could find out.

Then we all piled back in the van and I was rather rudely instructed by one of the men with Elijah to sit in the row closest to the driver's seat with Whitney and Jack. It wasn't that there was anything wrong with that except that I felt this unusually strong urge to sit next to Elijah, to be close to him.

I was attracted to him, of course, but this felt different somehow. I'd been attracted to other men before and I hadn't felt this way. It was almost like an instinctive need to be near him, as strange as that sounded.

Whitney and Jack whispered quietly to each other as Oliver talked to the woman driving, the two men behind me were silent, and Abby and Elijah spoke quietly in the back. I leaned my head against the van window and closed my eyes for a second. So many things had happened since I got up this morning, it was all starting to feel a bit overwhelming, but the motion of the van helped to soothe me and before long, I must have fallen asleep.

At least I assumed I did, because the next thing I knew, I was being woken by a warm hand on my shoulder. "Liz?"

The deep tone left me in no doubt who it was, and my eyes shot open to find Elijah sitting next to me, a look of perplexed amusement on his face. "You're a very deep sleeper," he commented, making me blush. How long had he been watching me?

Then I looked around and realized that everyone else was gone. We were the only two people left in the van, which had obviously stopped moving. I really must have been out of it to miss all of that.

"Where... uh, where is everyone?" I asked, wiping my face quickly to make sure I didn't have any drool on my chin.

Elijah's amusement grew deeper as he watched me try to look calm and collected, a smile playing at the corners of his mouth. "They've gone ahead. I told them we'd catch up, but I need to talk to you first."

"You do?" *Oh my God, why is my voice so squeaky?* I tried not to wince in embarrassment at the sound of it.

He nodded, the smile disappearing as his grey eyes looked deep into mine. I thought I'd never seen eyes quite that colour before, until I remembered that Oliver's must be the same. I had just never been this close to Oliver's face before.

"There's something happening between us, Liz," he said, leaning in even closer, and my heart felt like it was going to beat out of my chest. "I know you feel it too."

"I do feel... something," I managed to agree, hardly able to believe this was happening. He was looking at me like he wanted to devour me. No one had ever looked at me that way before.

"I tried to fight it," he continued. "But it's no use."

Wait, what? Why would he try to fight what he was feeling? I didn't understand, but before I could ask, his lips were on mine and every question or thought or idea I had ever had disappeared.

I'd kissed other men before, but in that moment, it didn't feel like I had. This felt like something completely new as his lips moved against mine, his hands gently cupping my face. And then his tongue pressed against my lips insistently, and when I let them part to allow him in, my whole body ignited.

Electricity raced through me, making me more aware of every part of my body than I had ever been before. Somehow, I was clutching at his strong shoulders, though I didn't remember my arms moving to get there. His firm muscles flexed and rippled beneath my touch as his hands moved away from my face, down my neck, his fingers trailing lightly across my collarbone.

"I want to see you, Liz," he whispered, his mouth never fully leaving mine. "All of you. Will you let me?"

I swallowed hard with both excitement and nerves. No man had ever seen me naked before. I would have gotten naked for Liam, but he never gave me the chance. *Thank God.*

"Here?" I asked, looking around at the van and our surroundings. I couldn't tell where we were parked, but a quick glance out the window showed me it was quiet and deserted.

He gave me a smile as he reached into his pocket and pulled out a set of keys. "I've locked us in. No one's going to disturb us."

He planned this. That thought sent shivers down my spine again and this time I was the one who kissed him, trying to pull him to me, but he was so strong and solid that I ended up pulling myself towards him instead. *Whoa.* What was it going to feel like to have that body on top of me? *Inside of me?*

I whimpered into our kiss. The mere thought of being pinned beneath him was enough to send a wave of desire through me stronger than I'd ever felt before. Elijah growled – *he actually growled!* - as he pulled back from me.

"Let me see you," he whispered again, his eyes filled with longing.

I didn't stop to think. It didn't matter that I'd only met him an hour ago. It didn't matter that he was the twin brother of my best friend's boyfriend, which would have been a little weird if I did stop to think about it. But I didn't, I just pulled my shirt up and over my head, more thankful than I'd ever been about anything that I had decided to wear my black lacy bra this morning instead of the plain white one I usually went with.

His grey eyes grew darker as they roamed across my exposed skin, and then he leaned down, placing a kiss on my collarbone, then just lower, and lower until his face was buried between my breasts.

"Elijah," I moaned as my body continued to light up beneath his touch.

"Eli," he corrected me, looking up at me with an intense gaze. "Call me Eli."

"Eli," I repeated breathlessly, and he smiled in satisfaction before focusing back on my chest that was still right in front of him.

Without taking his eyes off it, his hands slid up to my shoulders, pulling my bra straps down my arms, and then he pulled the top of my bra down too, letting me spill out into his waiting mouth.

"Oh, God," I gasped as he sucked my nipple hard, his tongue swirling around it like he needed to taste every inch. The throbbing need for him between my legs was getting worse and somehow he seemed to know it. His nose twitched and he looked up at me again, releasing my breast from his lips with a pop.

"Take everything off," he commanded, no longer asking politely. His need was clearly as strong as mine was, and I was powerless to disobey him. Not that I wanted to. I wanted to do exactly what he told me to do.

As quickly as possible, I unbuttoned my jeans, lifting my hips off the seat to pull them and my panties down, trying not to let him see just how wet they already were. Then I reached behind my back to undo my bra, pulling it the rest of the way off so that I was completely naked for him.

His eyes widened in wonder as he looked me over, examining me as if I was some kind of treasure. Then he kissed me again, ever harder this time, and I met him just as desperately. Our tongues danced and tangled as his hands roamed across my naked skin, down my shoulders, up my thighs, cupping my breasts and brushing my nipples, until there wasn't any part of me he hadn't touched except where I wanted him most.

He must have heard my silent plea because his hands slipped between my knees now and began a slow, teasing climb up my inner thighs, getting closer and closer to my aching centre.

"Do you want me, Liz?" he teased, his lips leaving mine only to brush against my cheek and then my ear, his breath hot against my skin. "You want me to fuck you with my fingers?"

Oh my God, yes! I had never wanted anything so badly.

"Please, Eli," I begged, spreading my legs wider. I could feel his smile against my cheek as his fingers brushed against my tender skin and...

"Ow!" My head banged against the glass of the van window as we went over a bump in the road.

My eyes flew open to find Whitney and Jack both looking at me in concern. "Are you okay?" Whitney asked sympathetically as I rubbed my sore head. "You looked so happy in your sleep, I didn't want to wake you. But we're almost there, it should just be another ten minutes or so."

My hands went to my chest and the clothes I was still wearing. I wasn't naked. We were still driving and Eli and I had never been alone.

It was all a dream. Just a stupid, unreal, amazing dream.

I could have cried in frustration.

As I tried to compose myself, I couldn't stop from glancing back at Elijah in the back seat where he was now sitting with Oliver. I had missed him and Abby switching places somehow. And when Elijah's eyes met mine, his nose twitched again, just like it had in my dream.

He couldn't read my mind, could he? I didn't think that was an ability that werewolves had, but suddenly I wasn't so sure. From the look he was giving me, I couldn't help thinking that he knew exactly what I had just been dreaming about.

172

Chapter Thirteen

~**Oliver**~

Elijah looked away from me as I told him how our mother thought we were cursed. At first, I thought he was surprised or overwhelmed by what I'd just said, but then I realized he was actually staring at Liz, who was looking back at us too. His nose twitched and his eyes narrowed as he watched her. When I turned to look at her fully as well, she spun back around in her seat, her cheeks a deep shade of red.

That was weird.

"How do you know that woman?" Elijah asked, his voice deeper than it had been, with an emotion I couldn't quite place.

"Liz?" I asked in confusion. Why was he focused on her right now, after what I'd just said? Was he simply trying to change the subject? I didn't understand, but in any case, I answered as succinctly as I could. "She's Abby's friend."

"They look a lot alike," he mused, his focus still on the back of Liz's head. "But she's human."

I really didn't see how any of this was relevant. "Did you hear what I just said? About the curse?"

His head snapped back to me, finally giving me his full attention again. "Of course I did. You and me, cursed. I got it."

What the hell was this guy's problem? "And that doesn't worry you at all?"

I didn't really believe in it either, but at least I didn't dismiss it completely out of hand.

He gave a small huff of derision. "I'm about to become the most powerful wolf in the world, I don't think I have much to worry about. Besides, we've met now and we're both still here. So what's the problem?"

I still didn't really believe anything to do with this source of power either, but if there was even a little truth to it, if he was going to gain some kind of additional power, it was all the more reason for me to be concerned. "Well, the thing is, we won't just fall over dead. According to the curse, or at least what our mom told my dad about it, eventually one of us is going to kill the other."

That was the first thing I'd said that really got his attention, but not in a good way. Suspicion immediately crossed Elijah's face. "What is that supposed to mean?"

I didn't think it was rocket science. "Just what I said. Apparently, in our family, in our mother's family, whenever there are twins, one kills the other, usually by accident."

"So you came here to kill me?" His eyes widened as he looked around the van, and his pack members were immediately on full alert as well, tuned into his body language. Liz looked back at us again too, almost like she could tell something was wrong.

"No!" I exclaimed in frustration. Why would he jump to that conclusion? "Of course not. If that's what I wanted, would I be telling you all of this? I just came to talk to you. You have as much of a right to know these things as I do."

His eyes moved rapidly back and forth as he thought things over. "A curse... on twins..." he repeated almost to himself before pulling out his phone.

Now what? Why couldn't he stay focused on our conversation for two minutes?

But to my surprise, he simply pulled up a photo on his phone and handed it to me. The text was a bit difficult to read, but I could pretty much make it out. Someone was mourning the death of their child, a twin, and then there was talk of a curse and a king, and the source, which I could only assume was the same artifact we were currently on our way to find.

"That's from the book?" I guessed as I handed the phone back to him.

Elijah nodded. "Our mother's book, the one that belonged to her family. So whether this curse is real or not, it seems like the idea of it has been around for a long time."

That same uneasy feeling I'd had when my dad first told me about the curse settled over me again. Was there actually something to this?

And if it was true, did I trust Elijah not to try to kill me?

At least the text hinted at a way out. It suggested returning the artifact might stop the curse. But who would we return it to? The Alpha King was long dead. And would Elijah really be willing to give it up anyway?

Before I could respond to him, my own phone buzzed in my pocket, and I pulled it out, intending to put it on silent, but my fingers stopped when I saw what it was: an email from Jenny, with the subject line "Another letter".

My eyes went from the phone to Elijah, who was watching me closely. "What is it?" he asked.

He's got a right to see this too, I thought. I had come here to share what I knew with him after all. It was no good keeping it to myself.

"It's a letter that our mother sent to Jenny. Do you want me to read it out loud?"

He nodded, trying to appear nonchalant, but I could see the curiosity in his eyes, the same curiosity I was feeling too. The last two letters had revealed so much. What would this one tell us?

I read the brief note from Jenny first.

Hi Oliver,

Sorry this took so long, but I found this letter I think you should see. I hid it from the Alpha, for rather obvious reasons, and it took me a while to remember where I'd hidden it.

I'm not sure if these are the answers you're looking for, but I hope it helps.

That only piqued my curiosity further. What would she have hidden from Alpha Adrian, and why? A quick glance at Elijah told me he wanted to know as much as I did, so I carried on reading.

~Letter from Nicole~

Dear Jenny,

Thank you for your letter. I think you know how much it means to me to hear from you, but in case you don't, let me say it again: I couldn't do this without having you to confide in.

I am feeling a bit better now. I still have rough days, of course. Last week Oliver said his first word: mama. Patrick was so happy, but the only thing I could think about was whether Elijah would ever have a reason to use that word at all.

It's a bitter pain, but the more days pass, the more I think I made the right decision. Looking at my beautiful Oliver, I can't bear the thought of anything happening to him, and I feel the same about Elijah, even though I can't see him for myself.

You asked me in your last letter how I could be so sure that my family's bad luck with twins wasn't just an old superstition. Well, there is something I have never told you, but I think I am ready to tell you now. I know I can trust you to keep it between us. No one else can know about this, and especially not Patrick. I couldn't bear it if he ever found out.

As you know, I grew up in the Seven Hills pack with my parents. But what you don't know, and what I didn't know until my 17th birthday, was that I had a sister. A twin sister.

Twins run in my family, which perhaps is why the curse was placed on us. Or is it the other way around, and we tend to have twins because of the curse? I can't say. All I know is that my parents believed in its power enough that they gave my sister up for adoption. She was taken and raised by another Beta's family in a distant pack, to keep her safe. To keep us both safe.

No one was ever supposed to know. But my mother told me later, after everything had happened, that the curse seems to find a way. Even when twins are separated as we were, they end up coming together, running into each other randomly in the most unlikely of places.

That was how it was for me and my sister, at least. Her name was Carol.

Adrian and I went to Portland to go dress shopping on the day of my birthday party. He wanted to buy me something nice to wear. I went into the dressing room to try something on, and before I even had it zipped up, I could hear Adrian saying how much he liked it. Confused, I finished getting dressed and hurried out to find him talking to a girl who looked exactly like me, trying on the exact same dress I was wearing.

This was before we had our wolves, so there was no strong pack scent to tell us apart. I didn't blame Adrian for mistaking her for me. I would have done the same.

We were both shocked and confused as we stared at each other. Neither of us knew that we had a twin, so you can imagine what a surprise it was. But I did know about my family's history, so when she leaned in close to me and whispered, "Are you from a pack too?", I knew that she was also a werewolf and that she must be my sister. It couldn't be a coincidence. The resemblance was too strong.

Carol hadn't grown up knowing about the curse, of course, so she was confused and hurt about why we were separated and why our parents had given her up when they kept me. I invited her to come to my birthday party that night and she looked surprised as she said it was her birthday too, and then we both laughed. Of course it was. She had no plans though, so she agreed to come and talk to our parents herself.

On the drive home, I was worried about my parents' reaction and if there was any truth to the curse at all, but Adrian was in high spirits. I finally asked him what he had to be so happy about, and he grinned at me in a slightly sickening way.

"Twins usually share a mate," he reminded me. I had heard that myself, but I'd never paid much attention to it since I never thought it would apply to me. "So if you and I are mates, like we should be..."

He trailed off, but I heard enough of the glee in his voice to turn my stomach. He was happy I had a twin sister so that he could have both of us as mates. For the first time, I secretly wished that maybe he wouldn't be my mate after all.

When we got back to the pack, I didn't tell my parents what had happened. I knew they would go straight to the Alpha, Adrian's father, and demand Carol not be allowed in. I figured they were just being paranoid and if she showed up in front of them, they would have to talk to her and give her answers.

I got ready for the party and Adrian came to my door to pick me up, still wearing that same self-satisfied smile on his face. "Happy birthday," he told me, giving me a kiss. "Just one more year."

We'd been saying that for a while, how we couldn't wait to turn 18 so we'd have the mate bond that we'd been sure we would share, but after how he had been in the car earlier, I couldn't bring myself to return the sentiment this time.

The party was a big success. You were there, Jenny, you probably remember. I waited and waited for Carol to show up, but even after we had cut the cake, there was still no sign of her. I was getting more and more worried but I couldn't tell anyone what was bothering me. No one knew that Carol was supposed to be coming at all, no one except Adrian, of course.

Finally I couldn't take it anymore and I told him I wanted to go looking for her. He reminded me that we had no idea where she was and no way of contacting her. Maybe she just changed her mind about coming.

But I didn't think that was true. Something was wrong. I could feel it.

With a little more begging from me, he gave in and we slipped away from the party. We took Adrian's car and headed out through the forest, off the pack land and onto the main highway.

It was only a couple of miles from our border territory that we found the car, its headlights still on, slammed into one of the large redwood trees that lined the highway. Adrian swore as we approached and ran out of the car to go and see if he could help, but I stayed where I was. I knew there was nothing we could do.

I knew it was too late.

Carol died on the side of that highway because I invited her to my party. She died because of me. When Adrian came back to the car, he was shaken too, more upset than I'd ever seen him. He told me he would call the police and ambulance, but that we should go so that no one would ever know we were there. He didn't want there to be any questions about what we were doing there or why I looked just like the woman in the car.

He didn't want anyone to know it was my fault, which it obviously was.

As he got back in the seat next to me, he handed me something he'd taken from her car. It was a small wrapped present that had been next to her on the passenger seat. A birthday present for me.

He promised me that night he would keep my secret, that no one would ever know how I caused my sister's death, but the guilt of it has been so hard to bear. I can't tell you how many times since then I have woken up at night from a nightmare where I am back in those dark woods, the headlights of the car shining into the trees, but this time, I go with Adrian to the car. I see my sister's twisted, broken body behind the wheel, and then her eyes snap open and she tells me she wishes she never met me.

Please forgive the tear stains on this letter, Jenny. I have never written this all down before, and it somehow makes it more real. Until now, that night existed only in my mind, but now, it is on this paper too.

But you see now, don't you, why my boys need to stay apart. Adrian knows it too. He has promised me that if either of them ever learn about the other, he will keep them separate. He will do everything he can to ensure they never meet.

I know it's a long shot, but I ask the same of you, Jenny. If by some miracle, you ever meet Oliver, don't let him see Elijah. Take him to Adrian instead. Adrian will know what to do.

I need to rest now. Reliving all of this and writing it down has really drained me. Keep well, my dear friend, and please keep sending me news of Elijah whenever you can.

All my love,
Nicole

~Elijah~

I had trained myself a long time ago how to hide what I was feeling, and how to feel as little as I possibly could in the first place, but I had never felt as close to cracking as I did right now. Emotional assaults were coming in from every angle, battering me on all sides, and I didn't know where to focus my defenses the most.

First there was everything Oliver had said about our parents, bringing up a million questions that only my dad could answer. I hadn't spoken to him in a long time and I hadn't wanted to, but right now, I almost wished he were here.

I was still mulling that over when the scent of Liz's arousal nearly ripped me straight out of my seat. Why the fuck was she turned on right now? I turned to look at her and she looked back at me and for a second, all I could see was her face and the longing in it. Everything else faded away until it was as if we were the only two people left in the van.

She's feeling something for you, Abby had told me. Was that why she was aroused, because of me? For just a fleeting moment, I wanted nothing more than to go and do something about it.

Then Oliver started speaking again and I snapped at him, frustrated with everything that was happening and with how in control he seemed. Of course he could be calm and collected about this. He had a loving family and a werewolf mate, and he was apparently content to think the source was just a myth. At that moment, I almost envied his blissful ignorance.

And now, he had just read the letter from our mother.

I had never heard her voice before, not a single word. Hearing her words in Oliver's voice wasn't the same, of course, but it still meant more to me than I could have imagined.

I knew there must be more to the whole situation than what was in that letter, more to her relationship with my dad than I could guess at, but there was one thing that came across to me louder than anything else.

She had missed me.

She had thought about me, at least once in a while. She wrote to Jenny about me and she asked Jenny to send information back.

That was more than I had ever known before.

Why didn't she keep in touch with my dad directly? Why couldn't I talk to her, even if I couldn't see her or Oliver? Why didn't my dad ever tell me any of this? Why didn't anyone tell me anything?

My whole outlook on life was built on the fact that my mother didn't want me, and now it seemed that wasn't true. Or at least, it wasn't the full story.

Oliver was frowning too as he scrolled back up on his phone, reviewing parts of the letter he had just read aloud.

"She says that she asked your dad to keep us apart," he murmured, reviewing the section with his eyes as he spoke. "But when I went to talk to him, he put me straight in touch with Storm, and she led me to you. There was no hesitation on his part."

We both turned to look at Storm in the driver's seat, unaware of the scrutiny she was under as she chatted away to Abby.

"My dad put you in touch with Storm?" I repeated in disbelief. How on earth did they know each other? Storm had never once mentioned to me that she had any connection to my father. I didn't understand how it was even possible.

But Oliver nodded in confirmation. "He said she would know where to find you."

Just one more question to add to the pile, I figured. For now, I tried to focus back on the previous question, about why my dad would have wanted us to meet in the first place.

"Maybe he doesn't believe in the curse," I suggested, though it was purely a guess since I had never been able to understand anything my dad did. "Maybe he only said it to humour her."

Oliver's frown deepened. "But Mom says how shook up he was when they found her twin. He saw the effects of the curse first-hand, so why would he doubt it? It doesn't make any sense."

Welcome to my life.

That wasn't the only thing I had noticed in the letter either. "She also mentions how twins usually have the same mate," I said, and Oliver's eyes immediately widened before darting up to Abby once again. His agitation was almost palpable and I was tempted to let him sweat it out for a little longer, but in the end I didn't. I put him out of his misery. "But I don't feel anything for your mate."

He exhaled in obvious relief. "I never even thought of that."

I hadn't either until the letter had mentioned it. It was something wolves often joked about when they were young; everyone wanted to be mated to a hot pair of twins. But I hadn't thought about it in years, since I never thought it would apply to me.

And apparently it didn't, even though I was a twin. Yet another question that I didn't have an answer for. It would be nice if we could start getting some fucking answers at some point.

"Eli!" Storm's voice called out from the front seat and everyone else went quiet.

"Yeah?" I called back, not sure if I was grateful for or annoyed by the interruption. There was still so much I needed to work out.

"We're here."

Everyone immediately turned to the windows, trying to see where 'here' was. My heart beat faster and my wolf was on high alert too. Was this really it? Was the source here? After all this time, was I finally about to hold it in my hands?

I should have felt only excitement. This was what I'd been working towards for years, after all. But the last hour had shaken the foundations of more than a few things I thought I solidly knew, and so my feelings were far more mixed as Storm parked at the river's edge and we all climbed out of the van.

"These are the coordinates we worked out based on the map of the hurricane's path and what we know about settlements in the area at the time," Storm told me as I walked over to her, Julian and Matthew standing close guard behind me. "Is it what you were expecting?"

Looking away from her, I did a quick survey of the area. It was completely uninhabited, an untouched part of the riverside close to where it opened into the wider river that led into the sea. Surrounding us, there was only grass, some rocks, and a few scattered trees. There were no obvious hiding places where the source would have been secured, but that was probably a good thing. If it were obvious, someone would have found it a long time ago.

Was it what I was expecting though? I didn't know how to answer that. Nothing about this day was going as I expected it to.

"Elijah?" The soft voice of my mate broke through my thoughts, and I turned around to find her standing just behind Julian and Matthew. She looked so tiny compared to them, so fragile, and a strong protective need rose up inside me.

"What?" That came out harsher than I meant it to as I tried to control my urges, and Liz winced a little at my tone. But to my surprise, she didn't back off. Most human women would when I spoke to them that way.

"I just wondered if there was something I could do to help? What are you looking for?"

She wants to help me? Why?

No one ever did anything just for my benefit. People helped me if I paid them to, and my pack members did what I asked them to because I was their Alpha, but nobody helped me for no reason at all.

But once again, Abby's words came back to me. *Get to know her.* She'd told me to give Liz a chance, and maybe it was worth a shot.

"I'm looking for a full moon," I blurted out, to the surprise of both Storm and my men. Obviously none of them had expected me to answer honestly. "The text says the full moon will show the path."

Liz frowned as she looked around, and I knew what she was thinking. It was the middle of the day. How was the moon going to show us anything?

"Maybe it's a metaphor?" she suggested tentatively. "In literature, a full moon usually means maturity or a moment of truth. A realization or an illumination."

Illumination. That was the word the text used. *The full moon wilt illuminate the path.*

"What else could it mean?" I asked eagerly. She might be onto something here.

"Well, the moon is usually feminine," she continued, warming up to the subject as she realized how interested I was in what she was saying. "That's why it's called Luna. Even Shakespeare called the moon 'her'. And in China, the full moon is associated with family, the coming together of family."

How did she know all this? I couldn't help but be impressed.

And hearing her say the word Luna affected me in a way I couldn't quite explain. How much did she know about wolves like me? She might not know she was my mate, but did she know what an Alpha was? Did she know that as the Alpha's mate, she would be a Luna?

I shook my head and tried to focus back on the rest of what she said. So the full moon was a woman or a moment of realization?

Or maybe both?

As I looked back to my clever human mate who was still mumbling to herself as she reviewed all the knowledge in her head, I began to wonder.

What if Liz *was* the moon? What if, in order to find the path to the source, I needed my mate?

Chapter Fourteen

~**Abby**~

I had some new information for Oliver and I was sure he had some for me too as we regrouped outside the van. Elijah, his men and Storm had all gone a short distance away, presumably to talk about where to start looking for the artifact, while Whitney, Jack and Liz stayed close to the van. I kept my voice down as I let Oliver in on what I had found out.

"Elijah thinks Storm's employer wants the artifact," I told him, summing things up as quickly as I could. "But her only instruction is to make sure he doesn't get it."

I had taken the chance to ask her exactly how she was involved in all of this while we were sitting in the van together, and she surprised me by admitting easily enough that she had no personal interest in the whole hunt at all.

"I'm not even sure if the damn thing really exists," she told me. "But Adrian and I go back a long way. When he asked me to watch out for Eli, I couldn't really refuse."

"So Adrian is your employer?" I asked curiously. He had put us in touch with her, of course, but I hadn't been entirely certain that she wasn't also working for someone else.

"In this case, yes," she told me. "But I'm a free agent most of the time."

After everything that had happened since we met, I was more intrigued about her life than ever, but I knew for right now I needed to focus on the artifact. "So why doesn't Adrian want Eli to get the source?"

Storm shrugged. "He's never said. But you've met Eli now... if this thing's for real, do you really want him in charge of all wolves in the country?"

I grimaced a little at the thought and Storm laughed before changing the subject.

She hadn't told me exactly how she and Adrian knew each other, but I thought it was still information that might be useful to us anyway, and Oliver agreed before briefly filling me in on the new letter he'd just received from Jenny.

My heart went out to Oliver's mom once again. She must have carried so much guilt about her twin's death. Maybe that was even what caused her mental illness in the first place? Even if not, it couldn't have helped.

Then Oliver told me about how she said Adrian had promised to keep the boys separate and I frowned.

"But Alpha Adrian encouraged you to go and find Elijah," I pointed out when he finished. "He all but drew a map."

Oliver nodded. "I know. That struck me as odd too. There must still be something we're missing."

I hoped it was only one thing, but it felt to me like there were still a lot of loose ends. I had a feeling there was still more than one secret waiting to come out.

And speaking of secrets, I figured I should probably tell Oliver about Liz and Elijah being mates, for a start. Just as I was about to open my mouth, I glanced over to where our friends were standing, but only Whitney and Jack were there now. *Where did Liz go?* I spun around frantically only to see her talking to Elijah, the two of them in the middle of what seemed to be a fairly intense conversation.

"Give me a second," I said to my mate before hurrying over to his brother and my friend. *He better not be rejecting her.* I didn't know if I was physically capable of kicking his ass, but if that's what was going on right now, I was willing to try.

I walked up to them just in time to hear Elijah ask her if she knew what a mate was. I didn't know why he was bringing it up, but I didn't think it was for anything good.

"I don't think this is the time for this conversation," I interrupted, examining Liz's face carefully to see if he'd upset her in any way. It didn't look like he had, thankfully. She just looked confused.

"Mate?" Liz repeated curiously, completely ignoring me, her eyes fixed on Elijah. "Well, it's the word used for the sexual partner of an animal."

Of course she would throw out the dictionary definition. That was my friend: if it was found in a book, she would know about it.

Elijah seemed to find it a little amusing as well. For the first time since we'd met him, he almost smiled. "That's true. And wolves are a kind of animal."

"Okay, hold on," I tried again, stepping directly between them so they couldn't continue to talk around me. "We came here to look for this artifact, right? Let's take care of that first."

"It's all related," Elijah said, looking down on me in frustration. "I think I need my mate to help me find it."

He needs his mate? A sinking feeling settled in my stomach as I began to understand what was happening. "So that's why you're going to tell her? Just so you can use her to get what you want?"

"Tell me what?" Liz spoke up from the other side of me. Her confusion had only grown as she looked between Elijah and me.

Elijah opened his mouth to respond but I cut him off. Whatever explanation he was going to give wasn't what Liz needed right now. This was a time for girl talk if there ever was one.

"I'll tell her."

His eyes narrowed as he growled at me. "It's none of your business. I don't need you to interfere."

I could see that the distance between them was bothering him. He was trying to hold himself back, but now that the idea of accepting her had entered his head, even if it was for the wrong reasons, it was going to be even harder for him to resist.

Still, I stuck to my guns. "I disagree. It is my business. You're my brother-in-law, almost, and she's my friend, and I don't think you're in the best frame of mind to handle this right now."

"Handle what?" That was Oliver who had just walked over to join us after checking in with Whitney and Jack.

"Talk to your brother for a minute," I instructed him, avoiding the question. "Liz and I need to have a chat."

Ignoring Elijah's continued protests, I pulled Liz over to a small group of rocks a small distance away, out of earshot of the others, and told her to sit down while I perched down on another one.

"What's going on, Abby?" she asked, a mixture of concern and annoyance in her voice. "Why won't you guys just tell me what this is about?"

"I'm going to," I promised. "Right now."

At least I thought I was. Now that it was just the two of us, I wasn't entirely sure where to start. I thought back on everything we'd talked about earlier until I remembered something that might be a good segue.

"Do you remember on the way down here, you asked me if Oliver and I started dating because we're both werewolves?"

I started dating because we're both werewolves?"

She nodded. "Yeah, and you said no."

"Right. We didn't start seeing each other only because we're both wolves. We started seeing each other because we're mates."

She gave me a curious look. "How could you be mates before you started seeing each other?"

"It means something different for werewolves," I explained. "It's closer to what humans call soulmates. It means we were destined to be together. Each wolf has a mate chosen for them, planned in advance, and when you meet that person, you just know it."

Liz was hanging on every word, completely enthralled. "So you knew right away that Oliver was your mate?"

I nodded. "I did, but I tried to fight it for a while. Mostly because I was seeing Liam at the time."

Her face scrunched up in disgust at the mention of his name and we both laughed. It had taken a while, but we could laugh about it now.

"How do you know?" she asked. "That someone is your mate?"

"Well, your wolf tells you, for one thing," I said. "That's the biggest giveaway. But there are other things too, like the way they smell, or how you're connected emotionally, or how your bodies seem to spark against each other, like an electric charge."

Liz's eyes widened and I knew then that she had already experienced something from that list, though I wasn't sure which one. "And that only happens if you're supposed to be with someone?"

I nodded. "It's fated, and it's a really special connection."

"And this only happens between werewolves?" she asked.

Now we were getting to the point. "Usually. But not always."

A spark of realization flashed in her eyes and Liz looked over at Elijah who was talking to his men while Oliver and Storm stood nearby. "So Elijah and I...?"

She knew it, but I could see she was embarrassed to say it out loud, so I filled it in the blank. "Are mates. Yes. If you both want to be. There are ways to sever the connection if it doesn't work out."

She swallowed hard, thinking things over. "And he knows about it?"

I nodded. "He would have known it right away. I think he must have known since San Francisco."

I only realized that after I had spoken to him and he confirmed they were mates. When I was sitting in the front seat next to Storm, I remembered the way Elijah had stared at me on the stage at the book festival. He hadn't been looking at me at all, I realized. He was looking at Liz.

"San Francisco?" Liz repeated the words with a bit of hurt in her voice. "He knew all that time? Why didn't he say anything?"

That was a really good question and one I couldn't answer. "I think he's a little distracted with everything else that's going on. This thing he's looking for, whatever it is, it's really important to him. And now, based on what he just said, I think he wants you to help him find it because you're his mate. He seems to think he needs you to find it."

"So that's the only reason he was going to tell me," she deduced, the pain in her voice growing stronger. I wished I could argue with her, but that's what it seemed like to me too, and the last thing Liz deserved was to get used by another selfish bastard who didn't really care about her. We'd both had enough of that to last a lifetime.

"That's why I wanted to tell you first," I explained. "It's still up to you whether you want to help him or not, but I thought you should have all the facts first."

A range of emotions played across my friend's face: hope and disappointment, longing and frustration, happiness and anger. I couldn't begin to guess which one she was going to settle on.

"I think I understand," she finally said, getting to her feet. "Let's go see what he has to say."

~Liz~

I didn't know how to describe what I was feeling right now. It wasn't quite the same feeling of despair I had all those months ago when Abby sat me down at my work and told me Liam was a lying, manipulative piece of shit, but it wasn't all that far off either.

A man I had feelings for, one I thought might care for me too, was trying to use me. It was heartbreakingly familiar.

And once again, Abby got to be the bearer of my bad news. I knew it was because she cared about me enough to tell me the truth and that she didn't want me to get hurt, but it didn't make it much easier to take.

Just when I thought I might finally be in line for something good to happen to me, it turned out to be far more complicated than I could have ever imagined. I still wasn't sure I completely understood all of this mate stuff. There had to be more to it than what Abby had told me in the limited time we had, but I understood one thing perfectly clearly.

There was some mystical force telling Elijah that he and I were meant to be together, and he had hidden that fact from me until he thought I might be useful to him.

If it was just that he hadn't told me today, I might have understood. But he had known since San Francisco? That was a week ago! Shouldn't he have been excited when he saw me again today?

I remembered how in my dream he told me he was trying to fight what was between us. How did my subconscious know that? Abby suggested we might be emotionally connected somehow, so was I able to sense what he was feeling without even realizing it?

And why would he be fighting it in the first place? If he didn't have a damn good reason, I was going to tell him exactly where he could shove his request for help.

Elijah and Oliver were arguing about something as Abby and I walked back over to them but they both stopped talking as we approached.

"I'm sorry, Liz," Oliver said a little sheepishly as he looked between Elijah and me. "I didn't know you were his mate."

He didn't? Then how did Abby know? I thought maybe it was something all werewolves were able to sense.

I shook my head to push those questions aside. There were other things I was far more interested in right now. "It's okay. You're not the one who should have told me," I replied to Oliver, pointedly ignoring Elijah who was standing right beside him.

From the corner of my eye, I could see him grimace. "Liz, can I talk to you? Alone?"

The last word was obviously directed at Abby who was standing supportively beside me.

"It's up to you," she whispered to me. "I'll stay if you want me to."

I appreciated that, but I needed to do this on my own. "We can talk," I told Elijah, giving Abby a small nod to let her know I was okay.

She went over to Oliver while Elijah moved towards me. "Come with me," he said as he started to walk away, then he paused for a second to wait for me. "Please."

Keeping my distance from him, we walked side by side back over to where Abby and I had just talked, but this time we didn't sit down. I was too agitated to sit. I wanted answers and I wanted them now.

Elijah pursed his lips a few times, opening his mouth to speak and then closing it again. Finally he seemed to decide where to start.

"So Abby told you that you and I are mates," he said. It wasn't a question but I nodded anyway. "Did you know about mates before?"

"I didn't know werewolves existed until earlier today," I told him honestly. "It's been a bit of a wild ride, Elijah."

One side of his mouth quirked into a half-smile. "I can only imagine. And you can call me Eli."

That was what he'd said in my dream too. Once again, I didn't understand how my subconscious had known things I wasn't consciously aware of.

"So how are you mixed up with those two if you didn't know about wolves?" He pointed over at Oliver and Abby who were talking to the red-haired woman now.

"They go to college with me," I explained. "Abby's in most of my classes."

This time Eli gave a full smile. It made him look even more like Oliver, if that was possible. "You're kidding me. They go to college with a bunch of humans?"

I shook my head, trying not to smile back. There was something infectious about his smile. "It's true. At least I think most of us are human. Up until today I thought we all were."

He gave a further huff of amusement, and then sighed. "Look, Liz, I haven't handled this very well, I realize that. This has been a crazy day for me too and I'm still trying to make sense of it all. But the reason that we're here, this artifact I'm looking for, it's really important. If you could help me out with the rest of this clue, it would really mean a lot to me."

He must be telling the truth about the kind of day it had been. I had helped the others to free him from some men who had kidnapped him, after all. I hoped this wasn't a typical day for him.

But even so, it didn't explain everything. And how could I be sure he wasn't only saying this now so I would agree to help him? Would he leave me behind as soon as I wasn't of use to him anymore?

I still had some questions for him first before I agreed to anything.

"Why didn't you talk to me in San Francisco?"

Eli's eyes widened at the question, like a deer in the headlights. "What do you mean?"

"Abby told me you would have known we were mates from the first time you saw me. I know you saw me there, so why didn't you talk to me?"

"There was a lot of stuff going on that day too," he tried to tell me. "The men who took me today, they had been at that festival, and..."

"Don't bullshit me, Eli." His eyebrows raised in surprise as I cut him off. "People I trusted a lot more than you have told me better lies than that. Now tell me the truth."

He swallowed and tried again. "Abby was up on the stage with you. I didn't know who she was, but I knew she was a werewolf, and I was afraid she was..."

"Nope." I interrupted him again, crossing my arms in disapproval. "I don't buy that you were afraid of tiny little Abby over there. If you can't be bothered to be straight with me, then I don't think we have anything else to talk about."

As I turned to go, he reached out to grab my arm, and as his fingers made contact with my bare skin, there was a spark of electricity followed by a soothing tingling sensation all the way up my arm and through my whole body.

Whoa. When Abby mentioned sparks, I thought she meant that odd electric sensation I'd felt earlier when he was next to me, but this was a completely different level.

Eli seemed to feel it too, as he immediately pulled his hand back as if I'd burned him.

It was hot all right, but I still wanted to hear his explanation. "Well?" I asked, trying not to show how much his touch had affected me.

He seemed to be struggling a little bit too. "I didn't speak to you that day..." he trailed off but I couldn't tell if he was trying to come up with another lie or if he was just embarrassed to continue, but finally he finished the sentence. "Because you're human."

"And that's a bad thing?" I didn't understand what he meant by that.

"It's not great," he offered, almost as a joke. He seemed to wait to see if I would smile, but when I didn't, he carried on. "Look, I'm not just any werewolf. I'm the Alpha of my pack, I lead hundreds of people, which is why these guys do exactly what I tell them."

He gestured over at his friends, but I didn't turn to look. I already knew what they looked like. I was only interested in Eli right now.

"And more than that, this thing we're looking for today, it's going to make me even more powerful. I'm going to have tens of thousands of wolves answering to me, hundreds of thousands even. I figured I needed a strong, powerful wolf by my side as well. And you're... well, you're not even a wolf at all. You're just a human."

I didn't think being called "just" a human would ever sting quite this much. It was hardly my fault, nor was it all that I was. "You don't know anything about me," I couldn't help pointing out.

"I know," he quickly agreed. "You asked why I didn't talk to you that day, you wanted the honest truth, and that's the reason why. But since then, as the days went by, I thought about you. A lot. But I didn't have any idea where to start looking for you, so I thought I had lost you forever. And then with you turning up today, here of all places, helping to rescue me, helping me with the clue... well, maybe it's a sign. Perhaps I was wrong before. Maybe I jumped to conclusions too quickly."

My heart beat a little faster, driven on by his words and the look in his eyes. I wanted so badly to believe what he was saying, but I couldn't trust him yet, not fully. If I let myself fall for him, I was going to fall hard, I didn't have any doubt about that, and I wasn't sure my heart could survive another crash landing.

"Please, Liz," Eli said, moving closer to me as he reached out and brushed his hand against my face, sending those warm, exciting tingles through me once again. "I know you can help me. Are you willing to try?"

~Oliver~

When I walked up to Elijah and Abby facing off, I didn't have a clue what was going on. Once Abby excused herself from our conversation, I had gone over to check on Whitney and Jack, who were both un-derstandably confused about what was happening now. I filled them in as best I could before I noticed Elijah and Abby arguing, and I quickly hurried over to see what was happening.

Things weren't any clearer when Abby and Liz walked away from us to go talk in private, so I turned to my brother and demanded an explanation. "What was all that about?"

His lips tightened in frustration, his nostrils flaring with repressed emotion. "That woman is my mate."

What? "Liz?" I asked in shock. "Are you sure?"

He glared at me. "You think I would say so if I wasn't sure?"

Fair enough. But still, I was shocked. "What are the odds of that?"

How could he be mated to my mate's human friend, on the other side of the country from where he lived? I was still incredibly relieved that he wasn't also mated to Abby, which honestly hadn't crossed my mind until he mentioned it in the van earlier. The idea of sharing her with anyone made me a little sick. So if it was Liz instead of Abby that was Elijah's mate, I couldn't really complain, but it still confused me too.

Did it have something to do with how much they looked alike or how they shared the same interests? It just seemed like far too big a coincidence that of all the women in the world, it should be someone close to us and so similar in appearance to Abby that people often mistook them for sisters.

"The odds are astronomical," Storm interjected, clearly having been listening to us the whole time. "I'm willing to guess that's not what happened here."

We both turned to look at her, identical looks of confusion on our faces. "What do you mean?" Elijah asked. "Is it some kind of trick?"

Storm's eyes rolled so hard I was afraid she was going to fall over. "No, you idiot. That girl's your mate. But I don't know if she was originally meant to be."

"What do you mean?" I asked, repeating Elijah's question from a few seconds ago.

"Mate bonds aren't static," she explained, looking at both of us like we were ignorant children. "If your fated mate dies, you're given a second one. If you get rejected, you get a second chance. People might not accept or reject their mate, leaving things in limbo. Nothing is as settled as we like to think it is, it can change at any time."

I supposed that was true. I hadn't ever really thought about it in quite those terms before.

"But nobody died here or got rejected," I pointed out before realizing maybe I was assuming too much, so I turned to Elijah. "You didn't reject anyone, did you?"

He shook his head. "No, I never had a mate until I saw her."

"Nothing changed with him," Storm agreed. "But your actions might have changed it."

She was looking right at me, but I pointed to myself anyway just to confirm. "My actions? What did I do?"

"I can't be certain," Storm demurred. "But I've heard stories about twins where one of them met their fated mate first, and the bond between them grew so strong that it severed the bond to the other twin."

Could that really happen? Abby and I did have a very strong bond, not only because we were meant to be together but because we genuinely loved and liked each other as people. She wasn't just my mate, she was my best friend. She was everything to me.

"So if the bond between Elijah and Abby broke before they even me t..." I said out loud, trying to work it out, and Storm helpfully completed the thought.

"Then perhaps it attached itself to someone close to her who was quite similar to her."

So Liz was Elijah's mate *because* she was Abby's friend? She just happened to be in the right place at the right time? This was a lot to take in.

Elijah seemed to think so too as he replied to Storm. "So because he met our intended mate first, I get the knock-off human version?"

How dare he speak that way about my friend, or about any woman in general? "You son of a..." I took a step towards him but Storm quickly put herself between us.

"Calm down, both of you. Elijah, grow the fuck up. Oliver, don't let him rile you. He says shit like that to get attention, I don't think he actually means it."

I wasn't at all convinced of that, but either way, Elijah looked over to where Abby and Liz were, his eyes softening slightly at the sight of his mate. *Does he care for her or not?* I really couldn't tell, and I could only imagine how confused Liz was.

Then Elijah's eyes widened and I realized our mates were coming back over to us. Liz looked a little pissed off, which I was pleased to see, then she and Elijah went off to talk, leaving Abby and I with Storm, and I quickly filled Abby in on what Storm had just suggested.

"So I should have been his mate too?" Abby asked, her own eyes wide as she looked over to where Elijah stood before turning back to Storm.

The older woman shrugged. "It's just a theory, but it makes sense to me."

It made sense to me too. At least there was one thing that did.

"How is Liz feeling?" I asked. I couldn't imagine what was going through her head to learn that she was someone's mate when she only learned about werewolves in general earlier today.

"I think she's a bit overwhelmed," Abby confirmed. "But she's tough. She won't let Elijah walk all over her."

I hoped not. He'd obviously had people giving in to him for far too long. He needed someone who wouldn't take any of his crap.

"So are things always this eventful around the two of you?" Storm asked, giving us both a teasing smirk.

"Us?" I asked in disbelief. "It's only been since we met you that things have gotten crazy."

That made Storm laugh. "If that's true, then maybe we can blame it all on Eli."

That sounded like a good plan to me, and it brought my thoughts back to the reason we were all here in the first place. "So what exactly is this thing we're here to find? Do you know?"

"I've seen the text," she said. "There's supposed to be a key and a 'receptacle', whatever that means. And only a worthy wolf can claim it. It's all very vague, and I suspect it's actually nothing like what Eli thinks it's going to be at all."

A new thought crossed my mind and I frowned as I thought it over. "Abby told me you're supposed to make sure that Eli doesn't get the source, that Adrian hired you to keep Eli from it."

Storm nodded. "That's right."

"Then why are you helping him?" She had arranged his rescue and driven us here. He wouldn't have gotten anywhere near it if it wasn't for her. "Why are you doing any of this?"

Before she could reply, the sound of engines cut through the air, disturbing the still silence of the surroundings. "Oh, fuck," Storm muttered under her breath, and Abby and I looked at each other in alarm.

"What?" Abby asked, getting the word out before I could. "What is it?"

Storm's lips tightened and for the first time since I'd met her, she actually looked nervous. "It's Reeves," she explained as the bikes came into view, a half dozen of them. "Things are about to get a whole lot more complicated."

Chapter Fifteen

~Elijah~

Liz had just opened her mouth to reply to my request for help when I heard the engines, and Julian immediately linked me.

'It smells like Reeves, Alpha. I'd recognize his rotten stench any-where.'

Fuck. That was the last thing we needed right now. How the hell did he find us?

'Get the humans into the van,' I ordered. We didn't need to be worried about protecting them too. The rest of us could shift and take care of ourselves.

"Eli?" Liz was staring at me in concern as I closed the link. "What's wrong with your eyes?"

There wasn't time to explain mind-linking to her right now. "I'm fine, but you need to go get in the van with your friends. It's safer there."

"Safer?" She was looking confused, and I realized that she must not have heard the bikes yet. Human hearing was really poor, yet another weakness.

"Those men who had me before, they're here," I explained as I put my hand on the small of her back to push her towards the van. Once again, the sparks of our bond flamed up, sending a hot wave of desire through me.

The first time we touched, it was like an explosion. I'd heard about the mate sparks, of course, all wolves have, but I never knew it would feel like that. I even wondered if, because she was human, I wouldn't feel them at all, but obviously that wasn't the case. They were there and as strong as I could have possibly imagined. The idea of more of our bodies connecting, every part of them connecting, feeling like that all over, was almost overwhelming.

For the first time, I really let myself imagine being with Liz, not as just a human, but as a person, and I had to admit, the thought wasn't unappealing. Maybe even more than appealing, if I were being honest.

But I still had to focus on the source. I couldn't forget what I was here for and what all this was about, and right now, I needed her help on that. So when I touched her the second time, when I did it on purpose, it was to remind her of what was between us. I thought I was prepared for it that time, but it affected me almost as much as the first. And now, with my hand on her back as we walked briskly towards the open door of the van, I was more than a little tempted to just follow her inside and kick everyone else out and see exactly what it felt like with a few less clothes on.

If our lives weren't in danger, I might not have been able to resist.

But as it was, I helped her up into the van, told the three humans to stay down from the windows, out of sight, then closed the door and locked them all inside. When they were secure, I turned back to the others.

"We can't let Reeves get the source."

"Agreed," Storm said, her expression more grim than I'd ever seen it before. "Have you got a plan?"

Not much of one, unfortunately. "We don't have any weapons, unless you've got some hiding somewhere?" I wasn't surprised when she shook her head. "So we'll have to shift. I can communicate with my pack members, so wait for my signal."

Everyone agreed and we all stripped down and shifted, running off into the tall grass to hide just as Reeves and his men pulled up.

My heart pounded painfully as I watched them approach the van containing my fragile mate. Not quite as fragile as I had first thought, I had to admit, smiling a little at the memory of how she'd just stood up to me and demanded answers. But physically, she was still more than vulnerable.

I was worried they were going to try to break into the van, but instead they held up some kind of scanner to it, and then Reeves motioned at them to keep going.

They must have been scanning for werewolves, I figured, though what kind of device could do that, I didn't know. Since they hadn't found any, they were content to leave the humans inside alone, which was just what I'd been hoping for.

At least Liz is safe. Now I just needed to worry about the source.

"I'm guessing you haven't found it yet, Eli," Reeves called out to me though he couldn't see my location. He knew we wouldn't have gone far. "Or else you wouldn't all be cowering from us."

A rumbling growl started in my chest but I forced myself to silence it. I couldn't give away my position.

"You're not the only one who knows how to use a tracker," he smirked, clearly trying to get a rise out of me. "We stuck one on you as soon as we took you. You were never going to get away from us."

Fuck. Exactly how many trackers were on me?

"And if you want to keep hiding, that's fine. We've got everything we need to find the source right here."

As he spoke, two of the men with him had set up some kind of larger scanning device and were starting to walk around the area.

'What the fuck is that?' I asked Julian and Matthew by mind-link.

Matthew was the most up to date on technology, so he offered his opinion. 'Some kind of radar or electromagnetic scanner, Alpha. It'll show them anything buried in the area.'

I hadn't ever bothered looking into anything like that since I was sure I could solve the clue once we were here. But Reeves obviously wasn't interested in following the path that the clue mentioned. He was going to bulldoze his way in and find it himself.

'What do we do?' Julian asked, and for once, I wasn't entirely sure. There were about the same number of them as there were of us. They had guns, but we had speed and strength. There was a good chance we could take them out, but when was the best time?

Most importantly, they had the scanner, and as I watched the men work, a new thought came to me. 'We wait,' I answered Julian. 'We let him lead us to it, and then once he's found it, we go in.'

My men agreed and we all stayed where we were. I could just see Oliver's wolf in the distance, his eyes on me, waiting for me to make a move. I tried to nod at him to let him know I had a plan, but I wasn't sure he could see me.

My eyes moved back to the van as I followed my earlier train of thought to its logical conclusion. *If Reeves leads me to the source, maybe I won't need Liz's help after all.*

I tried to tell myself that was a good thing, that I didn't need to rely on anyone else, but the truth was that part of me had wanted us to do this together. It might have been a good thing for us if she felt invested in the source too. After all, if she was going to be part of my life...

My thoughts trailed off as I realized what I was thinking. I was seriously considering accepting her. I wasn't sure exactly when that started happening but the idea of her as my mate no longer disappointed me. In fact, there was even part of me that found the notion a little bit exciting.

I hardly knew my own mind anymore.

Concentrate, I reprimanded myself. There would be time for worrying about all of that later. And sure enough, no sooner had I forced myself to focus, then the men holding the scanning device shouted over to Reeves and he hurried over to join them. They must have found something.

That was our cue. 'Now!' I ordered my men through our link, and we shot off through the grass with Abby, Oliver and Storm not far behind.

Gunshots rang out along with the shouts of the men as they tried to cover each other, but I kept my eyes firmly on Reeves. He had pulled out his own gun, though even from this distance I could tell it wasn't a regular one. What it was loaded with, though, I couldn't begin to guess.

Just as he took aim at me, I dodged left, tackling one of the men holding the scanning device instead. We rolled around on the ground as he tried to shake me off, but I clung on, digging my claws into his chest. As long as I was attached to him, Reeves wouldn't shoot.

Or so I thought. A loud shot rang out, from very close range, and the man on top of me went rigid before collapsing on top of me, his body literally falling to pieces.

What the fuck? Did he really just shoot his own man? And what did he shoot him with to make him literally fall apart like that?

As I scrambled out from beneath the remains of the man's body, Darryn Reeves was standing over with me with his weapon pointed right at me.

"Shift now," he ordered. "Or my face is going to be the last thing you ever see."

Not having much choice, I assumed my human form again. 'Report,' I linked with Julian. I wanted to know what else was happening, but I didn't dare take my eyes off Reeves.

'We got three of them,' he replied. 'Plus the one Reeves killed. That just leaves him and one other.'

Those were much better odds, but Reeves knew how to play them. "If any of them makes a move against me, you die. You know I'll do it. Call them off."

Obviously if he had no problem shooting someone he knew, he could easily do the same to me, so I called out the instruction to the others, telling them to stand down.

"Get one of your mutts over here to dig," he instructed, pointing at the ground beneath us. "They'll be faster than my shovels."

I scowled at him, but the truth was, he was right. I linked Matthew to come over and he began to dig at the spot Reeves pointed out while Reeves continued to point his weapon at me.

"What's this really all about for you?" I couldn't help asking. After the conversation Storm and I had on the plane and the short talk Reeves and I had when he was holding me, I was more curious than ever about his motivation.

He must have thought he was close to getting what he wanted because this time he actually answered me. "You bastards killed my sister."

Ah. A dead family member. Perhaps I should have guessed, it was a common enough backstory for a villain, and I had no doubt that Reeves was the villain in this scenario.

"So some random wolf attacked your sister and you've decided to take down all werewolves?" I asked. "Seems like a bit of an overreaction."

Reeves narrowed his eyes at me. "Not just some random wolf. She died because of her mate."

Huh. That was more interesting. His sister must have been human, so why would she have a mate? It wasn't that it was impossible, of course, since my own human mate was here with us, but it still wasn't common.

As if he'd heard my unspoken question, Reeves kept talking as Matthew continued to dig, the hole getting deeper and wider by the second. "He was a stuck-up Alpha asshole just like you. Thought he was better than everyone else and definitely thought he was too good for a human mate. He told her all about wolves and the mate bond and he slept with her just for good measure, then he rejected her and broke her heart."

An uncomfortable feeling washed over me as my eyes flitted quickly to the van concealing my own human mate inside it. The idea of her heart breaking over me made me feel sick. "It shouldn't have bothered her that much," I told Reeves. "Humans ditch their partners all the time, and it's not like she would have felt the bond that deeply."

"You don't fucking know what she felt," Reeves contradicted me angrily. "She was his mate, she was tied to him, and when he rejected her, it tore her apart."

Was that really true? I didn't think it was possible for humans to feel it that strongly.

"She went crazy," he continued. "She was so desperate to see him again and try to get their bond back that she tried to track him down on his pack land, but when he was told that she was there, he told his wolves she was an intruder and ordered them to kill her."

Damn. That was cold, and that was coming from me. No matter what, I could never hurt Liz like that.

"Before all this happened, she'd been dating my best friend," he told me, his story still not finished, apparently. "He went to try to avenge her, and guess what happened."

I wasn't sure if that was a rhetorical question, but I answered it anyway. "They killed him too."

"They killed him too," he repeated in agreement. "That's when I learned all about you sick fuckers and the rules you live by. I took out that Alpha and his pack, but it's not enough. I want you all wiped off the face of the earth."

I had to respect his conviction even if I obviously didn't agree with it. He was a man who wouldn't stop until he got what he wanted. Just like me.

It was too bad only one of us was going to get it.

'Alpha.' Matthew's voice spoke up in my head and I looked over to see his wolf in a decent-sized hole now, where he had uncovered the top of a small, wooden box.

Was that it? It was smaller than I would have imagined, but I knew that power came in all shapes and sizes. Once again, my eyes went, almost against my will, to the van where my mate was concealed, but this time I froze when they reached it.

The door was open and I couldn't see anyone inside. Where the fuck had they gone?

~Liz~

My heart was racing as Eli closed the van door behind me. He'd told us to stay down so we all obeyed as we heard the motorcycles approaching.

"What's going on?" Whitney asked, and I could hear the fear in her voice, echoing the way I was feeling too. But my fear wasn't for myself, it was for Eli who was still outside.

Those men are here for him, aren't they? They had wanted him before and they must have followed him here somehow. So why shouldn't he be the one to hide?

I remembered him saying back when we stopped before, when Oliver told him they were twins, that he wasn't going to worry about taking care of us if something happened. But now that we were in that situation, he hadn't hesitated. He made sure Whitney and Jack and I were safe while he stayed out there and protected us.

What was I supposed to make of him? He seemed to say one thing and do another, to be drawn to me one second and then denying me the next. Which one was the real him?

"I don't really know what's happening," I answered Whitney honestly. "But Eli's in trouble."

They both gave me a funny look. "Eli?" Jack repeated. "You guys are on a first name basis?"

I didn't really know how to explain to them what was going on between us and I suddenly had new sympathy for how Abby must have felt trying to explain things to me. "It's kind of a long story," I said weakly. "But we need to help them."

"How are we supposed to help?" Whitney whispered. The bikes had stopped just outside the van and we could hear the voices of the men now, so I held my finger up to my lips to stop our conversation, and they both nodded at me in silent agreement.

"Check the van," a man's voice said just outside the window, making me jump. For a second I thought they were going to break in, and I looked around desperately, trying to find a weapon, but I couldn't see anything that would be useful. Then the voice spoke again. "Use the wolf detector."

Wolf detector? What was that?

I held my breath as a shadow crossed the van and a beeping noise, almost like the sound of a metal detector, sounded just outside.

"All human," another voice replied.

"Leave it, then," the first man said and they moved away, the three of us inside the van breathing a heavy sigh of relief.

We stayed where we were for a few more minutes, the voices of the men outside getting further and further away until finally I couldn't take the suspense anymore. Getting to my knees, I tentatively peered over the bottom edge of the van window.

As the volume of their voices suggested, the men had moved further away. A couple of them were holding onto some kind of equipment that they moved across the ground while others were looking over the territory, guns in their hands.

Fuck, this was serious. Whoever these guys were, they weren't messing around. There was no sign of Eli, or Oliver and Abby, or any of the others.

I whispered what I could see back down to Whitney and Jack as I continued to watch. No one seemed to be paying any attention to us anymore, which was one good thing at least. Then there was a shout, the men with the equipment seeming to get excited about something, and immediately all hell broke loose.

Wolves came running out of the grass and the men were shooting at them and my heart was in my throat as I watched it all unfold, helpless to do anything to help my friends. Whitney and Jack both got up too, just as desperate to see what was going on as I was, even though it probably would have been safer for all of us to stay down.

Then someone knocked on the van window behind us, and all three of us screamed. Thankfully the sounds of the gunshots and fighting outside meant that no one heard us, but it didn't stop the painful pounding of my heart as we spun around to see what was going on.

Jack immediately jumped up to shield Whitney and me, but I peered around him to see who was there. I don't know who or what I was expecting, but it certainly wasn't an older version of Oliver and Eli.

What the hell?

"Who is that?" Whitney whimpered from beside me, and once again, I had no answer for her.

"Come out of the van," the man said to us through the window. "I'm on your side. Hurry, we can help the others."

Whitney, Jack and I all looked at each other nervously. Eli had said to stay inside and it definitely seemed safer here than it did out there with bullets flying around, but I did want to help. And this man must be related to Oliver and Eli, he looked far too much like them not to be. Where on earth had he come from?

Making up my mind, I reached for the door handle, ignoring Whitney's yelp of disapproval. I might not know what I was doing, but I did know that I couldn't just sit back if there was something I could do to help.

I was worried the door opening would draw attention to us, but everyone was so caught up in their own fight, wolves against humans, that no one noticed. The three of us slunk out of the van and circled around the other side as quickly as we could.

The man waiting on the other side gave us all an appraising look as we approached. Closer up, he looked even more like Eli, and I was almost certain I knew who he must be.

"Are you Oliver and Elijah's father?"

He smiled, but it didn't reach his eyes. "It's that obvious, is it?"

I simply nodded, trying to take this all in. If I was going to have any kind of relationship with Eli, I supposed I would get to know his father eventually, I just never expected it to be under these circumstances. And especially not when he was half naked, which I couldn't help noticing.

He was in excellent shape for a man of his age, as the muscles on his chest, arms and stomach clearly demonstrated. Thankfully, he was wearing pants, though I noticed there were several other pieces of clothing on the ground around us. They must belong to the other werewolves, I figured, to Eli and his friends and the others too. Did that mean the pants his dad was wearing weren't his? Did he come here as a wolf?

I had so many questions but this didn't seem like the time, not when there was still fighting going on just on the other side of this van.

He seemed to recognize the urgency as well since he didn't waste any time on introductions. Instead, he held out his hand to us, displaying a half dozen small blister packs, each with some sort of liquid inside.

"This will take care of those men," he explained. "Whatever you do, don't touch the liquid yourself. Press the pack against their skin and pop it open. When it makes contact, it will knock them out."

Seriously? I had never heard of anything like that, and I read a lot.

My disbelief must have shown in my face because he almost laughed as he looked at me. "Trust me on this. They'll work."

"Why can't you do it?" He was obviously stronger than Whitney and me, at least, and probably faster too.

"They can't know I'm here," he replied vaguely. "Not yet, at least."

That really didn't explain anything. I exchanged glances with Whitney and Jack and they looked just as unsure as I did. But what choice did we really have? If there was a chance it would help, I had to try.

The sounds of fighting and gunshots had died out on the other side of the van now, so with all the determination I could summon, I grabbed two of the packs from the man's hand and Whitney and Jack quickly followed suit.

"Remember, don't get it on yourselves," he repeated. "Good luck."

Giving him a nod of thanks, I turned back and peeked around the van to see what was going on. The fighting had indeed stopped. There were a few bodies lying on the ground, and panic rose inside me at the thought that one of them might be Eli, Oliver or Abby, but I quickly realized the bodies were fully clothed, which must mean they were the human men. Were they actually dead? I had never seen a dead body before.

For a moment I was tempted to change my mind and just get back in the van, but when I went to look back at Eli's father, he was gone. The pants he had been wearing were on the ground, and I could just make out the grass moving in the distance, no doubt the result of a wolf running through it.

This day could not get any stranger. If it weren't for the strange liquid in my hand, I would have thought I'd dreamt that whole encounter.

The three of us all took one last look around the van. There were still a few wolf-people, but some of them had changed back into humans too. Two of them were standing next to one of the human men. They must be Eli's friends, I figured, though they had their backs to us.

They were also completely naked.

And so was Eli.

I spotted him now, in the distance, being held at gunpoint by one of the men. Why wasn't anyone helping him? Anger and desperation flowed through me and I turned to my friends firmly.

"You take that one," I told them, pointing to the man closer to us. "Once he's out of the way, I'll go for the other one."

To my surprise, they didn't argue with me. I was prepared to fight, nobody had ever just obeyed me like that before. Something in my tone must have told them I meant business.

I watched as they crept over towards the men, careful to stay out of their line of vision. The wolves spotted them, but they made no move, obviously recognizing that we were trying to help. Whitney managed to get almost right up behind the human man before anyone noticed they were there, and Jack quickly grabbed him to hold him still while she pressed the pack in her hand against the back of his neck.

I still wasn't sure if I expected it to work, but to my amazement, the man dropped to the ground almost instantly and completely silently.

Eli and the man holding the gun on him didn't seem to have noticed anything. They were still talking between themselves intensely.

It was up to me now.

I had no training for this sort of thing, but I had my friends on my side and my mate to save, so with one last deep breath, I made my way over towards them as quietly and calmly as I could.

~**Abby**~

My breath caught in my throat as I watched Liz creep closer to the man I figured must be Darryn Reeves. We'd never been formally introduced, but as he was the last one standing amongst the team and the one who had been speaking to Elijah earlier, I had to guess he was the ringleader.

I had no idea what kind of weapon he was holding or what Whitney and Jack had just done to that man to get him to collapse like that. I would have asked them but I was still in my wolf form. I tried linking with Oliver to ask him but he didn't know any more than I did.

It felt like we only understood half of what was happening, but there was one thing I did know for certain: Liz was risking her life to try and save Elijah.

He damn well better appreciate that.

There was nothing we could do now but watch and hope that she could get to Reeves without being noticed. Reeves and Elijah were talking, Reeves' attention completely wrapped up in whatever they were discussing, but then suddenly Elijah turned to look at the hole where one of his wolves had been digging and then he glanced over at the van. His eyes widened as he saw the open door, and of course Reeves didn't miss his reaction. He spun around when Liz was only a few steps from him.

"Owooo!" I tried to call her name to warn her, but of course it only came out as a howl. I had forgotten I was still a wolf.

Oliver reacted faster than me, starting to run towards them to protect our friend, but Reeves was quicker than all of us. In a matter of seconds he had Liz securely pinned against him, her back to his chest, his arm wrapped tightly around her body so she couldn't move and his customized gun pressed against her temple.

"All of you stay back!" he barked out, looking around at the whole group, taking in, perhaps for the first time, that he was on his own now. "Another step and she dies."

Oliver's wolf froze and so did everyone else. The frustration in Reeves' face was clear as his eyes scanned the scene, trying to decide what to do next, and worry for my friend filled me as his finger twitched nervously on the trigger.

"Calm down," Eli said to him, his voice carrying across to us easily over the open space. "Don't hurt her."

Though his words were calm enough, there was a tremble in his voice that I didn't miss, and apparently Reeves didn't either.

"What is she to you?" Reeves demanded, clearly looking for an angle he could use against Eli.

"She's human," Eli replied, not entirely answering the question, thankfully. I didn't want to think about the danger Liz would be in if it was known she was Elijah's mate. "She's got nothing to do with this."

He said that, but even from a distance, I could see his jaw clenching, the muscles in his cheek twitching as he watched his mate with a gun to her head. He was panicking inside, no question.

"She's just like your sister," Eli added, which meant nothing to me, but apparently it did to the man with the gun. "She got dragged into this against her will."

Reeves grimaced a little, the words obviously affecting him, but then he seemed to dismiss them, tightening his grip on Liz even more. "She won't get hurt if you all do exactly what I say."

My eyes went to my friend's face. She was doing her best to stay calm and to keep still, but I could only imagine how she was feeling. What could I do to help? I looked over at Oliver but he was looking equally lost. We were simply spectators here, as frustrating as that was.

"Liz, look at me," Eli addressed her directly. "He's not going to hurt you. We'll work this out."

She nodded, almost imperceptibly, but enough that I saw it and I was sure Eli did too. It seemed to relax him a tiny bit at least.

"Alpha." The voice came from inside the hole, and though I couldn't see down it, the fact that he was speaking told me the wolf who had been digging had shifted back to his human form. "The box?"

Eli swallowed hard, looking down into the hole and then back at Reeves. "That might be it, but we won't know for sure until we open it. What's your plan here?"

"It's simple," Reeves snarled back at him. "You want the girl? Then give me the source."

~Elijah~

This was all my fault. I wasn't sure what Liz had been trying to do, but if I hadn't given away the fact that something was wrong when I looked at the van, she might have been able to do it. Now she was being held at gunpoint and the sight of Reeves holding her, never mind having a gun against her head, was driving me insane.

She had tried to rescue me, again. First she helped to break me out earlier, and now this. Seemingly unaware of her own weakness, her own *humanness*, she put herself directly in harm's way for me more than once, for a man who had tried his best to deny our bond since the moment we met.

What would make her do that? It was a kind of selflessness I'd never come across before.

Except maybe in my mother's letter.

Seeing Liz's efforts suddenly put my mother's actions in a new light and it was as though a shadowy part of my life had finally been illuminated. My mother had suffered from being away from me, or so her letter suggested at least, but she did it anyway. She did it because she thought it was best for both Oliver and me, not because she didn't want me or because it was easier for her, as I'd always been told.

She cared for me, and it seemed that, for some reason I didn't fully understand, Liz did too.

Was that what family was truly meant to do? Was that what having a mate would mean?

It was a glimpse of a world I had never truly believed in before. I thought that everyone was just out for themselves, like my father and like me. That was why I needed the source, because no one had my back. I had to protect myself and this was the best way I had come up with to do that. Once I had the source, I would never have to feel vulnerable and abandoned again.

But my mother's letter had shown me that view was flawed. I hadn't been abandoned, at least not like I originally thought, and there were people who had my back. Liz had just proven that, and in their own way, so had Oliver and Abby. They didn't have to be here at all, and yet they were, not for the source, but for me.

And if I was wrong about those things, then maybe I was wrong about other things too.

Maybe I had it all wrong.

Those were the thoughts flying through my head as Reeves offered me the trade: Liz for the source.

Suddenly I knew what I had to do.

If the source was in that box, I couldn't let Reeves have it. Trading it for Liz's safety would be selfish of me, just as selfish as Reeves' own motives were. He intended to destroy as many wolves as possible with it to avenge his sister. Thousands of lives measured against one. If I chose Liz over the source, I would be no better than him, and I wouldn't be the mate that she deserved.

She had shown me how selfless she was, and I needed to be the same.

No matter what, I couldn't let it fall into his hands.

I only prayed that Liz would understand. I had to do this, not for myself, but for her. *For us.*

"Matthew," I called out to my warrior who was still in the hole, holding the box. "Give me the box."

~Oliver~

"Are you fucking kidding me?"

The words were out of my mouth as soon as I shifted, getting back to my human form so that I could have a word with my brother. A few choice words, actually.

He couldn't seriously be choosing that damn box over his mate?! What the hell was wrong with him?

I couldn't remember ever being so completely mystified by anyone's actions before. There were people whose actions I despised - Abby's ex Liam, for example, or Jared, the obsessed maniac who nearly killed her - but at least I understood their motivations. Elijah was a complete enigma to me.

"Stay back," Reeves snapped at me, his eyes widening a little when he saw who I was. He hadn't seen me in my human form yet today. He knew I existed, of course, after our meeting in San Francisco, but he obviously hadn't expected to find me here today, and he looked back and forth between Elijah and me as if he was seeing double.

I couldn't really blame him. We looked even more alike without our clothes to tell us apart.

In any case, I was far more of a threat to him in my wolf form than I was now, and he seemed to remember that as he turned his attention back to Elijah. "Don't do anything stupid, Eli. Do you really want this girl's blood on your hands?"

Eli didn't even flinch at the threat to his mate. "I'm not making any choice just yet. I just want to open the box," he told Reeves. "We don't even know for sure what's inside, it might not be the source at all. Maybe some kids buried a time capsule out here twenty years ago."

If that were true, why wouldn't he just give it to him? It was obviously a bluff and Reeves saw through it too.

"Then I'll open it and find that out myself," he countered. "Give it to me."

He gripped Liz tighter and she inhaled sharply, either in surprise or pain, I wasn't sure which. The sound made Eli's fists clench but he still didn't give in.

"We'll let someone neutral open it then," Eli suggested. "Like those humans."

He pointed over at Whitney and Jack, both of whom looked startled to be included in this.

"They came here with you," Reeves pointed out. "They're hardly neutral."

"I've never met them before today," Eli told him. "And they know nothing about the source."

I couldn't believe they were discussing this so calmly after Reeves had just threatened to kill Liz. How was Eli not losing his mind?

Reeves looked over at me as if looking for confirmation of what Eli had just said, so I gritted my teeth and agreed. "He's right. They're friends of mine, they don't know him or anything about any of this." Before I let them anywhere near that thing though, I wanted more information, so I turned to Eli. "Is it dangerous?"

He just smirked at me. "I thought you didn't believe in the source. If it's got no power, then there's no danger."

Every word out of his mouth grated on my nerves. I couldn't wait to punch him right in his smug face when all this was over and we were all safe. After I let Liz have a go, of course.

"We can do it," Whitney piped up, taking everyone by surprise. "If it will help Liz, we can do it."

Well, at least someone was thinking of Liz, even if it wasn't the one person who should be.

"Put it on the ground between us," Reeves instructed, and the man in the hole hopped out, placing the box where he was asked to, before Reeves turned back to Whitney and Jack, speaking to them sharply. "You two, come on."

My friends walked forward hand-in-hand. I tried to catch their eye to let them know I was there to protect them, but they both avoided looking at me, probably not least because I was naked. This whole thing had to be incredibly strange to them. How were we going to go back to just being friends after all of this? How could they ever look at me or Abby the same way? When I asked them to help this morning, I had no idea it was all going to get so out of hand.

~Liz~

I was doing my best to remain calm but inside I was fuming.

I still didn't know exactly what Eli was looking for but one thing was clear: it was more important to him than I was.

He was content to let this man kill me rather than give him whatever was in that box.

That probably should have terrified me, but the truth was, I was too angry to be afraid. I wanted to survive right now simply so I could have the pleasure of telling Eli right to his stupid, handsome face exactly what I thought of him. He thought I wasn't good enough for him? That I was expendable? Well, he was the one who wasn't good enough for me.

Liam had made me feel worthless and I wasn't going to let any man do that ever again, mate or not. Any daydreams, or real dreams for that matter, that I might have had about us being together were now a thing of the past.

I was still going to save his stupid life if I had half a chance, but that was the last thing I was going to do for him. The pack his father had given me was still firmly clenched in my fist, where I prayed it wouldn't break before I had a chance to use it. If the man holding me loosened his grip at all, I would try to use it on him just like Whitney and Jack had done to the other guy. So far, his grip was like a vise though. I couldn't move an inch, much less get my hands free.

But now the man's attention was focused entirely on the box on the ground, as was Eli's, and I was waiting for any sign of distraction. If I was going to get a chance, this seemed like the time it would happen. I had to be ready to act if there was the slightest opportunity.

Whitney knelt down next to the box as Jack put a supportive hand on her shoulder. He looked up at me with a nod, as if to say they weren't going to let me down, and I appreciated it more than I could say. I knew they had my back, and so did Abby and Oliver, though I still wasn't sure exactly which wolf was Abby. And Oliver, well, I was almost getting used to the fact that he was standing there naked, as was Eli. Neither of them seemed to think it was odd, and I supposed in the grand scheme of things, it was hardly the most important thing going on right now. But it was still weird, I couldn't entirely lose sight of that.

The box was dirty, obviously, from having been in the ground, but as Whitney brushed her hand across the top of it, I could see that it was sturdy and made from a beautiful wood. This wasn't something hastily constructed, it was a quality item. It seemed to have some kind of latch on the front, which she turned and then slowly opened the lid.

Everyone leaned forward, trying to get a look at what was inside, but from where we were standing, the lid blocked the way. Whitney reached her hand out as if she was going to pick something up from inside, but Eli quickly called out to her in a sharp tone.

"Don't touch it. Just turn the box around so we can see."

Her hand froze in mid-motion and she nodded before doing as he asked, turning the box so it was facing us.

Inside was a golden locket on a thick gold chain, with a large pendant in the shape of a crescent moon.

My eyes went to Eli, who was staring at it as though it held the answer to all of life's mysteries.

Was that it? Some gold? Did he want it just because it was valuable?

Was my life really worth less than a piece of jewellery?

"The source must be inside the locket," the man holding me said, his voice as full of awe as Eli's face was. "It needs to be opened."

"A key and a receptacle..." Eli muttered, still staring at it in almost a trance-like state until he shook himself and looked back at Whitney. "We need the key. Is there anything else in the box? Anything at all?"

She turned the box back towards herself. "Can I pick it up to look beneath it?"

Eli and the man holding me looked at each other, apparently both considering their options. "It must not have any power until it's open," Eli suggested. "I don't see the harm."

"Fine," the man agreed. "But keep it where we can see it."

Whitney obeyed as best she could, turning the box so both men could see as she gingerly picked up the locket and examined the rest of the box. "There's no key," she announced, turning the locket over in her hand. "And no keyhole in the locket anyway."

"There has to be," the man holding me muttered, leaning closer to her. "Let me see..."

His grip on me loosened just enough to move my hands together, and that was what I'd been waiting for. I grabbed the pack with both hands, pressed it against his arm, and broke it open.

"What the...?" he growled, jerking away from me, but then his grip loosened further as whatever the liquid was began to take effect. As he pulled away, his arm brushed against my hand and I felt a cool, tingling sensation where the liquid droplets seeped into my skin.

The man collapsed behind me, and the world began to grow dark.

"Liz?"

The last thing I heard before falling to the ground was Eli calling my name.

Chapter Sixteen

~Elijah~

My whole body went cold as Liz fell to the ground, only seconds after Reeves had toppled over behind her.

What the fuck just happened?

One second they were both fine and the next they were... I didn't even know what they were, and that fucking terrified me. I didn't see any blood but I couldn't understand what only happened to them and not to anyone else.

For a moment I was frozen to the spot, unable to move as the others all shouted her name and ran towards her. I tried to move my body but it felt weighted down even as my wolf howled at me to do something. Finally I began to move towards her, my heart pounding in fear, but in the next moment, Oliver was blocking my path.

"Stay out of the way," he ordered angrily. "We'll take care of her. You've done enough."

Sure enough, I could see over his shoulder that the other humans were already next to her, along with a silver wolf that shifted into Abby as she approached. There was a stricken look on her face as she looked at Liz's limp body that I was sure mirrored my own. As I watched, Abby lifted Liz's head onto her lap while the other human woman checked her pulse. I searched their faces for signs of panic or grief, but they just seemed concerned, not devastated.

Liz must still be alive then, at least.

Would I feel it if she weren't? I hadn't marked her, of course, but I could have sworn when she was looking at me a moment ago, I could feel her anger burning inside me.

Anger that was directed at me.

She obviously thought I had chosen the source over her and the idea that she might die thinking that nearly broke me.

"She's my mate," I growled at my brother, trying to push past him but he wouldn't budge. He tried to push me back but he couldn't move me either. We were at a stalemate, equally as strong as each other.

"You could have fooled me," he snarled back. His eyes were filled with anger and for a moment, he looked just like our dad. "If you'd just given him the damn box, she'd be fine."

"I couldn't do that," I argued. "You don't understand."

"You're right about that," he agreed, though I could tell he didn't mean it the same way I did. "I don't understand anything about you."

"Oliver," Abby called out. "Come take a look at this."

He turned and I took the opportunity afforded by his distraction to go around him. In a matter of seconds, I was kneeling down on the ground next to Liz. Her glasses had slipped down her face as she fell, so I gently pulled them off.

Without them, she looked younger, even more innocent somehow. The need to protect her was almost overwhelming.

"What's wrong with her?" I asked the other human woman who was still holding onto her wrist, keeping watch on her pulse. "Is she going to be alright?"

"She's breathing," she confirmed, and my own lungs filled with oxygen as I inhaled in relief. "But unconscious, obviously."

Meanwhile Oliver had kneeled down across from me, on the other side of Liz and next to his mate to see what she had called him over for. "She dropped this," Abby said, pointing to something shiny on the ground. Oliver reached for it, but the human man quickly reached out to stop him.

"It's one of the packs the man gave us," he said, addressing Abby and Oliver. "He said not to get any of the liquid on ourselves but Liz must have touched it."

It felt like they were speaking in code, and I didn't have the first idea what any of that meant. "Pack? What pack?" I asked.

The guy who'd been talking looked over at me suspiciously, like he wasn't sure if he should answer me, but when Oliver nodded at him, he complied. "I don't know what was in it, but he told us it would knock anyone out if it came into contact with their skin."

I still didn't know who 'he' was, but I looked over at Reeves now. "So he's just unconscious too?"

Oliver shuffled over and checked his pulse and nodded in confirmation to me. "He's alive. I have no idea how long they'll be out for though. I've never heard of a liquid that can do that, and I'm a chemist. If it exists, I should know about it."

A chemist? *Seriously?* Just like my dad?

I had questions about that, but this wasn't the time. We didn't know how long Reeves would be out for so we had to make use of whatever time we had. First things first, I picked up the gun he'd been using and walked over to the river's edge, tossing it as far as I could into the deep water. At least now if he somehow got away from us, he couldn't blow us to pieces. That was one consolation.

Then I went back to the group, which now included Julian, Matthew and Storm who had all shifted back too. Storm was handing everyone's clothes back to them, so I quickly redressed while the others did the same.

"Find something you can tie him up with," I instructed my pack members, gesturing to Reeves' unconscious body. Liz's friends were still down on the ground with her, and as much as I wanted to push them away and take care of her myself, there were still some other things I needed to do first.

I needed to secure the source.

Taking one last look at Liz, I forced myself to turn away.

"I can't believe she got the drop on him," Storm said as she came up to me, glancing back at both Liz and Reeves. "Pretty impressive for a human. I thought you were a goner for sure."

I didn't miss what she was trying to do, drawing my attention to Liz's bravery, but it was hardly necessary. I knew how impressive it was without her help, and besides, what was going on between me and Liz was none of her business.

"He gave me his reasons for wanting the source," I told her, changing the subject to Reeves instead.

She was interested in that, as I knew she would be. "What were they?"

I didn't have time to go into it all, so I gave her the highlights version. "His sister got screwed over by some asshole Alpha who rejected her because she was human, then had her killed. Reeves claimed he took out the whole pack in revenge and then vowed vengeance on our whole species."

To my surprise, instead of smirking as I'd expected her to, as was typical for her, Storm's face went pale. It made her red hair look even redder. "Did he say where this was? Or when?"

What did that matter? I didn't understand her reaction. "It didn't come up."

She opened her mouth to ask more questions but I'd wasted enough time. As Julian and Matthew returned with seatbelts they'd ripped out of the van to tie up Reeves and his one remaining henchman, who was also still unconscious, I picked up the box with the locket.

It wasn't exactly what I was expecting, but then no one had ever known exactly what the source was. I supposed a locket was just as likely as anything else.

As I picked it up and held it in my hand, a strange chill passed through me, and I noticed Oliver shiver at the same time.

That was strange.

He seemed to think so too because he came to stand next to me now, looking at the locket in my hand. "You should destroy that damned thing," he said. "It's a menace. Look how many people have died here today because of it."

He gestured at Reeves' men scattered in the grass around us.

"And your mate could have been next, not that you would have cared."

I growled at him. He had no idea what I cared about. "Stay out of this. It doesn't have anything to do with you."

"Actually, it has everything to do with him. With the both of you."

The words came from a new voice, and all of us, wolves and humans alike, turned to find its source. My mouth dropped open when I saw who it belonged to: pretty much the last person I would have ever expected to see here.

"Dad?"

~Oliver~

Elijah looked just as shocked as I felt to see Alpha Adrian coming towards us. Where the hell had he come from? He was naked, so clearly he had just shifted, but how long had he been here?

For a moment I wondered what Whitney and Jack would think of this new development, my naked biological father turning up out of the blue, but then I realized it was pointless worrying about that. We were so far past normal by now, another layer of insanity couldn't do much harm.

The wind was blowing in his direction, carrying his scent away from us, so even as he got closer, I still couldn't smell him very well. That explained how he was able to sneak up on us but it still didn't address why he was here at all.

Adrian's eyes were fixed on the locket in Eli's hands as he drew closer. "That's it, isn't it?" he asked, his voice full of the same wonder that Eli's held whenever he spoke of that damned 'source'. "You can feel it."

That last statement wasn't a question. He seemed certain that it was true, and he wasn't wrong.

When Eli picked it up, an unusual sensation passed through me, a shiver down my spine that had no cause I could think of, unless there was some truth to the legend after all. Eli seemed to be affected the same way.

Was this golden locket really a source of power? What did all of this mean?

"This is the source," Eli confirmed, his voice even colder than usual as he looked at his father. In contrast to his tone, his face held a hint of triumph. "You thought I was wasting my time all these years but you were wrong. It does exist, and now it's mine."

I don't know what I expected Adrian's reaction to be but I certainly didn't expect him to laugh. And yet, that's what he did, causing Eli to frown, the smug look on his face vanishing completely. Obviously he hadn't been expecting that either.

"Of course it's real," Adrian told him. "Why else would I have set you down this path in the first place?"

Eli's frown melted into confusion and caution. "Set me down this path? What the fuck are you talking about? You never wanted me to look for it."

Adrian gave his son a look of derision. "After all this time, you still believe that? Do you really think it was just a coincidence that I took you to that conference where you first heard about it?"

I didn't know what conference he was talking about, but Elijah obviously did. His face grew slightly paler.

"You planned this?" he asked, uncertainty in his voice. "But... you wouldn't give me the money I asked for. You fought me over it. You lost the pack."

That part of the story I did know, and I was just as curious what Adrian's answer would be as Eli was.

"I had to let you believe I didn't want you to go after it," he explained, his eyes gleaming coldly. "You've always been so stubborn, Eli. If I told you I wanted you to find it, you would have run in the opposite direction."

I could hardly believe what I was hearing, though I was beginning to understand where Elijah got his perverse logic from. "You manipulated your own son like that?" I asked incredulously. "Why?"

"Manipulating people is what he does best."

Storm's contribution to the conversation made both Eli and I turn to her in surprise. I had never seen her looking so hard and cold. Usually she had a slightly bemused air about her, as if she found everything a bit funny, but there was no humour in her face now as she glared at Alpha Adrian.

"Stephanie," he greeted her, seeming to find her anger amusing. "Long time no see."

Stephanie? Eli and I exchanged confused glances.

"It's Storm," she growled at him. "And I've done everything you asked. It's time to hold up your end of the bargain."

His end of the bargain? Wasn't he simply paying her? That's what I had assumed, but as I thought back to her elaborate house in San Francisco, I realized that didn't really make much sense. Why would she need to work for Adrian if she was so well off? There was obviously more going on between them than I'd realized.

And more than Elijah had realized too. He looked back and forth between the two of them, his scowl growing deeper all the time. Apparently he liked being kept in the dark about things as much as I did.

"How do you two know each other?" he demanded.

"She could have been your stepmother," Adrian answered him, a smirk still on his face. "If I'd accepted her."

Eli's eyes went wide in surprise, and I was sure mine looked just the same. "She was your mate?" I asked. Had he rejected her? It sounded that way, but then why was she helping him?

"She *is* my mate," Adrian corrected me. "My second chance mate. We've just never made it official."

"And we never will," Storm snapped at him before turning to Eli and I to fill us in. "He refused to accept me but he wouldn't reject me either. I've been stuck in limbo for the past eight years but he promised me if I kept you safe until he got to the source that he would finally release me."

Her words earlier came flooding back to me, suddenly making a lot more sense. *Mate bonds aren't static. Nothing is settled, it can change at any time.*

Had he really kept her hanging on like that? For what?

Okay, maybe I couldn't really talk since I had also rcfused Abby's attempted rejection when we first met but I would have accepted it eventually if she really meant it. How selfish did a person have to be to keep their mate dangling on the hook for so long?

And if Storm was Adrian's second chance mate, what happened to his first one?

I still had a lot of questions.

"So it's time now to keep your word," Storm continued, turning back to Adrian. "But I want one more thing too."

Adrian raised his eyebrows at her. "You're not really in a position to make demands."

She ignored his reply and pointed to the still-unconscious Reeves on the ground. "I want him."

What? I looked over at Elijah to see if this made any sense to him but he looked just as confused as I felt.

Adrian, however, seemed to understand what she was asking for. "So you figured out who he was, did you?"

Storm's face turned even more livid, which I wouldn't have thought possible. "You knew? You had me following him around for years and you knew who he was the whole time?"

"Who is he?" I asked, unable to contain my curiosity any longer.

Storm was so lost in her anger that I didn't know if she'd answer me, but she did. "He's the son of a bitch who slaughtered my whole pack."

Clearly there was more I was missing, but understanding dawned on Elijah's face. "It was your Alpha who rejected his sister?"

"Not only my Alpha," Storm replied, her voice almost breaking as her fury combined with pain. "My brother. He could be a cold bastard too, I know that, but he didn't mean for the girl to die. The border guards got carried away. And even if he should have been punished for what he did, the whole pack didn't have to pay for it. Innocent men, women, children..."

She broke off as her eyes filled with tears, and I was shocked at the change in her from her usual collected, self-assured persona.

"I only survived because I was away at the time," she continued once she'd regained control of herself. "But I was the only one who did. All that was left of the pack resources passed to me."

That's where her money came from. It made sense, but what a terrible way to get rich. I could feel Abby's empathy inside me as she listened silently to all of this too, still kneeling on the ground next to Liz. She couldn't stand to hear of anyone suffering this way.

"And when I went to the Alpha Council in search of help, I had the terrible luck to run into my mate, who never had any intention of being with me."

She sneered the word 'mate' as her gaze turned back to Adrian, and Elijah and I followed her glare. He was still regarding her coolly, unbothered by her emotion.

"That's enough reminiscing," he told her coolly. "You've done what I asked of you, so you've served your purpose now. So fine, you can have the human. And I, Adrian Reynolds, former Alpha of the Seven Hills pack, reject you, Stephanie Blakeney."

Storm staggered beneath the weight of his words, bowing her head and clutching at her stomach as the bond severed, but when she raised her head again, it was in triumph. "Finally," she muttered, before turning and walking over to Reeves' sleeping form. "How much longer will he be out?"

"It depends how much of the liquid got into his bloodstream," Adrian replied calmly. "But likely a few hours."

Storm nodded. "Good." Then she leaned over and hauled him up, slinging his limp form over her shoulder. Once again, just as I had been the first time we met, I was impressed with her strength. She gave Elijah and I one last look as she stood back up. "I hope you both come out of this alright. Whatever he says, believe the opposite. It's been nice knowing you."

And with that, she walked away without a backward glance.

~Elijah~

As Storm walked away, I tried to make sense of everything I'd just witnessed.

Storm and my father were mates? I never knew he had found even one mate, let alone two.

Why hadn't he accepted her, or, if he really didn't want to, rejected her instead? Thanks to my own refusal to acknowledge my mate, I knew exactly what that felt like and I knew how the pull had nearly driven me crazy so many times in just the last week. How could he have lived with that need for his mate for years and not given into it?

And why wouldn't he just accept Storm anyway? Sure, she pissed me off at times, but she wasn't *that* bad.

Then again, what drove my father to do any of the things he did? It was something I'd never really understood and it made even less sense to me now.

How many other things had he hidden from me?

I still had a million questions about the other things he'd said, how he had wanted me to find the source the whole time, that he had manipulated me into wanting to look for it by pretending he didn't want me to, and that Oliver was important somehow in finding it. But first, I had one other very important question to ask.

"You're the one who gave the humans that liquid?"

Oliver and Abby's friends said a man gave it to them, and when Storm asked my father how long the effects would last, he'd answered immediately, indicating he knew exactly what she was talking about. So he must have been the one behind it, and I needed to know exactly what it had done to my mate.

"It's my own creation," he answered me proudly. "Pretty impressive, isn't it?"

It was, actually, but I was hardly about to admit that to him. Oliver opened his mouth to respond, but I cut him off. Whatever he was about to say could wait. "The human woman over there, she got a bit of it on herself. How long will it keep her unconscious?"

He didn't even glance in Liz's direction, apparently unconcerned about whether she was injured or not. It couldn't be more clear he didn't deem her worthy of his attention. "If it was just a small amount, maybe twenty minutes. Not much more."

That was a relief at least. It had been about ten minutes so far, so it shouldn't be much longer. Hopefully I could do what I needed to do with the source before she regained consciousness, so that when she was awake, I could dedicate all my attention to her as I wanted to.

As I should have done all along.

Everything Reeves had told me about his sister and then what I'd just learned about my father and Storm showed me exactly how much of a fool I'd been for treating the mate bond so cavalierly. It didn't mean less to Liz because she was human. She was feeling it too, and either because of it or maybe just because of who she was, she'd tried to help me over and over again even when I gave her no encouragement.

She was a far less selfish person than I was, and I saw it clearly now. I had to give her an honest chance or I had to let her go, as kindly as

I could. There was no middle ground, no pretending it didn't matter, because it did. It mattered a lot.

But first, I had to deal with the source.

"What do you know about it?" I asked my dad, holding the locket up by its chain so he could see it. "How long have you known?"

I thought he had learned about it the same time I did, at that conference all those years ago, but apparently that was a lie and I was tired of all the lies. It was time for some truth now.

"I heard the stories from your mom's family," he explained, his eyes glued to the locket as it swayed gently in the wind. "But I did honestly think it was just an old family legend until her sister told me otherwise."

Her sister? Did he mean her twin? "Carol?" I asked, remembering the name from my mom's letter.

For the first time since he'd arrived, my dad was taken off guard. "How do you know that?"

I was hardly about to answer that, not when I had so many questions of my own that still needed to be addressed. "What did she tell you?" I asked instead.

According to the story my mom had told in her letter, my dad and Carol couldn't have had much time alone together. They had spoken very briefly at the clothing store and that was it. When would she have had a chance to tell him anything about the source?

"She said the curse the Alpha King placed on twins in your mother's family was to prevent them from ever accessing the source. It needs both twins to unlock it, so as long as one of the twins dies, the source would never be able to be opened."

The same chill from before spread through me as I looked down at the locket, and from the corner of my eye I saw Oliver shudder again too. Was that true? We had to open it together?

"When did she tell you this?" Oliver spoke up, stealing the words right out of my mouth. "You only knew her for less than a day before she died."

Once again, my dad was startled that we knew as much as we did, and I sent a silent thank you to Jenny for getting us that information. It might not have completely levelled the playing field but at least we knew which questions to be asking.

My dad looked back and forth between Oliver and I, trying to gauge his response. I could almost see the wheels turning in his head. "Just tell us the truth," I snarled at him. "At this point, what do you have to lose?"

That made him smile, even though the smile was cold and humourless. "I will tell you, because it's important that you both know. You need to understand as much as possible so you can unlock the source's power."

Something in the way he said that made me shiver again, this time not because of the locket. Why was he so keen on us unlocking it anyway? Surely if we unlocked it, the power would be ours. What did he have to gain from any of this?

Those were still questions I wanted answered, but for now I waited on the information he'd promised.

"I guess you know that Carol was your mother's twin and they met on their 17th birthday?" Oliver and I both nodded to confirm we did. "And then she was in an accident on the way to your mother's party."

So far this all matched up with what our mother's letter had said but it didn't explain when he had talked to her.

Luckily, I didn't need to ask. He answered that question now. "When we got to the scene, your mother was too upset to leave the car, so I went alone to see if there was anything I could do. Carol was very badly injured, but she was still alive, just barely."

She was? Why hadn't he told my mom that?

"Her eyes were glazed over and she spoke to me like she was possessed. She told me she'd had a vision of the future. Some people have their lives flash before their eyes before they die, but apparently, she saw your lives instead."

Oliver's lips started to curl in disbelief, but I was hooked. What had she seen?

"She told me that Nicole and I would have twin boys and that if we could manage to keep you apart until you were both 21, until now, that you would be the ones to finally find the source. She told me the stories were all true, that it would give the bearer the power to bend other wolves to his will, that it would make him the most powerful wolf that had ever lived."

"And you believed her, just like that?" Oliver asked and I looked at him in confusion. *That* was his question? Was he always so skeptical?

"She was dying," my dad reminded us. "What reason would she have to lie to me? I'm not even sure it was her speaking, or whether it was her ancestors speaking through her. Either way, she made me promise I would keep you apart, no matter what, and when I agreed, she stopped fighting, and she died right there in the front seat of her car."

So he was honouring a deathbed promise? Was there actually something selfless behind his separating us after all? This was all so much to take in.

"What about when Nicole turned out not to be your mate?" Oliver asked, still sounding unconvinced. "Didn't you question this vision then?"

"I did," my dad admitted. "While Nicole was gone on the exchange, I turned 18 and I met my mate. But I was convinced that wasn't the plan for me, that I was meant to be with Nicole instead, so I rejected my mate. I assumed your mother would be my second chance mate, but instead, a few weeks later she called me to tell me she'd found her mate and wasn't coming back. So yes, I questioned it then. I didn't understand how we could still have children when she had a different mate. But then she came to me to ask for my help and suddenly it was all clear again. I knew that she would have twins, and I convinced her to give one of you to me so that I could keep you apart, just as I'd promised Carol I would."

I blinked quickly as I tried to process all of this. He really had planned this. He had known all along.

"Who was your mate?" I blurted out. Perhaps it wasn't the most important question right now, but it was still one I wanted answered. I wanted to know everything.

My dad turned his cold eyes on me. "It was Jenny."

Jenny? Once again, that long-forgotten memory of her comforting me as a child came back to me. Was that why my dad didn't want her around me? Because if he hadn't been such an idiot, she could have actually been my adoptive mother? Was that why she felt protective of me, why she stayed with me when I fought my father over the pack?

How different would my life have been if he hadn't rejected her? How different would *his* have been?

"None of that is important right now," my dad continued, sweeping it all away with a flick of his wrist. "We're wasting time. This is the moment we've all been waiting for, what you were born for."

Oliver looked distinctly unimpressed with that summary of the worth of our lives, and for once, I had to agree with him. It was important, yes, but it wasn't all we were good for.

"Open the locket," my dad urged, not noticing our reaction or perhaps just not caring. "Oliver, Elijah, it's time. Unleash the source."

Chapter Seventeen

~**Abby**~

I had managed to keep silent through all of this so far: through Alpha Adrian's sudden appearance, through all the revelations about his relationship with Storm and the heartbreaking story of how she had lost her entire pack, and through everything Adrian had just told his sons about the curse, about his mate and about why he had wanted them kept apart in the first place.

But when he instructed them to open the locket and 'unleash' its power, I couldn't keep my mouth shut any longer.

"Keep an eye on her," I instructed Whitney and Jack, placing Liz's head gently back on the ground. She hadn't shown any signs of stirring yet, though based on what Alpha Adrian had said, she shouldn't be unconscious for too much longer.

Then I jumped to my feet and marched over to where my mate and his brother stood, both of them looking at the locket, Elijah with anticipation and Oliver with trepidation. Walking past them, I placed myself firmly between them and their father.

"What's in this for you?" I demanded of the former Alpha. "What do you get if they open it?"

From everything we'd just witnessed and everything Oliver's mom's letters had told us, it was clear to me now what kind of man Adrian was. He said he had 'convinced' their mom to give him one of the boys, but according to Nicole, he had actually blackmailed her and used her own guilt over her twin's death against her. I was sure there was more he hadn't told us too.

It couldn't be more obvious that he was selfish and manipulative and nothing like Oliver at all. They may look alike but that's where the resemblance stopped. More than ever, I felt sorry for Elijah, not just for growing up without a mother but now also for growing up with a father like that, one so unlike Oliver's adoptive one. I had never appreciated Alpha Patrick more than I did right now.

"Abby, was it?" Adrian asked, looking at me with thinly-disguised disdain. He clearly didn't appreciate my interference. "What's in it for me is to help my boys to reach their potential. This is what was destined for them and it's my privilege to help them achieve it."

"No one's life is completely predestined," I argued back as Oliver came to stand beside me, his solid warmth boosting my strength, as always. "Nothing is written in stone. They can make their own choices, it's why we all have free will, so stop pressuring them. They'll open it if and when they want to, not because you say so."

My argument seemed to make no impact whatsoever.

"One of them will die if they don't open it," he answered coldly. "I would guess within hours. It seems the older the twins are when they meet for the first time, the quicker the death occurs. Is that what you want, to sentence one of them to death?"

He was goading me, I knew that, but I growled at him anyway. "Of course not. But there must be another way to break the curse."

"A way that no one else has discovered for hundreds of years, but you expect to come up with it in a matter of minutes?" he asked, his tone just as mocking as his expression.

"Maybe," I shot back, refusing to back down even as he scoffed at me. "Oliver and Elijah are both smart and strong. If they work together, using the information they both have from their mother's book, I'm sure they can figure it out. And you still haven't answered my initial question. What's in it for you?"

I didn't for a second believe that he had done all of this out of the goodness of his heart, that he had rejected his initial mate and insisted on raising a son alone, simply for the benefit of the sons he hadn't even met yet when all of this started. There had to be something else behind it, something that benefited him personally, but I couldn't figure out exactly what it was.

"I will be the father of the most powerful wolves in the world," he answered, making it sound like I was the crazy one for asking. "And you will be their mate, so I don't understand why you're objecting to it."

Their mate? Of course. He must think that Elijah and I were also mates because of Elijah and Oliver being twins. Obviously that wasn't true, but I decided not to correct him. Letting him know that Elijah had a human mate didn't seem like a wise move right now, not when he was already trying to control his sons' actions. Who could say what he might try to do to Liz?

And did he really think being their father was going to win him any special treatment? Elijah hadn't spoken to him in years from what we understood and Oliver barely knew him. Neither of them had any reason to show him favour. There had to be something else we were still missing.

"How do we open it?"

That question came from Elijah, and I didn't miss the glint of satisfaction in Adrian's eyes as he turned to his son. Obviously he thought he was making progress. "You need to use the power of your twin bond to feed energy into the locket. One of you will send your strength and the other will receive it, and the one that has your combined power will be able to open it."

None of that sounded good to me and, to my surprise, Elijah seemed to agree. His face immediately turned wary, giving me a feeling that he knew something I didn't. A quick glance at Oliver's expression told me that if there was a secret, he didn't know what it was either.

"We don't have any bond," Oliver pointed out, looking between Elijah and Adrian.

"You do," Adrian argued. "It's just dormant because you've been apart for so long. You'll need to access it somehow."

A light of understanding crossed Adrian's face as he turned from his sons to me.

"Actually, perhaps you might be able to help."

"Me?" I asked in surprise. What did it have to do with me? "How?"

"You have a bond with them both," he pointed out, incorrectly. "So you might be able to act as a bridge between them. Perhaps... yes, perhaps you are the key to this whole endeavour."

~Elijah~

Oliver's eyes widened in alarm when my dad said that Abby was the key and he put a protective arm around her, as if it put her in danger somehow.

And he wasn't entirely off base. She would be in danger *if* she was the key, but she wasn't. My dad was wrong about that.

I'd already figured out what the key was. Now I just needed to explain it to my brother and decide what we should do next.

"The three of us need to talk about it," I told my dad. "Alone."

He scowled but somewhat surprisingly didn't argue with me. He must have realized that he needed our cooperation if he was going to get whatever the hell he was after.

"Fine, but do it quickly. Remember, the clock is ticking. The curse doesn't want you to get into that locket, so the longer you take, the more opportunity you give it to strike you down."

That was a little dramatic, but also not too far off the mark. After all the new information I'd learned today, I had no doubt the curse was real, so I needed to tell Oliver what I knew and hopefully he could help me figure out what to do next.

Because that was one thing my dad was right about. If we didn't figure out how to break the curse, one of us was going to die, and I didn't like those odds.

After a quick glance at Liz to check that she was still being cared for and hadn't regained consciousness yet, I led Abby and Oliver a short distance away where we could speak without being overheard.

"You can't open it for him," Abby insisted as soon as we were sure we were in the clear. "I don't know what he wants but it's nothing good."

"I'm aware of that," I told her drily. She really didn't think much of my intelligence, apparently. "I think he knows exactly what will happen if we open it."

"What will happen?" Oliver and Abby asked in almost perfect sync.

"One of us will die."

Confusion flickered across both their faces. "But I thought one of you will die if you don't open it," Abby said.

"That too," I agreed. "It's called a curse for a reason. We don't have a lot of good options here."

"Tell me everything you know." That was Oliver, his face deadly serious. He obviously didn't want to die any more than I did, which was the main reason I was going to have to trust him, even if it went against everything I had ever been taught.

"The text says there will be a key and a receptacle," I told them both. "I thought it meant literally, but apparently nothing about this is literal."

I remembered Liz's definition of the moon and a new wave of understanding washed over me. The book said the full moon would illuminate the path, and Liz had done just that. She'd shone a light into my life and shown me the way. She literally was my moon.

My Luna.

"So I am the key, like your father said?" Abby asked, looking uncertain.

"No, he's wrong about that. Oliver and I are the key and the receptacle. My dad just said one of us has to send power to the other. So the one sending is the key, the one receiving is the receptacle. But that's not all the text says. It says that only one of those two things can be preserved, which I think means that only one of us will survive the transfer of power. And it suggests only a worthy wolf can possess the power once it's been opened."

As much as it pained me to admit it, I couldn't guarantee that I was more worthy than Oliver. If the power was somehow going to use our worthiness to determine who lived and who died, once again, I didn't particularly like my chances.

"So what can we do instead of opening it?" Oliver asked. "If we don't open it, we're still at risk from the curse, according to you."

He still didn't believe in it? I didn't know what else I could say to convince him, and there wasn't time anyway. "The book suggested that the curse could be broken by returning the source to the rightful owner."

"Don't waste too much time," my father's voice called out from a distance, reminding us he was still waiting. We all turned to look at him as he spoke, but none of us bothered to respond, turning our attention back to each other again.

Abby's brow was furrowed as she looked at me. "But the rightful owner is long dead, isn't he?"

"Of course. I suppose it would have to be one of his descendants. Perhaps they passed down the rightful ownership of it just like the curse was passed down in our family."

Abby nodded, placing her hands on her temples as she searched her memory. "Okay. I'm pretty sure there are genealogical records on the great wolf lines in some of the books at your pack's library, Oliver. If we go back there..."

"We don't have time for that," I cut her off. "And both of us getting in a car right now is not a good idea. We know what happened to Carol."

"What was the Alpha King's name?" Oliver asked, his voice far more quiet and contemplative than either mine or Abby's. "Was it Cedric?"

"Yes, I think so." I couldn't completely remember from all the things I'd read about the source, but that sounded familiar. "How do you know that?"

"My mom..." he began, then caught himself. "*Our* mom used to sing a song when she was doing things around the house. It was all about King Cedric and his many children, listing them all and making silly rhymes about them."

My heart began to beat faster and from the look on Abby's face, she immediately understood the significance too. "Do you think she was giving you a message? A clue about who the source needed to be returned to?"

Oliver and I looked at each other, the same wonder and amazement reflected in his face that I was sure was showing in mine. "It might be," he admitted. "Does that mean she knew about all of this too?"

"She definitely knew about the curse," Abby reminded him. "So maybe she knew more than that too. Maybe she was giving you a way to protect yourself, and your brother too."

Abby gave me a smile as she called me Oliver's brother and a strange warmth spread through my chest. It felt almost like... belonging.

"So what was the song?" I prompted him. "How did it end? Maybe the last person in it was the last known descendant."

Oliver began to hum the tune, mouthing the words as he went, trying to remember, while Abby and I waited as patiently as we could.

"I think it got to someone named Flora Alonso or Alonsa, something like that, somewhere in New York," Oliver said when he had finished reviewing it all in his head, and frustration crossed his face. "That narrows things down a little, but not enough."

He was right. Based on the timeline we had, we didn't have time to go searching a whole state for someone. And that was assuming she was even still alive, since it must have been twenty years ago our mom learned that song.

'Flora Alonso?'

A voice repeated the name in my head, but it wasn't my voice, and it wasn't Abby or Oliver's either. It almost sounded like...

'Liz?'

I looked over to where she was still lying on the ground, still unconscious with her human friends watching her.

I must be hearing things. There was no way she could be in my head even if she was conscious. She wasn't a wolf, and I hadn't marked her and...

'Yes, it's me. Are you looking for Flora Alonso?'

How could this be happening? I was more confused than I had been at any point so far today, and that was quite a high bar to surpass. But as it seemed to be real somehow, I answered her.

'Do you know someone by that name?'

'I do. She's my mother.'

~Oliver~

I was desperately racking my brain for other ideas about how we could track down the King's descendant when Elijah suddenly took a step backwards, his eyes wide. He looked over at Liz and then back again, his brow furrowed and his head inclined as if he were listening carefully to something.

Abby and I exchanged glances. 'Is he okay?' she asked me through our link.

'No idea,' I answered honestly, but at least for the first time, I was starting to feel like we were somewhat on the same page. We still had a long way to go, but we seemed united in the opinion that Alpha Adrian was not to be trusted and that the source needed to be returned rather than opened. That was all good news.

But we still had to figure out who to return it to and I didn't have any idea how we were going to do that in whatever limited time we had available to us.

Then Elijah's head snapped up and he looked at us with both disbelief and something that almost looked like happiness on his face. "It's Liz," he said, completely out of nowhere.

"What's Liz?" Abby asked, mirroring the question in my own mind.

"The rightful owner of the source," he exclaimed, growing more excited by the moment. "She's a descendant of the Alpha King."

Did he hit his head or something? He wasn't making any sense.

"Liz can't be the King's descendant," Abby pointed out gently. "She's not a werewolf."

"I know that," he agreed, sounding a bit annoyed that we weren't as excited about this as he was. "I don't know how it's true, but it's true all the same. She just told me so."

Okay, now I was completely sure he'd lost the plot. "The woman who's lying over there unconscious just told you she's descended from the Alpha King?"

"Yes," he growled, obviously not appreciating my tone. "Well, not exactly. She told me Flora Alonso is her mother."

"How did she tell you?" Abby asked, sounding just as unsure as I was.

"I just heard her in my head," he told us. "Look, I can't explain it either, but I know what I heard. It was her. So if we return the locket to her, we can end this all right now."

"What about the source?" I couldn't help asking. "You've wanted it all this time and now you're just going to give it away?"

That didn't fit in with anything I knew about him so far.

"I've always felt a need to find it," he said. "Since the first time I heard about it, I knew that it was my destiny, and I thought it was because possessing the power would give me everything I was missing in my life. But after today, after everything that's happened, I think maybe that wasn't the reason. Maybe I needed to find it because it would lead me to her."

He looked back towards Liz with such tenderness that I could hardly believe my eyes. 'Are you seeing this, Heels?' I asked her in my head.

'I am,' she answered gleefully as she tried not to smile. 'It's wonderful.'

"That's enough stalling," Alpha Adrian called out. His shout was an unwelcome intrusion into our conversation and a reminder of the danger we were still in. "Hurry, before it's too late."

"What do you want to do about him?" I asked Elijah, gesturing with my head towards my biological father. He'd obviously been planning and scheming for this for a long time, I didn't think he was just going to accept our refusal to open the locket and desire to return it instead. Elijah may have had a change of heart, but I was pretty sure Adrian hadn't.

"We'll need to do what he just suggested," Elijah answered. "Stall until Liz wakes up and we can return it to her. That should break the curse and then he's got nothing to hold over us. There are five wolves here against him. He wouldn't stand a chance."

Hopefully it wouldn't be too long before Liz regained consciousness. It must already be close to twenty minutes since she collapsed, which was the amount of time Adrian had said she'd be out for. I was still very curious about the compound he had created that could knock someone out like that, but I recognized that this wasn't really the time to indulge my scientific curiosity. Maybe I could get my hands on some of it later to test in the lab, since Adrian wasn't likely to be willing to share his formulas with me directly once we thwarted his plans for us.

"How do you plan to stall?" Abby asked, still focused on the more immediate issue.

"We'll pretend to be trying to open it," Elijah suggested. "You try to keep him talking. Maybe you can find out more about what he actually wants while you're at it."

"Is that okay with you, Abby?" I didn't want to put any pressure on her or make her do anything she wasn't comfortable with.

"If it's going to help you, then of course," she replied with determination. "I'll do whatever I have to. I'm not going to let you die, either of you."

I never for a moment thought she would. "I love you, Heels."

"I know," she teased me, giving me a wink.

Our plan in place, we walked back over to the others. "Any change?" I asked Whitney and Jack about Liz when we were within easy talking distance, but they both shook their heads.

"Her pulse is still steady," Whitney confirmed. "But she hasn't moved yet."

Okay. That meant we had a bit more time to kill, and we just had to hope that no crazy accident would strike either of us down in the meantime.

"Which of you is transferring the power?" Alpha Adrian asked, barely concealing his excitement as we stood before him.

We hadn't discussed that, but I stepped up to offer. "I am."

"Then Eli needs to hold the locket in his palm," Adrian instructed. "And you put your hand on top of his."

My brother and I looked at each other and each gave a small shrug of our shoulders. It looked like we'd have to do that much if we were pretending to go along with all this. Eli did as our father said, putting the locket in the centre of his hand and holding it up to me, palm up, and I covered it with my hand. The source was trapped between us.

"Now use your bond," he continued. "Transfer the power."

We still didn't have any kind of bond, but obviously we weren't about to tell him that. Instead we both stared at our hands, as if we were trying to make something happen.

"How do you know exactly how to do all this?" Abby asked, trying to distract him as she'd promised.

"I told you," he muttered at her, keeping his eyes locked on us. "Carol told me."

"That was a lot of detail for her to go into," Abby pointed out. "You must have only had a couple of minutes with her if she was that close to death. But she told you all about the curse and your boys and keeping them apart and bringing them back together and how to unlock the source? It sounds like it would have taken a lot longer than that."

"It doesn't matter," he claimed, trying to brush her off, but Abby wasn't giving up that easily.

"It does matter. How do we know this is going to work if we can't be sure where you got the information from? You're asking your sons to trust you but you're not being open with them. Maybe their bond isn't strong enough to do what you want because they don't know the truth."

'She's pretty good,' an amused voice said in my head, and my eyes went wide.

'Elijah?' It sounded like my brother, but how was he linking with me?

His eyes widened too, letting me know he definitely heard me too. Suddenly my hand began to feel warmer, and his must have as well because we both looked back down at our joined hands at the same time. Slivers of light were beginning to show between our fingers.

This couldn't be good. Had we somehow activated our bond just by touching the source at the same time?

Meanwhile, Abby continued questioning Adrian, unaware of what was happening between us.

"I think you got the information from somewhere else," she guessed. "Why won't you just tell us where you got it from?"

"Fine," Adrian growled, finally looking at her, obviously annoyed with her pestering. "Carol told me about the boys, but Nicole told me how to open the source. Does that make you feel better?"

My mom had told him that? Why? If she wanted us to return the source, if she went to all the trouble of teaching me the song, why would she tell Adrian how to open it?

Abby was clearly thinking along the same lines. "When did she tell you that? How did it come up? It must have been after the boys were born, because she wouldn't have known before then that you were going to have twins together. I didn't think you spoke very much after the boys were born."

That was what my mom's letters had suggested, and Abby was absolutely onto something. But unfortunately for all of us, the source began to glow brighter, and Adrian's attention was immediately drawn back to it, making him forget all about Abby's questions.

"This is it," he said, his eyes gleaming brightly. "Finally."

'How do we stop this?' I asked Elijah in my head, watching the growing light with alarm.

'Just let go,' he suggested.

I tried, but I couldn't lift my hand. It was like it was being held in place, stuck to the source like a magnet.

"Oliver?" That was Abby, sounding worried, and I didn't know what to tell her. I was worried too.

But then I realized she wasn't looking at me. She was looking over to where our friends were, and both Elijah and I turned to follow her gaze.

In our distraction, we had missed another big change. Liz was no longer unconscious.

In fact, she was standing up now and looking right in our direction, her eyes glowing with the same colour light that was emanating from the source between our hands.

~**Liz**~

Everything was dark around me. It felt like I was floating, weightless and peaceful, and even though I couldn't see anything, I wasn't really afraid. I felt safe and protected, like there was someone watching over me. Somehow I knew I wasn't alone.

Gradually a voice pierced the deep stillness. It took me a moment to realize it was Eli's voice, and a longer moment to realize that he was saying a name.

My mother's name.

I repeated it back to him, and he answered me, asking if I knew who it was. Of course I did, so I told him she was my mother, and then his voice faded away again.

It was a bit strange, but I was so comfortable and content that I didn't worry too much about it. I was happy to go back to my peaceful floating, leaving the rest of the world to deal with itself for a while.

Or at least I was until another voice spoke to me, one I had never heard before.

"It's time, Liz," the woman's voice said. "Time to wake up now."

I groaned in protest. It was much nicer here where I was, where I didn't have to worry about friends who could turn into animals, strange men with guns who were trying to kill them, or handsome men who pretended to like me but really didn't. Here, I didn't have to worry about anything.

But the woman wouldn't leave me alone. "Your birthright is waiting," she insisted. "It's time to go and claim it."

Birthright? What on earth was she talking about? The only things I'd inherited were my father's poor vision and my mom's button nose.

"They will give it to you," she continued, ignoring the fact that I hadn't given any indication I was interested. "All you have to do is ask."

"Who are you?" I finally grumbled back. "What do you want?"

"I'm your ancestor. My name is Adelena, and I was mated to the Alpha King Cedric."

Okay, now I was sure I was dreaming, which was a shame, since it had been so pleasant up until this point. But I was curious to see what else my brain could come up with. "What's an Alpha King?"

"The Alpha is the head of a werewolf pack," she replied. "And the King is the head of the Alphas. Or he was, until we lost the source."

None of this was really making sense to me, but I supposed I should have expected to be dreaming about werewolves after everything that had happened today.

"So you're a werewolf too?" I asked.

"Of course," she answered. "Just like you are."

"I think you've got the wrong girl," I scoffed. "You probably want my friend Abby. She's the special one, not me."

"I'm not wrong," Adelena maintained. "Your wolf is dormant, just like all the wolves in our family for so many years. It was our punishment."

"Punishment?" I repeated. Despite myself, I was growing more curious about the whole thing, even though I knew it still couldn't be for real. Maybe I could write a book about it later though. It sounded like it would make a good story.

"We lost the source," she explained. "The great gift that the moon goddess gave our family. It was entrusted to us to rule over the other wolves, and when we didn't protect it sufficiently, our wolves were taken from us until our power is returned to us."

"*You* ruled over the other wolves? I thought it was your mate who was the King?"

"He was, but only because he was mated to me. Ownership of the source has always passed down through the females. We are the ones with the true power."

I liked the sound of that. It would be nice to feel powerful for once, but I still didn't believe a word of this. "If that were true, why is this the first time I'm hearing about it?"

"Because you've never been this close to the source before. It's here. Your mate has it in his hands." She sounded almost triumphant. "Ask him to give it to you, and you will become who you were always meant to be. You will finally carry on my legacy. It's time now, Liz. Wake up."

"Come on, Liz, wake up." The words were the same, but it was another voice that said them. This voice was much more familiar to me.

My eyes opened to find Whitney and Jack both hovering over me. A look of relief and happiness crossed their faces as they saw me looking back at them.

"Thank God," Whitney whispered. "We were so worried about you."

I appreciated that, but my attention had already been directed to what was going on just behind them. Oliver's and Eli's hands were clasped together as a bright light shone from between their fingers.

A light that seemed to be calling to me.

Ask him to give it to you.

Whitney and Jack tried to tell me I needed to lie down a while longer, but I ignored them both, getting to my feet and walking towards the two brothers, my eyes locked on the light between them. Suddenly they both turned to look at me, and I could see their shocked expressions in my peripheral vision, but I couldn't look away from the light.

Mine, a voice inside me said. It wasn't Adelena and it wasn't Eli. It was entirely new, and I knew somehow that it was a part of me, something waking up inside me.

"That belongs to me," I told them calmly, only aware that I intended to say it as the words came out of my mouth. "Give it to me, please."

Oliver smiled with what looked like relief and looked over at Eli, who was staring at me in amazement.

"What is this?" a man's voice called out, shrill and panicked. "Who is she?"

"She's the rightful owner," Abby replied from somewhere in the distance, satisfaction in her voice. "The source belongs to her and they're going to return it to her. That will break the curse."

"No!"

The man's cry was so full of rage that it snapped me out of my trance and for the first time I looked over at him. It was Eli's father, the same man who had given me the liquid that had knocked me out in the first place, but he no longer looked friendly or helpful. He hardly looked like Eli or Oliver at all. His face was twisted in anger and frustration as he glared at me.

"I've come too far and sacrificed too much to let you ruin this now," he snarled before reaching down into the tall grass.

The light coming from Oliver's and Eli's joined hands had become so bright it was nearly blinding. I had to shield my eyes as I looked back towards them.

"We have to stop it," Oliver cried out, looking at his brother. "Give it to Liz, now!"

But Eli's eyes were fixed on his father, and as I turned back to him too, I could see what he had picked up from the ground.

A gun.

It was one of the guns that the human men had been carrying. One of them must have dropped it during the fighting earlier.

He aimed it straight at me and pulled the trigger.

As the loud bang of the release sounded, the world around me seemed to go into slow-motion. I could see Abby crying out, trying to warn me, but there didn't seem to be anything I could do. My body was rooted to the ground, frozen in space as the bullet came hurtling towards me.

The light between Eli and Oliver flashed even brighter and then it seemed to travel up Eli's arm, into his chest, and Oliver collapsed onto the ground.

Eli's eyes met mine, just for a fraction of a second, glowing unnaturally brightly, and then, far faster than should have been possible, he was at my side, pushing me out of the way of the oncoming bullet, and I hit the ground hard.

Eli's friends immediately had Eli's father pinned to the ground, disarming him, and Abby was at my side just as quickly. "Are you okay?" she asked, searching my face for any sign of pain. "Did it hit you?"

"I don't think so." I hadn't felt anything other than the impact of the ground, but I checked myself over anyway. There were no apparent injuries.

"Abby." Jack's voice was sombre, and she and I both turned to look at him. He was standing not far away, his arm around Whitney who was covering her mouth with her hand. "It didn't hit Liz."

Something in his voice made my stomach drop, and I followed his gaze downwards to the crumpled body next to me.

Eli's body. With a bullet hole right between his eyes.

258

Chapter Eighteen

I had never felt as helpless as I did looking down at Eli's lifeless body. Shock and disbelief washed over me, leaving me cold and numb, and I could only imagine how Liz was feeling.

How could this be happening? We'd only just met him, only just started to get to know him, and now suddenly he was gone?

There was no way he could have survived that shot, even if the bullet wasn't silver, which I was pretty sure it was. Reeves' men had known they were going up against werewolves, after all. They would have been prepared.

I turned to Oliver, expecting to see the same stunned expression on his face that I was sure was on mine, but he wasn't beside me like I expected him to be. I turned further, and when I saw him lying on the ground, all thoughts of Eli immediately flew out of my mind.

"Oliver?"

My heart was in my throat as I raced over to him, kneeling at his side. He was still alive, I knew that for sure. I would feel it if he weren't. But what happened to him? I'd been so focused on Adrian and then Liz that I had lost track of what was going on with the source. I had seen the bright flash of light when the gun went off, but my eyes had stayed on Liz, praying she'd be okay.

As I knelt down, I saw the locket on the ground now, close to Oliver's unconscious body. It was open and empty.

Did that mean the source had been released? 'Unleashed', as Adrian called it? Then where was it?

Eli said one of them would die if it was opened, and apparently, he was right. Tears stung my eyes as the reality of it began to sink in, but I forced myself to concentrate on my mate. If Eli was the one to die, then why was Oliver knocked out too? Was he going to be okay?

"Eli?" Liz's anguished cry pulled my attention back to her even as I cradled Oliver's head in my hands. She had fallen to her knees now too, her posture almost identical to mine, her with her mate and me with mine.

I wished I could be there to support her, but I couldn't leave my mate either. I'd never wanted to be in two places so badly in my life.

"Let me go!" Adrian's furious voice called out and, to my surprise, the men holding him did just that, stepping back and bowing their heads.

As if he was their Alpha.

My eyes widened as I thought it over. Perhaps, if Eli was dead, Adrian *was* the Alpha again. Would the authority revert to him as the former Alpha? Or would it go to Oliver, Eli's sibling? But Oliver was from another pack, not to mention unconscious, so I had to admit, I wasn't sure how it would work.

Whatever the case, Adrian was free again and walking over towards Eli and Liz, with the other members of the pack following behind him.

"Oliver?" I shook him gently, trying to wake him up. "I need you now, please. Wake up. We have to stop him."

I still had no idea what Adrian was intending to do, but he looked like a man on a mission, and I knew without a doubt that whatever he was planning, it wasn't going to be good.

~Liz~

The ground was hard beneath my knees as I knelt next to Eli, but I barely noticed it. I couldn't see or feel or think of anything other than the man lying in front of me.

If it weren't for the almost perfectly round hole in his face and the small trickle of blood from it, it would almost look like he was sleeping. I reached out to touch him, but drew my hand back at the last second. It felt like if I did, that would make this all real, and I wasn't sure I could handle that.

Since the moment we met, he'd been determined to deny the connection we were meant to have. Just a short while ago, he was ready to trade my life for whatever was inside that locket, the power that apparently was supposed to be mine.

And now, he took a bullet for me? He laid down his life to protect me, without me even asking him to. Why had he done it?

I wanted to shake him and ask him, to see him looking at me with those intense, grey eyes, but they were closed now, and I knew I would never see him looking at me again.

My tears fell to the ground, falling straight from my eyes as I bent forward, my grief too strong for me to stay upright. Inside my head, there was a strange keening noise, almost like a cross between a whimper and a howl.

Mate, the voice whispered between whimpers.

"Get out of the way."

A rough hand pushed me to one side as Eli's father knelt down beside me. He picked up Eli's hand and I shuffled back out of respect. I was grieving, of course, but I had only known him for a day, when it came down to it. His father had far more right to be here than I did.

"Where is it?" he muttered to himself. For a moment I thought he was feeling for a pulse, but his hands went to Eli's torso, pulling up his shirt and placing his hands on his bare chest. They rested there for a second before he growled in frustration. "No! It has to be here."

"What does?" I asked in consternation. What was he looking for?

He turned to me, his face dark with frustration. "Did you take it?"

Was he actually accusing me of stealing something from Eli's body? After he was the one who had just shot and killed his own son, even if it was by accident? Why wasn't he upset about *that*? What was wrong with this man?

"I didn't take anything."

He obviously didn't believe me, and he grabbed my face with both hands, holding me tightly while he searched my eyes.

"No, you don't have it either," he finally snarled, pushing me backwards so hard that I almost fell over as he turned back to Eli, examining his body again.

It's still inside our mate. That same voice in my head spoke to me again. *The silver is weakening it, but it's there.*

The silver? Did that mean the bullet?

Yes. Take it out and the source will come to us.

Take out the bullet? How was I supposed to do that? And what did I care about this mysterious source now anyway? If I didn't have my mate, what was the point of being a werewolf at all?

The source will give you more power than you can imagine. Power to control, and power to heal.

Heal? Did that actually mean...

Hope began to push through some of the despair inside me, as much as I tried to stop it. That was crazy, wasn't it? Eli wasn't injured; he was dead. How could he be healed?

How can you be a werewolf?

Touché. Apparently my new inner voice was a comedian now.

"What are you doing?" The words came from above us, and Eli's father and I both looked up to find Oliver and Abby standing there, holding hands. His posture was slightly stooped, but Oliver's face was stony and hard. He wasn't looking at me though, he was staring at the man who must be his father too.

The man jumped to his feet. "You're alive?" He sounded surprised.

"I wasn't supposed to be, was I?" I'd never heard Oliver sounding this cold or full of anger. "You knew that. You knew that transferring my strength to Eli would kill me."

"But... it didn't," his father pointed out weakly, though that hardly seemed the point if he had thought it would.

"Only because we didn't fully complete the transfer," Oliver explained. "If we had, I'd be dead, and it wouldn't have bothered you one bit."

They didn't complete the transfer, so he has some of the power in him, the voice in my head told me. *You can use it to help your mate.*

"Oliver?" He immediately looked down at me, his face softening into compassion and sorrow as he saw both me and his brother. "I need your hand."

He didn't question the request or hesitate. In a moment he was kneeling at my side, holding his hand out to me. "Take what's yours, Liz."

I didn't know exactly how this would work, but I knew instinctively that it would, and as our hands connected, warmth flowed from Oliver's hand into mine, spreading through my whole body. My skin seemed to vibrate as energy surged beneath it.

And that was only part of it? What would it feel like if I got the rest?

When the flow had stopped, I let go of Oliver's hand and turned to Eli. "What is she doing?" his father asked, but no one answered him, partly because none of us knew, and partly because it was none of his business anyway.

Placing my hand over the hole in his forehead, I closed my eyes and pictured the bullet inside. I imagined my hand as a magnet, pulling it back, sucking it out towards me as the palm of my hand began to glow warmer.

And then the bullet was in my hand, as if by magic. And to my surprise, it hurt, like it was burning my skin.

"Drop it," Abby urged me as I looked down at it, frozen in pain. When I didn't immediately move, she grabbed my wrist and flicked my hand to the side, sending the bullet flying into the tall grass, and immediately the burning stopped. "Silver is harmful to wolves like us," she explained, giving me an encouraging smile.

Like us. I almost smiled too, but I knew I still wasn't finished. I still need to claim the rest of the power that Eli had taken, and then, hopefully, if the voice inside me wasn't lying, I might be able to heal him somehow.

I reached for his hand, but before I could touch it, Eli's father grabbed the other one first, and with a bright flash, the power flowed into him instead.

~Oliver~

The bright flash of light that passed between Elijah's body and Alpha Adrian made me wince, bringing back memories of just a few minutes earlier when Eli had taken my energy, and the source, into himself.

As events began to unfurl around us, quicker and quicker, Liz suddenly regaining consciousness and asking for the source and Adrian threatening her with the gun, Eli and I were still unable to break apart.

'I need to save her!' he shouted in my head through our newly-established link. 'Let go.'

'I can't,' I told him for the tenth time at least. I wasn't lying. I was glued to it, feeling weaker and weaker by the second as my energy drained into the locket between us, and I suddenly knew exactly how this was going to end.

It was going to take all my energy until I had nothing left.

I was going to die, just like Eli had said one of us would, and there was nothing I could do to stop it.

Just when I felt my knees start to buckle, Adrian raised the gun, and the light flashed as Eli broke away somehow. I had no idea how he managed to do it when I couldn't, but at that moment, I didn't have the energy left to figure it out. I blacked out before I even hit the ground.

The next thing I knew, Abby was hovering above me. "Oliver, please, I need you," she repeated, over and over. "We've got to stop him."

"Stop who?" I murmured, my head still weak and sore. Her relief at hearing my voice and the love she had for me flowed through me, through our bond, and immediately I felt a bit stronger.

"We have to stop Adrian," she told me, and I could hear the urgency in her voice. "Eli's been shot, and he..."

"What?" Immediately I was getting up, even though I could hardly manage to support my own weight. Abby put her arm around my waist, letting me lean on her as much as I could.

"Adrian shot him. He's... he's dead, Oliver. I'm so sorry."

No. I tried to reach out to him through our link, the one we had just forged, but there was only silence on the other side.

Was he really gone? Was that why I didn't die, because he did instead? Did he break the transfer on purpose, to save me?

"Is Liz alright?" I asked, and Abby quickly nodded.

"He got to her in time."

So it was to save Liz, that was how he managed to break away. Perhaps that explained how he was able to do it. The mate bond was stronger than just about anything else on earth, and I should know.

"But Adrian's over there now," she told me, pointing to my biological father, kneeling next to Eli's body, with Liz beside him. "I don't trust him."

I didn't either, not for one damn second. So with Abby still supporting me, we walked over together. Then I gave whatever power Eli hadn't managed to take to Liz and she somehow got the bullet out of his head.

I wasn't sure what she intended to do next, but before she could do anything, Adrian grabbed Eli's hand, the light flashed, and the source flowed into him.

Oh, fuck.

I still didn't understand exactly what this power was, but it almost seemed to be a living thing. It had wanted to escape from the locket, whether we wanted it to or not, and it must have been looking for a new home since Eli had no life force of his own left. With Adrian being the first one to touch him, the source latched onto him as a new host.

Adrian's face broke into a satisfied, unnerving smile as he stretched out his limbs, obviously feeling the power flow through him. I had felt it just a little bit when I got the remnants that were left when Eli broke away, so I had a vague idea how it felt, but I could also guess it was a lot stronger for him since Eli had taken far more of it than I had.

"At last," he whispered, his eyes shining brightly with anticipation.

The rest of us were all too stunned to say or do anything, except for Liz, who lunged towards him across Eli's cooling body. "No! I need it, I have to save him."

Save him? Elijah was past saving, and it broke my heart to think she didn't know that. But on the other hand, I could hardly blame her. If it were Abby lying there, I wouldn't accept it either.

Adrian stepped back, his expression turning colder as he looked at Liz. "You're too late. It's mine now."

"Then you save him," she begged. "Please. I don't care about the power, you can keep it. I just don't want him to die."

The pain and heartbreak in her voice made my chest tighten, and I could see the tears in Abby's eyes.

"He's already dead," Adrian replied icily, turning away to face his other pack members who were both watching warily. "It's too late."

"You won't even try?" I demanded. I didn't think he could actually bring him back, but surely making an effort wouldn't hurt anyone, and at least Liz would know there was nothing more that could have been done.

"This was the way it was always meant to go," Adrian told me, a chilling smile spreading across his face. "Count yourself lucky that Carol's vision wasn't entirely correct."

"You thought we were both going to die," I said as the realization washed over me. "You kept us apart all these years just to bring us together now, when it suited you, so we could both die and you could take the power for yourself."

I had met power-hungry people before, people like my father's former Beta who tried to take the pack from me, but this was a whole other level. Adrian fathered two sons and raised one of them, knowing the whole time that he was intending to sacrifice us both for his own personal gain. I didn't think I had ever met anyone more purely evil.

Even though I was still weakened, I couldn't just stand there and argue with him anymore. I had to do something.

I lunged towards him, intending to shift, but halfway through the motion, he held out his hand and I immediately stopped as if I was frozen in place.

Adrian's smile widened as he watched me struggle against the invisible restraints that seemed to be holding me. "What part of 'source of all power' don't you understand?" he laughed. "I'm untouchable now. All wolves are subject to my power. Get on your knees."

Against my will, my knees began to bend, and soon they hit the ground, as Abby did beside me and the other pack wolves on the other side of him. Liz was kneeling already, not because of his order, but even she bowed her head beneath the weight of his authority.

"You're just as weak as your mother," he taunted me as I tried and failed to even raise my head to look at him. "She wanted to bring the two of you back together, you know. She thought she could break the curse and protect you. She was going to tell your father everything."

She was? I hadn't known any of that. If that was her plan, why did it never happen?

"That was when she told you about opening the source," Abby guessed, her head also bowed as she addressed the ground, though her words were clearly meant for Adrian. "She told you that if you did nothing, they would both die. She wanted to save them, but you only saw the opportunity."

"Very good," Adrian sneered. "You are a clever little girl. I'm sure I can find a good use for your talents in my new pack."

The idea of him anywhere near my mate made me growl, but the sound got choked off as Adrian raised his hand to me again. Everything in my body was subject to his authority.

Whatever doubts I had that this source was real were obviously wrong. I had never experienced anything like it.

"Did she know you wouldn't help her?" Abby continued, her voice strong despite her subservient posture. "Is that why she killed herself?"

"How should I know why she slit her wrists? She was always unstable. It was lucky for me in the end that she wasn't my mate after all. At least I didn't have to suffer when she died."

Like my father did, I thought. I didn't remember a lot about that time, but I did remember coming across him once, late at night when he thought he was alone, with tears streaming down his face. He turned away to hide it from me and neither of us had ever spoken about it again.

With a great effort, Abby managed to raise her head just enough to look Adrian in the eye, surprising both him and me with her strength. I could feel the anger radiating from her now, it was clearly where she was getting her resistance from, but what had made her so angry?

"How did you know she slit her wrists?"

Adrian was caught off guard by the question for just a second. "It... it's common knowledge," he stuttered before growling. "None of this matters now."

But Abby wasn't finished yet. "It's not common knowledge. Oliver thought she died of an illness and so did his pack. Alpha Patrick kept her mental illness a secret from everyone. The only way you would know that was if you were there yourself."

Could that be true? I didn't see how it was possible, but Adrian didn't deny it.

"I don't think she slit her wrists at all," Abby said, her voice growing even stronger by the second. "I think you did it for her, to make it look like she had. You killed her, just like you killed your son and tried to kill my mate!"

She got to her feet, and Adrian took a step back, clearly surprised by the power coming off of her, as was I. How was she doing this? I still couldn't even lift my head.

"You robbed my mate of his mother, and his brother. The source is meant for a wolf that is worthy of ruling others, and you are the most unworthy man I have ever met. It doesn't want to be in you. It's seen just how black your heart is and it's fighting to get out."

As soon as she said that, Adrian grimaced, almost as if her words had made it come true. His hand clutched at his chest, trying to control the pulsing energy inside him.

"You will never control it," she told him. "It wasn't meant for you. You've built your whole life on a lie."

Adrian opened his mouth to try to reply to her, but he wasn't able to. It seemed to be taking all of his energy just to keep himself together.

"Whitney, Jack!" Abby called, and suddenly our friends appeared directly behind Adrian. I hadn't seen them approaching since my head was still bowed, but as they did, I immediately understood. They weren't affected by the source. They weren't wolves, after all, so it had no power over them.

Adrian turned to look at them in surprise, and with one swift, perfectly placed punch, Jack knocked him to the ground. The forces holding me down began to weaken.

"Liz," Abby instructed next. "Take it!"

With a roar of determination, Liz crawled towards Adrian, falling to her stomach at the last minute and grabbing his hand that lay on the ground.

A blinding light flashed, making me close my eyes against its brightness, and when I opened them again, the invisible bindings on me had gone completely. Immediately, I raised my head to see Liz with her arms outstretched, her skin almost glowing, while Abby smiled at her in satisfaction.

"Heels, what the fuck was that?" I asked as I got back to my feet. "What did you do?"

Adrian appeared to be unconscious now, though whether it was from Jack's punch or the loss of the source, I couldn't say. The two Seven Hills pack wolves were at his side, already working between themselves to restrain him.

Abby turned to me with a radiant smile. "Something in the source spoke to me," she explained. "It recognized me and it told me what it could see in Adrian's heart. Apparently my family used to protect the source from misuse. We were guardians of it, as Liz's family were the owners. They were our cousins."

Cousins? I looked back and forth between my mate and her friend, the one who had always bore such a strong resemblance to her. This was unbelievable. Were we really all connected by this artifact we didn't even know existed until a week ago?

There were so many new questions, not to mention the things Abby had just revealed about Adrian, but for right now, there was only one thing on all our minds.

With her newfound power settled inside her, Liz knelt down beside Eli's lifeless body and placed her hands on him, trying to somehow bring him back from the dead. There was nothing the rest of us could do but hold our breaths and wait.

~Elijah~

When I saw my father raise the gun, I knew without a doubt what I had to do.

At first I'd been intending to destroy the source so it wouldn't fall into the wrong hands. Then, when it was revealed that Liz was the owner, I planned to give it to her, of course. But now, with her life in danger, I only had one choice. I had to take it myself. I was too far away and the bullet too fast. Claiming the power as my own was the only way to reach her in time.

Giving my brother one last apologetic look, hoping this wouldn't cause him any harm, I broke the connection between us. Then I looked at Liz, and in my mind's eye, I pictured myself beside her, pushing her out of the way, and without even realizing I'd moved, I was suddenly there. She hit the ground, and then the world went black.

That was the last thing I remembered.

When I opened my eyes again, I was lying on the ground, and a quick look around told me I was no longer beside the river in Connecticut. Instead, I was in the forest on my pack's territory. Birds sang in the trees above me and the air was filled with the mild spiciness of the redwood trees. Everything was peaceful and calm, and I felt at home in a way I wasn't sure I ever had in the past.

How did I get here?

"Eli?"

Someone said my name and I sat up, trying to determine where it came from. In the trees, just a short distance from me were two women I had never seen before. They looked very similar to each other, almost identical, though one was a bit older than the other.

The older one came towards me, the younger one trailing behind her, and both of them were looking at me with concern written across their faces. "What are you doing here, sweetheart?"

Sweetheart? This woman couldn't be much older than I was, why was she talking to me like...

Like...

Suddenly, something in her face looked familiar. It was something I had seen before, but only in the mirror, and with a flash of realization, I knew exactly who she was.

"Mom?"

Was I dreaming? What was this?

As I got to my feet, the other woman came to stand beside her, and I realized who she must be too. When I spoke her name, it was a statement, not a question.

"Carol."

She nodded at me, giving me a sad smile as her eyes focused on a spot just above my eyes. "Hi, Elijah."

I thought I understood. They were twins, but she looked younger than my mom because she had died younger. They were both dead, and if I was here with them, then...

I must be dead too.

Fuck.

"What happened?" my mom asked, her brow furrowing in sadness as she looked at me, examining my features carefully. "You shouldn't be here."

"My father happened," I muttered. "He was trying to kill my mate and it looks like he got me instead."

My mother's eyes widened in disbelief and horror. "Adrian did this to you?"

She reached up and brushed her thumb lightly across my fore-head, between my eyes, and a flicker of pain passed through me. That must have been where the bullet hit me, I supposed.

As she pulled her hand back, I could see red slash marks along her wrist. "I knew how corrupted he had become, but I never thought he would..."

I cut her off, reaching out to take hold of her arm, holding her wrist up so I could see it. "Did he do this too?"

I wasn't sure how I knew, but it suddenly seemed clear to me, and I wasn't at all surprised when she nodded at me. "I asked him to bring you to me. I was tired, so tired of the lies and secrets and I wanted to talk everything out with my mate and find a way we could all go forward together. But when he came, he came alone, and he made sure I never asked for you again."

Tears pricked my eyes at the desperate sadness in her voice, and I had to ask the question that had been on my mind all day, ever since Oliver and I had read her letter. "So... you did want me?"

As soon as the question was out of my mouth, she threw her arms around me. "Always. I missed you every day, Eli."

It was the first time I ever got a hug from my mother, and I broke down as I felt the warmth of her embrace, crying like I hadn't in years, like the little boy who used to cry himself to sleep, holding my pillow and pretending it was her.

I had no idea how long we stayed that way, but when she finally pulled back from me, her eyes were red and puffy too. "Did you meet Oliver then?"

I nodded, clearing my throat as I tried to catch my breath. "Just today. We didn't get a lot of time together, but he seems like a good guy."

He did, I had to admit. He had tried to warn me and help me, not asking for anything in return. I finally saw that clearly, now that it was too late to do anything about it. If we'd had more time, we might have been friends.

"And your mate?" she asked tentatively, searching my face. "What was she like?"

I hardly knew how to answer that. "I only really met her today too. But I think... I think she was amazing."

That was the thing I regretted most of all about dying. I would never get a chance to tell her that, or to find out for myself just how amazing she was.

"I'm so sorry," Carol spoke up, her own face reflecting our sadness too as my mom and I both turned to her. "I tried to warn him what would happen if he didn't change, but he obviously misunderstood me. He thought that was what *should* happen rather than the worst-case scenario."

"There was nothing you could have done," my mom told her sister firmly. "Adrian's flaws are his own, they weren't caused by you or me. Or you, either."

She addressed that last part to me.

"If anything could have saved him, it would have been you, Eli, but he was just beyond saving. I didn't know how far gone he was until it was too late or I never would have let him take you."

The truth in her words seeped into my soul, healing parts of me I hadn't even known were broken. She had wanted to protect me. She had tried, and my father killed her for it.

"I'm so proud of you," she added, her eyes watering again as she took my hands in hers.

Right now I didn't feel like there was very much for her to be proud of. "You shouldn't be. He raised me to be just like him, to care only for myself. I wasted years trying to find the source just to make myself stronger. In the end, I'm no better than he is."

My mom shook her head vigorously. "That's not true. You sacrificed yourself for your mate, and by doing so you saved your brother too. He would have died if you hadn't."

I supposed that was true. I hadn't really thought about it. One of us was always going to die.

"Adrian would never have done that," she continued. "It would have never even crossed his mind. You're not like him, Eli. Maybe you went down a wrong path for a little while, but your heart is good. I can feel it."

Even if that were true, I couldn't see what good it did me now. It was too late to make things right with anyone. They would all remember me as the cold, power-hungry man I had been.

There were no second chances for me.

No sooner had that crossed my mind than a bright white light appeared beside us, making all of us wince.

"What is that?" I asked, assuming they would know. They'd been here a lot longer than I had, after all.

My mom and her sister both looked at the light in wonder. "I think...
I think it's a doorway," my mom said breathlessly. "It's for you."

"A doorway?" I repeated in confusion. "To where?"

"Back," she said simply, all traces of sadness gone as her face shone
with happiness. "You can go back, Eli. You don't have to stay here, not
yet."

This wasn't making any sense to me. "But... I died," I reminded her.

She laughed, and it sounded just like my laugh. "Do you *want* to stay
here? Or do you want to go back to your mate?"

Liz? I looked towards the light, trying to see what was beyond it.
Could I really see her again?

"Eli?" As soon as she crossed my mind, I could hear her calling me,
from far in the distance. There was a sorrow in her voice that tore at my
heart. "Please, come back. I need you."

"Go," my mom urged me, nudging me forwards. "You can make it
right, Eli. Be better than you were. Better than he was. Don't waste this
chance."

"I won't," I promised her, looking back once more at her happy,
tear-stained face. "I love you."

"I love you too, my beautiful boy." She ran towards me and hugged me
once more. "And tell Oliver I love him too, please."

"I will." With tears in my own eyes, I looked towards my aunt, who had
used her last breath trying to save me, even though it hadn't worked.
"Thank you."

She nodded in understanding. "Good luck, Eli."

I took one last look at them, committing them to memory as much as
I could, and then, with a deep breath, I stepped into the white light.

Chapter Nineteen

~**Liz**~

The energy flowing through my body, and from my fingertips into Eli's body, was like nothing I'd ever felt before. It seemed to hum beneath my skin, warm and electric, and it was making the little voice that had been talking to me louder and stronger too. That voice kept urging me on, to call for my mate and bring him back from wherever he'd gone.

'Please, Eli', I called out to him in my head, over and over again. 'Please wake up.'

I was aware that everyone was watching me. Oliver and Abby had their arms around each other, his around her shoulder and hers around his waist, fitting together as perfectly as if they had been designed for each other. And I supposed, in a way, they had. That was what a mate was, wasn't it? Someone you were meant for.

I still wasn't entirely sure mine wanted me at all, but I knew that either way, I had to try to save him. I had to do everything I possibly could.

"I don't think it's working," I heard Whitney whisper to Jack. They were standing quite far away from me, too far for me to be able to hear them whispering, but somehow I heard it anyway. Everything seemed sharper and more intense now, every sound and every smell.

Was that because of the power inside me?

In a way, the voice in my head said. *The source has restored my strength. I'm your wolf, Liz, and you have all my senses now. There are a lot of new things you can do.*

My wolf? I remembered how I had teased Oliver this morning about having multiple personalities, when he told us he and Abby were werewolves. It looked like I wasn't that far off the mark. Was I really going to have this other voice in my head from now on?

You'll get used to it.

Maybe I would. But it would be a lot easier if I had someone to help me figure it all out.

"Eli?" I said out loud this time. "Please, come back. I need you."

"Liz." That was Oliver this time, his voice gentle and sympathetic. "I think he's gone."

A whimpered cry escaped from my lips, and almost immediately Abby was in front of me, kneeling on Eli's other side. "It's okay," she told me. "Keep trying. We can wait as long as you want."

Although I knew she meant to be supportive, I heard the words she wasn't saying. She didn't think it was going to work either. She just wanted me to feel like I had done all I could.

And I couldn't blame her for thinking that. Nothing had changed since I started.

Nothing except...

Suddenly Eli's skin beneath my fingers began to feel warmer, like the blood had started moving again. Abby gasped as the colour began to return to his cheeks and Oliver stepped forward, squinting down at Eli's forehead as the bullet hole began to close up all on its own.

"Is he..." Oliver began, but before he could even finish the question, Eli opened his eyes.

Relief flowed through me, relief and hope and nervousness all at once. How was he going to react when he realized I was the one with the power he had come all this way to find? Would he resent me for taking it? Or would he only want me now because I had it?

"Where is he?" Those were the first words out of his mouth as he shot up to his feet, taking us all by surprise. Whitney and Jack both gasped while Elijah's pack mates broke into genuinely happy smiles.

"Alpha," they both greeted him, bowing their heads.

Eli didn't pay any attention to them though. He was only looking for one person, and he didn't relax at all until he saw his father lying on the ground.

"Is he dead?" he demanded, addressing the question to anyone who would answer.

"No," Oliver replied, going to stand beside him. "Just unconscious."

"Then I'm going to kill him," Eli snarled, taking a step towards the man on the ground, but Oliver quickly blocked his path.

"Hold on. You were dead yourself two seconds ago, and before anyone kills him, he needs to answer for what he's done, and not just to us."

"He killed our mother!" Eli cried out, still trying to push past his brother, but Oliver held fast.

"I know that," Oliver answered, looking confused. "Abby just figured it out. But how do you know?"

"She told me," Eli explained. "Our mother just told me exactly what happened."

Abby and I exchanged anxious glances. Maybe the bullet was still messing with his brain somehow? How could his mother have told him anything?

Oliver clearly had the same concern. "Calm down for a minute," he suggested. "You've just been through a big trauma. The danger's over, so we can all take a minute to breathe. Adrian's restrained, Liz has the source, there's no need to rush into anything else."

Eli seemed to tense slightly at the mention of my name, and he finally looked over at me, for the first time since his eyes opened. There was something new in his eyes, something I couldn't quite interpret, but I had a guess what it meant.

He hadn't looked for me until Oliver said I had the power. I should have known.

But he still didn't speak to me now. He turned back to his brother instead, taking a deep breath, just like Oliver had suggested. "I'm sorry. I've got a lot to process right now."

Oliver nodded sympathetically. "I get it. A lot just happened. But I'm glad you're okay, Elijah."

To my surprise, and to the surprise of everyone else gathered there too, Eli looked a little emotional at that. It was a look I hadn't seen on him before. "Thank you. And I have a message for you. Mom said to tell you she loves you."

Oliver's eyes widened, a mix of confusion, hope and disbelief on his face, and Eli laughed.

"I forgot, you're a scientist. You won't believe it if you don't see it, right? Well, you don't have to believe me, but I really did see her. She told me a few things, but that's the most important one for you to know. She loves you."

"That's amazing," Abby said, going to stand next to Oliver as she smiled at Eli.

"It was," he agreed, stealing another glance at me before turning back to Oliver and Abby. "Look, I'd really love to get out of here, but can Liz and I have a moment to talk first?"

They both quickly nodded. "Of course," Abby assured him. "We'll get everyone back into the van and then we can all go home."

Home? I suddenly felt like I didn't know where that was anymore. Where did I belong? I wasn't human after all, apparently, but I didn't have a pack either. I felt caught between two different worlds, the one I had always known and this new one that I didn't really understand. Where was I meant to go now?

Oliver helped Elijah's friends pick up Adrian's limp body and Abby, Whitney and Jack all walked away too, heading for the van. That left me and Eli alone in the grassy field.

"You saved me, didn't you?" he asked quietly. Once again, I was amazed at my hearing. Before today, I never would have heard him from this distance.

"It was the power inside me," I tried to explain. "I still don't know exactly what it does or why I have it, but my wolf said it was strong enough to heal you, and it did."

"Your wolf?" he asked, looking at me in wonder. "You have a wolf?

"Apparently," I told him. "I've just met her. She talks a lot."

Eli laughed, his face relaxing as he did, and my heart constricted a little. I wanted to hear that laugh more often, but I still didn't know what he wanted to talk to me about or what he was thinking. What was the point of this?

"I wasn't going to let him kill you, you know," he said suddenly, completely changing the topic. "Reeves, I mean. That was never my plan."

Was he telling me the truth? Before when he lied to me, I could tell, but this time I wasn't certain. "You could have fooled me," I pointed out.

Eli grimaced at my disbelief. "I know, and I'm sorry it looked that way. I just couldn't let him get the source. You must know by now how strong it is."

I certainly did, and I had to admit, although I still didn't know exactly who that man was or why he wanted it in the first place, based on his actions towards Eli and the others, I had to assume his intentions hadn't been good.

"I was going to give it to you," he continued, taking a step closer to me. "When I realized you were the rightful owner. I just didn't have a chance."

I wanted to believe that, but there was one thing I still wanted to know more. "Why did you take that bullet for me?"

"Because I would do anything for you," he said simply. "You're my mate, Liz."

He said it like it was obvious, but I knew it wasn't. He must be leaving something out.

"You didn't seem so keen on that fact when I first showed up," I reminded him.

He winced again. "I know. I was an idiot. Not just about that, but about a lot of things. You have no reason to believe me. I know I'll have to earn your trust, but I'm willing to do that. I'm willing to do whatever it takes to prove to you that I want to be worthy of you."

Worthy of me? The words healed my wounded heart a little, but I still had one very big, nagging doubt. "Is this all because of the power? Because of what will happen if you're my mate?"

His face scrunched up in genuine-looking confusion. "What do you mean? What will happen?"

Did he really not know? He knew so much about this power, I found it hard to believe he didn't know what it would mean for him to be mated to the person who held it.

Since I couldn't ask him straight out, I decided to test it a bit by feeding him something false. "Apparently my mate will be more than a wolf. He'll have the ability to change into different kinds of animals."

Elijah blinked a couple of times in surprise, and then a hesitant smile spread across his face as he stepped even closer, just a few feet from me now. "Really? That does sound pretty cool, but it has nothing to do with why I want to be your mate, Liz."

My mouth twitched upward at his reaction. It seemed sincere, like he believed me, and he didn't look like he knew anything else about what being my mate would give him.

"It's good that you don't care about that, because it's not true," I confessed. "I just wanted to see how you'd react."

This time his smile was even wider, though a bit sheepish. "I deserve that. And a lot more than that, really. But I promise, I'm going to be better, Liz. I want to be better. For my pack, for my brother, and especially for you. Please say you'll give me a chance."

There was truth in his grey eyes as he took the last few steps, closing the distance between us completely. My doubts began to melt away beneath the warmth of his gaze.

"Are you willing to try?" he asked, hope and nervousness battling in his eyes.

I didn't answer him with words. I kissed him instead, and the whole world seemed to explode around us as my body lit up like it had in my dream of him, but even stronger. Sparks flew from his fingers as he gently cupped my face, deepening our kiss until it felt like we were sharing one breath.

When we finally broke apart, I knew for sure what my answer would be.

"You've got one more chance," I told him, smiling up at that handsome face that was looking at me with such awe, I could hardly believe it. "Don't mess it up."

~Abby~

I tried to keep an eye on Liz and Elijah as they talked but there were a lot of other things to sort out. We finally got a chance to introduce ourselves properly to the other wolves from the Seven Hills pack, who told us they were Julian and Matthew, and they loaded the still-unconscious Adrian into the back of the van. We needed to head back to the spot where we had left our car before we left Connecticut behind for good.

I had assumed without even asking Oliver that we were heading back to the Jade Moon territory, but I asked him about it now once we had a minute to ourselves.

"What do you plan to do with him?" I gestured to the back of the van where his biological father was tied up.

"I'm going to let my dad decide that," Oliver explained, his eyes dark with anger as he followed my gaze. "Adrian killed his mate, after all. If there's anyone who has the right to decide how he pays for that, it's my dad."

That made complete sense to me and I didn't envy Adrian one tiny bit. Alpha Patrick had a softer side that I had seen a few times, but he could also be hard and cold when he had to be. I could imagine that Adrian was not going to receive any mercy from him, and rightfully so.

"Do you think Eli really saw your mom?" I asked Oliver next. Eli seemed so certain of it but I could tell that Oliver had doubts.

"I'm not sure," Oliver replied. "I've read things about people who claim to have seen the other side. Some scientists think it's all hallucination, a chemical reaction in the brain. But he seems to think he did, and I guess that's what's important. It would be good for him to think he saw her, whether he actually did or not."

"He said she told him to give you her love," I reminded him gently. That had to mean something to him too.

And sure enough, my mate's eyes softened at the thought of it. "Maybe she did," he agreed, and I felt certain that, even if he didn't fully believe it, he wished it were true.

Liz and Eli joined us then, and I tried to gauge from their expressions how their talk had gone. They weren't holding onto each other or anything, but neither did they look angry. That gave me a little hope.

"You can take the back seat, at least for now," I offered. "Oliver's going to drive."

"Where are we going?" Eli asked. His hard, demanding tone from earlier seemed to have dissipated. He sounded much more like my mate now.

"We're going to my pack," Oliver told him. "We can talk things over and you can meet my dad, and then you can figure out what you want to do after that."

Eli nodded slowly. "Okay. That makes sense."

He started to turn away to get into the van, but then stopped and looked back at us with something new in his eyes.

"Thank you, both of you, for coming here today. This would have all ended a lot differently without you here."

It would have, but on the other hand, I felt certain this was the way it was meant to go. Maybe some things really were predestined after all.

Oliver also looked a little moved by the unexpected gratitude, and his voice was a bit huskier when he spoke again. "I'm glad it went the way it did," he said simply. "Now let's get out of here. I've had enough of this place to last a lifetime."

We all got back into the van and, with one final look at the remote location where so much had just changed, we headed back onto the road.

~Elijah~

It must have taken hours to get to Oliver's pack lands, but the only way I knew that was because it was dark by the time we arrived. Otherwise, it really only felt like minutes.

We had to go back to pick up Abby's car first, then she, Oliver and their human friends went in that vehicle while Julian and Matthew took over driving the van we were in, leaving Liz and I alone in the back. Well, alone other than my still unconscious father, but that was alone enough. It gave us a chance to talk privately at least, and we did.

I'd never just sat and talked to a woman like that before, but then I was never interested in getting to know anyone like this. Before I had always wanted something from them, but this time I just wanted to know her. There wasn't anything she said that wasn't interesting to me and when she laughed, I couldn't help smiling too. My cheeks were sore before we were even halfway to Oliver's house. I'd never smiled so much in my life.

How did I ever think she was plain or unappealing? The more I looked at her, the more fascinated I was by all the little features that made her unique. The slope of her nose, the pink in her cheeks, the spot on her neck that was made to bear my mark... I couldn't stop staring at them all. And when she licked her lips to moisten them, I found myself back in that moment by the river, back where she kissed me for the first time.

I'd kissed plenty of women before, but not like that. Her kiss was sweet and tempting, but almost innocent somehow. She must have kissed other men too, and I wondered how many? Had she loved any of them? I wanted to know, but I was afraid of the answer. All my life, all I'd really wanted was for someone to put me first, to be the most important person in the world to someone. I had tried to achieve that through power, first by being Alpha and then by going after the source, but I could see now that it wouldn't have given me what I really wanted. But maybe, just maybe, my mate could.

"You aren't seeing anyone else right now, are you?" I finally blurted out when I couldn't take it any longer.

Liz looked surprised at the question, but then she gave me a smile. "No. Abby was though, when she met Oliver. Did you know that?"

Of course I didn't know that. I didn't really know anything about them, but I also didn't care about them right now. I only wanted to talk about her.

But Liz wasn't finished yet. "Actually, Abby was seeing the same guy I was. Or at least, we both thought we were seeing him. Turns out he was actually with someone else the whole time."

What? My confusion must have shown on my face because Liz laughed again.

"It's kind of a long story," she shrugged.

"I've got time," I told her. We were going to be in this van for a while still, so there wasn't any better time to hear it.

A little hesitantly, she told me the whole story, and my blood boiled at the idea of anyone using my mate that way. I couldn't believe Oliver didn't rip the guy limb from limb, but Liz explained that Abby wanted to get revenge her own way and that they'd worked together to do just that. I had to admit it was a clever plot in the end, but I still thought it would be far better for this asshole's health if he never crossed paths with me.

"Why did he choose the two of you?" I asked. Was it because they looked alike? Did he just have a type?

"It was because we were both virgins," Liz explained, her cheeks turning even more pink than usual. "He must have thought we'd be more naïve."

My heart beat a little faster. "Were?" I asked, not even realizing I was saying it out loud until it had come out of my mouth. The idea that she might still be, that no man had ever been with her that way, meant more to me than I had ever realized it could.

Although I knew logically it made no difference, somewhere in my heart it felt like it would mean she had waited for me, even if she hadn't known it was me she was waiting for. Like I could be her first real love. Suddenly I regretted every casual encounter I'd ever had. I had only ever been thinking of myself, not my future mate and how it might make her feel.

Shame flashed through me, but I remembered my mother's words too. I had taken a wrong path, but I had a second chance to make it right. I could do better now.

Liz swallowed a little nervously. "Well, Abby's not anymore, obvious-ly."

Obviously. Mated wolves didn't usually keep their hands off each other for very long. Which led me to the second part of my question.

"But you are?"

For a second she looked almost embarrassed, but then she seemed to think better of it. She squared her shoulders and lifted her head up, giving me a confident glare from behind her glasses. "Is that a problem?"

It wasn't a problem at all. In fact, it was just about the most amazing thing I'd ever heard. And if I had my way at all, it wasn't going to be the case for long.

~Oliver~

It was late by the time we pulled up in front of the Jade Moon pack house. It had been a really long day and I knew it wasn't quite over yet. There was still one very difficult conversation I needed to have.

Abby took Whitney, Jack and Liz inside to get them set up in guest rooms for the night while I went over to the van to talk to my brother.

"He's still out?" I asked in surprise, looking at Adrian's sleeping body in the back of the van. Whatever the source had done to him when it left his body, it really wiped him out.

"Luckily for him," Eli responded darkly. "If he'd started mouthing off on the way here, I'm not sure he would have made it here alive."

That was a good point. It might not have been the smartest idea to leave him and Eli in a confined space, but at least it had worked out in the end.

My brother and his pack mates helped me carry the unconscious former Alpha into my dad's office, and my dad wasn't far behind us, having been alerted to our arrival.

"Oliver, I'm so glad you're..." he said as he came into the room, but he trailed off as he caught sight of Eli standing next to me. His mouth dropped open and he blinked rapidly a few times at the sight of my twin before regaining control over himself.

"Dad, this is Elijah," I introduced him. "Elijah, Alpha Patrick West."

Elijah held out his hand to my dad, looking a little nervous all of a sudden. "Call me Eli," he requested.

My dad took his hand and shook it firmly, still looking at Elijah with keen interest. "Eli. That's interesting. Oliver never liked people calling him Olly."

They both looked over at me and I just shrugged. It was true. I still didn't like it. My brother and I didn't have that in common, but I was starting to see that there might be some things we did. Maybe we could find some common ground after all.

"Welcome to the Jade Moon pack, Eli," my dad said, turning back to my brother. "I'm glad to see that you're both okay."

Then he glanced towards the other men in the room and saw Adrian's slumped over body on the sofa, and his mouth fell open again.

"Is that..."

"The biggest son of a bitch who ever lived?" Eli filled in helpfully. "Yeah, that's him. My father."

"I feel like I've missed something," my dad said, looking back and forth between the two of us.

"Just a little bit," I told him wryly. That was obviously an understatement.

My dad called for someone to take Julian and Matthew to get settled in for the night, leaving Adrian alone on the sofa. He was still out cold.

The three of us sat down and Eli and I told my dad everything that had happened. Abby joined us partway through, adding any extra details she knew.

We went through the whole story before getting to the end and the last thing we had discovered, just before Adrian passed out. I knew it was going to be hard for my dad to hear and I thought I should be the one to tell him.

But to my surprise, Elijah stepped in. "Oliver doesn't believe me," he started, glancing over at me with a bit of a smirk. "But when I was dead for those few minutes, I went somewhere else, and I saw my mom there."

My dad leaned forward in his seat. "You saw Nicole?"

I could hear the longing in his voice and Abby obviously could too, as she squeezed my hand tightly. I could feel her empathy for my dad, for Eli, and for me too. She really could see all sides.

Elijah nodded. "She told me that just before she died, she was going to tell you everything. She wanted to tell you about me and find a way that we could all be okay, together."

He hadn't mentioned that part to me before, and I could see how much hearing it meant to my dad. He smiled, looking a bit happier, but he still didn't know the painful part yet.

"She called my dad," Eli continued. "She asked him to bring me here so that she could see me. But he didn't. He came alone, and when she told him what she wanted to do, he…"

He broke off, just for a second, the words sticking in his throat. I was ready to jump in if I had to, but my brother gathered himself and finished the sentence.

"He killed her. He was the one who slit her wrists. She didn't do it. She didn't want to leave you, or Oliver, or me either. It was all him. He took her away from all of us."

I could only ever really remember seeing tears in my dad's eyes one other time in my life, that night where I came across him crying just after my mom died, but I saw them gathering there now. Pain and confusion played out across my dad's face until one emotion settled there, pushing out all the others: anger. And I knew exactly who it was directed at.

"That's why we didn't kill him," I explained, gesturing at my biological father's body on the sofa. "His life belongs to you."

My dad nodded, but he was obviously too overwhelmed to say anything just yet. I wasn't sure I had ever seen him lost for words before.

Abby spoke up to bridge the silence. "Alpha Patrick, of course you have every right to do with him as you wish, but there are other people he's hurt too. He had two mates and he treated them both terribly. Perhaps they could have a say in what happens to him as well? It might help them find some peace."

Of course she was thinking of Jenny and Storm. I expected nothing less from my thoughtful mate.

Eli seemed impressed as well, giving Abby an appreciative look. "I can call Jenny," he offered. "I'd like to speak to her anyway. There are some things we need to discuss."

"And I'll get in touch with Storm," I said. "I've still got her contact information."

My dad nodded again, finding his voice at last. "I'll keep him in our holding cells until we hear from them."

He quickly linked members of his team to take Adrian there now, and arranged for one of the pack doctors to check on him too. He wanted him healthy and conscious for when the interrogation started.

When all that was taken care of, the four of us got to our feet. "You've all had quite a day," my dad said, looking at each of us in turn. "Why don't you get some rest and we'll regroup in the morning? Eli, you're welcome to stay here as long as you like. This was your mother's home and you'll always have a place here if you want it."

I could see that meant a lot to my brother as he nodded his thanks.

We said goodnight to my dad and went out into the hall, the three of us. "I'll show you to your room," Abby told Eli. "I've put you next door to Liz."

His eyes lit up at that, and I suspected that no matter how long a day it had been, he wasn't so tired yet that he wouldn't be seeing her again tonight.

I could understand that, of course. After everything we'd been through today, all the highs and the lows, there was nothing I wanted more in the world right now than to get my mate alone and show her just how happy I was to still be alive.

Chapter Twenty

~**Liz**~

I couldn't believe the size of this house. There were so many extra bedrooms, it was like a hotel. I was given my own huge room to spend the night, with its own bathroom, and Abby brought me some of her extra pajamas to sleep in.

"So this is where you're going to live when you're done with college?" I asked her once she had made sure I had everything I needed. "Oliver's going to be in charge here?"

"That's right," she said, taking a seat beside me on the bed even though I was sure she had a lot of other things to do. "He's going to be the Alpha, so he'll be in charge of everything, just like Eli is for his own pack. And I'll be his Luna, his partner, who helps him to keep everything running smoothly."

"So it's always the male who's in charge?" I asked, thinking about what my ancestor told me, about how my mate would be able to use my power.

"Not always," Abby contradicted me. "It depends on bloodlines, usually, and sometimes Alphas can choose their successors, like Oliver's father did with him."

"But most Alphas are male?" I pressed, and she had to concede that. "And if I decide I want to be with Eli, I would have to move to Oregon with him?"

That would be a huge change. How could I know if I was ready for that kind of commitment? And perhaps more importantly, how could I be sure he was?

"Eventually," Abby agreed gently. "His pack is there and he has a responsibility to them. So unless he decided to give that up…"

She trailed off, but I could fill in the blanks easily enough. Eli wasn't likely to give up power for anyone. It seemed very important to him and I was still struggling to understand how important I was in comparison.

She left me to go and join Oliver, and I got ready for bed, still thinking about Eli and the source and everything that had happened today. I must have gotten really caught up in my thoughts because a gentle knock at my door made me jump. My heart racing, I went over to open the door, and when I saw who was on the other side, my heart beat even faster.

"You weren't sleeping, were you?" Eli looked down at my pajamas, his eyes trailing across my body slowly, and I could feel my skin heating up beneath his gaze. The pajamas Abby had given me were surprisingly revealing, just a camisole with spaghetti straps and little satin shorts. She must have started buying sexier ones once she got a boyfriend… or a mate, I reminded myself. I was going to have to get used to that word.

My body reacted to his attention almost as much as if he had actually touched me. My nipples hardened and an aching started up, deep inside me. It didn't help that he smelled so damn good too. Ever since he came back from the dead this afternoon, ever since my wolf had come to me, his scent had changed. It was strong and enticing, like the forest on a rainy day, earthy and damp, and it made me want to bury my face against him and inhale until it filled me completely.

That would be weird, though. I forced myself to stay where I was, keep breathing normally, and just answer his question instead.

"No, I hadn't gone to bed yet," I assured him. "I was just thinking."

"About what?" he asked, sounding genuinely interested. He had really listened to me in the van on the way here too, and he really seemed to care about what I had to say. It was so different from the way things had been with Liam, or with anyone, really.

"About everything," I answered with a shrug. "It's a lot to take in."

He nodded, and I waited for him to say something else, but he stayed silent, looking over my shoulder into the empty room.

"Did you... want to come in?" I asked, feeling a little self-conscious about making the invitation. Was I assuming too much?

The smile that broke out across his face quickly confirmed that I wasn't. It was obviously exactly why he was there. "This is your first time in a pack house?" he asked as he followed me into the room, closing the door behind him. Suddenly the large room felt a whole lot smaller and every inch of it seemed to sizzle with energy.

"Yes," I said with a nod, trying to stay calm even though I was pretty sure he could hear my heart pounding. I could hear it too. "Is your house like this?"

"Not really," he replied, looking around. "It's a big house that the pack uses, of course, but that's the only similarity. The style is quite different."

His eyes landed on me as they completed their tour of the room, and the grey in them seemed to grow darker.

"Liz, I've been thinking about our conversation in the van."

We talked about a lot of things in the van, but from the look on his face, I was pretty sure I knew exactly what he was referring to. I played dumb anyway. "Which conversation?" I asked.

The corners of his mouth lifted. "About you being a virgin."

Oh, God. He couldn't be much more direct than that. But I still didn't know exactly what he had in mind.

"And?" I asked, my voice shaking slightly.

"And all I've been able to think about since then is doing something about it," he said, taking a step towards me.

The dream I'd had earlier today came rushing back to me. Was that really today? It felt like a lifetime ago already. But now the star of that dream was here with me, in my room, looking at me in just the same way he had then.

"But then I realized, that wouldn't be fair to you," he continued, and immediately it felt like cold water had been poured over my head, dampening the burning fire inside me.

"Fair?" I repeated, more than a little confused. What was he talking about?

"You told me how your professor used you," he reminded me, not that I needed reminding of it. "But he never did anything for your pleasure."

That was certainly true. Nobody ever had.

"Let me make up for it now," he suggested, his voice husky and deep as he took a step closer to me. "I want it to be all about you, Liz. Let me show you what it feels like to have a man worship you."

"Worship me?" I couldn't help repeating incredulously. I was hardly the type of girl any man would worship. But Eli was looking at me with such a potent combination of awe and lust in his eyes that I could almost believe he meant it.

"Please, Liz," he said, begging me. "Give me a chance to show you how good it could be if you let me in."

My wolf was howling at me to give in and my body felt drawn towards him like he had his own centre of gravity. How could I possibly resist?

"I did promise to give you a chance," I admitted, recalling our earlier conversation back on the grassy field, and Eli immediately grinned, a wolfish smile that sent a pulse of heat straight to my core.

In only two steps he was directly in front of me, his arms wrapping around my waist as he lowered his lips to mine. Tingling, zingy sparks flew everywhere our skin made contact, leaving me almost breathless with anticipation. And that was even before he kissed me.

Back on that field, I kissed him, but this time, he was definitely the one in charge. I found myself drowning in his kiss, losing myself in the feel of his lips, his tongue, and his teeth as they gently nipped at me. He pulled back for a second, but only to pull my glasses off before he kissed me again, even harder this time.

I'd never been kissed this way, so desperately, so needed. And I needed him too. I wanted him just as badly.

"Let me see you," he whispered, just as he had in my dream. "I want to see all of you."

This was moving fast, but then this whole day had been so crazy, I didn't even care anymore. I felt like a completely different person from the woman I'd woken up as this morning. I was strong and I was powerful, and if my mate wanted to please me, well, why shouldn't I let him?

I lifted my shirt up over my head and Eli exhaled in appreciation. I wasn't wearing anything underneath, I'd already taken my bra off to get ready for bed, and my nipples were taut and peaked now, well aware of the attention they were being given. But that attention was just starting as Eli bent down and lifted me up, his hands gripping my thighs and pulling me tightly against him, higher and higher until my breasts were level with his mouth.

"Oh my God." When his lips latched onto my nipple, sucking and licking at it, sending sparks of pleasure and need through me, it was a good thing he was holding me up because my legs wouldn't have been able to support me any longer. My fingers threaded through Eli's hair and he moaned against me, the vibration making my skin tingle even more. Apparently my touch was just as good for him as his was for me.

Carrying me like I weighed nothing, he walked over to the bed and laid me down. "I love it when you touch me," he told me, his eyes mere inches from mine. "But this is about you."

"But I want to touch you too," I couldn't help saying, and he laughed, a warm and deep sound that touched the heart of me.

"You will," he promised. "I really hope you will. But not tonight."

With a swift, firm movement, he pulled the little shorts down and tossed them aside, leaving me completely naked. For a moment he just stared at me, his eyes moving slowly across my body until I couldn't take it anymore.

"Eli, please," I said. I was the one doing the begging now. "Touch me."

That devilish smile, the one that was definitely going to get me into trouble, crossed his face again as he hastened to do my bidding. In an instant, his hands and his lips were everywhere, setting my skin on fire all over again. My whole body was burning and aching all at once, needing the relief that only he could bring me.

He hadn't lied to me. He really did worship me, exploring every inch, kissing and caressing me like I was some kind of goddess. I writhed beneath his touch shamelessly, and when he gently spread my legs and his tongue connected with my clit, I could swear I saw heaven. Was that what it was like for him earlier today, when he died?

My first orgasm was followed by a second and then, with his fingers inside me, a third. I was moaning incoherently, unable to form any thoughts other than *yes, oh God, yes.*

It would never have been like this with Liam. It would never have been like this with anyone other than the man who was made to be mine.

And when he finally took mercy on me, ending the onslaught of pleasure and laying down beside me, pulling me gently into his arms, I knew I really had no choice.

I had to take the leap of faith to be with him, whatever that involved. Just like our bodies, our lives were intertwined now, for better or worse.

He was made for me, and I was made for him.

~**Abby**~

"Oh, Goddess, yes!"

I had been trying to be quiet since we were in a house full of wolves with extraordinarily good hearing, but I couldn't help crying out as my body shuddered in the most exquisite release.

Oliver grinned as he kissed my forehead. "That's two," he teased, giving me just a few seconds to catch my breath before starting to thrust into me again.

He had a personal record he was trying to beat. The most he had ever made me orgasm before losing control himself was three times, but he really wanted to get to four, no matter how many times I told him it might be impossible. I certainly had no complaints if he wanted to keep trying though.

His strong arms were beneath my thighs, holding me with my back against the wall, and my arms were wrapped around him, feeling his muscles contract as his hips rotated. He knew just the perfect angle to hit my g-spot on the way in, then rub against my clit with the base of his shaft as he bottomed out.

It was absolutely amazing and turned me to putty every single time.

As the tension inside me began to build again, the pictures on the wall shaking with every strong thrust, I couldn't help wondering if Liz was having just as good a time as I was. For her sake, I certainly hoped so.

"Oh, fuck!" Oliver groaned as his own pleasure overwhelmed him, and the feel of him releasing inside me was enough to tip me over one more time too.

We stayed there for a moment, both of us panting, his cock buried deep inside me, until he finally leaned back, taking me off the wall with him and carrying me to the bed.

"That was still only three," I teased him as he placed me down gently.

"I'll just have to try again tomorrow," he laughed right back, climbing into bed beside me and wrapping his warm, solid body around me.

It was really the first quiet moment we'd had all day, since this whole crazy, incredible day started, and before I even realized it was happening, tears were slipping down my cheeks.

"Heels?" Oliver's arms tightened around me as he felt my sadness through our bond. "What's wrong?"

"So many things," I tried to explain, sniffling. "You almost died, for one. Eli did die, at least for a while. Your poor mom was murdered, your dad has been alone for so long, Adrian kept Storm hanging on for years, Jenny never got a second-chance mate... everyone has suffered so much."

Oliver gently turned me to face him, wiping the tears from my cheeks and brushing the hair from my face. "A lot of bad things have happened," he agreed, his voice full of tenderness as he looked down at me. "But think of all the good things too, Abby."

"Like?" I challenged. I still thought the bad outweighed the good overall. There was so much pain over so many years.

"Like, I've got a twin brother who might not be a total asshole after all," he started, making a little check mark with his finger on my cheek for each point. "Storm's free of Adrian now, and although it was hard for my dad to hear about my mom, I think in the end it will actually make him feel better. At least he'll know that she never made the choice to leave him. And what about Liz? Liz is a werewolf! And not just any wolf, she's some kind of powerful wolf descended from kings. I don't even know what that means, but it's going to be amazing for her. And she and Eli found each other. All of that is good."

He did make some valid points. "I suppose," I agreed as he brushed the last few teardrops from my eyelashes.

"And it's only going to get better," he promised, placing sweet kisses on my eyelids. "Now that we know everything that happened, we can all start to heal together. And that's where you come in. You always know how to make it better."

He was one to talk. He always knew how to make me feel better too. "I love you, Oliver."

"I love you too. Now, let's get some sleep," he suggested. "All this showing you my love has worn me out."

I poked him in the ribs, making him laugh, but I knew he wasn't exaggerating. I was exhausted, and I was sure he must be too. Once we both closed our eyes, it was only seconds until we fell asleep.

When I woke up, it was still dark in the room and Oliver was fast asleep. I closed my eyes to try to get back to sleep, but my stomach growled and I realized I'd hardly eaten anything the day before. We'd grabbed some food on the way home in the car but obviously it hadn't been quite enough.

I slipped out of Oliver's embrace and put a robe on before heading downstairs to the pack house kitchen. The whole house was silent, but as I approached the kitchen, I could smell someone else in there, someone not from Oliver's pack.

"Eli?"

Oliver's brother was sitting at the table in the dark, the light of his phone screen illuminating his face. He looked up in surprise as I said his name.

"Oh, hey, Abby. You're up early."

"So are you," I pointed out, walking over to him. "What are you doing?"

He looked back down at his phone. "I was trying to do some research."

"About?" I prompted, sitting down across from him, my hunger temporarily forgotten as my curiosity took precedence.

"About the Alpha Kings," he admitted somewhat sheepishly. "Liz is their descendant and she has the source's power inside her now, and I don't really know what that means for her. I was hoping I could try to figure it out, so I can help her."

My heart melted both at the sentiment and at the rather embarrassed look on his face, that face that was so much like my mate's but also completely unlike him too.

"What have you found out?"

"Well, when Cedric, the king who lost the source, lost his power, he was replaced by the Alpha council, and that's how wolf society has always been run here in America too. So even though Liz is technically the rightful queen, I don't know if anyone's eager to have a king or a queen again after all this time."

"What was your plan if you got the source?" I asked, which was something I'd been wondering about for a while now. "What were you going to do with it?"

He grimaced, looking more ashamed than embarrassed this time. "I was going to go to the council and demand their submission. I was going to take the authority whether they wanted me or not."

"Ah. I don't think Liz will want to do that," I deadpanned.

He looked at me in surprise, and then he laughed. His laugh was different from Oliver's, I noticed. Another way to tell them apart.

"No, I don't think she will," he agreed, still chuckling. "But I don't want her to lose out on what's rightfully hers either."

"What about you?" I asked. "What about your responsibility to your pack? Liz has a place as your Luna, doesn't she?"

They hadn't actually said they were accepting each other yet but it certainly felt like it was leaning that way.

"Of course," Eli quickly agreed. "But I feel that she's meant for something greater than that. If there's something she's meant to be, I want to help her reach it. I don't want to hold her back."

That was probably the sweetest thing I'd heard out of his mouth so far, but it seemed obvious to me he hadn't been in many real relationships so far. He was missing one rather important thing.

"You should talk to her," I suggested gently. "Find out what she actually wants to do before you decide what's best for her."

His eyes widened slightly, as if that hadn't occurred to him yet, but he nodded in agreement. "You're right. Of course. I will."

Eli got to his feet as if he was going to go do it right now, but then he turned back to me.

"By the way, Jenny's on her way here. She said she has a few things she wants to say to my father face-to-face. She caught the last flight last night."

That was good. The sooner we could get that all out of the way, the better. "Storm is coming too," I told him. "Oliver heard back from her right away. She'll be here later this morning."

"Then we can get this over with," he said grimly.

It was clear he thought Adrian's time was running short, and it didn't sound like he was too broken up about it. And for once, I couldn't really disagree. Although I still struggled with capital punishment among wolves, in this case, even I could see it was justified.

"It was nice talking to you, Abby," Eli said, sounding almost surprised that he was saying it. "I'll see you later."

He left me, and I grabbed a banana, downing it quickly along with some juice to quiet my rumbling stomach, and then I headed back to bed and the warmth of my mate that awaited me there.

~Elijah~

After I finished making Liz feel good that night, I held her until she fell asleep. It was something I'd never done before, going to sleep with a woman. Usually once the goal was achieved, the goal being a satisfactory orgasm for me of course, I wanted nothing more to do with them. But being next to Liz, having her in my arms, it gave me a sense of peace I wasn't sure I'd ever had before, other than perhaps for that brief moment when I woke up in heaven, or whatever place I'd gone where I'd met my mom and aunt.

But here in this world? Liz's embrace was the most peaceful place I'd ever found, and as I lay next to her, now more than ever, I was determined to prove myself worthy of it.

She had doubts about whether I wanted her or her power, I knew that. My change of heart about our mating happened to coincide with her ownership of the source, and I could see how she might misinterpret it. I had to admit it didn't look good.

And the more I thought about it, and especially after my conversation with Abby in the kitchen, the more certain I became of the best way to prove myself to her once and for all. Abby said I needed to talk to Liz about it, but I thought that was only partly true. I needed to prove myself to her first, and then we could talk.

When Liz woke up in the morning, I was already ready for the day, showered and dressed in some of the extra clothes Oliver had left for me in my room. We were the same size, after all. I had gone back down to the kitchen when it was a little livelier and gotten some fresh coffee and a muffin and some fruit and I brought it all back up to Liz's room.

"Eli?" She looked over at me, blinking in surprise. Too much surprise, I thought, considering I had spent the night here with her.

"Yeah? Is everything okay?"

Her face scrunched up in the most adorable confusion. "I can see you."

Now I was the one who was confused. "That's good, since I'm right here."

"No, I mean..." She reached for the glasses that were on the bedside table. "I can see you without my glasses."

She put them in and then winced, pulling them straight off again.

"Whoa, those are so strong." She looked down at them in consternation and then back up at me. "What's going on?"

I wasn't entirely sure, but I had a theory. "Maybe the source is healing you," I suggested. "Making you stronger the longer it's inside you. Do you feel different in any other way?"

She tilted her head to the side, as if listening to her body. "I just feel... really good."

"You look really good too," I couldn't help pointing out, smiling as she blushed at the compliment. "Come on, have something to eat and then we'll go outside."

"Outside?" she asked curiously as she took the muffin and took a bite. "What's outside?"

"You need to shift," I told her. "Your wolf must be dying to get out. She's been cooped up inside you since you turned 18."

Liz's eyes went adorably wide. "I don't know how to do that!"

I couldn't help laughing at her outburst. "That's why I'm going with you," I explained. "I'll help you, Liz. You don't need to worry, I'll be there for you."

I meant for everything, not just for the shift, and I was pretty sure she got that from the way the colour crept into her cheeks again.

When she finished eating, we found some loose clothes she could put on, since she'd need to be taking them off again soon anyway, and then we headed out to the woodland area behind the pack house. This was a nice territory, I thought, looking around Oliver's land for the first time in the daylight. It wasn't like the redwood forest at home, but it was nice all the same. I could get used to it.

"So what do I do?" Liz asked nervously. She did look different without her glasses on, but it was a good different. I liked being able to see her eyes better.

"You're going to let your wolf take control of your body," I explained. "She'll know what to do. It's an instinct they're born with."

She went quiet for a moment, and I was sure she was speaking to her wolf in her head. A couple of times, she nodded, which made me smile. It wasn't like her wolf could see her, after all. She'd get used to that with time.

Finally they seemed to reach an agreement and she looked over at me with a bit more confidence. "You'll stay with me the whole time?"

"Of course," I promised. "Now, take off your clothes."

Since she'd already been completely naked in front of me last night, the request didn't seem to make her too uncomfortable, and once she had removed everything, I took her hands, letting her feel the spark and warmth of our bond.

"Listen to your wolf," I instructed, keeping my voice as soothing as possible. "Give her control."

Liz closed her eyes, breathing deeply, and for a moment or two, nothing happened. Then, slowly, fur began to form on the surface of her skin, and I let go, taking a step back to watch the transformation. It was a privilege to be here for this, and when the shift was complete, I simply stared at her in awe.

Her wolf was a golden light brown, shimmering in the sunlight. It almost looked like she was made of light herself. She couldn't look any more regal if she tried.

As quickly as I could, I stripped down too and shifted into my own black wolf. We made a contrasting pair, her shiny golden colour and my jet black one, but somehow it went together perfectly too. My wolf was so excited to have his mate that he scampered around her like a puppy, looking for attention.

At least I can control myself a little better than that. Though perhaps I hadn't been all that different, worshipping between her legs last night.

We went for a long run, stopping a few times for our wolves to nuzzle and nip at each other, but they both seemed to accept that that was all they could do until Liz and I had fully mated and marked each other. I hoped that time wasn't going to be very far away at all. Maybe it would even be tonight. I could hope, at least. But first, we still had a few other things to take care of.

As we were returning to the pack house, Oliver linked with me. 'Jenny's just arrived. She's asked to see you.'

That was good. I had a lot to talk to her about, things that I wanted to clear up before I spoke to Liz about our future.

Liz and I shifted back and got re-dressed, then headed back inside. Abby was waiting for us and she offered to stay with Liz while I went to see Jenny, and then we would meet up with the others and my father.

Jenny was waiting for me in a small sitting room and she gave me a hug when I came in, which took me by surprise. She had never been the hugging kind, at least not since I was very young.

"So you know now that your father and I were mates," she began, diving straight into things. "But I imagine you have some other questions for me."

"I do," I confirmed. I had so many I barely knew where to begin, but I supposed the rejection was a good place to start. "Did you ever tell my mother? Did she know he rejected you?"

"No." Jenny shook her head firmly. "I never told anyone, not even Nicole. When it happened, she was away from home. She was here, actually."

She indicated the Jade Moon pack house around us.

"But we all thought she was coming back, and Adrian was so certain they would still be mates, so I didn't want her to feel badly, knowing he had rejected me for her. And then when they weren't mates, well, there didn't seem any point in bringing it up then either. And then when she got pregnant, things were even more complicated. There was just never the right time, you know?"

I could understand that. Sometimes small secrets seemed to take on a life of their own and grow into giant ones almost before anyone was aware it had happened.

"Oliver told me about the letters you sent him, the ones from my mom," I said next. "You mentioned you were a doctor? I've never known you as a doctor."

For my whole life, she had been the tough one in the pack, the one who led interrogations. No one wanted to get on her bad side. Picturing her as a healer was completely foreign to me.

Her smile was wistful. "I used to be. Then Adrian decided that I was abusing that position to get close to you. I don't know exactly what he was afraid of. Maybe that I would help Nicole to take you from him? I'm not sure, but he sent me away to be 're-trained'. That's when I learned the enforcement that I've done for the pack ever since."

So he'd not only rejected her, he took away her position too? "Why didn't you tell me this when I became Alpha? You could have gone back to what you wanted to do then."

"I was afraid," she admitted. "Adrian still had spies within the pack. I was afraid he would come back."

Even in exile, my father's reach had extended further than I realized. He'd controlled and manipulated all of us for far too long. "Well, you don't have to live in fear anymore," I assured her. "He's never going back there again. Whatever Alpha Patrick, you and Storm decide to do with him, even if he lives, he'll never be allowed to return."

She nodded, letting out a deep breath, like a weight had been lifted from her shoulders.

"You can go back to being a doctor if you want to," I continued. "But I'd like you to consider one other position first."

That got her attention, and she looked at me curiously. "What position is that?"

It was my turn to breathe deeply, before I said the words I never expected to say in my life. "I'd like to make you Alpha."

"What?" She couldn't have looked more confused, her eyes wide with surprise.

"I'd like to give the pack to you, Jenny," I told her. "You should have been Luna of the Seven Hills for all these years, and it was taken from you. I can't give you back any of that time, but I can give you the next best thing. Lead the pack for me. Take better care of it than I did."

"But... what about you?" Jenny was still confused. "Where will you go if you're not Alpha?"

A small smile crossed my lips. "You don't have to worry about me. I have a new queen to serve."

~Oliver~

My dad and I were already sitting in his office, talking over the previous day's events, when Elijah and Jenny came in. My dad got to his feet and greeted Jenny warmly, which surprised me until I remembered that they had met before. She had stayed here all during my mother's pregnancy, of course. As far as I knew, they hadn't seen each other since then, but they both looked happy to see each other again now.

"I can't believe Adrian killed her," Jenny murmured softly, looking between all three of us. "I had no idea."

That was obvious from the genuine look of sadness on her face, but I had never thought she did know about it. It was a shock to all of us.

With a slight shake of her head, she turned to me with a warm smile. "It's nice to see you again, Oliver. I'm sorry that I sent you straight off to Adrian the last time we met. If I had known..."

"None of us knew," I assured her, cutting off her unnecessary apology. If we were going to start apologizing for things Adrian had done, we'd be here all day. "His selfishness is almost incomprehensible."

She gave a huff of acknowledgement. "That's one way to put it."

There was a new light in her eyes since the last time I'd seen her, an excitement that seemed slightly at odds with the occasion, but before I could discover its cause, the office door opened again and my mate walked in.

"Storm's just arrived," Abby told us, turning back to welcome the last arrival to our rather unusual meeting this morning.

Storm stepped into the room behind Abby with her usual slightly cocky expression, but it quickly faded as her eyes landed on my dad. She stopped dead, mid-step, staring at him, her posture surprised and defensive, and Abby and I glanced at each other in confusion.

Storm didn't know my dad, did she? Why was she reacting to him like that?

Looking for answers, I turned to my dad, but he was just staring at her too, his eyes wide and his mouth hanging open. I didn't think I'd ever seen him lost for words like this.

I was just about to open my own mouth to ask what on earth was going on when he let out a low growl. "Mate."

Stunned silence filled the room as I looked from my dad to Storm to Abby, and back again. No one uttered a word.

Mates? Was that even possible?

My dad had already had a second chance mate and rejected her, years ago. It was incredibly rare for any werewolf to get another destined mate after that.

But maybe, because Storm had been the one to be rejected, her getting her second chance overrode my dad's previous actions?

Whatever the case, it didn't seem like they were faking it. They both looked completely shell-shocked and as I took in Storm's appearance again, looking at her bright red hair, tattoos and piercings through new eyes, the idea of her and my very traditional father almost made me laugh. He had once told Abby that she didn't look enough like a Luna to be my mate. Even though he'd had other reasons for trying to separate us, I knew he still had a lot of conservative ideas, and I didn't think Storm would fit into very many of them at all.

And what was she thinking? She had literally just yesterday gotten rid of the mate who had strung her along for years. She seemed pretty happy to gain her freedom at the time. Did she even want a mate after all of that?

"Do you want us to give you a minute?" my sweet, sensitive mate asked the couple who were still just staring at each other across the room.

"No, it's okay." My dad gave his head a shake, trying to collect himself. He came out from behind his desk and walked over to Storm. "I'm Alpha Patrick West. Welcome to the Jade Moon pack."

He offered Storm his hand to shake, and as she placed hers into it, a visible shiver ran through her body. Obviously she could feel the mate sparks between them.

"Storm Mayfield." Her voice had none of its usual bravado as she and my dad stood there, unable to take their eyes off each other, their hands still connected.

"Storm," he whispered, his voice barely audible. "I can't say it suits you. You seem more like the calm that comes afterwards."

I raised my eyebrows at Abby, who was trying not to grin, her eyes dancing in excitement. Who knew my dad could be so poetic?

Storm seemed surprised too. She slipped her hand out of his, turning away, but then looked over at him almost shyly. "You could call me Stephanie, if you prefer."

This time it was Eli who caught my eye, his expression showing he was just as shocked by the change in her as I was, or maybe even more so. He'd known her longer, after all. But that's what the mate bond did, it made you forget everything you ever thought you knew about yourself. I knew it, Abby knew it, and now Eli knew it too. He may think Storm was acting strangely, but I suspected he had no idea how much he himself had changed since we first met yesterday.

My dad cleared his throat as he turned back to the rest of us. "Well. Obviously Stephanie and I have some things to discuss later. But for now, let's focus on why we're all here. Former Alpha Adrian Reynolds is currently in our holding cell, accused of the murder of my mate, the attempted murder of both his sons, and generally being a manipulative, self-centred asshole. Does that sound about right?"

That summed it up pretty well for me, and everyone else nodded their agreement too.

"Just the first one of those things is enough to warrant his death," my dad continued. "But a quick execution seems too good for him. My son's thoughtful mate had the very clever idea of bringing all the people he's harmed here to help decide on the most appropriate fate for this worthless excuse for a wolf."

He gave Abby a nod of acknowledgement, and she gave him an encouraging smile back.

"He regained consciousness this morning and my pack doctors have been checking him over. He seems unharmed, for the time being. So before I have him brought up here, I wanted to know your thoughts."

Jenny and Storm looked at each other a little curiously, and I realized that, with the surprise of my dad and Storm learning they were mates, no one had introduced the two women to each other. Eli obviously realized the same thing because he stepped in to do it now while I marvelled at the strangeness of the whole situation.

My biological father's first and second chance mates together in one room, where the second chance mate was being given a second chance of her own with my adopted father. *You couldn't make this stuff up.*

"Well, he rejected me, as you all know," Jenny began. "But honestly, that wasn't the worst part. He took away the profession I loved and made me do something completely different instead, something that went against all my natural inclinations. So if I had to choose a punishment for him, it would be something that did the same to him, something that made him feel uncomfortable and unnatural for as long as possible."

Storm nodded in approval. "And because he kept me hanging on so long, I agree that a quick execution is not enough. Whatever the punishment is, it should be long and drawn out, so he has plenty of time to think about all the selfish and evil decisions he made."

My dad thought all that over. "I can't disagree with either of you, but the longer we hold him, the greater the chance he could escape, and that's something I can't allow. So long as he has his Alpha strength, he's a threat. So unless anyone has an idea on how we can eliminate that..."

A gentle knock at the door startled all of us. No one from the pack should be interrupting us, they all knew better than to disturb the Alpha during a meeting.

I was closest, so I went over and opened the door, and was even more surprised to see Liz on the other side. I almost didn't recognize her for a moment without her glasses on. She looked a bit less like Abby without them.

Abby had told me that Liz would wait with Jack and Whitney while all of this was going on, so I was immediately worried that something had happened. "Liz? Is everything okay?"

"Everything's fine," she assured me. "I just couldn't help overhearing your conversation."

Overhearing it? Through a closed door and whatever other distance was between us? What sense did that make?

"What did you hear?" Abby asked curiously, obviously having the same questions I did.

"About your dilemma," Liz explained. "How to properly punish Eli's father without him posing a danger to anyone else."

I still didn't understand how she could have heard any of that, but apparently she had, so I asked the next obvious question. "And?"

She gave me a shy smile. "I think I have a solution."

Chapter Twenty-One

~Liz~

Oliver looked confused when I said that I'd heard their conversation, and to be honest, I couldn't really explain it either. I had been sitting in a comfortable living room with Whitney and Jack, trying to fill them in on exactly what was happening between Eli and me, and what was happening to me in general, when I suddenly heard the conversation quite clearly in my head, starting with Eli introducing Jenny and Storm to each other. I didn't know who Jenny was, but I remembered Storm well enough from the day before.

Curious, I followed the voices until I found myself outside the door marked 'Alpha's Office'. I had heard every word and I knew exactly what the answer to their problem was, though how I knew it, I couldn't exactly explain.

Perhaps, like Eli had said outside when he helped me turn into a wolf, it was just a matter of instinct.

Changing into a wolf was the single strangest experience of my life. Although I could still hear and see everything as it happened, I no longer had control over my body at all. It should have been terrifying, but it wasn't at all. It was almost freeing to experience life as an animal, from a completely different perspective, and especially to go through the whole thing with Eli, who was as supportive and patient as I could have

"

possibly hoped for. He had promised to prove himself to me, and so far he was doing all I could ask.

And since then, it felt like the power inside me was growing. I could feel it humming beneath my skin, so strong that it was almost scary.

Once you've marked your mate, it will be better, my wolf told me. *He'll share it with you and help you to manage it.*

That was another thing I still didn't fully understand. Eli had told me a little about the concept of marking yesterday. I knew now that the tattoos on Abby and Oliver's necks weren't actually tattoos at all, like they'd told us, and I could smell that they shared a common scent, something that was unique to the two of them. I could also tell which of the other werewolves I saw around the house had a mate and which didn't. My nose could tell me far more than it used to.

It was all a little overwhelming.

But for now, I had to focus on what I had come here for. An older man was standing near the desk in the room, and he took a step towards me now. "We haven't been introduced," he said. "But you must be Liz. I'm Alpha Patrick, Oliver's father."

His father? For a second I was confused, but then I realized he must be Oliver's adoptive father, of course, the one whose mate had died. And I knew before he told me that he was the Alpha here because I could feel his strength.

I could feel so many new things.

Since he seemed to be the one in charge, I addressed myself to him. "That's right, I'm Liz, and it's nice to meet you. I didn't want to interrupt, but I think the obvious answer here would be to remove Adrian's wolf. Then he will be forced into doing something that's unnatural for him, as Jenny wanted, it would be for the rest of his life, as Storm wanted, and he wouldn't have any Alpha authority, or any wolf powers at all, to be a threat to anyone."

Everyone looked surprised by my suggestion, but nobody immediately contradicted me. They all took a moment to think it over instead.

"That does make sense," Alpha Patrick said. "But it's not a simple thing to do. We'd have to involve the Alpha council, and personally, I'd rather keep all of this just between us."

There was a general nod of consensus about that. "There might be another way," Oliver spoke up. "Remember how Reeves injected me with something that silenced my wolf? Maybe we could get our hands on that, if he can explain how it was made..."

"He's dead," Storm interrupted, unapologetically. "He won't be explaining anything."

Obviously she had killed him, but nobody seemed bothered by that. If anything, Alpha Patrick gave her a rather impressed look, which didn't seem to me to be the appropriate reaction to her killing someone, but then, this whole world was still very new to me.

"None of that is necessary," I stepped in to explain. "I can do it."

Everyone in the room turned to me in surprise, except perhaps for Eli, who just gave me a rather proud look.

"You can take away his wolf?" Abby asked, giving me a confused look. "How?"

"I don't know exactly," I admitted. "But I know I can."

Alpha Patrick looked at Oliver and I saw his eyes change the same way Eli's had yesterday. I'd asked Eli about that on the way home and he explained that it was something that happened when they communicated with each other in their heads. I could only guess that they were talking about me now, that the Alpha was trying to determine if I could actually do what I was suggesting.

Oliver must have backed me up because a moment later, Alpha Patrick nodded. "Okay. Let's bring him up here then."

Everyone broke into smaller groups as the Alpha sent out his orders. Oliver and Abby spoke to each other quietly while Storm and Jenny did the same, and Eli came over to me.

"Are you feeling okay?" he asked, a look of genuine concern on his face.

I didn't understand the reason for his question. Didn't I look okay? "I'm fine. Why?"

"I can feel the power coming off you," he explained. "It's stronger than this morning."

He could feel it too? "I think it's because of my wolf," I told him. "When I changed into the wolf this morning, I think it might have unlocked something."

"Shifted," he corrected me with amusement in his eyes. "You shifted, not changed."

"Same thing," I retorted, wrinkling my nose at him.

He laughed. "I thought you were a literature major. Aren't words your currency?"

I was almost surprised he remembered that. He really had been listening to me during our conversation in the van.

Before I could reply, the door opened and two large men entered, propping up Eli's father between them. He had some kind of silver chains connecting his arms, which seemed to be weakening him. I remembered what Abby told me about silver being harmful to wolves. I was starting to figure all of this out, slowly.

Alpha Patrick walked over and stood in front of him, his anger and disgust clear on his face. "You know who I am?"

Adrian looked at him with a defiance that, given his current situation, seemed ill-advised at best. "I assume you're Nicole's mate."

"Alpha Patrick West," the Alpha introduced himself, enunciating each word clearly. "Nicole's mate, Oliver's father, and now, the man who holds your life in his hands."

Adrian seemed unfazed. "Kill me then. What are you waiting for?"

He obviously thought that's where this was heading, and wanted to get it over with as quickly as possible.

But Alpha Patrick was not to be rushed. "There are a few other people who want to say some things to you first."

He stepped aside and Jenny and Storm moved forward together. Adrian's eyes widened a little at the sight of the two women side-by-side, but he quickly covered up his surprise with a sneer. "Is this whole reunion on my behalf?"

"I'm here to look into your pathetic face one last time," Jenny said, her voice strong and firm. "And to let you know that no matter what you did to me, you never broke me. I'll have a better life now that you're gone than you could possibly imagine, and once I leave this room, you will never cross my mind again."

"You're a piece of shit, Adrian Reynolds," Storm added bluntly. "And you deserve everything that's coming to you. But I do have one thing to thank you for. By getting yourself captured and bringing me here, I've finally met a man who will be a proper mate to me."

Adrian's bravado melted into confusion and then he looked over at Patrick in disbelief before turning back to Storm. "Him?"

Patrick stepped forward again, taking Storm's hand. "You've spent your whole life taking things that weren't yours. You tried to take Nicole for yourself. You took Eli. You took Jenny's profession, and you took years from Storm, and then you tried to take the source too. But you never once succeeded. Nicole was always mine, to her last breath. Eli is who he is in spite of you, not because of you. Jenny can live her life however she wants from now on and Storm has a home here with me. We will all live better and happier lives now that you're not a part of them anymore. And the source? Well, the rightful owner of it is here to deal with you now."

Everyone in the room turned to me as I stepped forward as confidently as possible, Eli right behind me.

Adrian looked truly shocked for the first time since he'd entered the room, his facade of indifference completely gone. "You?" he sputtered, looking me up and down. "But you were just a human yesterday! You can't be the owner of the source."

He couldn't know how his words mirrored the ones Eli had said to me yesterday, but I could see where Eli had got his prejudices from. At least he seemed to be willing to overcome them now.

"I was never *just* a human," I argued, seeing Eli smile out of the corner of my eye. "But that's exactly what you're going to be."

Reaching out, I put my hands on either side of his temples. The power crackled inside me as it flowed into him, knowing instinctively what it was meant to do. Adrian howled in pain or fear, I couldn't tell which, but eventually his howls turned into sobs. Weak, pathetic, and very human sobs. He suddenly seemed very small, and his wolf scent had vanished.

The power flowed back into me and I released my grip on him, taking a step back.

He looked up at me with a combination of panic and deep despair as his eyes darted back and forth. I suspected he was trying to reach his wolf, but he would find no answer. He was on his own now.

"Don't do this. Just kill me," he whispered, his eyes flitting between me and Alpha Patrick. "Please."

This time it was Eli who replied. "That might be the first time I've ever heard you use that word," he told his father coldly. "But it's far too late for that. You're not dying any time soon. You can stay here and work off your debt to Alpha Patrick. Since it's a debt that can never be repaid, that means you'll get to stay here for the rest of your miserable life. I hope it's a very, very long one."

Adrian's haunted eyes flitted around the room, looking for a single sympathetic face, and finally he settled on Abby. "This is too much," he pleaded with her. "They'll listen to you."

How he knew that, I wasn't sure, but everyone turned to her now and she took a deep breath. As long as I'd known Abby, she always tried to help other people, always tried to see every side in each argument. I, like everyone else, was curious to hear what she would say now.

But when she spoke, her voice was firm. "You lost any right to ask for mercy when you took my mate's mother from him. I have nothing to say on your behalf."

His last hope vanished, Adrian dropped to his knees, almost shrivelling before our eyes. He looked completely pitiful, but I was sure there wasn't anyone among us who pitied him. He had brought this entirely on himself.

"Take him back to the holding cell," the Alpha instructed the men who were still restraining him, though it was now hardly necessary. "I'll give him a few days to accept his new situation before I put him to work."

Adrian was led away and in the sudden silence the rest of us all looked at each other, no one quite sure what to say now.

It was Oliver who finally broke the silence, turning to Abby with a rather cheeky smile.

"So, that was our first week of summer vacation. What do you want to do next week?"

~Abby~

With Adrian stripped of his wolf and heading safely back to his cell, Oliver and I excused ourselves from the others to go and take Whitney and Jack back to town. They still had jobs and lives to get back to, as strange as it might seem after everything we had just been through together. Liz, on the other hand, was going to be staying at the pack house for a little while longer, at least until she fully came to grips with her new identity and until she and Eli came to some kind of decision about what to do next.

"How are you guys feeling about everything?" I asked, turning to face our human friends in the back seat while Oliver drove.

Whitney and Jack looked at each other for a moment, conversing silently with their eyes, before Jack answered. "Well, after everything that went down yesterday, the werewolf thing doesn't even seem like such a big deal anymore."

I had to smile at that and Oliver did too, his warm grey eyes looking over to meet mine for a second before returning to the road. "I promise you, this is not what our lives are usually like," I assured them. "It's generally pretty normal, other than the turning into wolves part."

"Honestly, I think it's kind of cool," Whitney said with a shrug. "It's like you guys have secret identities. We can be your sidekicks."

"Again, we don't usually need any sidekicks," I told her with a laugh. "But I appreciate that. And we're happy to be your sidekicks too, anytime you need us."

It was such a relief to know that they weren't completely freaked out by the whole thing. In fact, they were handling it all better than I could have hoped. We talked and laughed the rest of the way back into town, just like we always had, and when we dropped them off at their house, I was feeling pretty good about the whole thing. I knew they wouldn't tell anyone about us. And even if they did let something slip when they were drinking or something, it's not like anyone would believe them. They'd proven that to us well enough when they laughed at Oliver when he tried to tell them the truth.

Was that really just yesterday morning? It didn't seem possible. So much had changed since then.

After saying goodbye at their house, Oliver and I got back in the car to return to the Jade Moon territory, and I looked over at my mate with a combination of happiness, relief and sheer exhaustion.

"What is it, Heels?" he asked, glancing over at me curiously. "I know that look, you've got something to say."

"I was just thinking about everything," I told him honestly. "Your dad and Storm, for one. What do you think about that?"

Oliver smiled softly. "Honestly, I'm thrilled for him. He's been alone for so long and I'm pretty sure that life with her around isn't going to be boring. She'll keep him on his toes, just like you do for me."

I scrunched up my nose at his teasing, and he laughed. "And what about Liz?" I asked. "Her power is unbelievable. How did she do that to Adrian's wolf?"

I didn't know if she'd actually killed his wolf or just silenced him somehow, but either way, I'd never seen anything like it.

Oliver exhaled. "I have no idea. I've got to admit I was wrong about that source, it really is something. I hope she can control it. It would be easy to get drunk on that kind of power."

That was true, but I knew my friend. I didn't think that was too likely, but I did still have a few concerns about Eli. Although he was obviously making an effort to change, it would be tempting for him to fall back into old patterns. "Maybe I could go and talk to my parents," I suggested. "If my family was involved with guarding it, maybe they have some more information. Even just old family stories might be important."

"I think that's a great idea," Oliver agreed. "But let's just relax for a few days first, okay? I don't think I can handle any more excitement right now."

As soon as the word 'excitement' was out of his mouth, my familiar desire for him stirred up deep inside me.

"Oh really?" I gave him a challenging grin. "Not even a little excitement?"

"Heels." He shot me a look of warning as a low growl rumbled in his chest. "What are you up to?"

"I was just thinking about that little dead-end road up ahead," I teased him, knowing he would know immediately which one I meant. It was hard to keep our hands off each other for the whole of the drive between town and the pack house and we'd stopped there more than once before.

Oliver groaned at the reminder, and it wasn't long before we were pulling over and shedding all the necessary pieces of clothing. He slid over into the passenger seat with me, pulling me on top of him, and when I sank down onto his hard and ready cock, we both sighed in pleasure.

"Is this always going to feel so good?" he asked me, his face buried in my neck, sucking and nipping at my mark.

"I really hope so," I moaned. We'd been together for months already, and it was only getting better.

It didn't take long for us to both reach our climax, the combination of our need for each other and the slight thrill at the chance of being caught was more than enough to push us over the edge. We shuffled back into our proper seats and back into our pants, and then Oliver pulled back onto the road, heading for the pack house once again.

"You know, there's a good chance we'll have twins when we start trying for a baby," he pointed out, his mind obviously still lingering on our previous activity. "It does run in my family after all."

"As long as they're not cursed, that's okay with me," I replied, making him smile.

"Have you thought about when that might be?" he asked, giving me an uncharacteristically hesitant smile. "When you want to start having pups, I mean?"

The question took me by surprise, but I supposed with all the information about his own childhood that had come out, it wasn't completely out of the blue. "We're still both in college," I reminded him.

There might have been a slight disappointment in his eyes, but Oliver nodded in understanding. "I know. But with all the excitement in the last week, you haven't been forgetting to take your pills or anything...?"

"Oliver!" I crossed my arms at him. "What are you trying to say? Do I look pregnant to you?"

"Of course not," he quickly assured me, his eyes widening with panic at the idea he might have insulted me. "I just wanted you to know that I wouldn't be upset about it, if it happened. But if you're not ready, that's okay too. I'll be excited whenever it happens."

"You're crazy," I laughed at him. "How many 21-year-old guys are thinking about kids?"

"Only the ones who are crazy in love." He winked at me, then took my hand in his. "I promise I won't bring it up again until you do, but I just wanted you to know I'm excited about the idea. I love you."

"I love you too, Oliver." I leaned over to place a kiss on his cheek. I was sure I wasn't pregnant now, but knowing that he had been thinking about it did make me happy. I couldn't wait to have his pups someday. He was going to be an amazing father, and an amazing Alpha, and now with our new extended family, our future looked even brighter.

I really was the luckiest girl in the world.

~Elijah~

When the meeting was breaking up and Oliver and Abby had already left, I asked Alpha Patrick if I could speak to him privately. He was surprised and perhaps a bit frustrated with the request. He had, after all, just met his mate and I was sure he was anxious to speak to her, but I was acting on behalf of my mate too, so I couldn't put it off. I needed to know what my options were before I explained my plans to Liz.

Jenny, Storm and Liz all left together to give us some privacy, and I sat down across the desk from the man who could have raised me if things had gone just a little differently. I'd already seen enough of him to know that my life would have been pretty different had that been the case, but there was no point in regretting the past. Nothing could be done to change it now. We could only move forward, all of us.

"I'm going to be relinquishing my position as Alpha of the Seven Hills pack," I told him with no preamble. He had other places to be and so did I, so there was no point in beating around the bush.

He looked as shocked as perhaps only another Alpha could be. "Why would you do that? Who are you naming in your place?"

"I want to give the pack to Jenny," I explained. "I care about my pack, of course, but it was also my father's pack. There are a lot of memories tied up there for me, and I'd like to distance myself from him as much as possible. Jenny is a strong and capable leader and she deserves a chance to lead the pack that should have been hers as my father's mate anyway."

Patrick nodded, thinking it all over. "I can understand that. But what will you do instead?"

"Well, that's the other reason I'm doing it," I admitted. "My place is with my mate. She's going to need all the support she can get as she finds her place and learns to control her power, and I want to dedicate myself to her entirely."

A smile crossed his face. No doubt he was thinking of his own new mate. "Liz has no pack though, does she? If you leave your pack too, you will essentially be unprotected."

"That was exactly why I wanted to talk to you," I said. "I was hoping that perhaps we could stay here, at least temporarily, until we figure out where her proper place is."

This time his smile was more deliberate. "I think that's a wonderful idea, and I know Oliver will think so too. It would be nice for us all to get to know each other better."

I had been kind of hoping for the same thing, though I hadn't wanted to admit it to him. I was glad to hear him say it.

"Oliver and Abby are spending the rest of the summer here," he continued. "Oliver will be doing some preparations to take over as Alpha at the end of the next college year. I was planning on taking him with me to the Alpha council conference taking place in a few weeks. Perhaps you and Liz could come along then and we could make some introductions and sound out people's feelings about the return of the royal bloodline."

"You can feel it too, can't you?" I asked. Her power was undeniable.

"It is hard to miss," he agreed. "But it means others won't miss it either, others who might not want to have a queen back at all. We'll have to proceed very carefully to keep her safe."

We. It had been a long time since someone had my back for any reason other than that they had to, but Patrick had no obligation to me. He simply wanted to help, with no expectations in return. Like a real parent should.

"Your mother would be really proud of you," he added softly, almost as if he'd heard my thoughts. "She was so sad after Oliver was born and I never really understood why. Now I realize it must have been because she was missing you. I know my mate and I know how much love she had in her heart. She loved you, Eli, even if she never got to tell you so herself."

"I know." I really did. She had, after all, told me so, just yesterday. "But thank you."

He nodded. "Alright. Well, I'm sure you want to check on your mate, and I have someone I need to talk to as well."

"I've known Storm for a few years," I told him as we both got to our feet. "She's pretty unique. Life with her would be interesting."

"I've gathered that," he said a little wryly. "I'm looking forward to getting to know her for myself."

A strange warmth spread through my chest, and I realized after a moment's confusion that it was happiness, but not for myself. It was for Patrick. I couldn't really remember ever feeling joy on someone else's behalf before. My father had always encouraged me not to care about how anyone else felt, but it was actually kind of nice. This certainly was a whole new world for me.

We left the office and went to the kitchen together where we found the three women sitting at the table over a cup of coffee. "Do you want to join us?" Storm invited. Her usual smug smirk was missing. She was actually just smiling normally, and it kind of freaked me out.

"I need a few minutes with my mate," I replied, and Liz looked at me curiously. "If that's okay with her, of course."

Nice save. I was getting the hang of this, slowly.

Liz excused herself from the others and came over to me. "What's going on?"

"Let's talk in private," I suggested. "Maybe back in your room?"

Her cheeks flushed a little, clearly remembering what took place in her room the night before, and I definitely had intentions of continuing in that vein today if she was interested. But first, I really needed to talk to her.

Once we were alone, the door closed and locked behind us, I invited Liz to sit next to me on the bed. "I know we just met officially yesterday," I began. "And I know I didn't make the best first impression, but I meant what I said yesterday about proving myself to you, Liz. I'm not interested in power anymore or having people to control. That was the kind of life my father lived, and now that I've seen exactly what it did to him, I don't want any part of it."

"But you still have a pack to lead," she pointed out. "That's still a part of you."

That was the perfect set-up to tell her my news. "Actually, I don't. I'm giving my pack to Jenny."

Liz's lips parted in surprise. "What? Why?"

"I just told you why," I pointed out. "It's not about the power for me anymore. What's important to me right now is being there for you, and your life is here, not in Oregon. Your family, they're here in New York too, aren't they?"

Oliver's nursery rhyme about the source's owner had indicated her mother lived in the state, at least. "They were," she replied with a bit of sadness. "My parents died last year."

"So you're all on your own?" The protective urges I was already feeling towards her grew even stronger, so strong I could hardly stand it.

"I was," she corrected me gently. "Now I have you."

Her simple trust in me nearly brought me to my knees.

"You absolutely do." I took her hands in mine. "Liz, I want you as my mate. Not just because you're powerful, although you definitely are. There's no denying that. But I want you because you're amazing. You risked your life for me more than once even when you didn't really understand our bond or what was happening. You accepted the source without even knowing what it would do to you, and you used it to save my life. If I didn't want to dedicate myself to you after all that, I would have to be a complete idiot. And I don't think I'm a complete one, at least."

She smiled at me, a sweet, happy smile that filled my body with light. "I want you for my mate too, Eli."

I couldn't stop the grin that spread across my face, and I leaned forward to kiss her, but she put her hand on my chest to stop me. The sparks that flew between us were even stronger now than they'd been before, no doubt driven on by her new power.

"There's something I need to tell you first though," she said, looking up at me almost apologetically.

"What is it?" I couldn't imagine anything that would change how certain I was about this.

"Do you remember how I told you that being my mate would give you the ability to change into different animals?" she asked sheepishly, and I nodded, laughing too. I remembered. "Well, that wasn't true, but it will give you something."

"All I want is you," I promised, leaning forward again, but again she stopped me.

"I know. But if you become my mate, officially, then you will share in the source's power. It will divide between the two of us."

This time it was my mouth that dropped open in surprise. *Seriously?* All this time, all the years I spent looking for the source, and all I had to do to get it was accept my mate?

It was so ironic that all I could do was laugh. Liz looked a little startled at first, but then she joined in, smiling at me with genuine affection, the kind I'd never really had before.

"Does that mean you're okay with that?" she asked tentatively as our laughter died off.

"If it means I can help you, then absolutely," I told her honestly. "We'll share the burden and we'll share the responsibility. Everything I have and everything I am is yours now."

"Thank you," she whispered, her eyes welling with tears, and the sight of them almost killed me. "There's just one thing we have to do then, I guess."

"What's that?" I wasn't entirely sure where she was going with this.

"We have to transfer the power," she explained.

"And you know how to do that?"

"I do," she confirmed. "Apparently, I have to mark you."

~**Liz**~

Eli gave me a devastatingly sexy smile when I said I had to mark him to share my power, and my body immediately went haywire. My mind flashed back to what we did last night on this very bed and my cheeks began to flush as desire for him ran through me, strong and fast.

How could he affect me like that with just one look?

"Do you know how wolves usually mark each other, Liz?" His voice was low and deep, making my whole body vibrate to its frequency.

Was that a trick question? "You told me that we'll bite each other, with our wolf teeth."

"That's right," he agreed, still giving me that fiendish smile. "But what I mean is, do you know the typical context in which wolves bite each other?"

I really had no idea what he was getting at, but his tone of voice had my heart racing anyway. "No. What do you mean?"

I kind of pictured it being like a vampire's kiss. I was still more familiar with vampires than werewolves after all, so it was the closest thing I could think of.

Eli leaned closer to me, his grey eyes piercing into me. "It's usually done during mating. Or what you would call sex."

"Oh." That was all I managed to get out before my throat closed up, my arousal getting stronger by the second.

Eli didn't seem to mind my limited response though. He kept talking. "I would love to mark you right now, Liz, and have you mark me. I can't wait to let everyone know you're mine, but I want you to be ready too."

I swallowed, trying to breathe again. I appreciated that he was asking the question, and I tried to think about it logically rather than relying on my body for guidance. Was I really ready for this?

"And once we mark each other, that's forever?"

That was what I had understood from the things he'd said, but I wanted to be sure.

"Pretty much, yes. We'll be connected for the rest of our lives."

"And you're sure?" I couldn't help asking one more time. I'd been ready to give myself to a man once before only to find out he never had any intention of being with me at all, and the last thing I wanted to do was repeat my mistakes.

"Liz, I just gave up my pack for you," he reminded me, his tone teasing and patient. "My life is beside you now, and I'll wait as long as I have to until you're sure. But I'm sure right now."

He certainly looked sure. And if I was being honest with myself, I was too. So what was I waiting for? I'd decided last night to make this leap, so it was time to put my money where my mouth was.

"I'm sure too."

His face lit up in genuine happiness, just for a second, then quickly melted into something more heated. "In that case..." he began, but he never finished his sentence. His lips found mine instead and the whole world seemed to melt away.

The sparks between us were even stronger now, like pure electricity flowing from my body into his and then back again. When his hand settled on my hip, it sent a shot of energy directly into my centre, and my wolf howled in delight. Apparently she knew where this was going, and she was just as eager as I was to get ourselves mated properly.

Gently, Eli lifted me into his strong arms and then lowered me onto the bed, his lips never leaving mine. Impatient fingers pulled at my clothes, and it seemed I barely had time to blink before they were all crumpled on the floor. Only when I was fully naked did he stand back up, just long enough to undress himself too, and I watched in awe as he revealed his body to me.

I'd seen him naked in the field the day before, of course, but there had been quite a lot of other things going on. I hadn't had time to fully appreciate the magnificence of his sculpted body at the time, and of course, he wasn't aroused then. Now his cock was standing at full attention, hard and ready, and as he looked down at me, I knew that it was all because of me.

Me. The girl that had never been anyone's first choice now had this stunning creature, half god-like man and half animal, at her beck and call, and it made me feel powerful and desirable in a way I never had before. Strength and need battled within me, my whole body aching for the release only he could give me.

As he turned to the side, something caught my eye: a tattoo on the back of his neck. "What is that?"

His hand went to where my eyes were focused. "It's a tattoo I got to symbolize my dedication to my quest," he told me. "It was meant to be the path to the source, but now I realize, it was really the path to you."

My heart melted a little more at his sweet words, and I couldn't wait a moment longer. "Let me feel you, Eli."

His eyes darkened as he crawled back onto the bed, hovering above me, and his eyes closed in pure pleasure as I reached down to feel that incredible-looking cock for myself. It was hard and strong, and so big my fingers couldn't quite touch as I wrapped my hand around it. "Fuck, Liz," he groaned as I gently stroked him.

Seeing the way he reacted to my touch made me feel even more confident, and I gave him a teasing wink. "That's the plan, isn't it?"

He looked at me in surprise for a second, not expecting my teasing, and then he grinned, making my whole body weak with desire once more. "Don't mind if I do."

His words made me laugh, but only for a second. In the next instant, his lips were back on mine and he lowered himself onto me, letting our whole bodies connect, and the explosion of energy between us was the most intense thing I had ever felt in my life.

Hands and lips and tongues explored each other's bodies. When he lowered himself to kiss my neck, my wolf howled again in anticipation, and I knew without her telling me that it was the spot where he would place his mark.

But not yet. First we had to mate.

Eli's fingers slipped between my legs just as they had done last night, and my body arched towards him naturally. As he slipped one finger inside me, his tongue swirling around my nipple, I clung onto his shoulders to try to keep my balance, even though I was already laying down and there was nowhere I could fall.

"You definitely feel ready," he murmured as he trailed kisses back up towards my lips. "Are you still sure, Liz?"

I didn't think I could have refused him now if my life depended on it. My aching need had never been so strong. There was an emptiness inside me that only he could fill, I knew that with complete certainty.

He was made for me.

"I'm sure. I... I love you, Eli."

He froze, and for a terrible second I thought I had said the wrong thing. But when he raised his head and his eyes connected with mine, the desire and joy and love there was everything I could have hoped for.

"I love you too, Liz."

As his words lingered in the air, his cock drove into me, hard enough to push past the natural barrier of my virginity, and I cried out in pain and happiness all at the same time. He swallowed my cry with his kiss while his fingers moved to my clit, giving me pleasure again while my body got used to the feel of him.

Eventually my desire grew again, and despite the lingering discomfort, I needed more. My hips started to move against him and Eli quickly took the hint, his cock sliding out of me almost the whole way before he pushed back in again. It still hurt a little, but not as much. The third time it barely hurt at all, and after that I lost track of everything. I was far too lost in the taste and feel and smell of him, all my senses combining as the pleasure built inside me, growing stronger and stronger until...

"Eli!"

I called out his name as I came, and he didn't waste any time. His teeth lengthened and sank into my neck as I floated on the wave of my orgasm, and once again, instinct took over. Without even realizing I meant to do it, I grabbed hold of his head, exposing his neck to me and my wolf teeth found the spot they were meant to mark, drawn to it as if by magic. Eli shuddered as I marked him, his orgasm coming at the same time too, coming deep inside me as my teeth were in him.

When we finally broke apart, both breathing heavily, Eli flopped over onto his back beside me and grabbed my hand, holding it tightly as we both stared up at the ceiling, dazed and amazed by what had just happened.

'Did I hurt you?'

I heard the words in my head, but not with my ears, and I turned to look at him curiously. He was giving me a soft smile.

'Answer me in your mind. I can hear you now.' His lips didn't move at all.

'Really?' I tried out tentatively, and his smile widened.

'Really. Now please, tell me. Are you okay? Did it hurt?'

"A little bit," I answered him out loud. "But not for long. And it was more than worth it in the end."

That wasn't even the half of it. It was the most amazing experience of my life and the fact that it was only the first time of many to come made it even more incredible.

"It was amazing for me," he told me, his eyes shining with sincerity. "It's never been like that before. And your power came into me too, I can feel it now. How does it feel for you?"

I hadn't noticed until he asked, but now that he said it, the power inside me felt more under control. It felt manageable. "I feel good," I replied. "Better than good. I feel... whole."

His lips met mine again, but gently this time. "Me too. I thought I knew what was missing in my life, Liz, but I was wrong. It was you the whole time. You're the only thing I need."

The words were so sweet that I couldn't stop my tears, and Eli held me tenderly as I cried, overcome with joy and relief and just plain exhaustion.

It had been one hell of journey to get here, but finally, I had found the place I was meant to be.

~Oliver~

Abby grimaced as she came out of the bathroom the next morning, and I was immediately on alert. "What's wrong, Heels? Are you feeling okay?"

"Just cramps," she told me, holding her hand to her abdomen. "That time of the month."

Oh. I supposed that meant she definitely wasn't pregnant after all.

I couldn't really explain why I was suddenly thinking about it, but I supposed it had to do with finally having a brother after all these years. It got me thinking about what our lives would have been like if we'd grown up together, and that led to me thinking about the life that Abby and I would build for our own children. The thought of it really did excite me, but I knew she had a point. We were both still young, there was plenty of time for all of that later.

We didn't have to be in any rush. Neither of us was going anywhere.

Once we were ready for the day, we headed down to breakfast in the pack house dining room. Several of my friends were already there and we finally got a chance to greet them all properly and talk about what we were going to do over the summer. They all had a lot of plans and we laughed and joked with each other as usual. It was strange to think nobody had any idea of how close we had all come to disaster yesterday if the source had ended up with Reeves or with Adrian, with nothing to restrain them. I supposed they never would know. It was going to be our secret: mine and my brother's, and our amazing mates'.

Just as we were finishing up, Eli and Liz came in, holding hands, and I quickly introduced them to the others. My packmates were all shocked at his appearance, of course, but I kept the explanation short. "This is the twin brother I never knew I had, who was raised by our biological father."

It didn't answer all their questions, but it was a lot quicker than going into all the details.

Having absorbed that, the others left us and Abby and I sat down with Liz and Eli. Abby was almost bouncing with excitement and it wasn't hard for me to see why.

"So you've marked each other," I said, stating the obvious as they dug into their breakfast. "Congratulations."

"Thanks," Eli replied, giving Liz a tender smile. "We're pretty happy about it."

They certainly appeared to be. "So does that mean you're moving to Oregon?" I asked Liz curiously.

She looked at me in surprise before turning to Eli. "You haven't told him?"

This time Abby and I exchanged glances. "Told us what?" she asked.

"Jenny is the new Alpha of the Seven Hills pack," Eli replied, to my astonishment. "I completed the transfer last night before she left.

I could feel Abby's stunned shock through our bond, and it mirrored my own. That was a huge surprise. He really had changed, even more than I had realized. Giving up his position was a huge deal. "What are you going to do instead?"

"I don't know exactly," he admitted. "But Liz and I are going to stay here for the summer at least while we try to figure it out. I've already checked with Alpha Patrick and he said it was alright."

My dad hadn't mentioned that to me, but then again, I hadn't seen him since we got back yesterday. Nobody had seen him, or Storm either for that matter. I had a good idea where they were hiding, but given that it was my father, I didn't want to put too much thought into it. I was sure we'd get the most relevant details soon enough if they appeared bearing each other's marks the same way Liz and Eli had.

"That's wonderful," Abby said enthusiastically, squeezing my hand in excitement at the idea of spending more time with my brother and his mate. "We'll have a great summer."

Eli smiled at her. "Yeah, I really think we will."

Looking around the table, it was hard to believe the changes the last week had brought. My family was a little bigger than it had been then, with my brother, his new mate, and possibly a new stepmother as well.

But at the heart of it all, it was still me and Abby, and that was all that really mattered to me.

Whatever the future brought, we'd figure it out together.

~~THE END~~

The Story Continues...

If you enjoyed the book, please take a moment to
leave a review. Thank you!

Abby and Oliver's story continues in the final
book in the series, Mistaken Meanings.
Turn the page for a preview of the first chapter!

Mistaken Meanings

My mate snarled up at me, her golden-brown eyes narrowed in disgust.

"Is that the best you can do, *Alpha*?"

I hated when she called me Alpha. From anyone else, the word was a mark of respect, even though I wasn't technically an Alpha yet. I would be soon though, it was only a matter of time, and most of the werewolves in our pack treated me accordingly.

Not my mate, though. When she used my title, she did it sarcastically: a reminder that, in her eyes, I wasn't worthy of that title or worthy of her either, for that matter.

I fucking hated it.

I especially hated how much it turned me on.

"If it's so bad, why are you so wet for me?" I growled back at her, thrusting into her harder, our bodies slamming together without an ounce of tenderness. "There isn't a wolf on our territory who can't smell how aroused you are right now. The pups are probably asking their parents what that smell is."

I was exaggerating, of course, but only a little. She was definitely turned on. Her nipples were stiff peaks and her pupils were dilated, though she tried to hide it as she narrowed her eyes at me further.

The condom I was wearing was dripping wet with the proof of her excitement.

"If I'm wet, it's only because it's been so long since I've been truly satisfied," she lied, refusing to give me an inch even as she drew closer to her release.

"You're such a fucking liar. No one makes you come like I do, Marissa. No one ever has."

I pressed down on her clit as I pounded her even harder, and her legs began to shake.

"I hate you so much," she muttered just before her orgasm claimed her, and as she tightened around me, her pussy gripping my hard cock rhythmically, I lost control too.

"Not as much as I hate you," I managed to gasp as I emptied myself into the condom.

Before I'd even stopped pulsing, I pulled out, not wanting to stay inside her a second longer than I had to. Wordlessly, I pulled the condom off, wincing as it came loose, and threw it into the trash can next to the bed. She insisted that I wore a condom every time we had sex, saying she was far too young and beautiful to get pregnant yet; her words, not mine. When I pointed out that she could just go on the pill or something, she point-blank refused, saying I was the one who wanted to fuck her so I could take the responsibility.

She was always crude, never subtle, constantly over-the-top instead of understated. She was nothing at all like the woman I used to dream about ending up with.

That familiar pang of loss hit me again as I pulled my pants back on. After many months and countless sessions with our pack therapist, I finally understood what I had done wrong with Abby, more or less, but I still didn't think it fair that I couldn't have another chance. Instead, I was saddled with a mate who hated me, while the girl of my dreams was mated to another Alpha-to-be from a different pack. The whole thing wasn't right. *He* wasn't right for her; I was. She had just never been able to see that.

Marissa's phone buzzed as she finished putting her own clothes back on. We'd be expected at dinner shortly, but I had caught sight of Marissa in one of her ridiculously short skirts, flirting with one of the men who worked security in the house, and I had to remind her whose mate she was. I could swear she only did it to make me jealous, though why either of us should care, I really didn't know.

"Who's texting you?" I asked with that same unwelcome sting of jealousy, watching as she scrolled through the message. It looked to be a long one.

"One of my friends from the Jade Moon pack. They just had a pack meeting and there was big news."

The Jade Moon pack was Abby's mate's pack, but I refused to think of it as Abby's pack, even though that was where she was right now. Her place was still here, whether she recognized it or not.

"What's the news?" I asked, trying to pretend like I really didn't care. The thought that Abby might be pregnant crossed my mind, and for a moment, I thought I was going to be sick.

Thankfully, that wasn't it. "The Alpha's found a new mate. They're saying it's his third-chance mate?"

Marissa looked up at me in surprise, and I had to admit that was unexpected. Third-chance mates were pretty rare. Usually, once a wolf had exhausted a first and second chance, their only options were to take a chosen mate or remain mate-less.

I knew which I'd prefer.

Marissa was my chosen mate, though not chosen by me. We had been fated mates until I rejected her, but then my father and that fucking arrogant Alpha Patrick of the Jade Moon pack had insisted that I take her back. We reforged our bond through marking each other, but that kind of chosen bond couldn't compare to the strength of the fated mate bond, which had been severed forever when I made the rejection and she accepted it.

I still didn't regret doing it. I would do it again if I could. My actions towards Abby were the only things I would change if I had the chance to do it all over again.

The only reason I didn't reject her again now was because it would cast doubt on my 'rehabilitation', which was necessary if the Alpha position was ever going to be mine.

And now that asshole Alpha was getting his own fated mate, for the third time? Life couldn't be any more unfair.

"There's more," Marissa said, her excitement growing as she read on. She always loved a bit of gossip, like the shallow bimbo that she was. "Oliver has a twin brother! He's going to be staying in the pack too, with his new mate."

Oliver. I hated that name. I hated everything about that guy. Usually, I did my best never to think about him unless I absolutely had to, like when my insensitive mate brought him up. She didn't understand the depth of my feelings for Abby. She'd never even tried to.

Marissa was frowning at the phone now before she looked up at me. "Don't twins usually share a mate? Shouldn't Abby be mated to them both?"

The idea of another man having a claim on Abby when I had none made my anger flare once again. "You don't know anything about it. Why do you care?"

Her brief good humour evaporated as her eyes narrowed at me once again. "I care because it's my old pack. Why do *you* care?"

"I don't care. You're the one who brought it up. Hurry up and get ready for dinner."

Leaving her there, I made my way downstairs on my own and found my father just coming out of his office. I took the opportunity to fill him in on what I'd just learned. "I've just heard that Alpha Patrick has a new mate, and possibly a new son too."

That piqued his interest, as I thought it would, and he invited me into his office to share the details I had, which admittedly weren't many. It had taken a long time for my father to begin to trust me again after the fight I caused between our pack and the Jade Moon pack, but we were slowly getting there. He was starting to give me a few responsibilities again, small ones that I couldn't mess up.

I couldn't let him know I still had feelings for Abby. The full restoration of my standing in the pack depended on it.

He had never understood why Abby was so special. If he had, he would have helped me win her over, rather than standing between us every chance he got. I didn't think I could ever truly forgive him for that.

After I passed on what Marissa told me, my dad called over to the Jade Moon pack, putting the phone on speaker so I could hear it too.

"Alpha Patrick?" My dad smiled when the other Alpha answered, almost looking as though the man didn't make his skin crawl the same way he did for me. Had he really forgotten the defeat we'd suffered at Patrick's hands? "This is Alpha Easton from Forest Ridge. I hear congratulations are in order."

"Good news travels fast," the Alpha replied, sounding far more laid-back than he did the last time I'd spoken with him, here in this very room on the day of the battle I instigated. "Thank you, Alpha Easton. It's still very new, but she's an incredible woman. I'm very lucky."

I rolled my eyes and my father shot me a warning look. The message was clear: I was to be on my best behaviour. "My son is here too, he also wanted to congratulate you."

With real effort, I put on a conciliatory tone. "Congratulations, Alpha Patrick. I hope this is a blessing to you and your pack."

The Alpha's response to me was much shorter and cooler than it had been to my father. "Thank you, Jerrod."

"Forgive me for indulging in gossip," my dad continued, "but the rumour is you've also got another new addition to your pack?"

Alpha Patrick chuckled. "Let me guess: is this rumour's name Marissa?"

He wasn't stupid, I had to give him that much. When my dad confirmed it, Alpha Patrick laughed again.

"Well, in this case, she's right. Oliver's twin brother, Elijah, has joined us temporarily. I'm not sure how long he'll be staying, he was previously Alpha of his own pack on the west coast. I'm looking forward to having his input for as long as he's with us."

Wasn't that cozy? They were all one big, happy family, apparently.

My dad and Alpha Patrick exchanged a few more pleasantries before Alpha Patrick's phone rang again in the background. "Please forgive me," he apologized. "Word of my good fortune seems to be spreading."

"Of course," my father agreed. "Congratulations again. I'll see you at the Alpha council conference next week, I hope?"

"Certainly," Alpha Patrick confirmed. "I'll be there, along with Oliver and Elijah."

My ears perked up at that. If Oliver was going somewhere, there was a good chance that Abby would go too. The conference was somewhere I might be able to bump into her without being too obvious, if only I could find a way to be there too. My heart leapt at the thought.

They hung up and my father looked over at me thoughtfully, as if he were thinking along the same lines I was. Well, not exactly the same lines, of course, but about the conference at least. "Maybe I should take you along too, Jerrod. You've worked hard over these past few months and I'm proud of you. Do you think you could handle it? Being in the same room with Oliver West without losing your temper?"

I gave him the serene smile I'd been practicing in the mirror for months. "Of course, Dad. That's all in the past. Representing the Forest Ridge pack would be my honour."

He smiled too, accepting my reply at face value. "Good. We'll make plans to attend then, both of us. And our mates, of course."

Our mates? *Shit.* I didn't want Marissa there, but I couldn't think of a good reason why she shouldn't go. It didn't seem I was going to have much choice.

Although, maybe the idea wasn't a terrible one, all things considered. She'd always had a thing for Oliver. They'd even dated for a while before he met Abby. Maybe this was one time we really could work together since we both wanted the same thing: Oliver and Abby broken up.

How hard could it be?

~Abby~

Though keeping a straight face wasn't easy, I did my best as Storm came out of the dressing room wearing a floor-length pink dress and a deep scowl.

"I look like I've been dipped in cotton candy," she growled as I pressed my lips together even more tightly. She wasn't wrong, and I knew if I made eye contact with Liz, I would lose my self-control entirely.

Liz, Whitney and I were all sitting on the small couch outside the dressing rooms at the boutique Whitney had chosen. We were here to find the perfect dress for Storm's mating ceremony with Alpha Patrick later this weekend.

Storm came to me for help first, since her new mate was my mate's father, but I was hardly an authority on fashion. Liz wasn't much better, so we enlisted the help of our very trendy and fashionable cheerleader friend, Whitney, to lead the way.

Luckily, Whitney was undeterred by Storm's grumpiness as she leapt to her feet and circled around her, examining the look carefully. "The colour isn't quite you," she agreed, much to Storm's relief. "But I think we can work with the style, maybe just with longer sleeves so we don't see quite so many of the tattoos." Storm raised her eyebrows at Whitney, who quickly backtracked.

"They're amazing, of course, they just don't really go with the dress. So, pink is out, but what colour would you prefer?"

"Black," Storm immediately answered, to no one's surprise, but Whitney shook her head.

"This isn't a funeral. It's a... wait, what's it called again?"

That question was for me. As a human who had only found out about werewolves a couple of weeks ago, Whitney was still learning all the lingo.

"Mating ceremony," I supplied. "And Whitney's right, Storm. Alpha Patrick is very traditional, and although he said you could choose any colour, I don't think he meant black."

The mention of her mate softened Storm's expression considerably, making me smile. The way these two tough and guarded people turned to mush around each other was incredible. They were willing to do anything to make each other happy. That was the power of the mate bond: it made you reevaluate what was important and what was worth fighting for.

I should know.

"How about gold, then?" she suggested reluctantly, making an honest effort to cooperate.

Whitney pursed her lips, scanning Storm from head to toe. "I think it might clash with your hair."

Storm's hair was a bright red colour, much too bright to be natural. I had originally thought her hair, her piercings, and her many tattoos would have scared off Oliver's dad, who had once made a point of telling me I didn't look enough like a Luna. He later explained why he said it and apologized for it, but it didn't change the fact that he was a rather old-fashioned man and Alpha. A motorcycle-riding, strong-willed woman who looked like she'd stepped off the pages of a biker magazine hardly seemed like the ideal match for him after the untimely loss of his first mate, Oliver's mother. And yet, they seemed to work anyway. The Moon Goddess knew what she was doing, apparently. Considering my luck with my own mate, I couldn't really argue otherwise.

"Silver?" Whitney suggested, but this time, Storm and I quickly shook our heads.

"Silver is not a good colour for werewolves," I explained. "The metal is so painful for us that we try to stay away from it in general."

"Oh, right." I had told Whitney about that before, she had just forgotten, and I couldn't blame her. Learning about a whole other species and their culture was a lot to take in. "Well, how about red, then? We can find a shade that highlights your hair rather than working against it."

Storm agreed, so she went back into the dressing room to take off the pink gown while Whitney went to look through the other dresses to find something that would work.

That left Liz and me alone, and she leaned back in her seat, looking overwhelmed. "I can't believe they're having their ceremony already. They only met a couple of weeks ago!"

I knew what she was thinking without her having to spell it out more than that. Liz had discovered her own mate, Elijah, the same day Storm and Alpha Patrick met. And despite how much she loved him already, for someone who had grown up thinking she was human, committing to someone so permanently that quickly was hard to imagine.

But for werewolves, relationships worked differently. When the bond kicked in, it was hard to resist and rare for anything to happen to break that connection, apart from death.

Hopefully, that was a long way away for any of us.

"It's fast for humans, but not for werewolves," I told her now. "The bond comes first, and true love develops afterwards. It's a little bit backwards, I know, but in the long run, I actually think it's better. And because Alpha Patrick is an Alpha, the pack is eager to have his mate installed as their Luna too. You and I don't have to worry about all that just yet."

Although Elijah had been Alpha of his pack when he and Liz met, he gave up his position in order to dedicate himself fully to her as she learned how to embrace her werewolf heritage and the powers of her particular bloodline which had been hidden from her for so long. Her learning curve was a big one, and what their future together held was still not entirely clear.

"Okay, I've got a few different options for you," Whitney called out as she returned to the dressing room, passing the dresses in various shades of red to Storm. "One of these will work, I'm sure."

Despite Whitney's confidence, another hour passed before Storm finally emerged in the dress that was the clear winner, and all three of us got to our feet in excitement.

"It's beautiful," I assured her as she looked at herself in the mirror, turning from side to side as though she couldn't quite believe her eyes. The long red dress had a slit up one side and down one shoulder, revealing just a hint of Storm's tattooed arm. The bodice was form-fitting without being clingy, and with a rippled undertone of black that hinted at something unexpected, just like the woman wearing it.

"I actually kind of like it," Storm admitted. "Which can only mean one thing: we've been here so long that I've become delusional."

"Or this dress was meant to be," I countered. "Just like you and the Alpha."

"Thanks, Abby." She gave my shoulder a little shove which I understood was the equivalent of a hug from most people. We were very different people, but it felt like my new stepmother-in-law and I were going to get along pretty well. At least that was one person in the pack I didn't have to worry too much about winning over.

After dropping Whitney off at her house, Liz, Storm and I headed back to the Jade Moon pack land with Storm's new purchases. Whitney hadn't been able to sell her on heels, but at least she got some shoes that weren't full combat boots, so we were counting that as a win.

The pack house was rather quiet when we arrived, and as Storm left to hide her shopping bags somewhere that Alpha Patrick wouldn't find them, Liz and I went in search of our mates. They weren't in the Alpha's office, nor the kitchen, and not at Oliver's workshop either. Finally, I gave in and asked one of the guards if he'd seen them.

He answered us completely straight-faced. "They're both in the hospital."

"What?!" Liz exclaimed, her face paling as I asked the obvious follow-up question.

"Why are they in the hospital?"

The guard simply shrugged. "You'll have to ask them."

Luckily, the pack hospital wasn't too far away, so in a matter of minutes, we were standing in the waiting room with Alpha Patrick. "What happened?" I asked as he turned to greet us.

"They're fine," he assured us. "A few broken bones, nothing that won't heal."

"Broken bones?" Liz was still looking a little nauseated, but on this point, I could reassure her.

"Werewolves heal really quickly, remember? Those bones will be fixed in no time. But how did this happen, Alpha?"

His lips twitched a little in amusement. "They were arguing about who would win in a fight between them. It seems they were both right and wrong, given it ended in a tie."

Seriously? I really didn't understand men sometimes, but Alpha Patrick seemed to think the situation was funny. And I supposed Oliver *had* always wanted a brother, someone he could do stupid things like this with. The fact that they were both adults didn't seem to be stopping them.

We waited with the Alpha until we were told they were ready to see us, and Liz and I walked in to find our identical twin mates in side-by-side beds, both of them shirtless with various body parts bandaged and bruised faces. For a moment, I honestly couldn't tell who was who.

"Sorry, Heels," the one closest to me said with a sheepish grin, and I immediately went to Oliver's side. "We got a little carried away."

"You think?" I shook my head at him as I tried not to laugh. He looked both guilty and pleased with himself at the same time.

"Maybe we can play doctor when we get back to the house," Elijah suggested to Liz, making her blush.

"Eli! Everyone can hear you."

Elijah glanced over at Oliver and me, completely unconcerned. "So what? There's no way Oliver's not thinking the same thing."

I looked down at my mate for confirmation and he simply raised his eyebrows in invitation, making me shake my head once again.

Boys really would be boys, but I still couldn't be happier that this one was mine.

~Elijah~

With Liz supporting me, we made our way back to the room we were sharing in the Jade Moon pack house. The weeks that we'd spent here so far had been a lot more fun than I would have ever anticipated. Being here was kind of like a vacation, not having to deal with all the ins and outs of running a pack as I got to know the family I never knew I had. I spent a lot of my time with Alpha Patrick and Oliver, reviewing the pack's operations and making suggestions, but the final responsibility was no longer my own. I was essentially a consultant, and the role suited me very well. I never had any trouble giving anyone my opinion.

I was also enjoying the chance to get to know my mate and to support her as she grew more comfortable with all her new werewolf abilities. Liz amazed me more every day. Her whole world had been completely turned upside down, even more than mine had, and yet she took it all in stride. I had given up my pack, yes, but she had to accept that she was a completely different species from what she'd always believed. She gave up her job for the summer to stay with me until we could decide what to do next, and although I would support her no matter what she wanted to do, I had my own ideas too.

After all, I had been hunting for the source of power for years. I had a lot of plans for what I was going to do when I found it, and though some of those were immediately quashed when I realized that the source belonged to Liz and not to me, some of them were still valid. I still believed that the Alpha Council could be improved by having someone in charge, and who better than someone of the royal bloodline?

Liz was a queen without a throne, and I intended to build that throne for her, whatever it took.

"I can't believe you and Oliver did this to each other," she exclaimed as we reached our room and she helped me down onto the bed. "Are you sure you should have left the hospital already?"

"I'm fine," I promised her. "A good night's sleep and I'll be good as new."

That seemed to satisfy her. She trusted me when it came to all things werewolf, so she left it at that and moved on to making me more comfortable, taking off my shoes and then adjusting the pillows behind me. As she leaned over, her chest right at my eye level, I couldn't stop myself from bringing up my earlier suggestion once again.

"I wasn't kidding about playing doctor, though. What do you say, Liz?"

Though she rolled her eyes at me, I could see that hint of colour starting to rise in her cheeks. She was starting to get used to how much I wanted her, anytime and anywhere, but there were times like these when it still took her by surprise.

She honestly didn't know how incredible she was, and I didn't understand it. There wasn't a fucking thing about her that didn't turn me on. She usually kept her dark hair pulled back in a ponytail, but I loved the way it looked wrapped around my hands. Her hazel eyes seemed to see straight into my soul, and her body, soft and smooth, was my absolute favourite thing to touch.

"I don't think you'd be a very good patient," she said, trying to give me a disapproving look that held just a little too much desire in it to be truly convincing. "You never do what you're told."

"I promise I'll do exactly what you tell me *if* you help me feel better."

Clearly struggling against her better judgement, she looked me up and down. As her gaze passed over my groin, the blood rushed to that spot, making my already alert cock even harder.

I was always half-hard around her to begin with. It made life a little difficult at times, but I was learning to live with it.

"What kind of help do you need?" she asked, half-reluctant and half-curious, and I grinned up at her from the pillows.

"Well, most of my bones and bruises are healing, but there's this one spot that's getting more and more swollen as we're talking. I think you better take a look at it."

She might still be a little inexperienced, but she caught my drift immediately. "Oh, really? It wouldn't happen to be around here, would it?"

Her hand grazed lightly across the growing bulge in my pants, and even that small amount of contact made me groan. "You see, you're an excellent doctor. You identified the problem immediately."

This time she couldn't help laughing. "Well, you seem to have it all figured out. Maybe you can treat it yourself."

She was teasing me, of course. I didn't believe for a second that she'd leave me hanging. "I think you need to kiss it better."

"Why did I have a feeling you were going to say that?" Again, she tried to look reproachful, but she couldn't quite pull it off, not when her own desire was growing by the second.

She pressed down on me harder, making me groan again.

"Oh, I'm sorry. Does that hurt?" she asked, all faux innocence, and any other time, I would have grabbed her and thrown her down on the bed right there and then. However, at the moment, I honestly was still a little sore from the fight with Oliver. I couldn't do much other than lay here.

"My pants are getting too tight," I told her quite honestly. "It might feel better if you took them off."

Shaking her head at me, she undid my belt and unzipped my pants, pulling everything down to let my cock out, and I breathed a sigh of relief. That really did feel a million times better already.

Liz began to kneel down next to the bed, but I quickly shook my head. As much as I wanted her to touch me, I wanted to make her feel good too, and given my current aches and pains, that was going to be easier in my present position. "Not there."

She looked up at me in surprise. "I thought that's what you wanted?"

"Oh, trust me, I do. I just want you somewhere else."

Her look of confusion was adorable. "Where?"

"On my face."

Her cheeks flushed stronger this time, but she didn't even try to deny that she wanted it too. Standing back up, she quickly shed her own pants, revealing to me the beautiful curve of her hips and that fucking perfect junction between her legs, which was giving off a strong scent of arousal. Hers was the very best smell in the world.

Gingerly, she climbed up onto the bed, facing my feet, and straddled me until her sweet centre was directly above me. I grabbed onto her hips and pulled her the rest of the way down, inhaling her perfect scent until my mouth was watering. If I didn't taste her now, it honestly felt like I might die.

My cock twitched as desire flooded through me, and as my tongue connected with the warm, wet perfection of her, she took me into her mouth too, kissing me just like I'd asked her to.

Saying which was better was almost impossible: the way she tasted and felt as my tongue moved along all the little hidden parts of her, up to her sensitive clit that always made her shudder when I ran my tongue across it, or the way it felt as her own soft tongue stroked my swollen head, exploring each inch of it as she sucked and teased me.

Just when I'd lose myself in one sensation, the other would take over, until I honestly didn't know if I was coming or going – or rather, if I was coming or she was.

Liz's moans of pleasure were muffled by my cock in her mouth, just as the sounds from my own mouth disappeared against her skin while my tongue plunged deeper inside her. My thumb came over to assist, rubbing her clit as I kissed and sucked on her, the sparks of our mate bond adding to the already intense buildup of sensation. She wasn't taking it easy on me either, stroking me with her hand while she took me as deep as she could in her mouth, her other hand reaching around to gently stroke my balls, the twin feelings of need and desire inside me getting stronger and stronger with each movement she made until I couldn't take it anymore.

My whole body tightened in anticipation, feeling the moment of release building, and my mouth moved back to Liz's clit, sucking on it as I plunged my fingers deep into her. Her body shook just as my orgasm hit me, the world exploding around me like a bomb had gone off, like everything had been blown apart.

I came back to my body just in time to lower my lips back to her entrance. Not wanting to miss a single drop of it, I lapped up the sweetness that she dripped down onto my face as little aftershocks of pleasure ran through us both.

When we had both recovered, she gently climbed off me and turned back around so her face was next to mine. Running my fingers through her hair, I pulled her close to me, kissing her mouth just as I'd kissed her pussy a moment ago, tasting myself on her lips and letting her taste her own flavour on me.

I'd never imagined being so in tune with another person was possible, to feel like every emotion and sensation, good or bad, was shared between us.

Liz had given my life a new purpose, and I was determined to do her proud. I wasn't going to rest until everyone else knew what I had already accepted: this woman was made to be worshipped.

Keep in Touch

For more about my other books and to keep up-to-date with new releases, find all the links here:
https://linktr.ee/melodytyden

www.ingramcontent.com/pod-product-compliance
Lightning Source LLC
Chambersburg PA
CBHW051006180726
48291CB00006B/1998